Julia Notaro is a ps...
was brought up in .... work as a
trader for a major Japanese bank for several years. She
left the City to move to Japan, and now works there as
a teacher, living with her husband and their two young
children. She is currently working on her second novel,
and writes freelance articles for a variety of magazines
for the ex-pat community in Japan.

Short Change

Julia Notaro

POCKET
BOOKS

LONDON · SYDNEY · NEW YORK · TOKYO · SINGAPORE · TORONTO

First published in Great Britain by Pocket Books, 2000
An imprint of Simon & Schuster UK Ltd
A Viacom Company

I 3 5 7 9 I0 8 6 4 2

Simon & Schuster UK Ltd
Africa House
64–78 Kingsway
London WC2B 6AH

Simon & Schuster Australia
Sydney

A CIP catalogue record for this book is available from the
British Library

ISBN 0-743-40389-4

Typeset in Goudy Modern by
Palimpsest Book Production Limited, Polmont, Stirlingshire
Printed and bound in Great Britain by
Caledonian International Book Manufacturing Ltd, Glasgow

To my mother, who doesn't have a dog
and has never lived in Stratford

Acknowledgements

I would like to thank Nicky Biwaki who read the first ten chapters and urged me to finish the rest of the book; my agent Maggie Noach and Jennifer for their support and encouragement; Clare Ledingham and Rochelle Venables who told me to take out all the bad bits; and especially my husband and children who gave me space when I needed it; and last of all my in-laws who so willingly babysat for me when deadlines were fast approaching.

Chapter 1

L isa Soames put on her 'I am the employee of your dreams' expression as she looked in the shaving-mirror. She stood on tiptoe, tilting up her chin to get her mouth into view. Satisfied that she had removed all traces of breakfast from her lips, she licked her thumb and used it to straighten her eyebrows. She thought briefly about giving her whole appearance a check in a larger mirror, but decided she didn't have time; she would have to content herself with surreptitious glances in shop windows on the way to the station. In any case, if her interviewer was going to judge her solely on her appearance, she didn't want to work for his rotten bank.

She didn't want to work for his bank anyway. She didn't see herself working for a bank at all. Especially after what had happened to her father. She was sure his illness was due to working in an office for too long.

Her elder brother, John, didn't share her reservations. He had ridden into the City on the crest of the Big Bang, successfully establishing himself as a Treasury bond dealer. Having acquired a Docklands flat and a Porsche, he now viewed Lisa's unemployed state with a critical eye. Three years' sponging off the family while poncing around at university was long enough, he said. It was time for her to get a proper job just like him. To give her a kick-start, he had fixed her up with an interview at Haru Bank, a Japanese firm in the City.

Lisa wasn't at all grateful when she heard what he had done. 'But I don't know anything about banking,' she exclaimed, wondering which part of her character had made him think she was an ideal candidate to look after other people's money.

'You don't have to,' John assured her. 'Banks are crying out for dealers at the moment. They'll take anyone.'

'Even me?' Lisa wasn't convinced.

'If you wear some decent clothes they will,' said John, firmly pushing away the doubts that were beginning to crowd his own mind. He had believed that Lisa, being from the same gene pool as himself, must have a natural disposition to make money. Now he wasn't quite so sure.

'I don't want to work in a bank,' said Lisa. 'Banks are boring.' She could have added that she needed more time to recover from the traumatic experience of her first job since graduating, but she knew that would only make her brother angry.

'Dealing isn't boring. You get loads of money and you can get pissed every day. It's right up your street,' said John, confident that he had sussed out his sister's priorities in life. 'I'll tell you what,' he added, when she still didn't seem convinced, 'if you go to the interview, I'll take you out to lunch afterwards and you can drink as much as you like on me.'

Lisa liked the sound of that, so she agreed to go along with John's plan. On the train to Fenchurch Street, she found herself wishing that lunch with her brother came before her appointment at Haru Bank. She laughed when she remembered the edge a couple of vodka and tonics had given her during her last encounter with a corporate interrogator.

'Do you seriously think we'd give you a job with those shoes on?' her interviewer had asked her. She had looked down at her red patent-leather lace-ups, her lucky shoes which she'd worn for her finals at university, and then looked across at his worn grey slip-ons, which curled slightly up at the toes.

'A person who wears shoes like yours shouldn't really be making comments about other people's,' she had replied frostily and he, mistaking slight intoxication for forthright honesty, had given her the job.

The interviewer should have trusted his first instincts; Lisa had only lasted nine days. A woman who arrives at an interview wearing red patent-leather shoes, yellow socks, black trousers, a white shirt and a turquoise jacket bought for 10p at a charity shop is clearly not cut out to sell advertising space for a computer magazine.

She had just about managed to get through *Computer Update Weekly*'s one-week telephone-sales training-course, which had involved selling various imaginary products to different members of the sales staff and had culminated in the Gold Telephone Test on day five of the course. For it, Lisa had to telephone the sales manager, who wasn't known for his sensitive treatment of new recruits, and try to get him to buy a gold telephone. Lisa knew she didn't have the necessary qualities to succeed in tele-sales when she found herself giggling every time he picked up the phone. The angrier he got, the more she giggled, until finally, after her fifth abortive attempt, he had stormed out of his office and in a voice loud enough to make sure that all the sales staff and the people working on the floor above could hear, listed all the things wrong with Lisa's sales technique. He had then told her to start calling the C clients.

'What should I do if someone wants to place an ad?' Lisa had asked.

'I don't think you need worry about that,' he had replied dryly, and leaving Lisa to tackle the dusty contents of the C clients file, had gone for a very long, liquid lunch.

Computer Update Weekly had three categories of clients. The large companies that regularly placed adverts were the A clients; they were handled by the senior sales staff. The B clients were companies that occasionally placed adverts and were divided among all the sales staff except Lisa, who hadn't earned her spurs yet. The C clients were companies that had never used *Computer Update Weekly* before but were considered to be potential future advertisers. Success with a C client would earn Lisa some B clients and then she would start getting regular sales commission on top of her basic salary. She realised just how unlikely that was when she rang the first client on the list. The company turned out to be a one-tractor-owning Welsh farmer who put the phone down when she suggested he might like to place an ad in the following week's issue.

Lisa slowly cringed her way down the list. Each call had to be marked either negative or positive. A call became positive when you managed to get the client to answer in the affirmative twice. If Lisa asked, 'Do you have a computer?' and the client answered, 'Yes,' that was a positive response. At the end of the day, if she had lots of positive calls she would be praised for her sales skills even if she hadn't managed to sell any space. Whereas too many negative calls would earn a humiliating dressing-down from the sales manager at the daily meeting.

Too few calls were also frowned upon, as Lisa found out when she proudly showed her list of twenty calls at the end of her first full day on the phones. The sales manager didn't need to use words to convey his displeasure: one glance at his face told Lisa that she had to start dialling just that bit faster. Twenty calls in one hour was what he required, he said as he crumpled her call sheet into a ball and threw it back at her.

'I don't have any staff, so I don't need to advertise in your staff wanted section,' explained the owner of a very small business to Lisa on her second day of tele-sales. If it had been her first day, she would have given up and said goodbye at that point, but as she was getting hardened to extracting a positive response from a seemingly hopeless situation, she soldiered on.

'Couldn't you just imagine that you need to recruit some computer-programmers?' asked Lisa, hoping he had a sense of humour.

'Why would I want to do that?' came the reply.

Lisa sighed. Humourless and dense at the same time; this could be a tough one, she thought. 'Because I am having a very bad day,' she explained, 'and it would make me happy if you said yes.'

'OK.'

Lisa suppressed a groan. That didn't count. 'Now, imagine that you were expanding and that you wanted to recruit some computer-programmers,' she continued.

'Yes.'

One down, one to go, thought Lisa. 'Would you use our magazine to advertise?'

'No.'

'No?' echoed Lisa. 'Why not?'

'I've never heard of it.'

'That doesn't matter. Pretend you have.'

'OK.'

Lisa was proud of her self-control. 'And you would use our magazine to advertise if you needed staff.'

'Yes.'

She'd done it! 'Thank you very much. Goodbye,' she said, and she marked another positive call on her list.

After four days with the C clients, Lisa found that she couldn't pick up the receiver any more. She had become phonophobic. It wasn't the clients that she feared. It was the wrath of the manager and the contempt of her colleagues. She felt she had been marked out as a failure and couldn't bear everyone around her listening to her lack of success. At first, she had tried hard to seem bright and bouncy, as if she hadn't a care in the world, but gradually the strain took its toll and the lack of encouragement and the constant criticism from the sales manager became too much. She simply stopped making calls and sat staring at her phone instead. The manager, noticing her inactivity, hauled her into his office. She was a negative influence on the others, he said, convinced that harsh words would goad her into proving him wrong. They didn't. The following day she had just stayed in bed.

After that sorry experience, Lisa concluded that she wasn't cut out to work for a company that demanded she sat at the same desk, next to the same people, for a certain number of hours each day. This was quite a relief. It meant she no longer got nervous before her interviews and was able to enjoy them very much. Group interviews were especially good fun. She loved listening to the practised routines of her contemporaries who were frantically jostling to lead the pack in the hunt for well-paid jobs.

'Could you all please describe the qualities you think are necessary to work for our company,' said the manager at the magazine publishers who group-interviewed Lisa.

'Dynamic,' said shoulder-pads and too much blusher.

'Enthusiastic,' said navy suit and spotty chin.

'Loyal and dedicated,' offered grey suit, after a display of deep thought.

All eyes turned to Lisa, who was picking her finger-nails.

'How about docile and over five foot tall?' she muttered, not bothering to look up.

She'd noticed a large cross next to her name before she even sat down. It couldn't have been her clothes. She had dressed like a real businesswoman that day; she had also shaved her legs and worn lipstick. It couldn't have been her Essex accent, because she hadn't opened her mouth. It must have been heightism that had struck her off the list. Being three inches short of five foot was definitely one of the undesirable qualities that companies keep on their secret list of no-nos. After all, how could anyone be expected to have a serious business conversation with someone whose eyes were level with their belly-button?

Lisa knew that today's interview at Haru Bank wouldn't hold any surprises. Her height and her accent would overshadow her finer qualities. Nevertheless, it would be fun talking about herself and answering the standard interview questions like 'What are your faults?'

Was she really supposed to describe her faults?

Would anyone who answered honestly be given a job? Sometimes she liked to reply, 'I am sure that working for this company will enable me to overcome whatever faults I may have.' Or, if she didn't like the interviewer, she would answer, 'I smoke roll-ups, fart a lot and pick my nose.'

But today she decided to be on her best behaviour because she had never met a Japanese person before.

Lisa arrived exactly on time for her interview. Punctuality was one of the qualities that she had inherited from her father (even his daily bowel movement could be timed to the minute). That quality was not shared by her interviewer, Mr Ito, who kept Lisa waiting for over half an hour. She wasn't very surprised. Interviewers always arrived late. She suspected that it was another trick that the corporate world liked to play on the uninitiated interviewee and that there was probably a camera rigged up to record how she behaved during the unscheduled waiting-period.

In fact, Mr Ito had not intended to make Lisa feel uncomfortable. As the senior manager of the Treasury Department in the London branch of one of the largest banks in the world, he had many other things to occupy his time that were far more important than a meeting with a young graduate. Just before Lisa arrived, he had been asked to approve the provisional plans for the department's Christmas party, scheduled to take place in four months' time. There had been a long discussion as to whether there should be a choice of two or three main meals, and the wine that had been selected did not meet with his approval. Consequently, the meeting dragged on and Lisa had been left to wait.

She filled in the time by chatting to Babs, the assistant

personnel officer, a very friendly woman, who Lisa suspected was a highly trained industrial psychologist who would later report that Lisa's turquoise jacket, red shoes and yellow socks were three good reasons why she was unsuitable for a position in a major corporation.

Mr Ito arrived just as Lisa was about to go and claim her free lunch. He apologised for being late, glanced quickly at her *c.v.* and then read out the first of a number of questions he had written on a piece of paper and fastened to a clipboard.

'Why do you want to be the dealing-room secretary?' he asked without taking his eyes off the paper.

Lisa laughed at the idea. 'I don't,' she said. John had told her that the interview was for a trainee dealer position.

'You don't?' asked Mr Ito in surprise.

'No,' replied Lisa firmly. 'I want to be a trainee dealer.' She didn't know what a trainee dealer did, but she did know that any job with the word 'dealer' in the title meant she would get lots of money. She had no intention of being a low-paid secretary, especially as she couldn't type. Besides, the word 'secretary' conjured up the image of a girl named Tracey, wearing a tight skirt and a low-cut blouse, sitting at a typewriter painting her nails and being touched up by a middle-aged man bearing more than a passing resemblance to Benny Hill. Lisa knew that this was an unfair and inaccurate stereotype, but she couldn't help it. She had been subjected to the same media images as everyone else and so she couldn't be blamed if, to her, 'secretary' was synonymous with 'silly tart'.

Like most new graduates, Lisa suffered from the delusion that a degree was an automatic passport to a job with a fancy title and a big salary. Three years' arduous study at university, while trying to survive on a meagre grant, was supposed to have spared her a humble occupation. She expected the instant success that was due to people with her educational background.

Mr Ito, not realising the height of her expectations, gave it to her straight. 'Women don't usually do those jobs,' he replied without the trace of a smile.

Lisa glared at him as if he was something nasty she had just found stuck to the sole of her shoe. How could she be hearing such words? Not only were they out of date, they were also illegal. 'Well, I want to,' she answered angrily.

'I see,' said Mr Ito, and he wrote something on her *c.v.* in Japanese. 'Why don't you tell me about yourself?' he asked when he'd finished.

'Why don't you ask Babs?' retorted Lisa, annoyed that he had side-stepped the issue. 'I have spent half an hour talking to her and I have no intention of repeating myself.'

Mr Ito was astonished. It was the first time in London that he had interviewed someone who was reluctant to talk about themself. He continued with the next question on his list. 'Why did you apply for a job with us?' he asked.

Because you advertised for graduates was how Lisa usually answered this question, never failing to draw a frown on the interviewer's face, but she decided that Mr Ito deserved something a little more imaginative.

'Since I was a child,' she said, her voice throbbing with sincerity, 'I've dreamt of working for a large Japanese bank. I can't tell you how happy I was when I found out you needed trainee dealers, just at a time when I am searching for employment.'

Mr Ito was impressed. 'What is it about Japanese banks that attracts you?' he asked eagerly.

'It's the size,' answered Lisa quickly. 'Big banks have so many opportunities for someone like me.' Mr Ito wrote on her *c.v.* again. Lisa guessed it meant 'major bullshitter', and sniggered.

Noticing that it was almost twelve o'clock, Mr Ito decided to finish the interview with the last question on his list. 'Do you have any questions?' he asked.

'No,' replied Lisa, who was hungry.

They both stood up and Lisa, after giving Mr Ito a painfully firm handshake, turned and walked out of the room, thankful that her first and probably last encounter with a Japanese banker was well and truly over.

Chapter 2

——— ———

Lisa headed to the Broadgate Centre in a very bad mood. Her interview had left her feeling ashamed of herself. She should have walked out right at the beginning when Mr Ito made his sexist remark. Instead, she had just sat there and answered his questions until he decided the interview was over. It certainly hadn't taken her long to conform, she thought wryly, catching sight of her reflection in the windows of a bank. Underneath the unsuitable clothes she was becoming just like every other graduate anxious to secure a good job.

It was all Mr Littlewood's fault. He had been her social-science teacher at sixth-form college, and was so attractive that she had feigned a great interest in the delights of British government, fascism and sociological subjects like The Family and Deviance, in the vain hope of capturing his affection. She had spent hours on her homework and then lurked around the staff room at break, trying to engage him in conversations about how she could improve the already fine work that she had produced.

Being so young, she didn't know that nothing frightens

a man more than an intense, intelligent female. She would have been more likely to receive a chalky pat on the backside if she had pretended to be incredibly dense. As it was, Mr Littlewood never imagined that it was physical stimulation that Lisa had in mind when she approached him. He thought it was the need to satisfy her intellectual appetite that drove her to work so hard, and with this in mind he had encouraged her to apply for a place at the northern university he had attended, where she would be able to study social sciences in greater detail.

Lisa had followed her handsome teacher's advice, not realising that, after three years studying politics and sociology, there would be very few paths open to her that she could follow with a clear conscience. By 'clear conscience' she meant keeping to the extreme left-wing ideals that most students in her faculty acquired, either because the courses convinced them that to be on the left is the only way for a civilised human to be, or to avoid having their essays marked down by their tutors. Lisa had found herself leaning so far to the left that she would have fallen over if the practicalities of life, like finding food and shelter and being able to afford to go to the pub as often as she wanted, hadn't convinced her to refrain from taking up the alternative lifestyle of many of her contemporaries. She didn't want to be a squatter selling newspapers for the Socialist Workers, nor did she want to live in a mobile home and spend her days being chased through muddy fields by policemen in riot gear. She wanted indoor bathroom facilities and the usual comforts of modern living. The problem was how to acquire them without selling out her ideals.

If she wanted to earn money and keep her conscience clear at the same time, there were only a few careers open to a graduate in politics and sociology. The first was teaching, but she was tired of education and she wanted to do something that didn't involve being in a classroom full of screaming children. The second was to study at postgraduate level with a view to becoming a lecturer, but three years of being surrounded by intellectuals had cured her of wishing to be like them. They were all so weird, besides which it would be ages before she could get enough money to live decently. The third was to go into one of the caring professions, but she had enough problems of her own without trying to solve other people's. In any case, Lisa imagined that society's unfortunates could be violent, and she wasn't going to expose her delicate body to unnecessary abuse.

If Lisa was prepared to put her ideals aside, she could join those students who had, in their final year, begun growing out their strange hairstyles and reverting from peroxide blond and jet-black to good old safe and natural mousy browns. They had recognised that university was not real life and that what they had said and done in their three years as undergraduates would not be held against them on the milk round, as long as they now acquired a decent appearance and acceptable views. Words like 'career structure', 'promotion', 'fringe benefits' and 'ambition' tripped off their tongues, replacing old favourites like 'revolution', 'equality' and 'the masses'.

At first, Lisa had scorned those who so eagerly looked at the careers notice board each week to see which brewing-company or retail giant was visiting the campus to offer employment to a few of the willing hordes. She decided she wasn't going to be seen to have sold out: she would sit back and wait for the right opportunity to land at her feet. It didn't happen.

The months passed. Lisa missed the milk round, took her finals, got an upper second and found herself at the graduation ceremony with no plans for the future. She had gone back to live with her father and spent the summer looking for work, applying for any job that she was qualified for. She had no idea what she wanted to become. There wasn't one career that she could point to and say, 'That's what I want to do.' She just lived in hope that the right job would eventually find her.

Going to work at *Computer Update Weekly* had been a terrible mistake. She was glad her behaviour today had ensured that she wouldn't be making another one. She crossed the road at Threadneedle Street and looked up at the NatWest tower. Working in a bank, she decided, especially a Japanese one, was definitely not for her.

She arrived at the restaurant determined to enjoy her free lunch even if it meant listening to her brother's capitalist ramblings. Well, maybe lunch was not quite the word Lisa would have used to describe the fare that she was presented with. One bite of fish, a couple of peas and a slice of carrot, with a dollop of sauce, was a more apt description — and that was the main course.

'You were late so I ordered for you,' explained John apologetically. 'There's no time for a starter. I've got to be back before one.'

'I see,' said Lisa, staring down at the food on her plate. She picked up her glass of wine and took a large gulp. She couldn't really complain. John had just said he would pay; he hadn't mentioned the quantity of food she would be given.

'How did it go?' he asked, although he could tell by her outfit that the interview couldn't have gone well.

'Terrible,' said Lisa, stabbing at the carrot. 'They

had me down for a secretarial job. Imagine! Me a secretary!' She looked at John's reaction. 'You don't think I'd do a job like that, do you?'

John didn't think his sister would be doing any job at all if the last few months were anything to go by. 'They told me they were looking for trainee dealers,' he said, shrugging.

'Well, according to Mr Ito, they don't take on women for dealing jobs.'

'He was probably just saying that to let you down gently,' said John reassuringly. 'They'll soon hire a woman if they think she'll be any good.'

Lisa disliked Mr Ito even more now that she thought he had lied to her. 'Thanks for the vote of confidence,' she said. 'Anyway, I would never work for a horrible man like that. Not only was he sexist, he was also late, and when he did arrive he didn't even look me in the eye.'

'What did you expect from a Jap?' asked John.

Lisa flinched at the word but she knew her brother was just trying to wind her up so she didn't say anything.

John noticed her discomfort and smiled. He didn't have much sympathy for the leftie views she had acquired up north. 'Don't worry about Haru Bank,' he said. 'There are plenty of other banks we can try. We needn't bother with the Jap ones.'

'I'm sure it isn't only Japanese banks that employ sexist managers,' Lisa corrected him. 'I don't think that working in a bank – any bank, not just the foreign ones – is for me.'

'How can you say that when you don't know anything about it?' asked John. 'Wouldn't you like to have a life like mine?'

Lisa couldn't be bothered to argue over a lost cause. 'Time for another drink,' she said, pointing to her empty glass. 'Why don't you get a bottle in?'

'OK.' John walked over to the bar, leaving Lisa sitting alone looking slightly shabby among the expensive suits and carefully coordinated shirts and ties.

She thought of her father and wondered if he was spending his lunchtime in one of the bars in the City. She knew her aversion to banking stemmed from what had happened to him.

Dog, van, woman, car. Those were the words he had written down last Saturday after witnessing a crash. He had gradually lost his speech over the last ten years until one day he picked up a pen and began writing notes. At first, the notes had been full sentences but then, like his speech, they had become briefer and briefer. He could cope with nouns, but verbs and the little words that give meaning to a sentence were now beyond him.

Dog, van, woman, car.

Lisa had stared at the note and tried to guess what had happened. 'The dog ran in front of the van making it swerve and crash into the woman in the car?' she asked.

No. Her father didn't say, 'No.' He thumped the table. Thumping the table didn't always mean No. Sometimes he waved his hand to mean No and on those occasions thumping the table could mean Yes. But this time, as his thumping had an air of desperation, she guessed he meant No.

She tried again. 'The woman in the car was the one who nearly ran over the dog, and she swerved and crashed into the van?' No. Her father thumped the table and pointed to *dog*.

'The dog was in the van when it crashed into the

car being driven by the woman?' she asked hopefully. Thump, thump was the answer. Lisa didn't care any more. She wanted to give up, but her father was desperate for her to understand.

'The dog was driving the van and he crashed into the woman in the car?' she asked, hoping to inject a little humour into the situation before she lost patience and began swearing. But her father wasn't looking for laughs, and as he thumped the table Lisa realised that once again it was going to be a very long weekend.

'Sorry about that.' John interrupted her thoughts. 'Just bumped into a guy from Morgan's.' Seeing her look blank, he added, 'J. P. Morgan — you know, big American bank.' Lisa still looked blank. 'Oh, never mind,' he said. 'How are things at home?'

'Not so good. He's getting worse and worse,' replied Lisa.

'Oh, I wouldn't say that,' said John, always willing to doubt the severity of their father's illness. 'You've just noticed it more because you've been away.'

'No, he's definitely got worse since I've been back.' Lisa knew she wasn't imagining it. 'It would help if you came back more often,' she said: it was over a month since John had been home.

John shook his head. 'I've been so busy at work that I just crash out at the weekends. And anyway,' he added when he saw Lisa raise her eyebrows, 'he drives me mad. Last time I was over he wrote something down and I couldn't even read it.'

'Tell me about it,' said Lisa wearily. 'I had a great time on Saturday. There was an accident outside the house early in the morning. Dad woke me up to show me one of his notes about it. All it said was "woman, dog, car, van".'

'Sounds quite good for him,' said John. 'A woman in a car swerved to miss a dog and crashed into a van.'

Lisa smiled. 'Not even close.'

He tried again, 'A woman with a dog in her car skidded and hit a van?'

'Nope.'

'Fuck me,' said John, showing why he was useless when it came to dealing with their father. 'The van driver swerved to avoid the dog and crashed into the car.'

'No,' said Lisa, 'try again.'

'I give up,' said her brother. 'No, wait I've got it, the fucking dog was driving the car and he swerved to avoid hitting the woman, who was jogging, and then it crashed into a van? How about that?'

'That sounds fine to me. We're never going to know, anyway.'

'You're having me on!' John couldn't believe that Lisa had made him guess when she herself didn't know what had happened.

'No, I'm not. I gave up before I found the answer. I would have ended up screaming if I hadn't walked away.'

'Well, you won't have to be there much longer. You'll get a job and then you can move out,' said John, who couldn't imagine that his sister would live in Baneham with their father for any other reason than that she had to.

'But what about if he gets worse?' asked Lisa, knowing that it was a matter not of 'if' but of 'when'.

'He's fine. He was all right when you were at university, wasn't he?' said John, not wanting to think about the future. 'He's still working, isn't he? If he's working, he must be fine. Don't worry about it. Just sort yourself out. He'll get by.'

Lisa saw the sense in her brother's words. Their father was still managing to work; he wasn't confined to the house. What was the point in worrying about what might happen in the future? She had to stop thinking about it and focus on getting her own life sorted out.

'I wish I could look at it as clearly as you,' she said. 'You must take after Mo.' Their mother loathed her full name, Maureen, nearly as much as she hated being reminded that she was old enough to be the mother of two young adults.

John laughed. 'And the rest! The only thing we've got in common is the colour of our hair, and hers is dyed anyway.'

'Oh, I can see lots of similarities. Would you like me to make a list?' Lisa laughed too. It was a favourite joke of theirs to spot which of their parents they most resembled.

Mo had left home some years before to live with Ron, the man of her dreams. John had never forgiven her, but Lisa, having spent more time with their father recently, had come to understand why her mother had gone and, although she didn't like the life Mo was leading now, she no longer felt bitter about it.

'I'd love to hear it,' said John, making a show of looking at his watch, 'but unfortunately I've got to get back to work. Come on, drink up.'

'I'm in no rush,' said Lisa, who had the freedom of the unemployed. 'I'm going to take my time.'

'I'll leave you to it, then,' said John, getting up to go. 'Let me know when you hear something.'

'Don't hold your breath,' said Lisa. 'It was quite obvious that they didn't like me.'

'Oh, I doubt that,' said John, kissing her on the cheek. 'Who could fail to be dazzled by your charm?'

Chapter 3

——— ◄———

To her surprise, two weeks later Lisa was invited back for a second interview at Haru Bank. When Mr Ito had said that women don't usually work as dealers, he hadn't meant that women couldn't do those jobs, or indeed that he thought they shouldn't. With a daughter aiming to enter medical school in Japan, he believed strongly in equality. He was quite happy to have women dealing in his Treasury Department: the problem was that there weren't many women who, on experiencing the reality of the market, wanted to remain in it. There was only one female dealer at Haru Bank, Stephanie, who dealt fixed-date dollars. Mr Ito had all but given up on getting any more women in his department, but after Lisa's interview he concluded that she was perfect for the rough and tumble of the dealing-room.

Lisa was so amazed that her rudeness could be interpreted in a positive light that she decided to give Mr Ito another chance. His tardiness could just have been a Japanese custom and his sexist statement was probably the result of a poor command of the English language, she told herself, convinced that it wouldn't do her any harm to earn some money in a bank until she found out what she really wanted to do with her life.

On her second visit to Haru Bank, there were five interviewers: Mr Ito, three other Japanese managers and George, the personnel officer, who tried to give an air of professionalism to the occasion. 'Why did you stay at *Computer Update Weekly* for only nine days?' he asked, pen poised to note down her reply.

Lisa was taken aback. John had told her that the second interview was a mere formality to discuss her duties, salary and benefits. She hadn't prepared herself for a grilling and she immediately regretted writing on the application form that she'd worked for *CUW*. How could she answer George's question and come off looking good? She paused to think.

The Japanese managers saw this as a sign of great maturity, and were impressed. Everyone looked at her expectantly.

Lisa decided to be honest. 'It was a choice between money and my sanity, and I chose the latter,' she said.

The managers smiled, but George pursed his lips and wrote something down. Lisa wasn't bothered about him. He was too concerned about looking like a serious banker to have any real power, she thought.

Mr Ito asked the next question. 'Why do you want to be a dealer?'

'Because I would make a good one.' She didn't want to boast, but John had said that confidence was important.

'What is it about dealing that attracts you?' asked George. He could tell that she knew nothing about the markets and he wanted to catch her out.

The money and the booze was the first answer that popped into Lisa's head but she firmly suppressed it.

'I don't know, but my brother's a dealer and I'm sure that if he can be one, so can I,' she said.

The managers laughed, and George, who would have preferred someone taller with a reasonable knowledge of the financial markets, faced up to the reality of the situation. Mr Ito had made his decision before the interview had even started and this was just a matter of going through the motions. The other managers would be unwilling to question the wisdom of their senior manager's choice, even though Lisa was clearly unsuitable for the position. George, painfully aware of his lack of authority, decided to go along with them.

He handed Lisa a piece of paper. 'This is your starting salary and the benefits that we are offering you,' he said.

'It's not very much, is it?' Lisa was disappointed when she realised she wouldn't be moving to Docklands just yet.

'The amount will soon go up if you are any good at dealing,' said George through gritted teeth.

'I know that,' she said, 'but I had expected more.'

Mr Ito liked her negotiating skills. 'We can raise the amount by five hundred pounds,' he said.

Lisa, used to living on a student grant, thought it was a very large increase. She nodded in acceptance. 'What about a company car and longer holidays?' she asked hopefully.

'Don't push it,' muttered George.

'Trainee dealers start on a modest salary,' explained Mr Ito kindly. 'But once you become a dealer you'll earn much more. Can you start on the first of September at eight o'clock?'

'Yes,' said Lisa, who was becoming fond of Mr Ito. He was certainly much nicer than George. She found herself standing up and shaking hands across the table with her future colleagues. Lisa Soames, Trainee Dealer. It had a nice ring to it.

Sitting on the train to Baneham, she was surprised at how little her left-wing conscience pricked. Maybe if she had still been at university, she would have felt a little ashamed, but now that she was down south, and was no longer obliged to find a Marxist interpretation of everything from the existence of poverty in the modern world to the amount of grease that dripped from the sausage rolls in the refectory, she was able to convince herself that she was doing the right thing.

On the morning of her first day at Haru Bank, she rose at six o'clock and surveyed her wardrobe. Most of her clothes were from her university days. They looked very shoddy and washed-out. Black was the dominant colour and, although she usually favoured what she imagined to be the dark, mysterious look, she felt that today she ought to try for something a little brighter. She wanted to make a good impression on her colleagues, and yet she also wanted to be honest about herself. She wasn't into power-dressing, and comfort and neatness were high priorities. After she'd discarded all the garments that didn't meet these requirements, she was left with her black trousers, white shirt and turquoise jacket. Her lucky red shoes were left in the wardrobe because she now owned some shiny black lace-up brogues which would impress even the most traditional of City gents.

Lisa left the house at 7.05 a.m. She knew it was 7.05 because she left with her father and he always walked out of the front door at 7.05 precisely. His morning routine had been the same for as long as she could remember. From Monday to Friday he got up at

6 a.m. without the aid of an alarm clock. Then, standing at the kitchen sink, he washed and shaved. When they moved into the house, there hadn't been a mirror in the bathroom, so he had used the one above the kitchen sink. John had put up a small mirror in the bathroom when he had started shaving at least eight years ago, but by that time their father's morning routine was already established and to change it was unthinkable. Besides, there wasn't an electric socket in the bathroom, so he had to stay in the kitchen to blow-dry his hair. This was a daily habit that he had got into during the power cuts in the seventies. He hadn't been able to wash his hair in the evenings then so he had to do it early in the morning. He'd had collar-length hair in those days and, as it took a long time to dry naturally, he had blow-dried it. The routine had been established and, even though his hair was now much shorter and there wasn't very much of it, he still got the hairdryer out every morning.

After he'd seen to his face and hair, he put on his dressing-gown and sat down to breakfast. He ate a bowl of Kellogg's cornflakes with milk and sugar, followed by one slice of toast with Robertson's marmalade, and drank two cups of tea, PG Tips, loose-leaf, not bagged. Breakfast over, he washed up and then went up to the bathroom to clean his teeth, empty his bowels and open the window to let in some fresh air. He'd go into Lisa's room to get a clean shirt from the airing-cupboard, and then get dressed in his own bedroom. From Monday to Friday, he followed the same routine year after year . . .

By leaving at 7.05 and walking quickly to the station, they could catch the 7.23, which would arrive at Fenchurch Street at 7.40, giving Lisa twenty minutes to get to Haru Bank. If they had left at 7.00 they could have walked at a comfortable pace and still caught the train easily without breaking into a sweat, but Lisa's father had one morning left home at 7.05, and so had set the time of departure for the rest of his working life.

They strode along in silence. Lisa's father couldn't talk, anyway, and Lisa was too busy trying to keep up with him even to think about indulging in some friendly banter. As they approached the station, her father quickened his pace, Lisa broke into a trot and they headed towards the footbridge. Her father climbed the stairs two at a time. When he reached the top, he rushed across the bridge and shot down the stairs on the other side. Lisa, red in the face and gasping for breath, hurried along behind.

Her father headed for the far end of the platform, for the crack in the tarmac that he had chosen to stand on when he first moved to Essex over twenty years ago. Through wind, rain and snow he stood on that crack, even after British Rail built a large new shelter, just five yards away, to protect its customers from the elements as they waited, often in vain, for their train to arrive.

This morning someone was already standing on the sacred spot. Lisa's father wasn't deterred. He simply stood next to the intruder and shuffled along sideways until he had moved the offending body to the left. Then, ignoring the thick yellow stripe painted ten centimetres from the edge of the platform, he placed his feet either side of the crack and shuffled forward until his toes reached the edge. He leant forward to look down the tracks at the approaching train. As it pulled in to the station, he leant back ever so slightly.

There were no seats left on the train. Lisa stood next to her father and, as her breathing gradually returned to normal, she was overcome with a terrible realisation:

she was commuting to the City to go and work in a bank just like her father. What was she doing? She surveyed all those around her and she didn't like what she saw. The pale, sickly complexions she could understand and forgive. It was the general air of despondency that she couldn't abide. Not one person looked happy to be on the train.

She thought back to her undergraduate days, to the idealistic conversations that went on long into the night. She hadn't thought much about her future then, but she'd had the unshakable conviction that she was special and that her talents would be discovered and appreciated by many. She herself hadn't yet discovered what she was good at, but she knew she had talents that needed only the chance to emerge.

She promised herself that this new phase in her life was only a stopgap while she thought about what she really wanted to do. She looked hard at the faces around her and knew that she wasn't going to become trapped into the same unhappy existence as these poor fools, who only kept themselves going by thinking about their two-week summer holiday abroad. Lisa didn't want a life in which she was always longing to be somewhere else. She wanted her life to be so interesting that she didn't need to get away from it at all.

Just before Barking, the train slowed down with a high-pitched squealing of the brakes and then shuddered to a halt. In the carriage, there was no sound except the rustling of newspapers and an occasional sniff from some unfortunate soul in an ill-fitting toupée who had forgotten his handkerchief and who was becoming the most hated person in that confined space as everyone got more and more irritated at the unexplained delay.

After twenty minutes, Lisa's toes were numb and she

had given up hope of arriving on time. She looked at
her father for outward signs of the stress he must be
feeling at this interruption in his routine. Apart from
his thin lips turning downwards, you couldn't tell that
his nerves were screaming. Lisa wondered whether
this ability to keep up an appearance of calm was
the cause of his illness. Having such a tight rein on his
emotions must have messed up some vital mechanism in
his brain. She had never heard him shout and she had
never seen him lose his temper. Instead, his lips would
curve downwards and he'd turn in on himself. He was
the complete opposite of Lisa, who preferred outward
displays of emotion. Not that she had chosen to be like
that, it was just that she couldn't control her actions or
her tongue when provoked by life's irritants. She put
it down to the drop of Sicilian blood she had inherited
from Mo. In Sicily, her behaviour would probably be
viewed as a model of all that is restrained and calm.
Unfortunately, in England her outbursts were regarded
as signs of great immaturity and lack of self-control.

Without fanfare, the train started up again and
moved slowly into Barking. A collective sigh of relief
went round the carriage. Twenty minutes late wasn't
such a disaster.

'We are sorry to announce that due to points failure
this train will be terminated at Barking. Passengers are
advised to use the Underground trains to complete their
journey. We are sorry for any inconvenience caused.'

Lisa lost her father in the mad dash that followed
as the contents of one packed commuter train spilt
out onto the platform and made their way over the
footbridge to the crowded platform on the other side.
She completed her journey on tiptoe, hanging from a
bobble on a District Line train.

Chapter 4

———➤   ◀———

For someone starting out on a career they took seriously, being over an hour late on the first day would have been an absolute disaster. But Lisa wasn't at all worried. She thought it rather amusing, and it was with great effort that she managed to change her expression to one of serious intent when she encountered a flustered George in the lobby.

'We expected you at eight o'clock. Did you make a mistake with the time?' he asked angrily.

'It was the trains. Points failure,' she said, trying and failing to sound contrite.

Years of being a personnel officer had given George plenty of practice at smiling and being friendly on the surface. Underneath, he wanted to throttle the midget who had ruined his start to the day. He had spent the last hour pacing the corridors of the bank in case she had slipped in unseen. He could have forgiven her if she had shown some signs of being really sorry, but all she did was try to hide an ill-concealed smirk.

The other new graduate trainee dealer was sitting in the lobby reading the *Financial Times*. He wasn't upset to have been kept waiting by Lisa. She had blotted her copybook before they had even started and he could only benefit from that.

He held out his hand and smiled gleefully. 'The trains are terrible, aren't they? I'm Robert.'

'Pleased to meet you. I'm Lisa.' She smiled back at him, thinking how pleasant he seemed. She wondered if he understood the *FT*. He was the first person she'd met who read it.

George told them that they were going to have a tour of the bank, be introduced to all the staff, be photographed for their identity cards and then start work in the back office of the dealing-room. They would spend a few months there before being let loose with the bank's money in the world's financial markets.

As they set off on their tour he gave them a warning: 'Beware the smiling Japanese.'

Lisa immediately had a picture in her mind of a World War II kamikaze pilot in thick glasses, grinning wickedly before dive-bombing a hapless ship.

George guided them through the bank and Robert walked next to him, asking pertinent questions. Lisa, who couldn't think of any questions, was happy to follow behind and say nothing. She noticed that everyone they passed seemed very busy, either writing important-looking reports or having high-powered phone conversations. It was most impressive. If she had looked behind her, she would have seen all those people slump back into their seats and carry on with their normal early-morning routine of drinking coffee, reading the newspaper and chatting to the others in their section. The frenetic display of activity she was witnessing was the sudden rush to look busy that occurs in most offices when a senior manager makes an unexpected appearance.

They shook hands with the managers of all the different sections and Lisa instantly forgot who was who. The Japanese all seemed very nice and unthreatening, but George's warning had stuck in her mind and, as she shook hands with each one, her head was filled with images of little black-haired men inflicting various tortures on poor, innocent white people. Having prided herself on not being a racist, Lisa found it most disconcerting that she couldn't regard each one as a separate human being in his own right. But, as she wasn't used to the subtle differences that distinguish Asian features, the jokes about them all looking alike seemed quite accurate. Same hairstyles, same colour suits, same style of glasses; maybe they were mass-produced at a bank-worker factory in Tokyo.

They approached the dealing-room. When George opened the door, Lisa expected to hear the roar of busy dealers buying and selling financial instruments all around the world. Instead, the noise level hardly changed, because most of the dealers were sitting quietly eating their breakfasts or reading the newspaper. There was no attempt to look busy. They had no need to try to look important. They already knew that they were.

Lisa's eyes fixed on a rotund dealer wearing a candy-striped shirt and very loud braces. He was standing in front of his desk, phone in one hand, bacon sandwich in the other, barking instructions to his brokers. Physically, he was nothing to get excited about; too many pints of lager and late-night curries had put paid to that. But there was something in his manner that made him stand out. His belief in his own self-worth gave him charisma. He seemed so certain that he was the most important person in the room, if not the whole market, that those around him faded into the background. He

was Leo, king of the dealing-room. In his hands lay
the power to make or lose millions of dollars. That
power was enough to make one forget the large belly
overhanging his trousers, the balding head, the beady
eyes and the unhealthy complexion gained from spending
all day in the dealing-room and half the night in a bar.
He looked up and saw the newcomers.

'Oh my God!' he shouted, staring at Lisa. 'They've
employed a dwarf!'

Years of being the butt of short jokes had made Lisa
an expert in the art of the quick put-down. 'You're one
to talk,' she shouted back. 'The only way you'd reach
six foot is if you stood on a box!'

Unfortunately, Leo wasn't the type to congratulate
her on her wit. Instead, he threw his sandwich, and it
hit her squarely in the face. Lisa was left with a blob
of melting butter on her nose and half a rasher of back
bacon dangling from the lapel of her jacket.

She looked towards George for help, but he merely
shrugged and said, 'It's jungle law in this part of the
bank, I'm afraid.'

In any other place at any other time Lisa would have
fought back, but this was the first time she had been
in a dealing-room and the arrogance that seemed to
ooze from the pores of everyone in it had completely
wrong-footed her. Not only that, it was her first day
at work in *a bank*. She had always pictured banks as
very civilised places that employed decent, upstanding
citizens. She had never imagined that someone like Leo
would be allowed to work in one. He would be more at
home on a football terrace with a Chelsea scarf round
his neck, a can of lager in his hand and a Union Jack
tattooed on his forehead. What was a man like him
doing in a bank? If Lisa had come face to face with

a Yeti wearing a pin-striped suit and bowler hat, she would not have been more surprised. Therefore, her response to Leo's attack was uncharacteristically timid. She merely brushed the bacon off her lapel with the back of her hand and used her cuff to get the grease off her nose.

The morning's entertainment amused the local staff, and from that moment Lisa was known as the Dwarf. She had no problem with being short; she had always been so and it seemed perfectly natural to her. What bothered her was that people couldn't separate her from her height. Whenever she met someone, sooner or later, no matter who they were, they felt that they simply had to make a comment about it.

'Exactly how tall *are* you?' is what friends usually asked after they had known her a little while. They didn't consider it rude, although when she responded, 'About as many centimetres as your big fat arse,' they got the message.

'What's the weather like down there?' Lisa had heard this question so many times that she usually ignored it, knowing that the person who asked it was one of life's sad cases. Occasionally, when she was in a foul mood, she would reply, 'My height is the result of a serious childhood illness.' It wasn't true but it was effective in wiping the smile off the face of even the most insensitive of people.

'How nice, an armrest.' This was usually said in pubs by complete strangers, who soon found out that what they were leaning on was not just a convenient height, but also bit back.

'I've got a friend who is short like you' was a frequent comment by people who wanted to show that they understood her 'problem' and that they had sympathy

for her. Lisa put this comment in the 'I'm not a racist
– I know lots of black people' category. She wondered
if they would also say, 'I've got a friend who is really
spotty like you,' if she had terrible acne, or, if they
were talking to a man, 'I used to know someone who
had a penis just as small as yours.'

One good thing about Leo's attack was that it
instantly changed her attitude to the Japanese. She
realised that they, too, were victims of stereotyping,
and she felt a close affinity with them. Now that
she had rid her mind of the film *Tora! Tora! Tora!*,
she began to see how warm the Japanese were; she
felt a real soft and gentleness of spirit in each one
of them, which contrasted very strongly with the
'Look what I've just trodden on' sneers of the local
dealers – her fellow British citizens – who reluctantly
offered limp hands and didn't even make the effort
to mumble insincere words of greeting. Lisa hadn't
expected such a lack of friendliness. She tried not
to take it personally, but it was hard not to blame
her height.

After the introductions were over and Lisa and
Robert had got their ID cards, they were dropped
off at the Confirmation Section, the graveyard of the
back office. This, as Lisa later found out, was where
the bank placed its older clerks who had no chance of
promotion. Instead of firing them, Haru Bank, which
prided itself on looking after its workers, however
incompetent they were, thought it was kinder to put the
clerks out to graze in the Confirmation Section, where
they spent the years until their retirement checking
postal confirmations of past deals against the bank's
computer printouts. Sharing their fate were the young
school-leavers and the graduate recruits, who were

given a spell in the section to reduce their egos quickly to a manageable size.

As the work in confirmations was merely checking, and there was no chance of any local worker conspiracy which could sabotage the bank's good name, there were no Japanese in this section. This meant that the staff could talk as much as they liked, about whatever they liked, without fear that it would be reported to higher authority.

It was easy work. Grab a bunch of letters, check the name and location of the bank, plus the amounts, dates and interest rates, against those on the computer printout. Draw two lines across the letter and write 'CHECKED' in capitals, then go on to the next one, and so on, stopping every now and then to file away the letters.

Lisa worked very quickly, and Robert soon noticed that her pile of checked letters was much larger than his. He didn't want her to develop an advantage over him so he carefully watched how she operated.

'You aren't signing them,' he said after a few minutes.

'Why would I want to do that?' asked Lisa.

'So that they'll know who checked each letter. You're supposed to sign each one in the top left-hand corner when you've finished looking at it.'

'When did they say that?'

'When you weren't listening.' Robert shook his head and got back to his work.

Lisa's complacency was broken. What if someone went through the files and added up how many they had each done at the end of the day? As she hadn't signed any letters so far, she would have far fewer than Robert.

The paranoia that many office workers suffer from
had quickly taken a grip on Lisa. Just a few hours ago
she hadn't cared whether she worked at Haru Bank or
not, but now losing her job through incompetence was
something she wanted to avoid at all costs. It was as if
the invisible hand of conformity had reached out and
grabbed her by the scruff of the neck. One minute she
was Lisa Soames, idle left-wing graduate, and the next
she was Lisa Soames, conscientious office worker.

Sitting next to Robert, she felt like a fraud. He clearly
had more knowledge and experience than she did, and
when they discovered how useless she was at banking
she would be first publicly humiliated and then fired.
She tried to calm her fears by comparing her speed
with everyone else's. She was comforted to see that,
even though it was her first day and she was now
signing her letters, she was already much faster than the
others. She didn't know that the veterans deliberately
worked slowly to pace themselves. If they worked too
quickly they would run out of work, which might cause
either a reduction in their number or an increase in
their workload. The latter was very unlikely, as there
wasn't anything else the bank would trust them with.
But the possibility of Haru Bank losing its paternalistic
character hung over them and they feared management
might discover that they were merely taking up space.

Later that afternoon, Robert managed get himself
invited out with the lads in the back office for an
after-work drink. No doubt he'll be wheedling his way
into the dealing-room early, thought Lisa, imagining
herself ploughing through confirmations in the back
office graveyard for years to come while Robert, the
tall ex-public schoolboy, greased his way quickly to the
top. She vowed not to let herself get left behind.

Chapter 5

———— ➤ ◄ ————

It took only a few weeks for Lisa to forget that she had once existed quite happily without a full-time job. Now that she had one, her life was governed by the effort to keep it and to be promoted as quickly as possible. She thought that Robert, who had greeted her so nicely on her first day, was a slimy toad who was trying hard to keep her at the bottom of the pile. Lisa watched his every move and fiercely resented the ease with which he seemed to win people over.

Luckily, the Japanese didn't believe in promoting by merit. It didn't matter if it was Robert or Lisa who did the best work. They had joined the bank together and, as long as they showed up on time and didn't get drunk too often at lunchtime, they would advance together. Lisa would have avoided a lot of worry if she had known this. But she didn't and neither did Robert, so they spent their days watching each other instead of enjoying being paid far more than their simple work justified.

After a month, they graduated to the main part of the back office. Here, the deals were checked when they came from the dealing-room, so that any mistakes could be spotted before the deals came into effect. The section was run by Brian who, like Lisa, was deficient in inches. He was also short on locks, handsome features and an engaging personality. He was a man with very little going for him.

Brian's life was devoted to the running of his section. He knew that it was the most important in the bank and that, if it wasn't for his sharp-eyed vigilance, the bank would fall into the red because of the sloppy, careless work of the overpaid dealers. He hated the dealers; they refused to be grateful for the work he did keeping an eye on them, they refused to give him the respect he felt he should have, they never apologised for their mistakes, and they never said 'Please' when they asked him to do something. What irked him most of all was that, despite their faults, he couldn't help admiring them, and on a busy day he found himself going into the dealing-room as much as possible to soak up the exciting atmosphere.

He told himself every day that, given the chance, he could do their jobs just as well, if not better, but he had never been given the chance and now that he was thirty-five he never would be. No matter how well he did his job, he would never command the respect paid to even the most junior dealers. Like his work, he was dull and unexciting, and every time he passed from the quiet back office into the noisy, crowded dealing-room he was reminded of this. He wanted a piece of the action and knowing that he'd never get it made him hate those who did. He especially hated the arrogant trainee dealers, like Lisa and Robert, who were just marking time before going onto bigger and better things.

Brian's desk was next to that of the plant from Tokyo, Mr Sazaki, who was there to remind the staff that they worked for a Japanese establishment and to make sure that the section was run in a manner that would be approved by Head Office. Mr Sazaki had studied English to degree level at Wasada University and had a reputation among the Japanese staff of being able to speak the best English out of all the Japanese in the bank. In reality, his English had been confined to the works of Shakespeare, Dickens, Austen and other such notables and, even though his English vocabulary far outshone that of your average *Sun*-reading bank worker, he was incapable of holding even a simple conversation in English with the local staff. Their daily massacre of his beloved English language shattered his nerves and he spent his days with his head down, looking terribly busy and hoping that no one would talk to him. If it looked as though one of the local staff was going to approach him, he would rush out of the room and hide on the top floor of the bank. When things got too much for him, he used to beg his wife to ring the bank and tell them that he was ill. She did this gladly, providing he spent his resulting free morning giving her cunnilingus.

Mrs Sasaki's sexual appetite was no secret among the Japanese staff. Mr Sasaki had revealed all one drunken night in a bar in Tokyo. His colleagues sniggered whenever his wife called in to say he had another of his headaches, knowing full well that as she spoke Mr Sasaki was probably slurping away between her legs. Poor Mr Sasaki: at least in Tokyo he could escape to the office. In England, the office was hell too and he often prayed his five-year posting would be cut short. Until that unlikely event, he just had to keep dodging the local staff.

The other people in Lisa's new section sat at eight desks pushed together to make a large rectangle. On one corner sat Shirley, who had worked full-time in the bank for the last fifteen years. She was ten years older than Brian and five inches taller, so she regarded herself as the unofficial head of the back office. She controlled the mood of the room. When she was happy, there was occasional laughter and friendly banter, but when she was peeved the air was poisonous with her disapproval and the other staff worked in silence, anxious not to be the one who set off her famous temper.

Ten years ago, Shirley had had a punch-up on the floor of the coffee room with an unfortunate temp who had crossed her path. Her skill with her fists had become part of the bank's folklore and everyone feared her, especially as she hadn't even been reprimanded for brawling. The Japanese managers, unaccustomed to seeing two grown women rolling around the floor kicking and punching each other, had dealt with the situation as they saw best. Since not one of them was prepared to risk a punch on the nose from such a fearsome woman, they neither fired her nor reprimanded her. Instead, they made sure she was never promoted. So Shirley sat each day at the same desk, year after year, controlling the back office by the menace of her reputation. Lisa, knowing nothing about Shirley, had thought she looked reasonable, but Shirley, noting Lisa's short hair and *Guardian*, had branded her a communist leftie lesbo, and decided to keep a very watchful eye on her.

Opposite Shirley sat Dave, forty years old, plump and inoffensive. He was still smarting that Brian had seized the management position and knew that if he wasn't careful he would soon be banished to the back-office graveyard. In a vain attempt to put off the inevitable, he tried to look energetically involved in all that went on in the section. However, as most of what went on was

deadly dull, even he, with the fear of impending removal
hanging over his head, couldn't keep up a lively pace for
very long. By eleven o'clock, he was usually slumped in
his seat wondering whether to go to the Old Bull at
lunchtime with Len from the telex room, or whether
to ask that slim divorcee in accounts to accompany him
to the new wine bar near Fenchurch Street station.

Next to Dave sat Pam, a temp who had been there
five years. She had arrived one day, been given a
checking job and had never left. She sat, head down
all day, slowly working her way down the list of
deals. Occasionally she added an innocuous comment
to the general conversation, but mainly she was happy
to keep quiet and get on with her work. She had never
asked to be made full-time, so the bank, happy not to
have responsibility for her, had not given her a full-time
contract.

The rest of the section was filled by school-leavers,
who carelessly did their work as they chatted away
about holidays in Greece, romance and wedding details.
They all wished they were in the dealing-room and
lived for the day when they'd get the chance to
wheel and deal with those lucky people next door.
They pretended to one another that dealing wasn't
for them, but whenever they had the chance to talk
to Brian alone they reminded him of their true vocation
and begged him to speak to Mr Ito. Brian, unwilling
to admit that his power base was confined to his own
small section, never let them know they would have
more chance of dealing if they spent their time chasing
Mr Sasaki all round the bank.

There was a glass dividing-wall between the dealing-
room and Brian's little kingdom, allowing all its won-
ders to be clearly seen and heard. It was a sharp contrast

to the deadly dullness of the back office. Lisa tried to seem keen and interested in her new work but she soon became bored with the endless checking and with the chatter that accompanied it. Her only consolation was that Robert was still with her. Both of them spent much of their first morning in the section staring at the dealers through the thick glass and wondering how long it would be until they, too, were watched and admired by people less fortunate than themselves.

At coffee time, Shirley made her dislike of Lisa plain: she offered chocolate biscuits to everyone except the commie lesbo. The other staff, all too familiar with the subtle signs of Shirley's murderous intent, kept their heads down.

Lisa, being new and unwarned, said, 'Now I understand why office workers' hips spread so much in middle age,' and laughed loudly.

The others held their breath and waited for Shirley's heavy fist to smack the smile off Lisa's face, but Shirley had dominated the back office for so long that she was caught off guard by such blatant defiance and was too stunned to take immediate action. Lisa was pleased with her little triumph, but the other staff knew that Shirley wasn't so easily put down and that it would be only a matter of time before the beast rose again.

'Call for you, Lisa,' said a school-leaver.

She picked up the phone and smiled when she heard her brother's voice.

'How's it going?' he asked. 'I called the number you gave me and they said you weren't there any more.'

'I've just been moved.'

John was impressed by her rapid progress. 'What are you on? Money markets? Foreign exchange?'

'Nothing like that,' said Lisa. 'I'm still in the back

office, but I'm getting closer to the dealing-room. I can even see it from my desk.'

'Nice one,' said John, laughing as he imagined his sister in the quiet civilisation of the back office. 'Anyway, fancy a pint at lunchtime? I've got some news.'

'Good or bad?' asked Lisa.

'Depends which way you look at it. But listen, I can't say anything now. I'll meet you at the George at half eleven.'

'OK, see you then.' Lisa wondered if the news would benefit her. After a morning in her new section she needed a boost.

'I've been offered a desk in Singapore,' John told her. He didn't mean an ordinary office desk with three drawers on either side. To a dealer, a 'desk' is a team that deals in a specific financial instrument.

Lisa was upset. 'Are you going to go?' she asked.

'Well, the money's really good and I fancy a change, so I've told them that I'd like to try it for a year or so.'

'But you're such a racist,' protested Lisa. 'You'd hate to live abroad.'

'It won't make much difference,' he answered. 'Most of the dealers in the office out there are English or American.'

Lisa shook her head. He had no idea how terrible he sounded. She couldn't understand why it was that the markets made dealers so detached from the real world. What with her introduction to her new section and her brother's news, she was beginning to feel depressed. To lift her spirits she homed in on the one advantage she might gain from John's transfer.

'Can I live at your place while you're away?' she asked, picturing herself in his luxury Docklands flat.

'You can't afford it,' said John, treading all over her little daydream. 'I'm going to rent it out. Corporates will pay a lot of money for a flat like mine. I'll make a killing.' He was fond of his sister, but not fond enough to lose money in order to make her life easier.

'Thanks very much,' said Lisa bitterly. 'I'll return the favour next time.'

'Talking of favours, how are you doing in that job I got you?' asked John.

'It's very boring and I hate it,' she said grumpily.

'It'll be different once you start dealing. The back office is always dull, but you won't be there for long.'

Her disappointment that John was going away, combined with his refusal to let her stay in his flat, made her unwilling to look at things reasonably. 'How do you know? I could be stuck there for years,' she said.

'Don't talk crap. You're a trainee dealer. They have to put you in the dealing-room some time. Just keep pushing them.'

'Pushing them? It's hard enough just getting anyone to talk to me. They all hate me and there's this awful woman called Shirley who—'

'*Ssssshhhhhh!* Don't ever mention names in a bar. You don't know who could be listening.' John lowered his voice and looked around the pub.

Lisa quickly checked under the table for spies, but he failed to see the joke and continued to scan the room. Lisa stared at him. He had only been in the City five years and already he was showing strong signs of becoming as a nutty as their father.

'Don't worry about it,' she said. 'She's not even a manager or anything.'

'It doesn't matter. You don't know what she might become one day.'

Get out now, girl, while you're still normal, said the sensible part of Lisa's brain. Unfortunately, the voices of reason are always quieter than the pushier ones like greed, conformity and inevitability, so Lisa concentrated on finishing her drink and her tuna salad sandwich and then left her brother to walk back to work.

So, he was going to Singapore, she thought, wishing she could go too. She wanted to go anywhere except back to the boring back office. She tried to think positively; when she was a dealer and had built up a good reputation, she too would be able to work abroad in one of the world's financial capitals. She filled her mind with images of New York, Tokyo and Hong Kong and was able to convince herself that her time with Shirley, Brian, Pam and Dave was merely the shadow of a spider's web on a very successful life.

'Call for you, Lisa,' said a school-leaver.

She reached gladly for the phone, expecting John to tell her that he had changed his mind about the flat and that he would give her the spare keys at the weekend.

'Hello,' she said eagerly.

'Lisa, is the phone pressed right against your ear?' It wasn't her brother, it was a woman.

'Yes.' Lisa recognised the voice but couldn't place it. The caller hung up and Lisa sat puzzled. The school-leavers' sniggers made the penny drop. She rushed to the toilet to survey the damage. The paint on the earpiece had left a large black circle on her ear. Shirley had got her revenge.

A weaker person would have burst into tears and gone home, but Lisa was philosophical about the attack. She went back to her desk and carried on working. At least now she knew who was and wasn't on her side.

The other members of the section spent the afternoon quietly giggling at her, and the dealers came in one by one to laugh out loud. Even the local workers from other parts of the bank found excuses to come into the back office for a sneaky look, but, having better manners and more sensitivity, at least didn't laugh until they'd left the room. The Japanese staff came to look as well, but said nothing, putting the incident down as another strange local custom. The only person who said anything sympathetic was Robert, which proved to Lisa that, despite his slimy-toad exterior, he was a softie underneath.

When Lisa got home that night she washed the paint from her ear, changed her clothes and decided to have boil-in-the-bag kippers with two thick slices of white bread for tea; comfort food from her childhood which she liked to eat when she needed cheering up. Her father was having a boiled-egg night and he needed three slices of bread, one for soldiers and two to make a sandwich with the remains, so there was a tussle over the loaf. Lisa managed to get one thin slice and the crust, which she buttered thickly to make up for her disappointment.

The thought of going into work the next day filled her with embarrassment and spoilt the taste of her kippers. How should she behave? Should she ignore the incident, or should she get her own back? Abandoning her tea, she went and sat on the front doorstep, a favourite thinking-place, and looked up at the sky. If there hadn't been any clouds she could have gazed up at the stars and gained some wisdom from contemplating the size of the universe. As it was, the only light she could see was the glow from the street lamp opposite.

She focused on the Shirley problem. How could she

pay her back and come out smiling? At first, all she could think of were things that would get her either punched on the nose or fired. She wanted to avoid violence — she liked her nose as it was — and if she got fired it would be Shirley's victory. After a few minutes, feeling the need for alcohol to make her brain tick, she went inside and poured herself a large glass of whisky. As she drank it, a plan began to form.

Chapter 6

'Lisa, take that thing off your head.'

Brian was fed up with the temporary addition to his section. She'd been there only two days and she'd already managed to change the whole atmosphere of the room. It wasn't that she had upset everyone. On the contrary, her get-up this morning had caused merriment throughout the bank. Even Mr Aono, the general manager, had come to look, though he had at least had the dignity to pretend he wanted to speak to Mr Sasaki about the forthcoming golf tournament. Brian had had a laugh himself, but the point was, as he said to Dave by the coffee machine, 'She's not really cut out for this place.'

Looking at her now, Brian knew he was right. She simply wasn't 'one of us': her hair was too short, she always wore trousers, most of her clothes were black, she didn't read the right newspaper, and yesterday she'd said she hadn't got any shares and didn't intend to buy any. He shook his head. It might be amusing, but it also proved him right.

Lisa had got up that morning, fished out an old elastic bandage and wound it first round her neck and then round her head a few times, covering the ear that Shirley had marked. When she'd finished, she fixed the bandage with a pin and stood on tiptoe to see in the bathroom mirror if it looked good. It wasn't quite right . . . something was missing. After careful thought, she rolled up two pairs of socks and pushed them under the bandage so that they were over her ear. She looked in the mirror again. The bandage stuck out as if she had a massive carbuncle on the side of her head.

'Perfect,' she said, and she set off with her father to work. He was more concerned about getting to the station on time than with Lisa's appearance so it wasn't until they were sitting opposite each other on the train that he noticed she looked different. He pointed to the side of her head and she nodded to show that she knew.

Nobody in the carriage said anything, although Lisa heard a few titters here and there. She was pleased. That was the effect she had intended.

'What the fuck have you got on your head?' asked Robert when he saw her.

'I've had an allergic reaction to the paint,' said Lisa loudly. 'My ear's swollen up and full of pus.' Everyone laughed, and Lisa knew she had done the right thing.

It was such a contrast to the day before. Once again, she was the centre of attention and the subject of coffee-room conversation, but this time she felt able to laugh as heartily as everyone else.

Shirley didn't say anything at first. Lisa was effectively giving her the finger and she knew she deserved it. She realised her behaviour the day before had been unkind and that she was a little jealous of Lisa, who would soon be moving on while she would remain in the back office. If Shirley had been born twenty years later, she would have fancied her chances as a dealer; she was sure that she had more of what it takes than either Lisa or Stephanie, but she was too old now. At Lisa's age, she had already been married with a six-month-old baby. She had given up work as a bank clerk when she got pregnant and had stayed at home looking after the house and family until her second child was six. After that, she had still looked after the house and family, but she had managed to work full-time as well. It was now fifteen years since she had started at Haru Bank and she had no hope of promotion. All the future held for her was decline and, eventually, consignment to the back-office graveyard.

She had seen many young people come into the department. They stayed a while, learnt a few things and then moved on and up. Most of them were quite decent, but there was something about Lisa that had really hit a nerve. Perhaps it was her political leanings, shown by her preference for a left-wing newspaper, or maybe it was because she gave the impression that she thought they were all stupid to have stayed in a dull job for so long. Lisa hadn't said anything, but Shirley imagined that that was how she viewed them. Shirley knew she had gone too far by marking Lisa's ear, and she had decided to apologise to Lisa as soon as she got in, but once she saw her with the ridiculous bandage on her head and the socks poking through, all thoughts of saying sorry fled, and instead she took her place at her desk bristling with indignation.

She mellowed when Lisa, in a spirit of conciliation, handed round some sherbet lemons, helped Dave finish his *Sun* crossword and offered to go into the dealing-room to collect Stephanie's dealing-slips, a task so hated that they usually tossed up to see who had to go. Shirley

began to look at Lisa in a different way and she even
became quite sentimental when she realised that Lisa
was the same age as her son, Gary. Then a thought
struck her. How would he have coped if someone like
her had painted his ear on his first day in a new section?
It made Shirley feel very guilty for what she had done.
The truce came into effect when Shirley offered Lisa
a biscuit to go with her coffee. Lisa, who knew a
peace-offering when she saw one, responded in kind by
offering Shirley her newspaper to read at lunchtime.

Calm reigned in the back office once more and,
although the work was still deadly dull, Lisa realised
her time was not being completely wasted. Sitting on
the wrong side of the glass divide, she could now observe
the dealing-room in action and learn something about its
members.

Leo was definitely the king. On a busy day, when the
market was moving, it took a great deal of effort not to
stop work and watch him in action. He would stand up
with a phone in each hand and his eyes fixed firmly
on his screens, barking orders to his brokers, gradually
getting louder and louder and swearing more and more
until the market activity peaked and things began to
slow down again.

Being the king meant that Leo could show his rage
when he lost money. He could break his phone into
pieces by smashing it against the desk. He could kick
a chair across the room. He could even leave early and
stomp off to the pub – as he did once when he had made
a big loss in a very short time – and no one seemed to
mind. Or if they did, they never said anything to him
about it. His manager, Aki-san, treated him as an equal.
Occasionally, the two men clashed over strategy and
during those times Aki-san would pull rank, but he did

not try to curb Leo's unorthodox style. He realised that, if Haru Bank wanted to keep a dealer as good as Leo, they had to turn a blind eye to his bad behaviour.

Aki-san and Leo made up the Futures desk. Behind them, on the Money Market desk, sat the biggest team in the room. There was a dealer for each of the main currencies, and three dealers for US dollars. The only woman dealer in the room sat at that desk dealing fixed-date dollars. If Leo was the king, Stephanie, by virtue of being the only woman and because of her commanding presence, deserved the title of queen. She wasn't as dramatic as Leo. She never stood up to deal and she never let herself lose enough control to break or kick something. She had dignity and she always kept tight control of her emotions.

That didn't stop her being a force to be reckoned with. If a broker upset her in any way — and there were many ways to upset Stephanie, from not quoting fast enough to making a comment that she deemed to be offensive — she would refuse to deal with the broker's company again until one of its directors came to the bank personally to apologise. The brokers acted as intermediaries between the banks and they earned their commission on the deals they set up. Losing the custom of a major player like Haru Bank could mean the sack for the unlucky broker who had managed to upset Stephanie.

Of all the dealers in the room, Stephanie was perhaps the one most hated by the back office. She was rude, she always kept them waiting when they wanted something signed, and if a problem arose she would never admit that it might have been her fault. Brian especially hated the way she would come up to him and tell him to send a telex to a customer as if he had nothing better to do.

He often felt like pointing out to her that he was a
manager and was therefore far above performing such
menial tasks. He would have done so straight away if
he hadn't been so scared of her.

In fact, Lisa soon saw, Stephanie's behaviour to the
back office was exactly the same as that of the major-
ity of dealers. Lisa suspected Stephanie was disliked
merely because she was a woman. It was more or less
expected that the male dealers were rude and arrogant
because they had a lot of pressure in their job, not
to mention having to contend with their testosterone
levels. But Stephanie was a woman and women were
not supposed to be aggressive, arrogant or rude. Being
natural communicators, they were expected to be polite,
quiet and kind. Lisa wondered if she would manage to
be as loathed as Stephanie. If she did, it would mean
that she had become a real dealer.

Behind the Money Market desk, furthest from the
back office, was the Holy Grail of dealing desks:
Foreign Exchange, known to insiders as FX. This
was where fortunes were made and lost in the space
of a few minutes, or so it seemed to Lisa and Robert.
If they had known the markets better than they both
pretended to, they would have realised that the Futures
desk was the most risky, but because on a busy day FX
was the loudest desk — even louder than Leo — they
thought it was also the most exciting desk and they
longed to be on it. Lisa had plenty of time to dream.
Her work required very little concentration and, to keep
herself from keeling over in a bored stupor, she often
fantasised about her future life on FX.

One good thing about working in the back office
was that Lisa came to understand her father's life a
little better. Until now, she had thought his inability

to speak and his peculiar habits were for home use only. She had seen him as two people. The first was Mr Jolly Normal, his work persona and the lively young man she could see in the old photos of him before he got married. The second was Mr Jolly Strange, his home self. She had never imagined that this latter persona could possibly be the whole man. If it was, how on earth could he have kept his job?

Working at Haru Bank, she realised that he would be perfectly able to get by without speaking or writing properly. Mr Jolly Strange wasn't nearly so strange when set alongside the veterans of the back office, who all displayed signs of peculiar eccentricities. As long as her father was able to sit in a chair and sign his name – and that need be no more than a scrawl – he could probably hold out until he reached retirement age.

The big question was whether the years spent doing such boring work had caused his illness, or whether it had nothing to do with his job. Over the last five years he had had many tests to find out what was causing his loss of speech and his increasingly strange behaviour, but the doctors had eventually admitted that they would have no idea until he died, when they would be able to examine his brain in greater detail. Lisa always did her best to shut that image out of her mind.

Sometimes she tried to imagine what it must feel like to be her father. Did he realise what was happening? Was he gradually being locked inside his own body, or was the man himself gradually being lost along with his ability to communicate? It was easier to believe in the latter, because then he wouldn't be aware of the situation. That he might understand what was going on was too dreadful to contemplate.

Lisa didn't know whether her father's illness had

driven her mother away or whether the disease had
been caused by Mo's departure. She couldn't remember
exactly when he started to be not quite right. He had
changed so gradually that it was difficult to remember
what he had been like before he got ill. She didn't
know which parts of his behaviour could be put down
to his personality and which parts to the effect of the
illness. It was very difficult to pinpoint a cause.

Certainly the shock of having one's wife run off
with a flower-seller in the City was enough to make
anyone go nutty, but then again, the stress of living
with Lisa's father might well have made even the most
dutiful of wives look around for greener pastures. How
else could one explain Mo's love for Ron, the rotund
flower-seller with badly fitting false teeth and sweaty
armpits who had induced her to leave her two children
and her husband of fifteen years and move into his
three-bedroom council flat in Stratford?

Chapter 7

———   ———

Robert's great day came, without warning, after two long and weary months in the back office. The morning started the same as any other in Brian's little kingdom. Robert and Lisa had been given a large stack of checking to do and they were sitting at their desks quietly working when Mr Ito came in and said he wanted to talk to Robert.

Robert was gone for half an hour, and when he came back he looked insufferably smug. 'I've got FX,' he told Lisa, meaning, *Up yours, Shorty. I'm one of the big boys now.*

'Oh, well done,' replied Lisa, thinking, *I hope you get piles, you slimy, public-school toad.*

Robert had got a place on the loudest, flashiest desk in the dealing-room. When exchange rates were moving fast, the back office could hear — with fierce envy — the cries of the FX dealers as they bought and sold the major currencies. On a busy day, they often drew a crowd of admirers. The dealers pretended not to notice their inferiors hanging around, but the volume at which they shouted and the number of times they swore and made dramatic gestures couldn't be put down entirely to the pressure of the job. There was also an air of 'Look at me, aren't I wonderful?' Even when they were losing money.

The FX desk was run by Mr Sumida, a tiny little man whose size and welcoming grin often fooled those new to the bank into thinking he was as mild as a pussycat. But when he was losing money, or when those under him made even the slightest of mistakes, his roars of anger bounced off the walls and made those uninvolved mighty grateful that they hadn't got big enough balls to be on the FX desk.

Lisa and Robert had both fancied themselves capable of withstanding the pressures of working with Mr Sumida. The glamour of the job would surely compensate for working under such a tyrant, they thought. On the few occasions when they had come into contact with him they had tried to impress him with their intelligent conversation. They would have done better to try other means. Mr Sumida's English was so bad that he could hardly order a hamburger at McDonald's, let alone assess a person's aptitude for dealing during a casual conversation at the coffee machine. He did, however, take a keen interest in Lisa's breasts and if she had opened her shirt just enough to give him a glimpse of her cleavage, he would probably have done his best to see that she was on his team. As she hadn't, he had endorsed Robert's promotion to the desk because he looked the part and wasn't likely to rush off to the toilets in tears every time he got shouted at.

Robert knew he was going to be the general dogsbody for the FX desk, fetching coffee and sandwiches, sending telexes, inputting deals into the computer and taking care of jobs that would make Mr Sumida's life more comfortable, like going to the cashpoint machine or booking his rounds at the golf club. After a year, Robert might be entrusted with making small deals in the minor currencies, and eventually, if he did well enough, he would be given a dealing position of his own. He had a lot of hard work ahead of him, but he did have the chance to do well and he was determined to make the most of it.

Before Lisa could go and slash her wrists, Robert told her that Mr Ito wanted to see her too. Trying to look as if she didn't care what her fate was, she left the room as fast as she could without actually breaking into a trot.

Mr Ito was waiting for her in one of the little rooms usually reserved for meetings with visitors to the bank. Each room was furnished with a sofa and two armchairs placed side by side facing the sofa. Between the sofa and armchairs was a low table, which ensured that a comfortable distance was kept between the two parties holding the meeting. The gap between the table and the chairs was very narrow. This prevented those endowed with long legs from sitting with their legs crossed and thus flaunting their physical superiority. Instead they had to sit bolt upright, legs together, with the table top digging into their shins. The Japanese employees, who often had short legs, could sit in comfort, knowing that their long-legged adversaries' physical discomfort would become so great that they would, in the end, agree to anything, just so that they could get out of the room and stretch their aching limbs.

Being shorter than Mr Ito, Lisa felt no physical discomfort when she sat down. Her discomfort was purely emotional as she nervously waited to hear where she would be placed. Mr Ito, seemingly unaware of her feelings, put some papers on the table in front of him and slowly re-arranged them.

'Well, Lisa,' he said eventually, fixing his gaze on the middle of her forehead. 'You have been here two months now. Have you learnt a lot about banking?'

Lisa didn't think he wanted to know what she really thought so she chose to be diplomatic. 'Yes, working in the back office has been very useful.'

Mr Ito was pleased. 'You sound like you have been enjoying yourself.'

'Yes.' Lisa wondered if he was being sarcastic, or whether he thought checking was a deeply fulfilling experience. She imagined that Robert, the sycophant, had been gushing about how wonderful it was to sit in the back office with such stimulating people as Dave and Pam, checking the work of the glorious dealers, and that Mr Ito probably assumed she felt the same way.

'I have heard good reports about you,' he said. 'You are punctual and you are careful with your work. I am pleased to hear this. It is very important to be a careful worker in a bank.'

'Yes, I suppose it is,' agreed Lisa, who thought keeping awake despite being bored senseless was probably the best quality to have.

'What do you see yourself doing from now on?' asked Mr Ito, as if her new position hadn't already been arranged.

'I'd like to work on FX,' she replied, hoping there was room on the desk for two new trainees.

Mr Ito shook his head. 'I'm sorry, Robert is going on there,' he said. 'We are giving you BAs.'

Bastards! They aren't even putting me in the dealing-room, thought Lisa in a panic. Oh God! Sentenced to years in the back office doing BAs. Kill me now! No, better still, I'll kill my brother. Singapore isn't that far away . . .

She dragged herself back to the conversation. 'BAs?' It sounded like an abbreviation for a really dull job.

'Yes, on the Futures desk with Aki-san and Leo,' said Mr Ito.

'Leo?' Lisa hated Leo. He called her 'Dwarf' or 'Dwarfie', and he'd thrown a bacon sandwich at her. BAs: bloody awfuls. Was this some kind of punishment? What had she done wrong except be bored?

'Yes, and Aki-san,' said Mr Ito. 'He is a fine manager.' He was pleased to see Lisa's amazement. She was obviously thrilled with her good fortune.

'Thrilled' was the last word Lisa would have used to describe her feelings. 'What will I be doing exactly?' she asked suspiciously.

'You will be dealing bankers' acceptances. Eventually, I hope you will trade futures with Leo and Aki-san,' said Mr Ito. 'You must be very pleased.'

'Yes, I am,' said Lisa, who wasn't at all. Her pleasure at the news that she would be dealing straight away was outweighed by her dismay at hearing she'd be working with Leo. He'd disliked her from the moment he set eyes on her. Would he be nice to her now that she was on his desk? Lisa tried to believe that he would make her feel welcome. She'd be better off than Robert, she told herself. At least she wouldn't have to put up with a manager as fierce as Mr Sumida.

After the meeting, Mr Ito took Robert and Lisa into the dealing-room. Once again he introduced them to the staff, but this time he added that Robert would be assisting the dealers on Foreign Exchange and that Lisa would be dealing BAs. Lisa and Robert, each thinking they had come off better than the other, smiled when

Mr Ito said this. Robert was happy because he'd got
FX; even though he'd have to start at the bottom, the
potential for getting on was very good. Lisa believed she
had won because she'd be going straight into dealing. All
that slobbering and sucking up to people hadn't given
him any advantage over her at all, she thought. On
the contrary, by being given a dealing position, she
was obviously the favoured one, although she couldn't
work out what it was that had attracted the attention
of her superiors. She didn't realise that the decision had
probably been made in Tokyo and that personality,
intellect, or any other feature that she cared to think
up, had had absolutely nothing to do with it. Somebody
somewhere had, in all likelihood, taken the first name
on the list and placed it with the FX and then matched
the next name with the Futures team; the assumption
being that staff members of Haru Bank would be willing
and able to do any job they were assigned to.

Introductions over, Lisa found herself at her new
desk. She was placed on the left of Aki-san. On his
right sat Leo, whose greeting this time had a friendlier
tone; he merely grunted at her without taking his eyes
off his screens. The three of them sat on the left side of
the dealing-room with their backs to the other dealers.
At the opposite end of the room was the FX desk, and
running along the middle was the Money Market desk.
On Lisa's left was a huge tape-recorder taping all the
telephone conversations that went on in the room. As she
now sat nearest the machine, it was her responsibility to
keep it running throughout the day. When one of the
huge tapes ran out, she had to note down which days
had been recorded and then replace it with another
one. All the tapes were numbered and they were kept
in a large cabinet near Mr Ito's desk. Andy, a junior

dealer on the money market desk, who had previously done this tedious chore, and was thankful to have passed it on, quickly told her what she had to do and then skipped back to his desk. Lisa was mesmerised by the sheer size of the tapes, and was too busy worrying about how she was going to lift them off the reels to listen to Andy's explanation. Luckily, the tape was at the beginning of the reel and wouldn't have to be changed for at least a day. Lisa hoped she'd be at lunch when that happened, and that someone would do it for her.

She looked towards Aki-san and Leo for some guidance as to what she should do next, but they were both on the telephone, so she sat down at her desk and examined her new surroundings. First, she swivelled on her chair to see if it went all the way round; it did, very smoothly, which pleased her. Then she opened and closed her drawers. They were nice and spacious, just waiting to be filled with important documents. She checked out the people around her, Aki-san sat on her right and Andy was just behind her. Mr Ito's desk was about eight feet away. A little close for comfort, but Lisa thought he was kind, so she didn't mind. Finally, she stared at her desk. It was about four feet wide and two feet deep. On the far side it rose up into shelves, so when she was sitting down she couldn't see who was opposite her. She stood on tiptoe and leant over the top. The desk on the other side was empty. It was good to know that there was space on her left and in front of her; she wouldn't feel boxed in.

On the desk was a computer pad divided into coloured squares. Those in the middle were blue and had the abbreviated names of the larger banks printed on them. Along the top of the pad, there were red squares containing the abbreviations of different financial terms.

Some were familiar to her, like 'MM' for 'Money Market', 'FX' for 'foreign exchange' and 'Fut' for 'futures'. There were a few more that she didn't know anything about, like 'BA' and 'CD', but she was sure she'd find out about them during her training session. Along the bottom of the pad there were yellow squares containing the locations of the world's main financial centres: London, New York, Tokyo, Hong Kong, Frankfurt, Zurich.

On the left of the desk, there was a computer and a keyboard. Scary stuff: Lisa had very little experience with computers and this one looked shiny new and expensive. She reassured herself that she wouldn't be let loose on it without proper instruction.

On the back of her desk, between the shelves, there were two screens side by side. All the desks in the room had two or three of these black screens, which were filled with little green numbers that constantly moved. They were obviously essential to the dealers' survival because all the dealers sat with their eyes fixed on their screens. The only time they looked away was when they stood up to leave the room; all other tasks were carried out with at least one eye glued to the screens.

Lisa's hadn't been turned on yet, so, to show that she was in business, she reached forward and twiddled the knobs until she too could fix her eyes on the moving green figures. At first, she was dazzled by their greenness, but as her eyes gradually focused, she noticed that her numbers and screens looked very different from Aki-san's on the next desk. Did this mean she wouldn't be able to keep up? She noticed that her screens said 'page 212' and that Aki-san had a different page number. How did she change the pages? Looking to her right, she saw a black keyboard. Its colour probably meant it was connected to the screens. Dare she touch it? No, she would wait and ask someone later.

She switched her interest to the row of buttons above the screens. There were about fifteen of them, each with a light above it. Occasionally the lights flashed or abruptly went off, but mostly they just stayed on. Obviously something to do with the phones, but which was her line and how did she ring out? She had two phones and there were lots of lines but how did she connect the two? She was dying to ring someone and say, 'Guess what? I'm a dealer.' She decided to watch carefully the next time Aki-san made a phone call.

Underneath the screens, there were even more buttons. Each button had initials on it: 'MW', 'SHL' and 'DJW', standing for Maine Weaver, Shearson Lehmans and D. J. Walters. The buttons occasionally flashed and when one was pressed, which Lisa did gingerly, the light stayed on. When she pressed it again, the light went off.

'Yes,' said a loud voice behind Lisa. Andy leant forward, pressed one of his buttons, had a few words on the phone and then shouted, 'Who was in Fultons?'

Lisa sank down in her chair. Now she knew what those buttons were for. They were the direct lines to the brokers and security houses. If you pressed a button and then spoke into the phone, the brokers and dealers in the company linked to that button could hear you, via a loudspeaker box. Lisa could see these boxes on many of the dealer's desks and she could hear brokers calling out prices. So many things to find out. When would she start her training? She turned in her seat and looked for Robert. He was deep in conversation with one of his new FX colleagues, pointing at his instruments, asking questions, getting answers and looking very comfortable

with the whole situation. Trust him to find his feet
faster than she was doing, she thought. She looked
again at Aki-san who had just put down his phone.

'Lunchtime now,' he said. 'You like pizza. We go
eat.'

The word 'pizza' seemed to have a magical quality
because a few other Japanese managers, on hearing it,
stood up quickly, grabbed their jackets and followed
Lisa and Aki-san out of the room. As they hurried
through the bank, gradually gaining speed, they picked
up a few more pizza-lovers on the way and Lisa found
herself trotting down Lime Street with eight Japanese
men in dark suits, heading for the pizza pub.

Once inside, after a short discussion in Japanese, it
was decided that a half of lager each and three large
hot and spicy pizzas would just about fill everyone up.
Aki-san and one of the other managers went off to order,
leaving Lisa behind as the centre of attention.

Six friendly faces beamed at her and one manager
said, 'You do BAs now. You like working with Aki-san.'

As Lisa wasn't sure if this was a question, a command
or merely an observation, she had no idea what kind
of reply was expected of her. She just smiled and
nodded, hoping that the conversation would depart
from anything to do with dealing. She didn't want
her ignorance to be revealed quite so soon.

'We expected nice young lady, but we get you,' said
another manager. 'Why you no wear women's clothes?'

On second thoughts, maybe financial matters would
have been a safer topic. How could she answer that?
'If I wore "women's clothes",' she replied, 'I expect
you wouldn't be able to work. You would spend all
day looking down my blouse.'

The crowd roared and Lisa knew that she had got it

exactly right. They weren't interested in talking about work. They wanted to relax and have fun. Now that they knew she had a good sense of humour, they laughed and joked until the pizzas came.

Hot and spicy was an understatement. At the first bite, Lisa's lips went numb and her tongue got burnt. She glugged down her lager and looked around wildly for somewhere to spit out the offending mouthful.

Aki-san looked at her accusingly. 'You no like pizza,' he said. If she didn't like pizza, she was definitely suspect. He hadn't wanted a female on the desk at all, especially not a British one. If she failed the pizza test, he would cast her aside.

Spurred by his menacing expression, Lisa forced herself to swallow the offending lump. She wiped the tears from her eyes and, with a deep breath, took another large bite. Her first experience of kissing the boss's arse was painful indeed.

Back in the dealing-room, Aki-san gave Lisa a pep talk. 'You do BAs. Leo show you how. You work hard an' no make mistakes, OK.'

'Yes, sir.' Lisa felt the seriousness of his manner warranted a show of respect, so she added the 'sir', even though it was against her egalitarian principles.

'You no call me "sir". You say "Aki-san", OK.' He thought it enough that he spoke English to her; she could at least learn how to address him in the Japanese way. He felt his colleagues went too far in trying to be seen as international by adopting 'Mr'. It should be give and take on both sides.

'Yes, Aki-san,' Lisa replied. It was beginning to feel like the television drama *Tenko*. She wondered when she would be forced to kneel at his feet and kiss the floor.

'Leo now explain BA, OK,' said Aki-san.

Leo stood up, hitched his trousers, scratched his groin and headed for Lisa's desk. 'Right, Dwarfie, get me a coffee, black, two sugars, and Aki-san has it with milk and one sugar. Go easy on the milk, squirt.'

There had been a time in the not-too-distant past — just a few hours earlier, in fact, when she was in the back office — when Lisa would have told anyone exactly where they could stick their coffee if they'd spoken to her like that. But there was something about sitting in a dealing-room for the first time that robbed her of her fighting-spirit. The noise, the screens, the flashing lights and the large amounts of money that she had heard being dealt had overawed her and, instead of shouting something back at Leo, she obediently got up to get the coffee while he sat down in her chair. She wasn't so overawed that she didn't realise what had taken place. But she also knew that she relied on these two men to teach her about dealing and, as they had both made it clear that her status was lower than a bedbug's, it would be wise to go along with them until she found her feet. She could start fighting back once she had learnt how to deal.

'How's it going?' A friendly face in the coffee room was just what she needed. Only slimy Robert but at least she got a smile from him. He was a little flushed and he swayed slightly as he sugared his tray of coffee cups. The market was quiet, so the FX lads had been able to welcome him in style. While she'd been scarring her tonsils with chillis, he'd been slurping pink champagne, courtesy of an FX broker.

'Not so bad, but there's so much to learn all at once that—' Lisa stopped herself. Much as she wanted a shoulder to cry on, it wouldn't do to let Robert know how vulnerable she felt. She shrugged and gave what she hoped was a nonchalant smile.

Robert was sympathetic. 'You'll be fine, kid, no sweat,' he said, giving her a friendly pat on the shoulder.

His champagne-induced kindness would have brought a tear to the eye of a person with a weaker disposition, but Lisa was easily able to remain dry-eyed as she pressed the 'Tea' button. She would have liked to believe her mistake was due to being overcome with emotion, when in actual fact it was the expression of an unconscious desire not to be completely dominated by her senior colleagues.

Aki-san and Leo both spat out their tea.

'Fucking dwarf!' shouted Leo. 'Can't even get that right! Go back and get another one, you silly bitch.' To make sure that she didn't make another mistake, he wrote their order on her arm in black pen.

In the coffee room, Lisa wondered why it was that bank employees had the urge to mark their colleagues in black. She had never noticed her father coming home with strange markings, so perhaps it was just something about her that made her fellow workers itch to alter her skin tones. She comforted herself with the thought that at least Leo hadn't written on her face: maybe he had a sensitive side after all.

Bending down beside Leo for her training-session was not pleasant. He tended to press his face close to hers, and the fumes from his lunchtime whisky were decidedly off-putting.

'Right, Dwarfie, what you do is get the rates from the security houses in the morning, keep checking them through the day, add on a spread and give quotes to the customers.'

'What kind of rates?'

'Discount rates.'

Lisa was lost. 'Discount rates?'

'Oh Christ, she doesn't even know what a fucking discount rate is!' exclaimed Leo, and Lisa sank down a little lower.

She could tell that her training-session was not going to be fruitful. She wondered if Leo would be happier explaining how to use the phones. She thought about asking but he started up again.

'Look, here are the customers and their phone numbers. Here are their limits. When you do a deal, you input it into the computer, send off a telex to New York and fix a copy to the back of the deal slip, all right?' Having finished his lowly task, he got up and swaggered back to his desk.

A thousand and one questions raced around in Lisa's head. How do I input a deal? Where is the telex machine? What is a limit? New York? Where in New York? And what the hell is a BA anyway?

The excitement she had felt in the morning had vanished. Aki-san and Leo completely ignored her as they dealt. She tried to look busy. She switched different lights on and off. She pushed buttons and swivelled round on her chair a few times. She even got Aki-san and Leo three more cups of coffee each. It was no good. After a while she couldn't hide the fact that she had nothing to do and didn't know how to occupy her time. She had expected a training-period, or even a manual to study, but instead she was left alone to get on with things. If the back office had been bad, this was far worse.

Aki-san didn't believe in mollycoddling his juniors. If Lisa was to survive the market, she had to learn to find out things for herself. He might not speak to her all afternoon, but he made mental notes of what she was doing — or rather failing to do. He wanted to see her take the initiative, to demand information and ask lots of questions. He was very disappointed when she did none of these things. Mr Ito had been wrong when he said she was suited to the dealing-room; Aki-san had never seen anyone so out of place.

At five o'clock, Lisa looked towards Aki-san for permission to go. He ignored her as he had seemed to do all afternoon, so she quietly turned off her screens, cleared her desk, said 'Goodbye' to the back of his head and walked out of the room.

Chapter 8

——— ———

A very ragged-looking Lisa arrived at the bank the following morning. Her bowels had given out in sympathy with her nerves and she had spent the night racing to the toilet. She had planned to spend the evening blotting out all thoughts of Leo and Aki-san with a bottle of whisky, but the squitters had thwarted that escape. Instead, she had had to remain sober and swift of foot to stop her frequent eruptions from going anywhere except down the toilet bowl.

She wished she could have seen John, but he was now in Singapore and, from what she heard when he occasionally phoned, he was enjoying his new life very much. Lisa was angry with him for abandoning her at such a time. If things at work didn't improve soon, she vowed, she would fix it so that he never enjoyed anything ever again.

Aki-san and Leo were already at their desks when she got to the dealing-room. Judging by his bloodshot eyes and the way he was slurping black coffee as if even the slightest lip movement sent shooting pains to the top of his head, Leo had had a late night. His blue and white candy-striped shirt, which he had been wearing

the day before, was badly creased and on the breast
pocket there was a remnant of last night's vindaloo.
As Lisa approached the desk, he lifted his left buttock
and farted loudly. Lisa and Aki-san were surrounded by
an invisible cloud of noxious fumes.

Aki-san clapped his handkerchief over his nose and
turned to Lisa. 'What time this?'

She was ten minutes early. It was 7.50. It said so
quite clearly on the clock hanging on the wall in front
of them. Lisa knew that Aki-san could see it from
his desk. She also noted that he had on a rather nice
watch. Either his question had a hidden meaning or
the handkerchief had muffled his words.

'Pardon?' she asked.

'What time this?' Aki-san said again. 'It nearly eight
o'clock. You very late. Tomorrow you come at seven
o'clock, OK.'

'OK,' answered Lisa in shock. She had to start work
at seven o'clock. What kind of job was this?

Aki-san wasn't finished yet. 'Now, this your first day
dealing. You no make mistakes. You make mistakes and
I very angry. You get rate form and dealing-sheet and
you start, OK,' he said, speaking very clearly to make
sure he wouldn't have to repeat himself.

Rate form? Dealing-sheet? Lisa looked towards Leo.
She would have to ask him. She rose and crept over to
his desk.

'Whaddya want, Dwarf?' he growled when he
noticed her standing beside his chair.

'Can I have some rate forms and dealing-sheets,
please?' said Lisa, trying to sound a lot calmer than
she felt.

'In the drawer.' Leo pointed to the bottom drawer
on his right. 'Take one of each and photocopy them.'

Lisa located the sheets and headed for the copying-room. Perhaps if she lingered for a while she could delay the dealing bit, she thought. She met Andy by the photocopier. He smiled at her and to her astonishment his smile seemed to be genuine and even warm. So far the other local dealers had only sneered.

'Are you having fun?' Andy had warmed to Lisa, in the way that one target of abuse warms to another.

'Fun? With those two?' asked Lisa.

'Well, I don't envy you at all. They didn't want a woman on the desk and they're probably making things difficult on purpose.'

'Bastards! I think I'll poison their coffee.'

Andy laughed louder than the joke warranted and Lisa decided she liked him. She knew that she shouldn't trust anyone with her feelings. Her brother had warned her that dealers must be tough and that if she showed any vulnerability she would be destroyed. Her little joke sounded as if she was coping well, but she wasn't and she wanted to turn to someone for help. Could she risk asking Andy? He seemed genuine enough and he sat right behind her in the dealing-room. If he agreed to show her how things should be done she might be able to survive the day alongside Aki-san and Leo. But what if he was only pretending to be nice and then went into the dealing-room and revealed her ignorance? She would be seen as weak and feeble and she would have to leave. But then again, if she didn't have some help soon she would have to leave anyway.

She decided to take the plunge. 'Andy, could you tell me what a BA is?'

He tried not to laugh. 'Well, it stands for "bankers' acceptance". It's a sort of discount instrument, a bit like a CD.' He was amazed that she had sat in the dealing-room all day yesterday and hadn't even found out what she was supposed to be doing.

'How do you deal it?'

'Um, gosh, I don't know, I only do short-date dollars,' said Andy. He hadn't been dealing that long himself so, although he could tell Lisa what a BA was, he couldn't tell her what to do when she came into contact with one. 'Why don't you ask Leo?'

'Leo?' asked Lisa.

They both laughed at the waste of time that would be. Lisa was hugely relieved that Andy was laughing with her and not at her. Also, he didn't know much about BAs either. Maybe it wasn't such a rare thing for a dealer not to know much about the financial markets.

'Aki-san said I have to start dealing today, but I haven't the faintest idea where to begin,' she confessed.

'He believes in sink or swim. He's probably told Leo not to help you much just to see how you cope on your own.'

'I doubt if Leo would have bent over backwards anyway,' said Lisa.

'Yes, that's true,' agreed Andy.

Lisa could feel her tension draining away. Perhaps, later, Andy would show her how to use her computer. Full of renewed strength and vitality, she went back to the dealing-room and approached Leo.

'Right,' she said, 'where do I start?'

'You fucking what?'

Lisa steeled herself and asked Leo what she should do first. He told her to get the rates from a few security houses, add on the spread and then call up the customers with the rates. Andy showed her the direct lines to the security houses on the board in front of her and gave her the phone numbers of some of the other houses.

She took out a rate sheet and wrote the date at the top. Then she picked up one of her phones and looked at the buttons in front of her. She pressed the one that said 'DJW'. It began to flash. She waited for a voice on the other end of the line. Silence. She pushed the button again, and the light went off. She pushed once more, and it flashed again. She waited one minute, two minutes . . . her courage was beginning to slip. Just as she was about to hang up she heard a deep American voice: 'Good morning.'

'Good morning,' she answered, relieved that she'd finally got someone on the line. 'Can I have the BA rates, please?'

'Well, you're a nice change from Leo. What's your name, sweetie?'

'Lisa.'

'Nice to meet you. I'm Bob.'

'OK, Bob, can I have the rates please?'

'Well, you *are* in a hurry. I'll have to talk with Chuck and then I'll be right back.' He rang off and Lisa, cheered up by his syrupy tones, smiled to herself. She wasn't too thrilled with being called 'sweetie', but it was better than what Leo called her and, besides, Bob was American, so perhaps that was how they talked to each other over there. Despite his choice of words, she liked the sound of Bob. If everyone was as easy to talk to as he was, she might even begin to enjoy herself.

She pushed the next button.

'Hello.' Another male voice, English this time.

'Hello. Can I have the BA rates please?'

'Ones and twos twenty-two, threes twenty-four, fours twenty-six, fives twenty-seven, and thirty in the sixes.'

'Sorry, could you say it again?' asked Lisa, who

had only managed to scribble down the first few numbers.'

The voice sighed and slowly repeated the rates.

'Thank you,' said Lisa.

'You're welcome,' replied the voice, and instantly the connection was cut.

Who shoved the poker up your arse? thought Lisa shuddering. The short, sharp exchange had taken place with an ex-public schoolboy. She could tell by the tone of his voice, which had betrayed his unshakeable belief in his own superiority. It had been so strong that it had oozed down the line through every clipped vowel.

She turned to Andy with the numbers she'd been given. He told her that the one to six referred to one month, two months and so on, and that the other figures were the discount rate for each month. 'He hasn't told you the big figure because he assumes you know it — even though you obviously don't,' he added as Lisa raised her eyebrows.

'What do you mean?' she asked.

'Well, when he said twenty-two in the one month, he meant nine point two two, and so on,' Andy explained.

'Oh God! My head is going to burst,' moaned Lisa, and she turned sadly back to her desk to write the rates on her dealing-sheet.

Bob's light flashed. 'Hi, sweetie, here they are. Nine twenty for one and two months, twenty-three for the threes, twenty-five in the fours and fives, and twenty-seven in the sixes. Now, Chuck says that they are only good for now. If you want to deal you'll have to ring back and check.'

'Right, Bob.' Two *sweeties* in less than ten minutes. He was being so kind to her that he couldn't possibly mean anything bad by it. It was obviously another of the quirks in the market that she had to get used to. She was glad he'd told her that the rates could move. If he hadn't, she might have tried to deal with a customer and found the rate no longer existed. Thank God for Bob. His rates were a little better than the uptight Englishman's, which pleased her: she'd much rather deal with good old Bob any day.

She pressed the button for Maine Weavers and was surprised to hear a woman's voice say, 'Good morning, Leo darling. What can I do for you?'

'Good morning,' replied Lisa smiling. 'Sorry to disappoint you, but I'm doing the BAs now. I'm Lisa.'

'Ah, music to my ears. I was hoping I'd outlast him.'

'Pity me, I have to work with him.' Lisa had never met this woman, and the whole conversation was being recorded on the giant tapes turning slowly round and round beside her, and yet here she was putting down a colleague. Not very professional, and John would have been horrified. But Lisa, after hearing two friendly voices, was sufficiently relaxed enough not to care about the consequences of such indiscretion.

'I'm Jackie, by the way. I'll just give you the rates and then we can have a chat.'

She read off the rates quickly and Lisa wrote them down. They weren't at all good.

'We aren't looking to do anything before the big figure this afternoon,' explained Jackie.

'I see,' said Lisa, thinking, *Big figure? Isn't it nine?*

'How long have you been at Haru's?' asked Jackie.

'About two months.'

'So why haven't I heard of you before?'

'Well, I only got into the dealing-room yesterday. I've been stuck in the back office.'

'And you're dealing straight away? How are you coping?'

'Not so bad,' said Lisa. 'Leo's been a great help.'

'Yeah, I bet,' said Jackie sardonically. 'Isn't there another woman dealer at Haru's?'

Lisa looked over her shoulder at Queen Stephanie, who was sipping a cappuccino. 'That's right, she's on the dollars,' she said, quietly so as not to be overheard. 'I've never really spoken to her.'

'I get the picture,' laughed Jackie. 'She's probably pissed off that she's not the only girlie in the room now—Oooops gottago,' and she rang off, leaving Lisa to contemplate her last remark.

She looked round again and saw that Stephanie was now talking to one of her brokers. So far she'd made no attempt to be friendly. Did she really see Lisa as a rival, as Jackie'd suggested, or had she been simply too busy to take much notice of her?

Aki-san interrupted her thoughts. 'Lisa, I have a customer on the phone. Give me the rate sheet.'

Lisa handed him the sheet, glad of the chance to hear how to give a quote. Aki-san added a five-basis-point spread to Bob's rates and read them off. 'You want to do thirty million dollars in six months? Hold, please.' He turned to Lisa. 'Check customer's limit.'

Lisa fumbled through her drawer, found the customer file and read that the customer had $100 million left on their limit.

'There's plenty of room, Aki-san,' she said. 'The six-month rate isn't firm, though. I'll just check it.' She pressed the DJW button.

Aki-san didn't wait for Bob to answer. 'Hello,' he said to the customer. 'Our six-months BA rate is nine thirty-two . . . OK, done. That's thirty million dollars in six months. We confirm by telex. Thank you very much. Goodbye.' He wrote out the deal slip and handed it to Lisa. 'Now you must cover it. When we deal with a customer we lend them money through BA financing. To cover the loan, we issue a BA and sell it. The spread is the profit. Now you go to security house and sell them the BA. You must have spread of five basis points. You must deal at nine point two seven or less.' He raised his hand as if to say that was the end of the conversation, and turned back to his own work. Lisa prayed that Bob's rate would be unchanged.

She went into Bob's line again. 'Can you do six months at twenty-seven? We've got thirty million.'

'Let me ask Chuck,' said Bob. 'I'll be right back.' The light on his button went off. Lisa stared at it nervously, waiting for it to flicker into action again. The moment it flashed she pushed the button so hard that her fingernail broke.

'Hiya, babe. We're at thirty-one now.'

Lisa wanted to scream. 'Thirty-one? Can't you do it at twenty-seven?'

'No way. Chuck's not looking to buy before the big figure.'

'Please ask him again,' said Lisa, trying not to sound desperate.

'How much did you say you got?'

'Thirty million.'

'OK, but he's a hard man to move.' Bob rang off.

Lisa felt her face burning red. What if she couldn't cover this deal? What would Aki-san do to her? It wasn't her fault — she'd tried to tell him the rate wasn't firm, but he hadn't listened. She pushed Jackie's button.

'Hello, back already?' said Jackie cheerfully.

'What's your six-month rate?' Lisa had no time for pleasantries.

'Thirty-two.'

'Oh God!'

'What's up, love?'

'I need twenty-seven.'

'Well, no chance of that. How much have you got?'

'Thirty million.'

'Thirty? Hang on.' She rang off and Lisa sat and stared at the button, praying that she'd be rescued. The light flashed and Lisa went into the line. Jackie said, 'We can do ten at thirty. That's just as a favour, mind.'

Lisa felt as if a pile of bricks had landed on top of her. 'Can I let you know?' she asked sadly.

'OK, but don't be long,' said Jackie.

Lisa looked at Aki-san. He was entering a deal into his computer. 'Aki-san.'

'Have you covered it?' he asked, without taking his eyes off the screen.

'Not yet.'

Aki-san stopped clicking his mouse and swivelled on his chair to face her. 'Why not?' he said very quietly.

Lisa tried not to crumple under his gaze. 'D. J. Walker's are at nine thirty-one now,' she said, alarmed at the shade of purple Aki-san had turned. 'But Maine Weavers can do ten at thirty,' she added quickly, hoping to avert an eruption.

'Thirty is no good,' said Aki-san loudly enough for a few heads to turn. 'You must get twenty-seven or less.'

'I can't,' said Lisa quietly. 'The market is too weak.'

Aki-san turned to Leo. 'Talk to Bob.'

'Trust the dwarf to fuck it up,' sneered Leo, and with a scornful laugh he pressed Bob's button.

Lisa put her head down and prayed harder. Much
as she'd hate it if Leo got the rate when she hadn't
been able to, it would at least get her out of this
jam. Her hopes were crushed when she heard Leo's
raised voice.

'Whaddyamean you don't like the fucking market?
Whydya give us twenty-seven in the first place then?'
He slammed the phone down. 'Fucking prat!' he said,
kicking his desk.

Things obviously weren't going well.

Aki-san went into the line. 'Bob, lovely Bob, we need
your help. Please give us twenty-seven . . . OK, I hold.'
This sweet Aki-san was new to Lisa. Just then his face
clouded over. 'You should check market before giving
quotes,' he shouted, and he angrily rang off.

Aki-san, Leo and Lisa called round all the other
security houses but they couldn't get better than 9.30.
Lisa hoped that Aki-san would accept a spread of two
points instead of five, but he was adamant.

'We issue BAs in New York branch's name,' he said.
'We agree to get at least a five-basis-point spread. We
don't get five basis points, we have very big trouble.'

Lisa was glad he had said 'we'. Even if there
was trouble, he wasn't saying it would all fall on
her head.

'Fucking dwarf. Why didn't you check before dealing?' said Leo.

'I didn't do the deal. It was Aki-san. I told him the
rate wasn't firm,' shouted Lisa. She was sick of the
both of them. It was Aki-san's fault not hers. He had
probably done it on purpose to see how she handled the
situation.

'Have you sent the rates to the other customers?'
asked Aki-san.

Lisa looked at him as if he was mad. Did he think she wanted to risk dealing with anyone else today?

'You must call or telex them and give them the rates,' ordered Aki-san. 'Tell them they aren't firm.'

'What about the thirty million deal?'

'We leave it open till the big figure. Then you cover it at the best rate you can get.'

'But what if the rates get worse?'

'Then you in big trouble,' said Aki-san grimly. 'You BA dealer. It's your problem.'

They stared at each other for a few seconds, until Lisa decided it was time to get a coffee. She stomped off to the coffee room. Back-office Brian was filling a large mug with 'BRIAN' printed on it.

'How's the world of dealing, then?' he asked.

'So-so.'

Brian was pleased to see the path to glory wasn't as easy as Lisa had imagined. 'Oh, that bad, is it? I thought you'd be loving every minute.'

'I didn't say I wasn't,' snapped Lisa.

He took a few steps back in mock terror. 'Well, you don't look as if you are.'

'Maybe I'm just sad to have left your little world behind,' replied Lisa sarcastically, and Brian skulked out, leaving her to decide whether she ought to get Leo and Aki-san a coffee too. She didn't want it to look as though she was crawling to them, but if she didn't get them one they'd probably shout at her. She got two more coffees and spat in each cup before carefully stirring it.

The rest of the morning passed quite quickly, considering the strain Lisa was under. She managed, with Andy's help, to get her computer on. He showed her how to input deals and how to use the Reuters dealing-system so that she could call up banks and deal with them on a screen. Occasionally a dealer would shout 'BAs!' and, either by phone or by Reuters, she'd answer a customer's call and give them quotes. She made the rates so bad that there was no chance of anyone else dealing with her. It was very quiet in the dealing-room because all the dealers connected with the dollar, were waiting for the figure which would come out at the start of the New York market.

Eleven thirty came and Aki-san sent Lisa out to get her lunch. He wanted her back in fifteen minutes so that he and Leo could have an hour's lunch before the figure. To cheer herself up, Lisa bought herself a large prawn and tomato wholemeal bap and a chocolate croissant. She got a glossy magazine from a news-stand and headed back to the bank.

'You cover desk, OK,' commanded Aki-san, and he and Leo strode out of the room.

The dealing-room was almost empty. Most of the dealers were getting a good lunch to prepare themselves for a hectic afternoon, and the ones who wouldn't be affected by the big figure went out anyway. Only Andy, Robert and Lisa, the three most junior members of the room, were left. Lisa took the chance to ask Andy what to do when a big figure came out and he explained that as soon as the announcement was made it would be relayed to them by the brokers via the boxes. The rates would move very fast, depending on the way the figure was interpreted.

'What is the big figure?' asked Lisa.

Andy looked at her and smiled. It seemed so long ago that he'd been as green as she was. 'Are you asking me what a big figure is? Or what today's big figure is?'

'Oh, they're different every day, then?'

He laughed aloud at this one. 'Oh, my God, Lisa. What did you do in the back office?'

'I checked deals.'

'Well, you should have been finding out a bit more about the market. You'll get buried if you're not careful.'

Lisa had a vision of Leo and Aki-san digging a big hole and throwing her into it, laughing as they shovelled dirt on top of her. 'Look, don't take the piss,' she said. 'I'm in enough trouble as it is. Just tell me what's going to happen.'

Andy stopped laughing. 'Today's figure is the US unemployment figure. If it's less than expected, the market will be pleased and the rates should fall. Then you'll be fine.'

'What about if the rates go up?' she asked.

'Well, that depends on whether the figure is seen as inflationary or not.'

'I see.' Lisa didn't see at all. Surely lower unemployment would be inflationary? She didn't want to ask Andy any more questions in case he laughed at her again.

Andy was relieved that Lisa was satisfied with his answer. In reality, the market was far more complicated than that, and quite often he had no idea why the rates were moving. He had learnt just to follow along with everyone else after a big figure. He didn't want to admit this to Lisa, because she might tell Leo and then he'd never hear the last of it. But then he saw that she still looked worried and added sympathetically, 'Don't sweat, Lisa. Watch what Leo and Aki-san do, and then copy them.'

'Thanks, Andy, but scratching me arse and breaking

wind isn't my style.' Lisa managed to laugh at her own joke and, feeling better, decided to ask Jackie for some advice.

Jackie warned her that the quotes would take longer because, as the BA market was based in the US, once New York opened she'd have to ask their New York dealers for quotes and then get back to Lisa. 'It would be quicker if you dealt directly with New York,' she suggested.

'Can I do that?' asked Lisa.

'I don't think it would be a problem. It's no different from dealing with us, we buy the paper for the New York office anyway.'

'Do Leo and Aki-san talk with them in New York?'

'No,' said Jackie.

'Maybe I'm not allowed to.'

'Honestly, it's no different from dealing with me. I'll give you the number of our guy out there.'

Lisa decided to speak to the dealers in New York and then ask Aki-san, when he came back from lunch, whether she could deal with them direct. She let it be known that she was looking to deal in six months and that if the rates fell they should call her. They were quite surprised to hear from her, as Leo and Aki-san had always dealt via the London offices, but they assured her that it would make no difference to the paperwork whether she dealt via London or New York. New York would just be a lot quicker.

To Lisa, it sounded too good to be true. If it was quicker, why didn't Aki-san and Leo deal that way? Perhaps she ought to stick with the London offices.

It was 12.45 and the dealing-room began to fill up. Just before the figure was announced, Aki-san and Leo came rushing in looking grim. They sat down and stared

purposefully at their screens. Lisa tried to ask about
dealing with New York but Aki-san waved her away.
If she had hoped for a pre-figure pep talk, she didn't get
one. She tried to look calm, but her face burned red with
fear. As the minutes ticked by, the whole room became
very tense and a small group from the back office stood
in the doorway to watch the action.

As soon as the figure was announced, it was shouted
down the boxes by the brokers and the room roared
into action. It was a lot better than expected and the
rates began to fall.

Lisa got straight on to Bob. 'Where's ya six months
now?'

'I'll get back. Hold on.' Bob rang off and Lisa swore.
Then Andy shouted, 'BAs on line one.'

Lisa went into the line. It was the New York dealer
from Jackie's firm, Maine Weavers. 'Hi, babe, it's Uncle
Ed here. You still looking for sixes?'

'Yes. I've got thirty.'

'How about twenty-four?'

Lisa looked across to Aki-san. He was busy dealing
Futures. She only needed 9.27. She was easily making
her spread. If the rates fell below 9.24 would he be
angry with her for not waiting? She made her decision.
'Done at twenty-four.'

'That's great. Have you got any more?'

'Well, I can call the customer and ask. How much
do you want?'

'Fifty.'

'OK, I'll be back.' She rang up the customer they had
dealt with in the morning and said she could deal at 9.30
now. Two basis points cheaper than in the morning, but
it would leave her with a six-point spread. They said
they could do another $30 million.

She put them on hold and got back to Ed. 'I can do thirty at twenty-four.'

'OK, that's done. I'm still after another twenty.'

'I'll see what I can do. Speak to you soon.' She went back to her customer, dealt $30 million with them and, after taking down the details, allowed herself a few seconds to bask in the glory of her own skill. It was easy. Why had she been so worried? The fact that the market could have quite easily gone the other way was something she ignored. She didn't like to think how it would have been if the rates had gone up. She called round a few more customers until she had found someone who wanted to deal $20 million in the six months. She completed the deal with Ed and then started doing her paperwork. Things were beginning to quieten down, and Aki-san asked her if she had covered the $30 million.

Lisa tried not to smile. 'Yes,' she replied quietly.

'Did you get twenty-seven?'

'No.'

'*NO*?' Aki-san roared.

Lisa enjoyed the moment. 'I got twenty-four.'

'Twenty-four? How you get that? The rates are back up again,' said Aki-san in surprise.

'A dealer from Maine Weavers in New York called me.'

Aki-san was amazed that she hadn't copied the way he and Leo dealt. 'Why you deal with New York when we have direct line to London office?'

'Because it was quicker,' said Lisa. 'I did another fifty million, too, but I only got six basis points on that.'

'Only six?' Aki-san's face broke into a rare smile. 'You did well.'

And that's how Lisa melted Iceman Aki-san on her first day dealing BAs. She also learnt that even the most competent of dealers can overlook the obvious.

Chapter 9

——— ▬

It would have been wonderful if Lisa could have shared her first day's dealing experience with her father. She did try to talk to him, and he looked at her for a few seconds; but it was time for him to make his dinner of sausages and tomatoes, and to delay that would be unthinkable. She found herself talking to his back and, as he didn't show any signs that he was listening to her, she soon gave up. She nearly called Mo but then remembered her mother didn't like to answer the telephone in case it was a pervert on the line. Mo's lover, Ron the flower-seller, usually went up the pub in the evenings, so he wouldn't be there to pick up the phone if Lisa did ring.

Her good friend Nicky, with whom she had shared a room in her first year at university, would be very understanding about her dealing-room triumph, but she was off round the world and the last Lisa had heard was that she had got to Sydney and met a man with big muscles called Jeff. As for her other university friends, the ones she'd been told would be friends for life, she had been quite relieved at graduation that she would never have to see them again. Three years of listening to their whines and moans had almost persuaded her that it would be a good idea to bring back National Service; there were too many young people who didn't know when they were well off. She, of course, was not included in that category. She knew that she definitely wasn't well off and that her problems made those of her contemporaries fade away into insignificance, but she never whined and moaned about them. At first, she had tried to join in the discontented rumblings of those around her, but her revelations had shocked rather than invoked sympathy, and she had learnt that it was better to keep quiet about her problems than to have to listen to the 'caring' but useless advice that was so freely given about how she should act and feel.

She was sad that she had no one to share her little triumph with. So sad that she decided to console herself with a Chinese takeaway and a bottle of wine, both of which she consumed in bed.

It was with great difficulty that she managed to get herself up at five o'clock the next morning. The house was freezing and there was no hot water. She tried to turn the heating on, but her father, sensitive to the balance of his routine, heard her tampering with the central-heating controls and came rushing downstairs. They tussled over the switches for a few minutes until Lisa, realising she would have to kill him before getting the heating on an hour ahead of schedule, gave in.

Walking to the station in the dark depressed her further. She resolved to move a bit closer to work. Maybe she could share a flat with someone? She quickly dismissed that idea. She couldn't face the hassle of racing all over London after work, trying to beat the competition in the search for the perfect flat complete with decent flatmates. Even if she was lucky enough to find a comfortable and convenient place, you could never tell how you would get on with your flatmates until you had paid the deposit, handed over the month's rent in advance and started to live with them. She had been caught out at university, when seemingly nice people turned into absolute horrors as soon as she had unpacked her boxes. Besides, the rents were so high in London. It was a total rip-off to pay so much for so little. In any case, why pay rent when she'd soon be able to buy a luxury Docklands place like John's?

However soon that time would be, it wasn't soon enough for Lisa. Spending the winter getting up early with no heating or hot water, not to mention going to and from the station in the dark, would make her really depressed. She had to move closer to work. She didn't like to leave her father alone, but her working day was so long that he wouldn't see much of her during the week anyway. She might as well move out, and go and see him at the weekends. At least that way they wouldn't be fighting in the mornings. She wished John had let her live in his flat; it would have been so much easier commuting from Docklands.

Then a thought struck her. She knew another place that was, although not quite so fashionable, equally close to the City: Stratford. She could go and live with Mo. The thought of it made her laugh. No, it was too ridiculous. She'd much rather stay where she was. She could never live with Mo and Ron. She would have to come up with another idea.

But as her train passed through the East End, the idea came back again. Would living at her mother's really be so bad? She hadn't lived with Mo for about eight years now, but maybe as they were both older, and hopefully wiser, it would work out well. It might even be pleasant to see more of her. Besides which, Stratford was on the Central Line, so it would only take about fifteen minutes to get to work.

Lisa was beginning to come round to the idea. She'd ask Mo if she could stay with her and Ron until she could afford to buy her own place. Life with Ron and his sweaty armpits wouldn't be pleasant, but it was a case of 'better the devil you know'. Anyway, she would hardly see him. He was usually out selling flowers or up the pub. At the weekends, he followed West Ham to both home and away matches. As for Mo, as a child Lisa had never really understood her, but now that she was an adult she might be able to accept her faults and develop a closer relationship.

By the time Lisa got to Fenchurch Street she had managed to convince herself that relocating to Stratford was a good idea. It was Ron's day for selling flowers outside the main entrance. Normally she would have avoided him by using the side door, but today she decided to go up to him and begin to smooth the way for her move.

'Good morning, Ron. Bit nippy, isn't it?' she said cheerfully.

Ron looked at her in surprise. 'Hello, darlin', how's it goin'?' She usually pretended not to see him; he wondered what she could be after.

'Not bad, can't complain. How's me mum?' Whenever Lisa spoke to Ron her Essex accent came back strongly.

'Same as ever — you know Mo,' said Ron with a laugh. 'You're out early, luv. Gotcha cleaning the office, 'ave they?'

'I'm a dealer now,' said Lisa proudly. 'We have to get in at seven.' She noticed the clock above the main entrance. Ten to seven. Aki-san would be angry if she

was late again. 'I'll have to be off now. Bye,' she said
and started to walk away.

'Well, take care of yaself, luv,' Ron called after her.
'Don't be a stranger. Come round and see us soon.'

'Yes, OK,' said Lisa, waving. Sooner than you think,
Ron, she said to herself, sooner than you think.

Well, that hadn't been so painful. He wasn't so
offensive really. It was only when he ate that her
stomach turned over. His badly fitting false teeth could
hardly handle anything firmer than a boiled egg. He
slurped, crunched and dribbled in a vain attempt to chew
properly, punctuating his efforts with loud, smelly burps
that robbed Lisa of any appetite she might have had left.
Could she cope with the revolting Ron? Would she be
better off freezing her socks off every morning at her
father's house? As it was only the beginning of November
and she had the whole dark winter to get through, it
didn't take her long to make up her mind. She would go
and see her mother after work.

She got into the dealing-room a minute before seven.
Aki-san and Stephanie were the only ones there. Typical,
she thought, it has to be my boss who gets in early. Why
couldn't it have been Robert's? The FX desk, as usual
at this time of the morning, was empty. The FX dealers
wouldn't start coming in until 7.30.

Aki-san smiled when he saw that Lisa had arrived on
time. 'Good morning,' he said and Lisa smiled back at
him. He isn't so bad, she thought.

Aki-san pointed to the tape-recorder. The tape had
run out overnight.

'What do I do?' asked Lisa.

'Get new tape,' said Aki-san.

'I don't know how to put it in the machine. Can you
help me?'

Aki-san sneered and turned away. So much for Mr
Nice Guy. Lisa looked round at Stephanie, who was
eating her breakfast. She went over to her. 'Can you
help me change the tapes?' she asked.

'Can't you see I'm busy right now?' answered Stephanie.
'You'll have to do it yourself.'

'I'm not sure what to do,' said Lisa, who didn't know
that Stephanie was above such things.

Stephanie sighed and replied, 'Go to the cabinet
where the tapes are kept. Take out a tape. Put it in
the machine and write down the time and number in the
book.' It was going to be one of those days, she could tell.

'Thank you very much, Stephanie,' said Lisa sarcastically. It sounded so simple the way Stephanie had said
it, but the tape machine had lots of buttons and the tapes
had to be threaded through a complicated system of slots
and tracks. Lisa didn't have a clue where to start. She
went and got a coffee, hoping Andy would arrive while
she was by the coffee machine. He didn't, and the
caffeine just made her want to bring up last night's
sweet and sour prawn balls.

She went over to the tape-recorder and pressed her
nose against the glass. Along the top of the machine's
casing there was a row of buttons in different colours.
Which ones should she press? She tried the door. It
wouldn't open. 'It's locked, Aki-san.'

'Get key,' he replied, not bothering to look up from
his work.

She looked in her desk drawers, but found no keys.
She tried Andy's desk, but it was locked. Well, that
solved her problem temporarily. She sat down at her
desk to start getting some rates.

'Why you no change tapes?' asked Aki-san as soon as
he saw her pick up the phone.

'I don't know where the key is,' answered Lisa and was dismayed when Aki-san handed her two small keys. She reluctantly went over to the tape machine, unlocked the door and stood for a short while, trying to look as if she was going about the task. Then she went over to unlock the cabinet that held the tapes and took out the first one.

'Oh no you don't!' It was Andy.

Lisa wanted to hug him. But she remembered just in time that dealers were meant to be tough, so she just gave him a casual grin. 'What's wrong with this one?' she asked.

'That's the last tape we used,' said Andy. 'If you tape over it, we'll have no record of the conversations of a few days ago. If there's a problem with a deal, and there isn't a conversation on record, you'll be in big trouble.'

There seemed to be an ever-growing list of ways she could land herself in big trouble. What was big trouble, anyway? Would the managers hold her down and pull out her fingernails?

Andy reached for a tape at the other end of the cabinet, and handed it to her. 'Always take from the left and put back on the right,' he said. 'Then you won't tape over recent conversations.'

'Take from left, put back on the right,' repeated Lisa. She decided to get a pen and paper and write down everything he said this time.

Andy showed Lisa which buttons to press and how to thread the tape through some very awkward places. She couldn't reach without standing on her swivel chair, which made the operation somewhat precarious. It also meant that Leo, on entering the room, was presented with a fine view of her rear end as she struggled to keep upright while holding a heavy tape.

'God, Dwarf, do we have to see your fat arse every time you change the tapes?' he said loudly.

There wasn't much Lisa could say in response, but luckily at that moment, she lost her balance and dropped the tape. It bounced off Leo's shoe and crashed into her desk. Everyone in the room stood up to see the damage.

Leo howled in pain and sat down, clutching his foot. 'Fucking dwarf!' he roared. 'She's broken my fucking toe! Why don't you fire the silly bitch?' His language plunged to new depths to illustrate the terrible pain he felt.

Lisa was still on the chair clutching the door of the tape-recorder. She was wary of climbing down in case Leo took a swipe at her. Aki-san helped Leo into a chair and Stephanie came up with the first-aid box. Lisa was amazed how quickly Stephanie moved when a male dealer was in distress.

With Leo at a safe distance, she got down off the chair and put the tape away. When she came back, Andy had finished putting the new one in and he handed her the keys to put in her drawer. Leo had his shoe and sock off and his foot propped up on his desk. His big toe was covered by a large sticky plaster, which hadn't reduced the pain, but instead served as a warning of what can happen when you allow a woman, especially a short one, to work in the dealing-room. He looked calmer now, so Lisa went over and apologised. A string of profanities followed her back to her desk but she said nothing. He was obviously in genuine pain. She had told him it was an accident, but actually she saw it as the firm hand of justice paying him back for being so unpleasant.

Mr Ito called her over to his desk. 'Are you enjoying yourself?' he asked, indicating that she should sit down.

There didn't seem to be any sarcasm behind the enquiry so Lisa decided to be polite. 'Yes, thank you.'

'I hear you did well yesterday. Aki-san was pleased.'

'I'm glad to hear it,' said Lisa, relieved that he wasn't going to tell her off.

'Aki-san is a very good dealer,' said Mr Ito. 'He will teach you a lot.'

'That's nice.'

'Leo is a very good dealer too. He is helping you very much, I hear.'

'Oh yes, I'm learning lots of new words.' Lisa tried not to smile.

'Well good,' said Mr Ito, happy that Lisa was settling in with only minor problems. 'Now work hard today.'

'Yes, I will,' said Lisa.

'Just one more thing,' said Mr Ito. 'Please remember to be careful with the tapes. They are very expensive.'

'Yes, Mr Ito.' She went back to her desk, trying to hide a smile. If that was the 'big trouble', she could handle it quite well. She wondered what Mr Ito would say if she spilt a hot cup of coffee on Leo's crotch.

Lisa survived the rest of the day without any more drama. The market was quiet after the previous day's excitement, and she was able to find out more about her job. She felt like Sherlock Holmes. Nobody sat down with her and gave her a step-by-step account of what she had to do. Instead she picked up snippets of information here and there by trial and error. She found that she enjoyed talking on the phone. Dealers from all over the world called her, and they seemed to warm to her straight away. In her own camp, she found that some local dealers were now quite polite. Her unintentional assault on Leo had won her a few secret admirers. Andy was openly friendly and Robert, now that he was no longer in direct competition with her, didn't seem half as slimy as before. Only Leo was downright rude, and he harassed her whenever she came off the telephone.

Lisa had had no idea that there were so many ways in which it was possible to be insulted and got almost worn out trying to think up witty replies. Nothing she said made him stop. At one point she looked to Aki-san for help, but all he said was 'You must learn to get along with each other.'

Leo took this to mean that he could do what he liked, so he kept up the teasing and the jokes for most of the day. After a while, Lisa ignored him, hoping that if she showed no reaction he'd find someone else to annoy. This didn't work either, and when five o'clock came she was very relieved to pack up her things and leave.

She walked to Bank station. There was a problem on the Central Line and she had to wait ages for a train. The first one was so crowded that she couldn't get on it. When the next one came, she found herself carried bodily along by the throng of people and, once aboard, she ended up by the door at the end of the carriage with hardly any room to move. A man stood facing her, pushing her back against the door. Lisa's face was pressed against his chest and every jerk of the train sent him leaning harder against her.

She felt his fingers settle softly between her legs. She thought at first that the hand was there accidentally and she wasn't sure how to react. If she shouted, would anyone do anything or would they just ignore her? Would the man be angry and follow her off the train at Stratford? Was she just imagining the assault?

The train stopped at Liverpool Street. The door near Lisa stayed closed. On the opposite side of the train more people got on, and Lisa found the hand was even more firmly stuck between her thighs. She couldn't even raise her head to see the face of the man who was becoming so intimate with her. He wasn't in a suit. He had on a plum roll neck and a leather jacket that smelt fresh and new. As the train set off again, Lisa fought with herself. Half of her said scream and the other half reminded her that she was tired and that her imagination was probably playing a cruel trick on her. The poor man probably didn't even realise he was touching her crotch.

When the hand started to unzip her fly, the voice of reason made a hasty exit. Lisa screamed, 'What the fuck are you doing?' and the hand drew away.

If she had expected crowd support she never got it. Everyone around her pretended that they hadn't heard anything and the man with the wandering hand simply turned his back to her. At the next stop he got off and, as the train pulled away, he caught Lisa's eye and stared at her blankly. He looked like the kind of guy that Lisa wouldn't mind being chatted up by in a pub. She was sick of men today. She needed a drink.

Mo and Ron lived on the top floor of a four-storey block of flats. There was a small lift, which frightened Lisa because the doors closed so slowly that she was always worried that someone would jump in and attack her at the last moment. By the lift was a flight of stairs, dark and completely enclosed. She always had the dilemma of which was the safer way to the fourth floor. After her experience on the train she felt she had had enough of tiny spaces for one day, so she climbed the stairs, frequently looking back to make sure she wasn't being followed.

She got to her mother's front door without further molestation and rang the bell. From within the flat there came a loud, manic barking and a dog flung itself against the door in an attempt to get to and destroy its unseen enemy. Lisa rang several times, but aside from the barking there was no response. She knew Mo was in because all the lights were on. Lisa pushed open the letterbox and bent down. She came face to face with the slobbering mongrel and she feared that in its overexcited state it would somehow manage to bite off her nose, but if she didn't call out her mother would never come to the door. She shouted a few times and Mo appeared in the hall.

'Oh darling! Come in. You must be frozen,' she said, giving Lisa a big hug. Having a drop of Sicilian blood from a distant ancestor meant that Mo found it almost impossible to speak and behave without high drama. A stranger witnessing Lisa's arrival could have been excused for thinking she had just completed a solo trip to the North Pole.

Lisa followed her mother into the kitchen. Mo was wearing a long, pink, satin nightie and matching robe. Her thick black hair was a curly mess and she had no make-up on except for some very bright pink lipstick, which had smeared itself round the filter of the cigarette she was smoking.

'God, Mo! Don't you even get dressed now?' asked Lisa.

'What's the point when I don't go outside much any more?' Mo had recently decided to avoid coming into contact with people she didn't know. She preferred to hold court in her flat, expecting friends and relatives to visit her. She only ventured out on special occasions like weddings and funerals, and even then she had to take a good shot of whisky and a couple of tranquillisers to set her nerves right before leaving the safety of her home. Some people called her agoraphobic, but Lisa put it down to a desire to seem weak and helpless because Ron liked her to be that way. When her mother really wanted to go somewhere, she never seemed to have much trouble getting out of the front door.

Further conversation was halted by the dog, which was barking itself into a frenzy. After a few minutes, it was swiftly kicked by Mo and shut into the nearest room. It scratched at the door and whined and moaned while Mo made cups of strong black coffee.

'Bloody mutt,' grumbled Mo. 'Ron thought he was doing me a favour bringing that thing into the house. It would give me some security, he said. Drives me bloody nuts, more like.'

'Why don't you get rid of it?'

'Oh, I couldn't do that. Ron would be ever so upset.'

'Stuff Ron! He doesn't have to put up with it all day.'

'Well, it's company for me.'

Lisa decided not to pursue the subject. The dog was obviously a cross that Mo wanted to bear, and to suggest a solution would ruin her chance to act like a martyr. 'Have you got anything to eat?' she asked instead.

'No, love. Ron's doing up the kitchen at the moment and the cooker's not working yet.'

'Surely you've got something in the fridge?' Lisa opened the fridge door and peered inside. 'Obviously not,' she said when she saw that it wasn't even turned on.

'Don't worry,' said Mo. 'Ron'll bring in some chips later. Why don't you have some toast until then?'

Just once Lisa would have liked to experience a normal family atmosphere, if such a thing existed. She thought that mothers were supposed to want to fill their offspring with nourishing food. Granted she'd

arrived unannounced, but she hadn't expected a banquet.
A sandwich would have been sufficient. As Mo didn't
show any signs of making the toast for her, Lisa got
up and put some ready-sliced bread in the toaster. There
wasn't any butter, but she found a pot of Marmite in one
of the cupboards. She looked around for a plate and a
knife. Mo pointed to some boxes in the corner.

'How long has this been going on?' asked Lisa,
managing to locate a dinner plate and a steak knife.

'About six weeks. Ron's useless at DIY.'

'Why didn't you get someone in? They could have
done it in a few days.'

'Oh, I couldn't have strangers about.'

Fuck, fuck, *fuck*! said Lisa to herself. She would go
bananas if she lived with her mother. What with the
rabid mutt and the lack of food, she couldn't see herself
lasting even a week before the men in white coats came
banging on the door. She spread Marmite on the toast
and sat down opposite Mo, who was lighting another
cigarette and offered one to Lisa. Lisa wasn't really
a smoker, but a puff of nicotine was very inviting
at the moment, so she took one to have after she'd
finished eating.

'Is everything all right?' asked Mo. Lisa didn't usually
visit unless there was a reason to do so. They always
managed to have a decent chat when they did get
together, but there was a barrier between them which
prevented them from feeling fully at ease with each
other. No doubt it had been erected about the time she
had chosen to live with Ron instead of her husband and
two children.

'Not really,' answered Lisa. 'I hate the people I work
with, John's in Singapore so he's not around to help me
out, I have to get to work by seven every morning and

Dad won't let me have the heating on. I think that's enough to start with, don't you?'

Mo shook her head. 'Problems? They're not real problems,' she said. 'You should try to live my life.'

'I thought we were talking about me,' said Lisa. 'We can get on to you after.'

'You don't know when you're well off, that's your trouble.'

Lisa was sorry she'd come. 'Look, Mo, I'm tired, I've had a long day and I'm not really up to this. Can we just drop it?'

'Fine, although I don't know why you came if you don't want to talk.'

'Do I have to have a reason to see you?' asked Lisa.

'No,' said Mo, 'but you usually do have one. I suppose you're after living here for a while to make it easier to get to work.'

Lisa acted as if it was the first time she'd considered it. 'That's not a bad idea at all,' she said. 'Have you got room for me?'

'I wasn't offering to put you up, you know. I've enough stress without having to worry about you coming and going at all hours,' said Mo, who didn't want to hand over the keys too readily.

'Oh, well, don't worry about it, then.' Lisa knew how to play the game as well.

'I didn't say I wouldn't,' said Mo. 'I was just saying that I don't know if I'm up to all the extra trouble it'll cause me. We've got two spare rooms, although the dog sleeps in one.'

'I wouldn't want to put the mutt to any inconvenience,' said Lisa sarcastically.

'I can't be doing with cooking and all that. You'll have to sort yourself out foodwise and pay for the

phone, and Ron'll expect you to help out with the
bills.'

'That's fine by me,' said Lisa.

'Well, that's settled, then.' Mo stubbed out her cigarette and reached for another.

It was that easy. Lisa would have been pleased if she
hadn't felt that she was making a rather large mistake.
But she wouldn't have to stay in Stratford for long. Now
that she was in the dealing-room she was doing lots of
overtime, and the bank would help her with a mortgage
once she had been there six months.

Lisa moved in with Mo and Ron at the weekend. She
felt guilty at leaving her father but his sister Millie,
twice divorced and fancy-free, as she described herself,
had promised to stay with him as much as she could,
so he wouldn't be completely alone. He showed no
signs of being bothered that she was going. He was
so contained in his world of routine that he didn't seem
to need anyone around. At least not with the day-to-day
running of the house. John had said their father was
fine when she was away at university, so why should
he be any different now?

But, no matter how many arguments Lisa thought up
to justify moving out, she still felt guilty. The only thing
that would ease the guilt would be if she changed her
plans and stayed in Baneham, but she couldn't face the
winter mornings getting ready in the cold. If he really
missed her, she would move back in the spring, she told
herself firmly.

Chapter 10

——— ———

Lisa soon found out just how tough living with Mo and Ron was going to be. The first indication came on Saturday afternoon, when she was moving in. Mo had been using the smaller of the two spare rooms as a dressing-room and Lisa, who had been given this room, discovered that not only the wardrobe but also the large chest of drawers was crammed full of clothes.

'Mo, why don't you clear out some of this junk?' she shouted in frustration when she saw that even the space under the bed was filled with boxes of Mo's things.

'It's all good stuff,' said Mo, coming to the doorway and watching as Lisa tried to squeeze some things into the wardrobe.

'Good stuff!' cried Lisa, throwing some clothes over her shoulder. 'Are you mad? You've got two pairs of hot-pants here. When are you going to wear them?'

'When I've lost a stone and firmed up my thighs,' answered Mo.

Lisa was too young to understand that most women have a wardrobe half filled with when-I-get-slim clothes. 'I've heard that before,' she muttered unsympathetically.

'I like clothes,' said Mo. 'I'd feel lonely without all my stuff.' She shuffled back to the kitchen, where the latest issue of the Freemans catalogue beckoned. She lit a cigarette and sat down at the table, intent on adding to her vast collection of little-worn frocks, suits and separates.

The dog, no doubt blaming Lisa for the swift kick it had received during her last visit, seemed determined to make things even more difficult for her. It spent the afternoon following her around, barking and growling. Lisa didn't kick it, though Mo recommended she should, because it looked as if its teeth would probably have sunk right through to the bone if she had. Instead, she filled its drinking-bowl with whisky and slipped a couple of Mo's pills in for good measure. The dog slurped up the whisky and promptly fell asleep. Lisa and Mo were able to have an hour's chat over black coffee and cigarettes in the kitchen before it woke up again.

Ron came home that evening in a foul mood. The Hammers had lost 3–0, which meant that when Mo asked him if he was going to work on the kitchen the next day he snapped at her. She shouted back at him and they had a blazing row.

'Well, I'm going down the pub,' said Ron.

'If that's the case, I'm going down the pub too,' shrieked Mo.

'It better not be the same one as me,' shouted Ron.

Mo poked him in the chest with her finger. 'Don't you worry,' she said. 'I've no intention of looking at your ugly mug all night.'

Ron marched out of the flat, slamming the front door behind him, and Mo, after quickly throwing on some clothes, stomped out a few minutes later. Her reluctance to meet the great British public didn't extend to the people who frequented the local drinking-houses. Neither of them had asked Lisa to go too. They had been so wrapped up in their row that they had quite forgotten she was sitting in the kitchen. She was left with the barking mutt for company, and it had such a raving headache from the whiskey and pills that it got very menacing. Lisa shut herself in her room and was kept awake till the early hours by the hound's growling and scratching at the door.

On Sunday morning, the flat was very quiet. Only Lisa stirred before eleven, when she decided to go out and get a newspaper. The dog followed her to the front door, carrying its lead in its mouth. Much as she detested the horrible hound, Lisa felt it would be cruel to leave him behind. Because of the domestic dispute, it hadn't been out for its evening walk and she thought it was probably desperate for a pee. She put the lead on, opened the front door and was yanked down the landing. The dog headed for the stairs and bounded down so fast that Lisa had to clutch the banisters tightly to prevent herself crashing head first after it.

Once they reached the road, there was no stopping the hound. It ran and peed at each lamppost in an orgy of frenzied urination, pulling the lead so hard that Lisa had no hope of restraining it. She just let herself be dragged along, hoping her arm wouldn't be pulled out of its socket. After twenty minutes of running, peeing and pooping, the dog was exhausted and Lisa was at last able to haul it towards a newsagent's. She bought an *Observer* for herself and a *News of the World* for Mo and Ron. Remembering that there was no food in the flat she bought some soft, white sliced bread in a plastic bag and a carton of long-life milk.

The walk back was very different from the mad

outward charge. The dog was thoroughly knocked out
and Lisa had to drag it up the road. Every so often it
stopped and lay down for a rest, and she had to lift
it up onto its legs and use verbal and physical abuse
to get it going again. When they reached Mo's block,
they took the lift to the fourth floor and Lisa carried
it along the landing to the flat.

Ron was sitting in the kitchen smoking a cigarette.
He looked quite perky for someone who had spent the
previous evening knocking back vast quantities of beer
and spirits. Lisa gave the dog a can of Pal and made tea
and toast for herself and Ron. She then settled down to
read the newspaper. However, the sound of gnashing
jaws and too much saliva being produced, as Ron and
the hound slurped and munched their way through
breakfast, disturbed her so much that she read the same
paragraph over and over again. She finished her toast
and went to her room for some peace and quiet. Ron,
however, had other plans. As soon as he had finished
his breakfast, he set about the kitchen like a man who
really knew how to handle Easy Fit Kitchen Units.

After ten minutes, his confidence was sorely dented,
and so were several of the units: he'd taken a hammer
to them when they refused to 'slot into place' like the
instructions had promised. There was so much crashing
and banging, punctuated by 'Fuck this' and 'Fuck that',
that Mo was forced to rise from her bed.

'You've put the doors on upside-down, you silly sod!'
she screeched.

Another row began and Ron flounced off up the pub.
Lisa and Mo spent the rest of the day in the kitchen,
smoking cigarettes, drinking black coffee and leafing
through clothing catalogues.

Lisa didn't feel very well when she set off to work on

Monday morning. The tension and the caffeine overdose, plus the lack of nutritious food, had left her much the worse for wear. When she got off the train at Bank, she decided to treat herself to a fried egg and bacon sandwich for breakfast with a cup of freshly squeezed orange juice. Leo was in the shop, buying a curried, chicken bap. He smiled at Lisa and stopped to chat as she waited to be served. 'Had a nice weekend, Dwarfie?'

'So-so,' answered Lisa warily. 'How was yours?'

'Oh, great! Me and the Sow went to the Cotswolds.'

'The Sow?'

'The girlfriend,' said Leo with a laugh. 'If you saw her you'd understand.'

Lisa couldn't imagine that anybody pleasant-looking would sleep with Leo, despite all his money, but she thought it was brave of him to admit that his girlfriend wasn't visually pleasing. The Sow might be ugly, but she had certainly pressed the right buttons with Leo. His eyes were shining and he grinned as he talked. Quite a transformation, in fact. Lisa was so astounded that at first she couldn't find much to say as they walked to Haru Bank, but after a few minutes she relaxed and told him about the dog she was now living with, and he actually laughed.

Aki-san couldn't hide his amazement when he saw the two of them arriving together. But Leo didn't let him be amazed for long. As soon as he got to his desk he turned into his usual boorish self, and Lisa went back to avoiding him as much as possible. But now that she had seen that he could actually be human, she was comforted. Perhaps one of these days he would forgive her for being a woman on the desk.

The day seemed full of pleasant surprises. Bob asked Lisa out for a drink that evening. She hadn't altogether forgiven him for letting her down on her first dealing day, but he was fun to talk to and he was unattached, so she agreed to meet him in a wine bar on Lime Street. She went into Jackie's line to tell her the news.

'Morning, Jackie. Guess what?'

'Leo's been run over by a bus.'

'No such luck,' laughed Lisa. 'No, I've got a hot date tonight.'

'Really?'

'No, not really, it's just Bob from D. J. Walker's. He's asked me out for a drink.'

'Oh, I see. A dealer thing is it?' said Jackie, annoyed that Bob was the first trader to take out the new BA dealer at Haru Bank. 'Do you do much with him, then?'

'Yes, he often has really good rates,' said Lisa, laughing at Jackie's jealousy. 'Have you met him?'

'Only once. He's quite a dish. You'll enjoy yourself – though not too much, I hope.'

'Oh no,' said Lisa. 'It's strictly business, you know, furthering relations and all that.'

'Talking of that, why don't we have lunch tomorrow?' Jackie didn't want any more security houses getting in before her. She would have taken Lisa out last week, but her partner on the desk had been off sick and she'd had to stay in every lunchtime.

'Sounds good to me,' said Lisa. 'I'll have to ask Aki-san first, though.'

'OK,' said Jackie. 'Let me know what he says. By the way, are you looking to do anything in the sixes? We're at twenty-five now.'

Lisa was pleased: Jackie's rate looked very competitive. 'I haven't got anything yet,' she replied. 'But I'll ring round and get back to you. Bye.'

A drink with Bob and a lunch date with Jackie, thought Lisa as she reached for her customer file. Her brother hadn't been lying after all. If this was being a dealer, she could get to like it. She picked up her phone to call her biggest customer, but before she started dialling, she noticed that someone was in Bob's line. It wasn't Aki-san, because he was over at Mr Ito's desk. She looked at Leo and saw him talking on the phone. She caught the words 'like a dog', and realised what was happening. Bob was checking up to see what she looked like. Lisa was decidedly put out. The fact that she had rung Jackie to find out what Bob was like had nothing to do with it. Women discussing men was never as cruel as men discussing women, she told herself angrily, as she clicked into Bob's line.

'What are you two saying about me?' she said aggressively.

'Now now, little lady—' Bob began.

'*Little* being the definitive word,' sniggered Leo and clicked out.

Lisa concentrated on Bob. 'How could you ask him about me?'

'Actually,' he said calmly, 'Leo came on the line saying he'd heard I was taking you out. So whose fault is it, Miss?'

'Well, you didn't have to listen to him saying rotten things about me,' answered Lisa, knowing that she was beaten.

'Who said I had? Now calm down. I'll see you later.' Bob clicked out of the line, leaving Lisa feeling foolish. She also felt quite excited. Not only was Bob handsome, but he was masterful as well. She giggled like a young teenager and spent the day in eager anticipation.

Determined to disprove Leo's description of her, she

went out at lunchtime and bought herself some new clothes. She didn't want to turn up in the black trousers and black roll-neck she'd worn to work, so she bought a dress in Dorothy Perkins. Her cotton knickers gave her a terrible panty-line, so she treated herself to some lacy ones and a pair of hold-up stockings.

After work, she changed into her new clothes in the ladies, and even gave her legs a quick shave. Satisfied that she'd do, she set off for Lime Street.

When she reached the wine bar, she bought herself a glass of white wine and found a seat at an empty table where she waited, rather nervously, for Bob. Her stockings were itching like mad and she wished she had bought tights instead. Not that she intended to let Bob's hands anywhere near her thighs. No, this was strictly a business affair. They were meeting to further their business relationship, she told herself firmly, knowing that she would never be able to survive on the desk with Aki-san and Leo if they found out she had allowed herself to be led astray by a dealer from one of the security houses.

Her feet were beginning to hurt. She had swapped her lace-ups for some black court shoes that squashed her toes. What with the shoes and the new underwear, she was thoroughly uncomfortable. Looking around the bar, she could see that most other women were similarly kitted out in such garments of torture and she wondered why women, herself included, who were succeeding in a man's world, still insisted on dressing in outfits that were so impractical and uncomfortable. Not to mention expensive.

The wine bar was gradually filling up and, as the minutes ticked by, Lisa began to fear that Bob wouldn't come. Perhaps he'd heeded Leo's words after all? Then she saw a man enter the bar and look around. Seeing that Lisa was the only woman sitting alone, he headed straight towards her. She stood up to shake his hand and looked up – and up and up. He was at least six foot four.

'You're not nearly as ugly as they said' was his opening remark.

Lisa gave him a swift kick on the shins. 'Go get me some more wine, you swine,' she said laughing and Bob hobbled to the bar.

Despite the bad start, they found it easy to talk to each other. Bob was twenty-eight, a native of New York. He had been in London for six months and said that, although he liked it very much, he had no intention of staying. He wanted to return to the States in the next two or three years. He was so friendly that Lisa told him about her troubles in the dealing-room. She knew she was saying more than was wise, but he listened so intently and was so sympathetic that she couldn't stop herself. After they'd finished their second bottle of wine, Bob said he had to go to his office to finish off some work and then perhaps they could have dinner.

What he didn't say was that he'd left his work unfinished so he'd have had a good excuse not to take her out if she'd turned out to be a fright. Fortunately, though, he found Lisa amusing and, although she wasn't the tall, leggy type he favoured, he thought she'd be acceptable company for one evening.

They left the bar and walked to the dealing-room at D. J. Walker. Lisa sat down at a seat by Bob's desk and tried to look comfortable. She was aware of the looks she was getting from the few people still at work, particularly from a woman who sat on the other side of

Bob, and she felt like standing up and telling everyone that she wasn't a floozy he'd just picked up, she was a dealer from Haru Bank. Before she could put the record straight, Bob turned to the woman next to him and said, 'I'm off now. Don't call me at home tonight.' He turned off his screens and stood up to leave. Lisa, trying to look as cool and professional as she imagined Stephanie would, followed him out of the room.

It was raining when they got outside. Bob, having the advantage of height, was able to hail a taxi very quickly. He told the driver to take them to Soho, then opened the door and stood aside to let Lisa climb in first. 'There's a great new Mexican restaurant,' he told her as he settled himself beside her. 'I thought we'd try it out.'

'Sounds good to me,' said Lisa, who had never eaten Mexican food before. Following Bob's example, she relaxed back into the seat and crossed her legs.

'My God!' he said in surprise. 'You've got hairy knees!'

Lisa put her bag over her legs. She hadn't realised that when she sat down the new dress would ride up or that Bob would pay attention to her legs. She felt like Guy the Gorilla.

Bob chatted away as the taxi made its way slowly up the West End. He had taken full control of the evening, but not in an offensive way, and Lisa felt happy to let him carry on. As she sat listening to him, she examined him closely.

His legs went on for ever and he wore expensive-looking black slip-on shoes. Lisa usually hated slip-ons, but they looked just right on Bob's fine-boned feet. He had elegant hands with long slim fingers. He wasn't conventionally handsome, because he had acne scars and his hair was turning grey, but there was a touch of the Clint Eastwood about his face which Lisa found very attractive. He wasn't in love with himself either, which added to his appeal. He was self-confident enough to command respect but he wasn't the type who looked at himself in the mirror every morning and smiled in appreciation. Probably the acne in his youth had cured him of that. He did have a certain style, though; his clothes weren't flashy but they were expensive and well-kept and Lisa, after being around such unrefined males as Leo and Ron in the last few days, was captivated.

The Mexican restaurant was packed out. A waiter showed Bob and Lisa to a seat at the bar and they drank margaritas and ate tacos with a hot chilli sauce while they waited for a table. Lisa had never drunk tequila before and she found the taste, combined with salt round the edge of the glass, very pleasant. She didn't think much of the tacos, though: they reminded her of stale crackers. Nevertheless, she was aware of how much alcohol she had consumed already and how little food she'd had since lunchtime, so she carried on eating them to prevent herself getting sick. After an hour, she had lost track of what Bob was saying, but she was sure it was interesting, so she nodded occasionally and smiled at him to show that she was with him in spirit at least.

When they were finally seated, Lisa could hardly focus on the menu, so Bob ordered for the two of them. Lisa thought the starter looked like green sludge and she ate it simply to line her stomach. The main course looked the same but there was more of it. Bob assured Lisa it was a very famous Mexican dish so she gamely took a bite, but she wasn't impressed so she just stuck to the tequila. After a while, she felt very very drunk and she

hoped that Bob was equally drunk so he wouldn't notice
that she could no longer string a sentence together. All
she wanted to do was to rest her head on the table and
go to sleep.

Because of the differences in their height and weight,
what had made Lisa completely drunk had only slightly
intoxicated Bob and he was sober enough to pay the bill,
get a taxi and direct it to his place. Lisa found herself in
Kensington in front of a four-storey white house with
black railings.

'Do you want to take the taxi back home, or do you
want to come in for a coffee?' asked Bob.

'A coffee, please.' The taxi ride with the windows open had slightly sobered her up. She was now
really thirsty.

'Well, come on in, then,' said Bob. He paid the driver
and Lisa followed him up the steps to his flat.

'This is great,' she said when they were inside. The
hallway was huge, with a high ceiling, pale yellow
walls and a white carpet. Lisa worried that her shoes
might leave dirty marks until she saw that in places
there were already some large stains.

Bob noticed her looking at the carpet. 'I had a party
last week,' he said. 'I'll have to get it cleaned or the
owner will go mad when she sees it.'

'Oh, it's not yours, then?' said Lisa.

'No, I'm just renting from someone who's working in
the States.' Bob led her into the living-room. It was large
enough to hold a dining-table with seating for eight, two
large sofas and still leave enough space for Bob to do at
least three cartwheels and a back somersault.

They went into the kitchen and Bob put the kettle
on. 'Can you get some cups?' he asked, pointing to a
high cupboard.

Lisa stood on tiptoe and reached up. As she did so, Bob came quietly up behind her, put his hands on her breasts and began kissing her neck.

The first kiss landed on target but by the second one Bob was kissing thin air. Lisa had turned around and slid out from under him. 'I've heard of fast movers but you're ridiculous,' she told him re-adjusting her breasts. 'I'll be waiting on the sofa for my drink when it's ready.' She walked haughtily to the living-room, ignoring Bob's chuckles.

'Sorry, ma'm,' he called after her cheerfully. He liked a woman who played hard to get. He couldn't wait for the second round.

Lisa knew she should leave. Bob was a dealer, it was the first time they had met, and if Leo and Aki-san found out she had gone back to his flat, they would probably throw her off the desk. Three good reasons for walking out of the door. But Lisa didn't go. Her sexual appetite had been unleashed and the tequila had rendered her good sense unconscious. She knew that sleeping with Bob would not be a wise thing to do, but she couldn't face bringing the evening to an end. He was good company and it was flattering that he fancied her. The thought that he might have made some kind of bet with Leo to get her into bed came into her head, but she pushed it out very quickly. Bob didn't seem the type of man who'd do that, she told herself. She convinced herself that she was waiting for the coffee, but really she was waiting for him to touch her again. The first time hadn't been unpleasant, it had just caught her by surprise. She would be more prepared the next time.

Lisa wasn't an expert in the art of seduction or she would have made the next move herself. She had slept with only one man before. His name was Ken and they'd been friends at university for a year before anything sexual happened. Since then she had, of course, fought off many a wandering hand at clubs and parties, but this was Bob, the man who gave her rates every day, the man who had a direct line to the dealing-room. If she did something stupid, he could easily use that line to make a fool of her. It was better to let him make the running. She draped herself across the sofa in what she imagined was a sexy pose and waited for the next act to begin.

Bob came in with the coffee and a plate of cookies, only to find Lisa stretched out and asleep. Her mouth was open and she was snoring slightly. He thought the kindest thing to do would be to put her to bed. He picked her up and carried her to his bedroom where he unbuttoned her dress and slipped it off. Her legs looked sore where she had been scratching the itchy bits on the hold-ups, so he began to peel the stockings down.

Lisa stirred and opened her eyes. 'Don't fuck me,' she said, then closed her eyes again and went back to sleep.

'Good night, sleeping beauty,' said Bob, kissing her gently on the lips.

The next morning, Lisa woke up and had forty fits. As she was still wearing her knickers and a bra she realised that, technically, she hadn't been a loose woman but she knew that if they found out about it at work, she would never hear the last of it. She must have been really drunk she thought, if she couldn't remember taking her clothes off. What had made her be so foolish? She looked down at the man sleeping next to her and knew exactly why she had drunk so much. He was gorgeous.

She lifted the covers and saw that he was naked.

'Oh, my God,' she said slowly, trying to remember exactly what had happened. 'I'm never going to drink again,' she vowed, when none of the previous night's events came back to her.

She took another look at Bob. He had a really nice body. She lifted the cover a little higher. He turned over, pulling the covers on top of him, so she didn't get much of a look at his penis. Had she touched it? She had never before been so drunk as to have sex without remembering it, and in any case, she told herself, if I had, I wouldn't have my knickers on now. Comforting herself with that thought, she slid out of bed quietly, hoping to escape before he woke up.

As she was buttoning up her dress, Bob began to stir. He caught sight of Lisa and looked at her for a minute as if trying to recall who she was.

'Good morning, Bob,' she said, hoping she sounded nonchalant.

Before he could answer, the alarm clock rang and Lisa, noticing the time, began to panic. 'Oh my God! It's six o'clock! What am I going to do?' she said, abandoning all hope of making a dignified exit and thinking only of what Aki-san and Leo would say when they knew what had happened.

'Just ride in with me, babe,' said Bob casually, smiling at her discomfort.

'Not bloody likely!' she said screeching when she caught sight of her dress in the mirror. Bob had just thrown it on the floor when he undressed her and it was all creased. 'Have you got an iron?'

'No, honey. Now just calm down.'

'Calm down! Have you any idea what Leo and Aki-san will do to me if they find out?' said Lisa, who felt like crying. 'Call a cab, quick!'

Bob reached for the phone and ordered a taxi. Lisa raced around picking up the rest of her belongings, which were scattered all over the flat. When the taxi came, Bob stood naked in the doorway to say farewell. He was bemused by the little dynamo he'd spent the night with and was sorry it wasn't a Saturday, because then he might have been able to get her to stay longer.

'Don't say anything about this to anyone,' shouted Lisa, as she got into the taxi. It wasn't until they were halfway to Stratford that she realised she had forgotten her stockings. She had left concrete evidence of her foolhardy behaviour. If Bob was anything like the male dealers at Haru's, he'd take great delight in holding them up as evidence against her. Should she go back and get them and be really late for work, or should she take a chance that Bob would act like a gentleman? In the end, she decided to press on back to her mother's flat. After all, stockings were just stockings. They didn't have her name on, they could be anyone's.

As it was so early it didn't take long for the taxi to get to Stratford. Lisa raced inside the flat, struggled with the dog for a few seconds, changed her clothes and then rushed back out. She made it to work with ten minutes to spare.

Almost before she'd sat down, Jackie was on the phone, eager to hear the details. She became more and more amused as Lisa whispered some of what had happened. 'We'll have a nice long lunch and you can tell me all about it,' she said.

Lisa didn't know what to do about Bob. What could she say to him after having seen him naked? Also, should she mention the stockings? Bob's light began flashing before she had time to make up her mind. She watched it for a few moments, thinking maybe it was better not to talk to him. Then Aki-san picked up the line and told her Bob wanted to speak to her.

She pressed his button and said a bright 'Good morning.'

'Hiya, babe,' he said. 'Did you get back all right?'

'Yes, thank you,' said Lisa, waiting for the teasing to start.

'You didn't pay the cab driver, did you?' he asked. 'I forgot to tell you it was on my account.'

'It's OK, he told me.' Lisa was relieved that he hadn't mentioned anything embarrassing. 'Thanks for taking me out,' she said, thinking how lucky she was that he was a gent.

'You're welcome. We had a fun time.'

'We certainly did. Do you have any rates?'

'Not yet. Chuck was in late — he's just doing them.'

'Well, get back to me when you're ready.' It was so easy that she wondered why she'd been worried.

'Will do,' said Bob. 'Oh and Lisa . . . ?'

'Yes?'

'You left something behind this morning.' He chuckled and Lisa pictured him growing two horns.

'Did I?' she said trying to sound calm.

'Yes. But don't worry, I've got them right here.' He rang off and Lisa suppressed the urge to shout, '*Aaaaaaaaargh!*' She could just see Bob with her stockings displayed on his desk like trophies, or maybe he had them hanging round his neck. Surely he wasn't going to tell everyone what had happened?

During the morning, while Lisa was torturing herself with nightmare scenarios, Leo had a dispute with one of his brokers over the price he'd paid for some futures. The broker claimed that he'd never quoted the price

that Leo said they had dealt at. Leo, maintaining that
the broker was wrong, shouted and swore down the
phone. Aki-san joined in after a while, but the broker
would not give in. The only solution was for Lisa to
check the tapes.

Lisa had a chart showing the numbers of the lines
that went to each desk. It was very straightforward.
Leo's lines were number 20 for direct calls and 21 for
outside calls. Lisa wound the tape back and switched the
line to number 20. Then she pressed play. Stephanie's
voice came booming out. According to the chart, she
was numbers 5 and 6 so Lisa didn't understand what
had happened. She switched to number 5 and got Andy's
voice — but he was supposed to be numbers 15 and 16.

Fortunately, before she went mad Andy explained
that the chart had been made a few years before and
all the numbers had since changed. The only thing Lisa
could do was to try all the lines until she found Leo's
voice. So she twiddled and listened for the next half
an hour.

'Haven't you found it yet, Dwarf?' shouted Leo across
the room.

'I can't find your line because all the numbers are
wrong,' she shouted back.

Leo got up, strode over to the machine and pushed her
aside. 'As you're so fucking useless,' he said, grabbing
one of the knobs and twisting it, 'I'll fucking do it
myself.' Ten minutes later, he was still twiddling the
knob backwards and forwards.

Suddenly, Lisa heard her own voice booming out like
a castrato on helium. She remembered what she had
been talking about with Jackie that morning and was
horrified that the whole room would soon hear of her
exploits. She rushed over to the machine.

'What's up, Dwarfie?' demanded Leo. 'Been a naughty girl, have you?' He pushed her away and turned back to the machine.

In desperation, Lisa bit him on the forearm and, when he clutched his arm in pain, tuned the knob away from her line. By a stroke of luck, she managed to get into Leo's line before his retaliatory swipe hit her on the side of the head and knocked her over. He turned his attention back to the tapes and Lisa got up and went to lunch, leaving him with the happy task of proving himself right.

'So you bottled out,' said Jackie, bitterly disappointed that Lisa couldn't give her a thrust-by-thrust account of Bob's sexual prowess.

'No, I fell asleep,' said Lisa, thankful that she had.

'A lame excuse,' Jackie said. 'You should have just enjoyed yourself. You wanted to, didn't you? What was the point of saying no?'

'Because he'd have told everyone about it.'

'So?'

'What do you mean, "so"?' asked Lisa.

'Wake up, girl! You've heard the men in the market. They don't respect any women. We're just dogs, slags and tarts to them.'

'And so I should just sleep around?' said Lisa sarcastically.

'Not necessarily, but it's hard for women dealers in the market.' Jackie was enjoying her role of mentor. 'You'll slip up sooner or later when you're drunk or lonely, so you may as well make sure it's with a decent guy. Trust me, I've been in the market for nearly ten years.'

Trust me. Lisa had already trusted Jackie by telling

her about last night. But she didn't know whether she could trust her enough to follow her philosophy of having sex at every opportunity just because that was what the men in the market thought you were doing anyway. In any case, she hadn't seen many men in the market that she could stomach sex with. Jackie grinned and, looking round the crowded bar, pointed out a few men she'd slept with. Lisa shuddered. Of course, if Jackie'd had sex with as many men as she claimed, they would have had to included some ugly ones, but even so . . . Judging by the exes Lisa could see, Jackie made no attempt whatsoever to distinguish between those men who really shouldn't be touched and those who had at least one physically attractive feature.

As she walked back to work after lunch, Lisa was deep in thought. *Trust me*, Jackie had said. But were all women dealers like Jackie, or was she sexually deviant? Surely dealers like Stephanie couldn't be having that much sex? Where did they get the energy? If other women did what Jackie said they did, why wasn't Bob upset with her for backing out? The sex question occupied Lisa all afternoon, and the time passed quite quickly. By five o'clock, she had concluded that Jackie's bonk-all philosophy wasn't at all to her taste. She'd rather wait and see if someone she really liked came along.

Chapter 11

Lisa soon put her nearly nude experience with Bob to the back of her mind because he never mentioned it again and always acted as if nothing embarrassing had happened. Instead, he became another person, besides Jackie and Andy, whom Lisa could ask for information. His kindness often made her regret that he felt no more than a brotherly affection for her. Indeed, in the brief moments when she imagined that a knight in shining armour held the key to a happy life, she enjoyed fantasising about what might have happened. If only she hadn't gone to sleep. If only Bob had a penchant for diminutive women. If only Aki-san and Leo were like him, her life would be a lot easier.

Unfortunately, Leo remained just the same. He spoke to her only if he wanted her to do something or if he was bored and fancied a little sport. With Aki-san, things were slightly different. He had watched her survive her first few weeks in the dealing-room and concluded that she wasn't totally useless. He felt ready to explain the art of predicting fluctuations in the market to her and he would have done so if he could have spoken to her in Japanese. He had mastered enough English to deal

effectively, but when it came to discussing the finer
points of the market, his grammatical failings made
him feel foolish.

'What's going to happen to the rates today?' Lisa
would ask, ever hopeful that he would melt enough to
impart some of his wisdom to her.

Aki-san would stop what he was doing, carefully
consider her question and then reply, 'They go up
because market weaker.' Sometimes he swapped 'up'
for 'down' and 'weaker' for 'stronger', depending on his
mood, but other than that he offered no explanation.

This lack of communication had its benefits, too, in
that he didn't expect Lisa to tell him why changes in
the price of gold or oil altered the rates, or how the
Fed's actions influenced the market. This was a relief,
because it was a long time before she even knew what
the Fed was. All that Aki-san demanded was that she
didn't make mistakes. He didn't take kindly to careless
errors, as she found out the first time she dealt the
wrong amount.

'Why you do fifteen? You only need to do five,' he
shouted when Lisa lent $5 million to a customer through
BAs and then, instead of selling $5 million's worth of
BAs to a security house, sold $15 million.

'It was busy and I had another call waiting,' she
explained quietly, hoping he'd lower his voice.

'That no good excuse,' shouted Aki-san even more
loudly. 'You find another customer, get ten million
done now.'

Lisa tried not to whine. 'I can't get the same rate —
the market's moved.'

'Why you no come to me before?' screamed Aki-san,
looking ready to tear his hair out.

'You were at lunch.' Lisa didn't dare tell him that

she'd done the deal at nine o'clock and hadn't found the mistake until an hour later. When she realised the size of her error, she had felt the blood drain from her face right down to her toes. So much money, she'd thought. What was she to do? She'd looked across at Aki-san and opened her mouth to say something, but no sound had come out.

Hoping the mistake would melt away, she had put the deal slip in her drawer and tried to carry on as normal. At lunchtime, when she was covering the desk, she turned to Andy for help.

'What do you do if you deal the wrong amount?' she asked.

'It depends who you deal it with,' he answered, wondering what she'd been up to. 'If it's direct and not through a broker, you could probably get them to change it for you.'

Lisa wished she'd admitted the mistake when she'd first discovered it. 'What about if the deal was four hours ago?'

'It could be too late.' Then he noticed how pale she was. 'What have you done?'

Lisa told him.

'Well, I wouldn't like to be in your shoes when Aki-san comes back,' Andy said, shaking his head. 'Who did you do it with?'

'Lakers Trust,' said Lisa sadly.

'Lakers? You don't usually deal with them, do you?'

'No, they rang up for the first time and as I had a customer on the Reuters and their rate was good, I did it with them.'

'Aki-san hates Lakers. He'll go mad if he knows you dealt with them.' Andy was going to make sure he was there when Lisa owned up. Aki-san's explosions were great fun to watch if you weren't the one who'd caused them.

'I think I'll run away,' said Lisa mournfully. It was better to quit than get fired, she thought.

Andy felt sorry for her. 'Why don't you ring them and ask them to change the deal?' he suggested. 'It probably won't be too late as New York isn't even open yet.'

Worry had robbed Lisa of any initiative. 'I can't remember who I dealt with,' she said, realising how pathetic that sounded.

'Goodbye, Lisa,' said Andy. 'I'll send flowers to your funeral.' He turned back to his work and left Lisa to imagine how Aki-san would react when she told him the bad news.

Leo came back from lunch first, and Stephanie, who had overheard the conversation with Andy, told him all about Lisa's problem. 'Oh, Dwarfie!' he called, walking over to her, 'You've really fucked up now.' He snatched the deal slip off her desk. 'You'll be out of here by two o'clock with a big imprint of Aki-san's foot up your arse.' He roared with laughter.

'Oh, fuck off,' said Lisa, and she stomped off to get a coffee.

'Get me one while you're out there,' called Leo.

Aki-san was sitting at his desk when she came back.

'Aki-san,' said Leo, 'Lisa's got something to tell you.'

After Aki-san had calmed down and stopped shouting, he ordered Lisa to ring up Lakers and get them to change the deal. 'You say if they don't change it, Haru Bank will never deal with them again,' he said, although he knew it wasn't much of a threat because Haru Bank hadn't been dealing with them anyway.

'I don't have the phone number,' confessed Lisa quietly.

More shouting.

When Leo had found the number, Lisa was told to start dialling. She sat at her desk, with Leo and Aki-san standing on either side of her. The weight of their stares pushing her lower and lower into her chair.

'Can I speak to the BA dealer?' she said when she had got through.

'Fucking hell! She didn't even get the guy's name,' swore Leo, kicking her chair.

'Hi! Skip speaking,' said the dealer.

'Hi, it's Lisa Soames from Haru Bank,' she said, wondering how she could forget a name like Skip. 'About that deal we did this morning.'

'The fifteen million in six months?'

'Yes, that's the one. Can you change it to five?'

'Why?' asked Skip.

'I made a mistake,' admitted Lisa, cringing with embarrassment. Leo snorted in contempt.

'I'll have to ask New York. Hang on,' said Skip, and he put Lisa on hold.

Tick, tick, tick . . . the seconds crawled past. The stress and the body heat from the two henchmen on either side made Lisa sweat. Her heart beat in time with the clock — thump, thump, thump — and she was sure that if the answer was no she would shrivel up and die.

'Lisa,' Skip said when he came back into the line, 'they said no, I'm afraid.'

'I see.' Lisa's mouth went dry, and she found it difficult to breathe. 'Can you hold on, please?' She

forced herself to look up at Aki-san. He seemed very
big this afternoon. Like a giant; a huge, angry giant
who had just discovered that Jack had stolen his goose.
'They said no,' she said nervously, expecting a thump
on the head.

'Keep trying,' he replied icily.

The chills that ran up and down Lisa's spine set her
brain ticking. She had an idea.

'Skip,' she wailed, '*please* help me. It's my first day
here and I haven't told my boss about it. When he finds
out he'll kill me, and I don't know what I'm going to
do.' The words came tumbling out and she gave a few
sobs for added effect.

'Look, don't cry,' said Skip. He wasn't used to
tears in the market, and Lisa's sobs reminded him of
his little sister back home in Buffalo. 'I'll ask New
York again.'

'Thanks,' sniffed Lisa and she sat back to wait.

'Good news,' said Skip coming back into the line. 'We
can change it this time, but you owe me one, OK?'

'Yes, Skip. Thanks a *lot*,' said Lisa, smiling as she
hung up.

Aki-san punished Lisa for her mistake by giving her
the silent treatment. He was famous for this. Andy
told Lisa that Aki-san once didn't speak to Leo for
six weeks. Lisa didn't think she could cope with being
ignored for that long. After two days of silence it was
already driving her mad.

'Aki-san,' she said, 'if I pay you, will you talk to me?'
He ignored her, but Lisa thought she caught a slight
flicker of interest on his face. 'How about fifty pence?'
she said.

Leo laughed. 'Try again, Dwarfie,' he said, sure that
Aki-san would never back down.

Lisa reached into her handbag. 'How about a pound?' she offered, taking a coin from her purse and holding it out towards Aki-san.

He turned to Lisa, looked at her for a few seconds and said, 'Two pounds and I speak.'

Lisa handed over the money and Aki-san smiled. 'You no make any more mistakes, OK,' he said.

'Yes, Aki-san,' said Lisa, silently vowing to double-check every deal.

Aki-san put the money in his pocket. 'Now get me a coffee,' he ordered.

'That's not bloody fair,' protested Leo. 'You didn't talk to me for weeks.'

'You no pay me money,' replied Aki-san coldly.

Lisa's performance with Lakers Trust so impressed Aki-san that he often got her to cry on the phone when they needed a good rate. It worked for a while, until the security houses grew wise to the fact that she wasn't sweet and vulnerable after all.

Towards the end of November, the dealers began to get ready for Christmas. The first sign that the Season of Goodwill was on its way came when Mr Ito plonked two large boxes of Christmas cards on Lisa's desk one morning.

'Sign these and pass them on,' he said.

There were about three hundred cards, all of the same design. The message inside was 'Greetings for Christmas and the New Year from Haru Bank'.

Lisa got out a black biro and began signing. Sometimes she signed at the top left, sometimes at the top right, or in the middle, or at the bottom left. She varied her signature, too, occasionally printing 'Lisa Soames' very plainly, at other times writing with great flourishes and underlining in red. She spent the whole morning on the task and was deeply thankful to hand the boxes on to Aki-san when she had finished.

Lisa became thoroughly unpopular in the next few days, as each dealer tried to get through the hated card-signing as fast as possible by always writing their name in the same place on each card. Unfortunately, as soon as anyone had got a rhythm going, they found it broken by Lisa's signature cropping up in 'my' place. There were loud sighs at first, which gradually degenerated to 'Fucking dwarfs' as the time went on. Lisa was relieved when the signing was over. She hadn't imagined that her fellow dealers would be so upset by such a little matter.

As soon as the cards were sent out, invitations began to arrive for Christmas parties. The first was being hosted by some money-market brokers at a very expensive Japanese restaurant near St Paul's, and everyone in the dealing-room was invited. On the day, Lisa caused quite a stir by turning up for work in her black Dorothy Perkins dress. It was the first time she had revealed her cleavage in the office, and the Japanese managers were thrilled. Her figure exactly matched their idea of a perfect woman – short with nice breasts – so Lisa spent the day being leered at by all the Asian gentlemen in the room.

Aki-san came to work in his best navy three-piece suit. It was a little tight, because he had gained weight since coming to England. He assured Lisa that it had been very expensive when his wife bought it for him six years ago in Tokyo.

'Is that why she didn't want to cut the legs?' asked Lisa, looking down at the ten-centimetre hems on each leg.

'What do you mean?' Aki-san bent over and examined his trousers.

Lisa tried not to laugh. 'Does she think you will grow,' she asked innocently, 'or is she hoping to pass the suit onto your descendants?'

'Ha, ha, nice one, Dwarfie,' chuckled Leo, and they shared a moment's glee at Aki-san's expense.

'This suit better than stupid English shoes,' replied Aki-san, lifting up his Church's shoe to show her a hole in the sole and scuff marks on the toes. 'Man in shop say last for ever. He lied.'

Lisa and Leo laughed again. 'Aki-san, you're supposed to get new soles put on them when they wear out, plus you should polish them every day,' she said. 'Then they really will last for ever.' She soon wished she'd kept her mouth shut because Aki-san, agreeing that it was a good idea to polish the shoes, sent her out to buy some black polish and a brush. When she came back, he presented her with his dirty shoes.

'Hold on, I didn't say I'd do it,' she protested.

'Here is two pounds,' said Aki-san, holding out the money.

'OK,' said Lisa, who knew a good thing when she saw it. Word reached the Japanese managers that Lisa was shining shoes, and she was presented with more and more pairs. She cleared more than £30 in an hour.

Later that afternoon, disaster struck Aki-san. He was practising his golf swing during a quiet spell when he split the well-worn crotch of his trousers. Lisa offered to repair them. 'Go and take them off in the toilets,' she said. 'When I've sewn them up, I'll bring them back to you.'

'No,' replied Aki-san. He had been in England long enough to understand the humour. 'You will run away with my trousers and I will have to stay in toilet. I keep them on and you sew them.'

Lisa went to the back office and borrowed a needle and thread. She could only get orange but Aki-san was happy that she had managed to find any thread at all; he wasn't concerned about colour coordination. Lisa threaded the needle and got down on her knees. Aki-san stood with his legs wide apart, his hands folded protectively over his manhood.

'Get your hands away,' Lisa told him. 'I can't reach the material.'

'No, you very dangerous woman,' said Aki-san nervously and he squealed in terror as Lisa pushed his hands out of the way and stuck the needle into the crotch region of his trousers.

At that moment, Mr Ito came in, accompanied by Mr Aono, the general manager. From the doorway it looked as if Lisa was forcibly giving Aki-san some kind of sexual favour. Mr Aono, who was aiming to retire the following year, clutched his heart. He had been warned about British women by his uncle, who had been posted in a female prison camp during the war. Consequently, during his five-year stint in England Mr Aono had tried to avoid contact with the local female staff as much as possible. He had recently been congratulating himself on his success. This assault on one of his younger managers by a ferocious member of the local staff was simply too much. He rushed from the dealing-room and hid in his office for the rest of the afternoon.

Once Mr Ito realised the truth behind Lisa's strange position, he laughed loudly and told Aki-san that perhaps it was time that he invested in a new suit. He said there were several shops in the area selling suits that accommodated the long-body, short-leg Japanese male physique perfectly. Aki-san agreed and said that when the sales started after Christmas, he would ask his wife for the money. She, like many of the other Japanese wives, controlled the family finances. Every month, she gave Aki-san an allowance to take care of his personal expenses, which included lunch money and enough cash for the obligatory drinks after work with his colleagues. She didn't like to spend much on his appearance in case he became attractive enough to tempt another woman to sleep with him. However, now that Lisa had had to handle the crotch of his trousers, Aki-san reckoned his wife would make sure he got a new suit.

When Lisa arrived at the broker's party that evening and looked around, she wondered why she had bothered to go. The restaurant was full of men in suits, several of whom made crass comments about her as she made her way towards the group of Haru bank dealers that had formed by the bar.

Andy handed her some champagne and introduced her to some of his brokers, who sported beer bellies of varying sizes depending on their age and experience in the market. They amused themselves by thinking up shortist jokes and were quite disappointed when Lisa failed to laugh at any of them. By the end of her second glass of champagne, though, she no longer found them offensive and she even managed a smile now and then. By the fourth glass, she had become like most other people in the room, talking loudly about nothing very much and never pausing for breath long enough to listen to anyone's reply.

'Have you tried the food yet?' asked Andy, noticing that she was beginning to sway. 'The sushi is wonderful.'

Feeling hungry, Lisa walked over to the buffet. She

had never tried sushi before and was wary of the delicate pieces of fish arranged on little blocks of rice. The first one she picked up had white fish on the top. She nibbled the edge and, as the taste wasn't unpleasant, she copied the Japanese managers who were dipping the sushi into soy sauce and then shoving whole pieces into their mouths. She found that if she swallowed the sushi quickly it was rather nice, but if she tried to chew it it tended to remain in the mouth too long and she felt the urge to gag. The red pieces, which she was surprised to find were tuna, were the easiest to swallow, and she ate five of them. Gaining confidence, she tried some octopus, but it was so chewy that eventually she had to spit it out into a well-placed flowerpot.

The next dish she tried was tempura: vegetables and fish fried in batter. It was very light and she ate three big platefuls, stopping only to reprimand a young broker who placed his clammy hand on her left buttock.

By 7.30 the party was getting rather bawdy, and all around Lisa saw rotund men with shiny red faces talking and laughing loudly. Most of the Japanese managers had gone home, although here and there she saw a few propped against the wall and being bored into submission by brokers who thought it good business sense to try to make friends with them. In fact, most of the Japanese managers spoke such poor English that they couldn't understand one word of a typical broker's conversation. If the brokers had known this, they wouldn't have bothered, but they were too drunk to notice that all the Japanese chaps ever said was 'Yes'. The brokers didn't know it meant *Yes, I can hear you*, not *Yes, I understand and agree with you*, so they talked on and on until the Japanese either staggered off home or slumped unconscious to the floor.

The champagne and the unfamiliar food made Lisa feel hot and dizzy so, as there weren't any seats, she went to a corner and sat down on the floor. She glanced across the room and saw Stephanie, looking very cool and elegant, holding court with about four brokers. Stephanie noticed her on the floor and signalled that she should stand up.

Lisa mouthed, 'I can't.' Not without help, anyway. She wished she'd left the party rather than humiliate herself in front of Queen Stephanie.

Stephanie sent a broker over to help. 'I've got orders to get you on your feet,' he said, crouching beside her.

'Thanks,' said Lisa, 'but I think I'll be sick if I move. I've eaten too much raw fish.'

'And drunk enough to sink a liner, I suppose,' added the broker. 'I'll tell you what. How about I carry you out over my shoulder and put you in a cab?'

'How about bugger off,' said Lisa, who didn't fancy leaving bottom first.

'God, what is it about Haru Bank? Why are the women so fierce? If I don't get you up, Stephanie'll take my line out. Like it or not, you're moving — now.' And with that, he hauled Lisa to her feet and took her outside.

'Now that wasn't so bad, was it?' he said once they were standing on the pavement. 'I'm Stuart, by the way, but you can call me Chopper. Everyone else does.'

'Oh God!' replied Lisa, and she threw up in the gutter.

'Welcome to the land of brokers' parties,' Chopper said wearily, rubbing her back as she spewed out the contents of her stomach.

'I want to die,' said Lisa.

'Yes, it happens to the best of us. You'll get over it.'

Chopper was unsympathetic. He'd been in the markets since leaving school eight years ago and he was used to dealers stuffing themselves with free food and drink. Lisa's vomiting didn't faze him one bit. It went with the territory, as far as he was concerned.

He hailed a taxi, but the driver didn't want to take Lisa in case she threw up in the back of his nice clean cab. He changed his mind when Chopper offered him £50. Lisa was lifted into the taxi and propped against the door, with the window open.

'If you have to be sick,' said the driver, 'put your head out of the window.'

'Let's do it again some time,' called Chopper as the taxi drove off. He took out his handkerchief and wiped Lisa's vomit off his shoes. 'Not a bad little tart,' he said to himself. 'Not bad at all.'

Lisa managed to get back to the flat without being sick, and flopped into bed fully dressed. The next morning she woke up with a monster headache and a carpet tongue. She couldn't face anything to eat or drink so she just changed her clothes and set off for work. She was sick three times on the way to the station but she managed the train journey without incident. In the City, she bumped into Leo who told her to eat an egg and bacon sandwich, as the greasy fat would help her stomach to recover. Knowing that he was an expert in coping with morning-after-the-night-before nausea, she took his advice and it worked: she stopped wanting to throw up, although she still had a headache.

'How was last night?' asked Jackie, her loud, cheerful voice jarring Lisa's temples.

'Don't ask,' she groaned.

'That bad, eh?'

'Oh God! If I ever see another plate of sushi again, I'll die.'

'You'll get over it. Try and have a drink at lunchtime. It'll make you feel better.'

'Are you nuts?' Lisa had vowed never to drink again, but when codeine failed to relieve her suffering she tried the alcohol cure. A large vodka and tonic at lunchtime helped her so much that she had another. In the afternoon, she no longer had a headache, she just felt very drunk. Fortunately, Aki-san had been drinking at lunchtime too, so he didn't notice the state Lisa was in, and nobody else in the dealing-room paid any attention either. It seemed to be agreed that during the Christmas season it was the dealers' duty to consume as much alcohol as possible. Not for enjoyment, of course, but for the sake of building good business relationships.

One of the highlights of the season was the dealing-room's own Christmas party, which was held on board a boat moored at the Embankment. After a whole day of drinking, starting with a champagne breakfast hosted by some futures brokers, followed by a liquid lunch with Jackie and a few drinks in the pub after work, Lisa found herself sitting next to a very sober and serious Mr Ito in the restaurant.

'I hope you are going to behave yourself,' he said, noticing how red and giggly she was.

'I certainly am,' she replied, reaching for an unopened bottle of champagne. She shook it and, when she uncorked it, put her thumb over the top and sprayed champagne all over Mr Ito's face. Dripping wet and stunned, he sat completely still. Silence gradually fell round the table and Lisa thought she might have gone too far.

'Ooops, sorry,' she said, trying hard to sound apolo-getic.

'Let me help,' said Aki-san, and he stood up. He produced a can of shaving-foam from his pocket, reached forward and sprayed it all over Mr Ito's glasses. The table erupted into hysterical laughter and the tone for the evening was set.

Lisa couldn't remember getting off the boat. She remembered the dancing, especially when Mr Ito came up while she was doing the twist with Leo and poured a drink over her head. But she couldn't remember much else.

As she walking to the station the next morning, her coat felt a little bulky down the front. She put her hand in her pocket and pulled out a man's white cotton vest. 'Oh my God,' she said, checking her other pocket in case there were underpants in it. Much to her relief, it was empty.

The dealing-room was quiet that morning, as every-one tried to work off the effects of the night before. Word from the restaurant was that Haru Bank was no longer welcome there. There was also a rumour that Mr Ito was missing. His wife had rung in saying he hadn't gone home, and everyone had visions of him lying dead in a gutter somewhere. Leo's late arrival solved the mystery. As Mr Ito had been too drunk to tell the taxi driver his address, Leo had been obliged to take him home. He said Mr Ito was still tucked up in bed and looked like he wouldn't be surfacing for some time.

Lisa hoped it wasn't Mr Ito's vest that she had in her pocket. She knew it didn't belong to one of the local dealers because there was Japanese writing on the label. She tried hard to remember where she'd got it, but most of the evening was still a blank.

'Did you get home all right?' she asked Andy casually.

'I think I ought to be asking you that question,' he said with a chuckle. 'I've never seen you so ratted.'

'What do you mean?' asked Lisa, worrying that she might have left pieces of her own underwear somewhere.

'Oh dear,' said Andy. 'You can't remember, can you? You're a bit young to be doing that already.'

'Of course I can remember,' said Lisa, beginning to panic.

'Tell me where we went after the restaurant, then,' teased Andy.

'After the restaurant?' asked Lisa. Had she managed to carry on drinking elsewhere?

'Lisa can't remember the cocktail bar,' said Andy loudly and laughter broke out all around the room.

Lisa heard several versions of what had happened the night before. In some, she'd peed in the gutter in front of everyone. In others, she'd taken her blouse off for a bet and Robert claimed to have seen her snogging with Mr Sumida. Leo claimed she'd let Aki-san put his hand up her skirt, but Lisa didn't believe him because Aki-san had never ever acted in that way towards her and anyway she'd been wearing trousers. As her list of her real and imaginary misdeeds grew longer and longer, Lisa knew that she couldn't risk asking about the vest. At lunchtime she rushed off and disposed of it in the toilets of the pub downstairs. She never did find out whose it was or how it had ended up in her pocket.

Christmas Eve in the dealing-room was another excuse for everyone to have a good drink. Traditionally, it was a half-day in the City. As they worked that morning, the dealers had under their desks all the bottles of champagne they had received from their brokers over the previous few weeks. As soon as the clock struck twelve and the managers had checked that everyone's position was closed, the room became a danger zone as corks flew in all directions. Staff from other departments gravitated towards the dealing-room and were at once handed plastic cups of champagne. As soon as everyone was merry, Aki-san pulled out his chair and ordered Lisa to climb onto it.

'You the youngest,' he said. 'You now sing.'

'Me? Sing?' Lisa wasn't drunk enough to not be horrified.

'Give us a tune, Dwarfie,' cried Leo as she was helped, or rather pushed, onto the chair. Everyone clapped and then waited in anticipation. Lisa, who hadn't even made the choir at her junior school, hated to disappoint them. She took a deep breath.

'Maybe it's because I'm a Londoner,' she sang. She was loudly applauded, not for her vocal skill but for her nerve, and for once Aki-san felt really proud of the most junior member of his desk.

Christmas Day saw Lisa in the accident and emergency room at the local hospital. After going down the pub with Ron at lunchtime, she had returned to the flat for Christmas dinner. Ron had got out the new electric carving-knife he'd bought for a fiver down the local and, in the process of thinly slicing the succulent white breast of the turkey, he'd managed to take off the top of his middle finger.

Five hours later, when they got back to the flat, Ron, despite having a large bandage on his finger and a sore behind from the tetanus jab, intended to resume carving. But the parts of the turkey that hadn't been eaten by the dog, or got blood on them from Ron's finger, were all dried up. They abandoned the bird and heated up some sausage rolls instead. The trials of the day exhausted the three of them and by ten o'clock they were in bed and fast asleep.

Boxing Day was a little more successful. Lisa went to her father's, and their and Aunt Millie's combined efforts produced a dinner which was, if not easily digestible, at least warm and free from bloody digits.

Looking back, Lisa was glad that she had made sure she got plastered nearly every day over Christmas, because immediately afterwards a new dealing-room regime started, one that soon made the dealers forget that they had ever considered themselves too important to behave properly.

Chapter 12

——— ◆———

Changes happen fast in a Japanese bank. One day the dealing-room was relaxing under the gentle regime of Mr Ito, and the next he had received orders to go back to Tokyo. A new manager, Mr Kimura, would be taking his place.

Aki-san had worked with Mr Kimura at head office and was very unhappy about his appointment. He didn't explain to the local staff what Mr Kimura was like, because that would have been disloyal to a Japanese colleague, but he gave Lisa such a black look when she asked him about their new manager, that it was obvious there was something not very nice about him. She tried to find out more, but all Aki-san said was 'Don't talk to me about that man.'

Mr Ito's farewell party was held a few days later. All the bank's employees were expected to attend, so at 5.30 the function room on the top floor was filled with staff from every department. Everyone held a glass of wine but no one was drinking. When Lisa took a sip, she was told that it was considered bad manners by the Japanese to drink before the party had been officially started by Mr Aono.

As soon as it looked as though everyone was there, Mr Aono and Mr Ito arrived. The former made a speech complimenting Mr Ito on how hard he had worked as senior manager of the Treasury Department and how sorry everyone was to see him go back to Japan.

Then Mr Ito stepped forward. 'Thank you very much for coming here today. I am very sad to be leaving. London has so many fine restaurants, theatres and museums that my wife and I were often arguing as to where we should visit next. We also enjoyed many weekends away in other countries. France was my favourite. The bank here is also very nice.' He paused and there was polite laughter at his little joke. 'I have made many friends in London and I have been very proud of the fine staff that worked for me. I will miss you very much.' He bowed and everyone clapped. Lisa felt quite overcome with emotion. This was the man who was responsible for the life she now led. She was sorry to have soaked him with champagne at the Christmas party. She raised her glass to drink to him, but Andy put out his arm to stop her.

'It's the Fure, Fure next,' he whispered.

'What's that?' asked Lisa.

'It's a Japanese Hip Hip Hooray,' said Andy. 'Aki-san is the youngest manager, so he'll do it. You'll enjoy this.'

Aki-san walked to the middle of the room. He planted his feet firmly apart, threw his head back and as he raised his arms slowly into a V shape he shouted, 'HA-RU BANK. HA-RU BANK.' The veins at the side of his neck bulged and his face turned bright red as he leant back as far as he could, pumping his arms into the air. 'FURE FURE HARU BANK,' he chanted over and over again. Around the room, the chant was taken up enthusiastically by the Japanese managers who began to clap in time. The local staff joined in, although with less enthusiasm because they would be teased later if they were too carried away by a Japanese custom.

Lisa got the giggles. The sharp contrast between the serious and restrained mood at the start of the party and the football-crowd atmosphere that had taken over was too much. It looked so funny, but as everyone else was taking the whole exhibition seriously, she forced herself to stop laughing and instead clapped along with her colleagues. After the chanting stopped, there was a round of applause and shouts of 'Kampai'. Then everyone drank as much as they could, as quickly as they could, and left. By seven o'clock, it was all over and Lisa was sitting on the train to Stratford wondering what would happen now that Mr Ito had gone.

She soon found out: Mr Kimura arrived the next day.

He made a little speech to the dealing-room. 'Good morning, everyone. I am happy to be the new senior manager of the Treasury Department. My last foreign posting was in New York, where I had the honour to work in the best overseas dealing-room of Haru Bank. The New York dealing-room is the most profitable of all our dealing-rooms, but not for long. With my help and with hard work, you are going to make the London branch number one.' Polite applause followed, and Lisa noted a sneer on Aki-san's face. Mr Kimura continued, 'I will be studying you all very carefully. Then I will teach you to be very skilful dealers. I am looking forward to running a smooth and efficient machine.' A few suppressed sniggers were heard at this last comment. Lisa didn't laugh, though; it sounded ominous to her. She was beginning to miss Mr Ito already.

He had believed in a hands-off management style, which meant he never troubled himself with the day-to-day running of the dealing-room. He had preferred to allow the dealers to work unsupervised at their own pace. As long as they didn't lose too much money or make big mistakes, they were left to their own devices. Long lunches were fine when the market was quiet, and arrival and departure times were not strictly monitored. Mr Ito hadn't let power go to his head. For him, being the top manager in the dealing-room meant that he was able to spend as little time as possible on actual banking. After years of wading through reports and feigning an interest in matters financial, he had at last risen to a position where he didn't have to pretend any more. Instead, he had been able to devote his energies to things that really mattered, like fine wines and food, travel and the appreciation of the cultural events that London offered. He had enjoyed his time as head of the dealing-room and his enjoyment had rubbed off on everyone else. This would not be the case with Mr Kimura, who was a dedicated banker. The success of the Treasury Department was everything to him and he believed in intervention at all levels.

During his first few days in office, he walked around quietly, closely observing the work that was going on. It was unnerving for the local dealers. As they talked on the phone, he would come up behind them, listen for a few seconds, and then place his hands lightly on their shoulders. He would massage their tension away very firmly and then offer soft words of encouragement.

He wasn't actually unpleasant to anyone — on the contrary, he was always gracious and spoke kindly — but he still made his staff uncomfortable. His silent and unexpected appearances meant they could not relax for a minute. He also put a stop to long, liquid lunches. He didn't actually forbid them, but the dealers soon found out he disapproved. When they staggered back, late and flushed with drink, he would be waiting for them at their desk with the new lunch appointments book. 'Write down where you went, who you met and what you discussed,' he would say, standing and watching as the dealer tried to hold the pen steady enough to write something businesslike. 'Now work especially hard this afternoon,' he would add, as he picked up the book and walked back to his desk.

After one week, Mr Kimura started to invite each local dealer over to his desk and spend half an hour intently questioning them about their job, their personal life and what they thought about the other dealers' performance, creating a level of suspicion that had not existed under Mr Ito.

Lisa sat nearest to him, so she witnessed most of what went on, but she couldn't hear exactly what was being said; she caught only the odd word here and there, and this made her more paranoid than if she had heard the whole conversation.

Then, one afternoon, her turn came. Mr Kimura called her over, but instead of making her sit opposite him, on the other side of the desk as was usual, he pulled up a chair next to his and patted it to indicate that he wanted her to sit close to him. She assumed this was because he wanted to talk quietly so that they wouldn't be overheard.

'You have been here a very short time, Lisa, but you have already done very well,' he said.

She was surprised. She never felt she was doing very well, she always felt she was just coping. As she hardly ever received praise from Aki-san, she automatically assumed it was because she was bad at her job.

'I would still like to learn more,' she told Mr Kimura, anxious to sound keen. She wanted to impress her new boss with her dedication, even if it was false.

'I've been talking to Aki-san,' said Mr Kimura, leaning so close to her that she could feel his breath on her ear, 'and we both think you are under-utilised. Soon I would like you to take on more work. Maybe you could start dealing futures.'

That was the last thing that Lisa wanted. Being on the same desk as Leo was bad enough. It would be horrific to do the same job. She didn't want to admit this to Mr Kimura, though, so she just nodded.

The conversation continued, with Mr Kimura asking her about the details of her work and what she liked to do best. Just when Lisa thought she was impressing him with her intellect, he suddenly placed his hand on her thigh and said, 'You are a young pretty girl in the market . . .' He paused as Lisa, revolted, moved her leg away from his hand. 'I want you to promise that you will not give yourself away for free. You are valuable and should make sure you get a good return.'

Before Lisa could reply, Aki-san came over and handed Mr Kimura a report to sign. Mr Kimura immediately wiped the leer off his face, told Lisa she could go back to her desk and fixed his eyes on the report.

When Aki-san sat down again he waited for Mr Kimura to leave the room, then turned to Lisa. 'He like young girls. Please be careful.'

His warning was well justified. When he and Mr Kimura had worked together at head office, Mr Kimura had taken full advantage of his female colleagues' reluctance to report sexual harassment. He often fondled the young female staff, and if they protested he claimed it was an accident. He had got away with it for quite some time, until an encounter with a new recruit in the main lift left him with a black eye and a bruised reputation. Mr Kimura claimed that he had been reaching forward to press a button when he had accidentally brushed against her, but the recruit swore that she had elbowed him in the face as a reflex reaction to his squeezing her breast from behind. After this incident, Aki-san had thought, Mr Kimura had reformed; but obviously he hadn't.

Aki-san didn't believe in babying his staff. He wanted Lisa to stand on her own two feet, hence his refusal to intervene when Leo started to bully her. They were on the same desk and Lisa, as the junior member, had to learn not to provoke Leo. Mr Kimura, however, was another matter. By placing his hand on her leg, he was showing that he had no respect for Aki-san. If he did have, he would not try to abuse a member of his team.

One of Mr Kimura's first innovations was to have a managers' meeting at eight o'clock every morning instead of the relaxed, informal gatherings that Mr Ito had preferred to hold in the evening when the local staff had gone home. The Japanese managers would all stand around Mr Kimura's desk, and Lisa watched with interest. She couldn't understand what they were saying, but she could work out the mood of the meetings and she could tell when Mr Kimura was telling someone off, which he seemed to do regularly. His manner to the Japanese managers was very different from the smooth way in which he spoke to the local staff. To the Japanese, he was very abrupt and he seemed to be bullying them. He usually started shouting at some point and the managers stood there, heads bowed, waiting for the storm to pass. Aki-san came away from the meetings in a foul mood, and Lisa spent the mornings creeping around him so that he wouldn't take his temper out on her.

One morning, after a particularly stormy meeting, at which Aki-san had borne the brunt of Mr Kimura's anger, he came back to the desk and said to Lisa, 'You must deal more. Kimura-san want more volume.'

'I'm doing my best, Aki-san, but the market has been very quiet lately,' said Lisa.

'No excuse,' said Aki-san firmly. 'You must be more aggressive.'

So Lisa tried shouting at her customers, but they didn't deal more, they actually dealt less.

The following week, Aki-san presented her with a large book. 'Kimura-san give you this. Write down all your calls and say what you talk about.'

'But I have at least fifty calls a day,' Lisa protested.

'This is his wish,' replied Aki-san. 'He also want a report on how to increase volume.'

It took Lisa so much extra time to keep a record of her conversations that her dealing volume went down again. She ignored Aki-san's request, going on the premise that if she forgot about it, maybe everyone else would, too. It didn't work. A few days later, Aki-san came back from a yet another stormy meeting with Mr Kimura and said, 'I want to see the report.'

'What report, Aki-san?' Lisa asked innocently.

Aki-san raised his arm as if to hit her and she dived under her desk to avoid the blow. When he brought his hand down on her desk with a loud thump, the crash caught everyone by surprise and heads turned.

'I'll have it done by tomorrow,' said Lisa nervously, crawling out from under her desk.

The trouble was that Mr Kimura was asking her for information she hadn't got. She didn't understand the market well enough to be able to offer any solution to the low volume of deals, and she had no idea why customers dealt with her on some days and not on others. There was no one in the dealing-room who knew very much about BAs and those, like Leo and Aki-san, who had experience never took the trouble to explain anything except the barest details. She asked Andy for help but he just shrugged.

'I think I'll just go and kill myself,' she said mournfully.

'Why don't you ask Leo?' suggested Andy. 'There's no figure today, so he won't be busy.'

'Bet you a fiver he won't help,' said Lisa.

'Done.'

She went over to Leo's desk. He was busy studying the attributes of the day's Page 3 girl. 'Whadya want, Dwarfie?' he asked, turning the smile on his face to a sneer.

'I was just wondering, Leo, if you could—'

'Fuck off and read a book,' he said.

Lisa decided to follow his advice. Taking the £5 note she'd won from Andy, she went to the bookshop in Leadenhall Market and, with the addition of another £25, bought a thick, heavy tome about the money market. She showed it to Aki-san when she got back and he gave her a faint smile of encouragement. As she sat there reading during the afternoon he often stood behind her with his hand on her shoulder to show that he was fully supporting her efforts. If he had looked at the page numbers occasionally, he would have noticed that they barely changed. After five minutes, Lisa's eyes had glazed over and, although she saw the words, she didn't register what they meant. Her money wasn't completely wasted though, for by the end of the day the book had found its purpose as a footrest and Lisa's legs no longer dangled from her chair. The report, however, was still not even started.

Lisa couldn't bear the thought of a sleepless night and then another display of anger from Aki-san in the morning, so she decided to take the bull by the horns and went over to Mr Kimura's desk.

'Can I have a word?' she asked.

'Certainly.' Mr Kimura patted the chair next to him and Lisa, moving it slightly back, sat down.

'About this report,' she said, going straight to the point.

'Yes. Is it finished?'

'Not quite,' she replied. 'I need more information from the customers.'

'Then you should speak to them more,' said Mr Kimura sternly. 'A good dealer should always know what his customers want.'

Lisa ignored the 'his' bit. 'They always seem so busy on the phone,' she said. 'They don't have time to talk for long.'

'You should make them talk,' said Mr Kimura firmly. He was getting tired of her excuses.

'I don't know them well enough to get them to have a long conversation,' confessed Lisa.

Mr Kimura stopped to think. He didn't want to be angry with her. She was still quite new to dealing and she was being very honest with him. The other local dealers would never have admitted there was something they didn't know about in the markets. He decided to help her rather than tell her off. 'Perhaps you should meet them,' he suggested.

'Most of them are abroad,' replied Lisa.

'Then you must arrange a business trip,' said Mr Kimura at once, and also at once deciding to accompany her — it wasn't often, he thought happily, that business and pleasure could be so easily combined.

Lisa's largest customers were in Scandinavia, so Mr Kimura decided that they would take a three-day trip to Sweden, Denmark, Norway and Finland. Lisa blinked at the thought of visiting four countries in three days. 'The secret is,' he told her, 'to fit as many meetings in as you can. This is not a pleasure trip. You are spending the bank's money and so you must work very hard,' he said, trying to convince himself as well as her.

'Yes, Mr Kimura,' she replied, the wind taken right out of her sails at the mention of hard work.

Mr Kimura saw her disappointment. 'Your colleagues will be very jealous of you if you just go and play. You must work hard to stop them feeling bad,' he explained.

Lisa didn't care what her colleagues thought; she wanted them to be madly jealous of her. But Mr Kimura had ordered that she must work hard so, sighing at the lost opportunity to go sightseeing, she filled in her schedule with as many appointments as she could fit into the three days.

As Oslo is very small, it was decided that it could be taken care of on the Monday morning. In the afternoon they would go on to Stockholm, staying there until Tuesday lunchtime, when they would fly to Helsinki. The Finnish appointments were for Tuesday afternoon and evening, and on Wednesday morning they'd fly to Copenhagen, returning to London in the afternoon.

Before the trip, Lisa had to go out and spend money to make herself look like the international businesswoman she had now become. She went to the Burberry shop and treated herself to a classic beige mac. Then she headed for Austin Reed and, after nearly fainting at the prices, whipped out her credit card, and bought herself a smart navy suit with some matching silk blouses. If she was to impress her customers, she had to look the part, she told herself over and over again, trying to justify the cost of looking good. Besides, she would soon be able to pay off her ever-growing credit-card bills when she started getting a big salary like John's. She stopped short of buying a briefcase; she didn't want to be one of those sad types who arrived at work clutching cases that contained nothing but a newspaper and a sandwich; she asked Andy if she could borrow his.

'I'll have to clean it out and give it to you on Friday,' he said, determined that she shouldn't see what he kept inside it.

'That sounds ominous,' said Lisa, picking up on his anxiety. 'Sandwiches gone mouldy have they?'

'Oh, nothing like that,' said Andy hastily, wishing that it was mere mouldy sandwiches that were making him nervous. He leant down to make sure his briefcase was locked.

'Whatever is it?' asked Lisa, her curiosity awakened.

'Nothing that you need to know about,' said Andy firmly, 'and if you ask again, I won't lend it to you.'

'Be like that, then,' said Lisa, taken aback. It wasn't like Andy to be so uptight. What did he have in there? She entertained herself with thoughts of what he might be hiding, plumping for something kinky as the most likely object. She began to view Andy in a new light, imagining him wearing a leather jockstrap and cracking a long whip. Or maybe wearing a giant baby's nappy, with an outsize dummy in his mouth.

The night before the trip, Lisa paraded in front of Ron and Mo in her new business gear. They were most impressed that she had climbed to such dizzy heights so soon. They were even more impressed when she told them that a car would be coming to pick her up in the morning to run her to Heathrow. Ron suggested they all go down the pub for a send-off drink, which resulted in a very late night of alcoholic indulgence. Consequently, Lisa wasn't at her best when she got into the car at 4.30 the next morning.

She met Mr Kimura at the British Airways check-in counter. He immediately gave her twenty official Haru Bank brochures and an assortment of specially wrapped Haru Bank gift pens, ties and scarves to put in her briefcase. They made it extremely heavy, and what with that and the bag containing her clothes and make-up, she felt thoroughly weighed down. She couldn't imagine how she would cope with lugging her heavy bags around for three days.

Once they had checked in, they marched at City pace to the boarding-area and sat down.

Mr Kimura asked what news she had listened to that morning.

'News?' asked Lisa, who only just managed to get up and dressed in time.

'Yes, news. Our customers will expect us to be up to date about the market. What will you tell them?'

'I don't know.'

'You don't know? How can they have confidence in you if you say that? You must never say you don't know. You must think of something to impress them.'

Mr Kimura was shocked. He hadn't realised that Lisa
was so inexperienced.

'Well,' said Lisa, making a big effort to shake
off her hangover and sound like a proper dealer,
'how about "The rates are looking quite firm today
although, depending on certain economic factors, it could
go either way"?'

Mr Kimura was pleased. 'Yes, that sounds good.
Write it down and learn it.'

All through the delicious champagne breakfast on
the plane and the complimentary drinks, he questioned
her about the economy and the financial markets. She
got quite flustered until she realised that he didn't
expect her to come up with anything original, but was
preparing her for the business conversations she would
be having over the next three days. The aim was for her
to be able to answer any question asked without saying
anything that could be used against her or Haru Bank
in the future. Lisa was learning to say a lot without
actually saying anything at all, a very useful skill to
have in the world of banking.

They landed in Oslo, quickly visited three banks and
then, feeling slightly confused after meeting so many
people in such a short time, headed back to the airport
for the flight to Stockholm. On the aeroplane, Lisa
had to write reports on the meetings. She got out the
business cards she had received and, so that she would
remember who was who and who said what, she wrote
a brief description of each customer on the back of the
relevant card. Mr P: tall, thin, loud check jacket. Mr
L: bald, with big belly. Ms W: young, very keen.

Mr Kimura saw what she was doing and pointed out
that Mr P was the bald one and that Ms W had been at
least forty-five. They spent the rest of the flight arguing

about what each customer looked like, so Lisa wasn't able to finish any of the reports. She didn't get a chance, either, to examine the bounty she had received, and had to wait until she was in the taxi. As well as some very slick brochures, she had been given two silk scarves in horrible tones, a blue fountain pen and a large key-ring with the Norwegian flag on it.

They checked into their hotel and dashed out again to meet two Swedish customers for dinner. The Swedes began the evening very seriously, asking lots of penetrating questions. Lisa was too tired to answer any of them but luckily, Mr Kimura, a veteran of such trips, was still able to string a sentence together and he covered for her admirably. They were introduced to the delights of reindeer meat, and as the drinks began to flow the Swedish chaps lightened up and became louder and louder. They insisted on going back to the hotel with Lisa and Mr Kimura, saying they should all go to the wonderful cocktail bar on the top floor. Three cocktails each later, and after some very rude Swedish jokes, Lisa and Mr Kimura staggered off to their rooms.

Over breakfast at seven the next morning, both nursing nasty headaches, Lisa and Mr Kimura looked at the day's schedule and groaned. What had looked so neat on paper was turning out to be a cruel endurance test.

As they slogged their way through the morning's appointments, they developed a kind of camaraderie. When Mr Kimura showed signs of flagging, Lisa covered for him by asking some simple questions about the Swedish economy. In return, whenever she looked as if she was going to keel over in her chair, he pinched her swiftly on the arm to wake her up again. Thus the two representatives of Haru Bank were able to get through their morning appointments in Stockholm.

On the plane to Helsinki, Lisa longed to rest but she had to write up her notes and get ready for the next round of meetings. The only time she would have to herself that day would be the thirty minutes between checking into their hotel later that afternoon and meeting some customers for drinks in the hotel bar in the evening. She kept herself going by imagining the pleasure of the long, hot shower she would take during that precious half-hour. Unfortunately, Mr Kimura had other plans. After they checked in, instead of going off to refresh himself in his own room, he insisted on going with Lisa to hers to discuss the afternoon's meetings.

'Did the first customer this morning say they had fifty-five million dollars to spare for BAs each month, or was it thirty-five million?' he asked.

'Thirty-five,' said Lisa.

'Are you sure? I thought he said fifty-five,' insisted Mr Kimura.

'If you say so,' said Lisa, who had found her bathrobe and was longing to get undressed.

'You'd better check your notes,' ordered Mr Kimura, wanting to be proved right.

Lisa didn't care any more. 'I'm sure if you thought they said it was fifty-five, that's what it must be.'

'You should check your notes,' ordered Mr Kimura.

Lisa's patience was at an end. 'There's no time for this, Mr Kimura. I have to take a shower,' she said firmly, and she bundled him out of the room.

Mr Kimura couldn't believe it when she shut the door in his face. He wasn't angry, though. He had liked having her hands on his body when she pushed him, and he saw it as a sign that she was beginning to warm to him. 'Maybe she'll be ready for a little fun after dinner,' he said to himself, and he went back to his room to imagine a naked Lisa soaping herself in the shower.

That evening, as they sat opposite their hosts at dinner, Mr Kimura realised that getting Lisa into bed that night would be harder than he thought. She looked tired and out of spirits. Their hosts were so dull that they might as well have been stuffed, and their conversation was equally enthralling.

Mr Kimura offered Lisa a piece of what he thought was delicious reindeer tongue from his plate and when she gagged and spat it out into her napkin, he realised that, to light the fire of passion, he would have to take control and turn the conversation from banking to something more sexy.

'I'm very interested to hear about your famous saunas,' he said to their hosts. 'We Japanese enjoy very much hot springs. I can imagine the pleasure of sitting in your wooden saunas and rushing out naked into the snow.'

Lisa choked on her wine, but the Finns' faces lit up as they delightedly told him every single detail they could think of about sitting naked in a hot room. Mr Kimura was fascinated and quite forgot that he was trying to excite Lisa's sexual interest. At the mention of whole families taking saunas together, he asked one of the Finns, a serious woman who apparently had a facial deformity that meant she could show no expression but po, about her own family.

'Did you,' he enquired, 'go naked in the sauna with your father when you were an adolescent?'

His wide, salacious grin and his obvious sexual inter-est in the subject were too much for Lisa. She slapped him on the arm and told him to control himself. The Finns, sensing that she was at the end of her tether, presented her with a scarf and Mr Kimura with a tie, and then quickly ended the meal.

In the taxi to their hotel, Mr Kimura decided to give it another try. 'Lisa,' he said softly, in what he hoped was a seductive voice, 'the hotel has a sauna. We would feel very refreshed if we went inside.'

'The only thing that would refresh me is a good night's sleep,' said Lisa, repelled by the thought of Mr Kimura in the nude.

'A sauna would take away your need for sleep,' he persisted. 'You would feel so good that you would be ready for anything.' He stroked her thigh gently, and imagined that she was reconsidering his suggestion.

Lisa brushed his hand away and moved closer to the door. 'You'll be embarrassed about this in the morning, Mr Kimura,' she said, trying to laugh it off.

Mr Kimura wasn't stupid; he realised she was rejecting him. The important thing now was to retain his dignity. 'Embarrassed about what?' he asked seriously. 'I think you misunderstood my intention.'

'Oh, I understood, all right,' answered Lisa. 'But I think it's the wine talking, don't you?' and with that she turned away and looked out of the window.

When they got back to the hotel they headed for their rooms, Lisa to have a good sleep and Mr Kimura, now that sex with Lisa was out of the question, to give himself some solitary pleasure by imagining well-built, naked Finnish girls taking long saunas with their lucky fathers.

Lisa, still queasy from the reindeer's tongue and Mr Kimura's advances, got up early so that she could breakfast alone. As she was finishing her cup of tea, she spotted him coming into the restaurant. Desperate for more time to herself before they left for Denmark, she slid down onto the floor and crawled out of the room on her hands and knees. This evasive action worked, and she had twenty precious minutes alone in her room before their departure.

Mr Kimura felt better, too. Having spent half an hour in the sauna before breakfast, he was relaxed enough to let Lisa get nice and merry on the complimentary champagne on their flight to Copenhagen.

Mr Nishioka from Haru Bank's Danish representative's office was waiting for them at the airport. Lisa was very pleased to see him. Now that there were two managers, she wouldn't have to say much at all. She sat quietly through their first two meetings, mentally preparing herself for their last engagement, a formal in-house lunch at one of the banks.

They were met in the bank lobby by a junior manager who accompanied them to the lift. In the entertainment suite on the top floor, three more managers, of varying levels of seniority, were waiting for them. There followed a few minutes' confusion, as seven people tried to introduce themselves to one another by presenting business cards, bowing and shaking hands. The problem for the Danes was that they knew how to greet a Japanese business man in the Japanese way, but they didn't know how to cope when the Japanese not only bowed but shook hands as well. In what order should they present cards, bow and shake hands? Also the distances required for the acts of bowing and shaking hands were different, and if one bowed straight after a handshake one had to shuffle rapidly backwards before bowing, or there might be an undesirable bumping of heads.

The Japanese had their own problems. How long was one supposed to shake hands for? Was it really necessary to grip so hard? And who should they talk to first? Should they all bow, shake hands and give cards one by one to the senior manager and then repeat the procedure as they worked their way down to the most junior? Or should they individually introduce themselves to the nearest manager and then swap over? If they had had time to discuss the introductions stage at a pre-lunch meeting, they would probably have come up with a solution. But they hadn't, and the resulting free-for-all of bows, handshakes and card-swapping caused such confusion that nobody was quite sure at the end who was who and who did what.

In the dining room they were offered drinks. Lisa had a vodka and tonic and the Japanese, wanting to conform to European business practices, ordered either gin or vodka as well. On an empty stomach the drinks took rapid effect and Lisa felt dizzy after just a few sips. Mr Nishioka turned tomato red, Mr Kimura began to sweat and their hosts, realising that it might be wise to get everyone seated quickly, told the waitress to start serving. The conversation began with an extensive discussion of the weather in Denmark, Japan and England, which took them all the way through the starters with white wine and well into the steak main course with red. Weather covered, the Danes asked a few questions about the economic policies of the Japanese government. Owing to the wine and the frequent changes of prime minister, the Japanese managers felt unable to answer immediately. They consulted in Japanese for a few minutes and then, unable to reach a consensus in such a short time, avoided the questions by asking about the health of each member of the Danish royal family.

Main course over, the conversation turned to the British government. Lisa, spurred on by alcohol, gave a spirited criticism of all that was wrong with the government's social and welfare policies. In a banking atmosphere, her views were blasphemy, but by now everyone was too drunk to care.

The dessert, a soggy trifle, was decorated with small silver balls that were expected to melt in the mouth. They didn't. Conversation stopped for a moment as everyone tried to cope with the rock-hard balls. The bad state of the average Japanese adult's teeth is well known, and this dental challenge in a drunken mouth was lethal. Mr Nishioka, being the younger of the two, managed to swallow his balls, though not without prior pain, but Mr Kimura got two firmly lodged in his false teeth. Lisa and the Danes, who all had good teeth, loudly crunched their balls and gamely carried on talking while the two unfortunates squirmed in their seats.

After coffee and brandy, lunch was over and the guests were escorted to the lift. After much bowing and shaking hands, someone remembered to press the button, and to pass the time until the lift arrived they had another round of bowing and shaking hands. At last, the lift came. Lisa, Mr Kimura and Mr Nishioka got in and their hosts waved goodbye as the doors closed.

Lisa and Mr Kimura felt tired but happy sitting next to each other on the plane home. They had two empty bottles of complimentary champagne in front of them and were about to start on some more. Lisa had kicked her shoes off and her feet were pressed up against the seat in front. Mr Kimura had undone his top button and loosened his tie. He looked at his young companion and felt sufficiently relaxed to tell her his vision for the future.

'I have a dream,' he said, his eyes misting over.

'Like Martin Luther King?' asked Lisa, giggling into her champagne.

'What?'

'Never mind, go on, old chap,' said Lisa, nudging him in the ribs.

'What was I saying?' he asked.

'About a dream.'

'Oh yes. I can see the whole row of desks by the window in the dealing-room filled with corporate dealers.'

'Corporate dealers?'

'Yes, like Citibank,' said Mr Kimura, wiping away a tear. 'I want to build a team of twenty or even forty dealers who will spend their time doing business with the big companies all over Europe.' He smiled as he pictured a long row of young, handsome men and women in candy-striped shirts, silk ties and low-cut blouses – the women would all have fine cleavages – sitting talking on the phone to companies like Fiat, Volvo, Eli Lilly and Shell. They would conquer the market with their speedy dealing and excellent economic advice, and he would stand before them, nurturing their growth. Eventually, in the corridors of head office in Tokyo, staff would no longer associate the name Kimura with elevator groping, but would think only of the great achievements of his corporate team in London. His photo would be in the company magazine as the manager most likely to become president of the bank in the next ten years.

'Where will you put them all?' Lisa's voice slashed its way through his vision. 'There are only six empty desks by the window. Everyone would get squashed up.'

Mr Kimura frowned as he pictured twenty good-looking young dealers, red in the face, pushing and swearing as each fought to get his or her backside on one of the six empty chairs. It wasn't a pleasant picture, although the women's wobbling breasts were quite exciting.

'We could expand the dealing-room,' he said firmly, raising his hand to stop Lisa asking where. 'I am starting small, with a local dealer and a Japanese manager. Now this is a big secret,' he said, lowering his voice. 'You mustn't tell anyone yet but I'm thinking of making you that dealer.' He smiled at Lisa, anticipating the rush of grateful thanks that would pour from her lush red lips.

'Does this mean I'll get more money?' she asked, picturing herself putting the key into the lock of her very own Docklands flat.

'Money!' spat Mr Kimura. 'You local dealers only think of money. It is a great honour for you. That should be enough.'

'So no extra money, then?' Lisa was disappointed.

'No! Well, maybe if you work very hard and show me good results, you might get more money.'

'I see.' Lisa saw it all very clearly. Lots more work and stress for bugger-all. How typical of her luck!

'Look, this very big chance for you. You should be very happy,' insisted Mr Kimura.

'I am. Thank you very much,' said Lisa, obliging him with a smile.

Mr Kimura was disappointed. He'd hoped her grati-tude might lead her to give him some . . . physical relief. Obviously the girl was hard to please. Never mind, he

said to himself. When she had had time to think about
the honour he was bestowing on her, she would look
at him with adoration. He only hoped that Mr Aono
would support his choice of Lisa as a corporate dealer
on the new, not yet agreed upon, corporate desk. Too
much champagne had loosened his mind as well as his
tongue. He shouldn't have told her she was to have a
new position merely because he had had too much to
drink and wanted to impress her. He vowed to give up
drinking altogether when he got back to London.

At Heathrow, Mr Kimura told Lisa she mustn't boast
about her trip in the dealing-room the next day. There
would be a lot of jealousy from the other dealers, and
she must be careful to let everyone know that the trip
had been hard work.

Looking down at her hands, blistered from lugging
around Andy's briefcase, which now contained umpteen
brochures, five silk scarves, three pens, one Norwegian
key-ring and several mini-bottles of wine and champagne, Lisa agreed that the trip had been hard work.
She promised she would try to remember what he had
told her.

She didn't, of course. The following day, proudly
wearing one of her tasteless new scarves, she swept
into the dealing-room like Joan Collins arriving at an
Oscars ceremony. As she handed out souvenir chocolates,
she acted like a returning hero and the other dealers, impressed with her acquired poise and confidence,
let her believe that she was. For a couple of days,
anyway.

Chapter 13

After spending three days together, Lisa and Mr
Kimura thought that they had reached a better
understanding of each other. Lisa realised that, beneath
Mr Kimura's professional-banker exterior, there was a
vulnerable man who had feelings, especially sexual ones,
like anyone else. But she still didn't like him and she
hated it if he came up to talk to her during the day.
When he put his hands on her shoulders to administer
one of his massages, she felt shivers of revulsion running
up and down her spine and it was all she could do to
stop herself from turning round and giving him a good
slap on the cheek.

Mr Kimura thought that in Lisa he now had an ally,
if not a potential lover. During the trip he had tried
to impress her with his knowledge and his talents.
He had also promised her a place on the corporate
desk. He was confident that, when he had finished
convincing Mr Aono and head office that a new desk
was required, she would take her place and feel truly
grateful towards him. He assumed it was now only a
matter of time before she succumbed to his charm and
allowed his hands to roam freely all over her naked

body. To give her a taste of things to come, he treated her to extra doses of massage. He knew how much she enjoyed them because she squirmed and wriggled with pleasure every time he placed his strong, firm hands on her delicate shoulders. He couldn't satisfy her for long, though, because he was often so overcome with desire that he had to cut the massage short and rush to the toilets before he came in his underpants.

The dealing-room had lost its charm under Mr Kimura. It was no longer a place where Aki-san could practise his golf swing during quiet moments, it was no longer a place where the hung-over could rest their aching heads on their desk and snooze undisturbed for a few hours, and it was no longer a place where Lisa could pretend she was enjoying herself. She had been able to bear Leo's abuse when she could go out at lunch times and drink herself silly. She had been able to put up with not really understanding what she was doing when there was no serious pressure to do well. She had even been able to put up with the loneliness of being one of only two women in a large group of aggressive, chauvinistic males when she was allowed to go about her daily business at her own pace. But now that Mr Slimy Kimura was breathing and slobbering down her neck, she felt that she was being pushed to the limit. Now that he had taken away the fun and replaced it with strain and tension, she didn't want to be there at all.

She felt like a fraud in the dealing-room. She had no real interest in the financial world and she found market reports and forecasts incredibly tedious. She'd tried very hard to develop an interest in what the rates were doing. She'd even begun to read the *Financial Times* in the morning, but the orange pages and the small print soon gave her a headache. When she overheard discussions about the importance of today's figure, or an interpretation of the Fed's actions yesterday, something in her brain switched off and she found herself thinking about what she'd like for lunch. On the days when she forced herself to take notice of the market, she could never predict what was going to happen. She was just pulled along without ever understanding why the rates were going down, or why indeed they should suddenly go up. This wasn't a major hindrance, because she didn't have to take a position when she dealt. Each deal she did was covered straight away by lending and borrowing at the same time, so she wasn't left exposed to fluctuations in interest rates. She could make money by just being quick, but she got no satisfaction from this because she always felt out of control.

Luckily, she didn't have the stress and worry that Aki-san and Leo had on the Futures desk, where they had to predict what was going to happen and take a position. Depending on whether they thought the rates were going to rise or fall, they either bought or sold futures, leaving themselves exposed to fluctuations in the market; the idea being that when they sold or bought to close out their position, the difference in the rates would give them either a profit or a loss. If during the day the market turned against them and their prediction was wrong, they had to cut their losses by closing their position as fast as they could. During those times, when the market was against them and they were shouting and screaming at their brokers, Lisa made sure to keep her head down. If she'd thought the insults she received during quiet times were bad, the ones thrown at her when the market was really busy were ten times worse. Lisa looked at Leo and Aki-san as, depending on how they'd been wrong-footed, they shrieked '*BUY!*' or '*SELL!*' and she wondered why they bothered studying the market at all. They would probably do just as well if they tossed a coin, she thought.

The unpredictability of the market got her down. She couldn't imagine that there ever would be a time when she knew it well enough to get things right. If she got to deal futures, and she didn't really want to, she could study all the market factors and still lose money. Alternatively, of course, she might make a profit, but what would the satisfaction be in that when it could easily be lost the following day? Besides, it wasn't her own money, it was Haru Bank's, and they weren't exactly generous in sharing it, at least not when she compared the salaries and bonuses they paid with those paid by other banks. Dealing only had a point to it if you could earn enough money to be able to retire at forty, and then go and do something that really interested you. Lisa couldn't see herself ever being good enough at dealing to command that level of salary, so there seemed no good reason to remain in the City.

She knew she had to find another career, but she couldn't think of anything she wanted to do. Also, if she left now she'd look like a failure: yet another woman who couldn't take the pressure. She hadn't been dealing long enough to say that she was tired of it and wanted to do something else. Leo would have a field day if she announced that she was going. She could just imagine his comments, foremost among them 'I knew we shouldn't have had a woman on the desk' and 'Trust the dwarf to bottle out'.

Perhaps if she knew what she really wanted to do, she wouldn't care what anybody thought about her, but she couldn't think of a single job to suit her. If her life outside the bank had been happier she might have been able to see a clear path leading to a satisfying career, but her life was such a shambles that she felt she was hacking her way through a forest of thorns by just getting up and dressed in the morning. She hadn't the strength to cut through to the right path for her future.

Lisa became thoroughly sorry for herself and probably would have continued in that vein until the spring, but fortunately one evening Ron came up with a suggestion that jolted her into action.

'Lisa,' he said, as he sat at the kitchen table, unwrapping his supper of cod, chips and pickled gherkin, and smothering it in salt and vinegar, 'I was talking to a geezer down the local, and he's got a brother who's trying to sell a flat. It sounds right up your street.' He shoved a handful of chips in his mouth and chewed noisily while Lisa, who'd only had toast that evening and fancied something more to eat, took in what he had said.

'I'm not looking for a place yet,' she answered, reaching across the table for some chips.

'Get yourself a plate an 'elp yourself, luv,' offered Ron. 'I should've got you both some,' he said, as Mo took some chips as well. 'Anyway, I just thought you might be interested, that's all. It's in Leyton up the High Road, not far from the station.'

'That sounds very nice, doesn't it, darling?' said Mo, breaking off some of Ron's cod. She was acting as if she'd just heard about the flat, but Ron had told her a few days before. They wanted their space back and had been asking around for the last few weeks to see if anyone knew of a place Lisa could buy.

Lisa suddenly had a thought. 'Are you trying to get rid of me?' she asked. It was nearly four months since she'd moved in and, although living there wasn't very comfortable, she had got used to it and she thought that her mother and Ron enjoyed having her around.

'It's nothing like that, love,' Mo said reassuringly. 'It's just that you need your own space to do the things you want to do.' *And so do we*, she could have added, but she didn't. Lisa was her daughter and she loved her, but she wanted to see her settled in her own life.

'Which means you've had enough of me here,' said Lisa angrily. 'Well, if that's the case, I'll go back to Dad's. I don't want to buy a place until I can afford somewhere really nice, and I'm not staying where I'm no longer welcome.'

'There's no need to be like that,' said Ron. 'You're a young woman. You should be out and about, not living with your parents. Why don't you just come and see the flat?'

'I'll think about it,' said Lisa in a huff. She felt like stomping out of the room to make a point, but the chips were really tasty and she was hungry, so she finished up what was on her plate before going off to her room.

So she was going to have to move back to Baneham and witness her father's gradual decay, she thought as she lay down on her bed. Since she'd left, he had definitely got worse. She wasn't sure if her leaving had quickened his decline or whether, now that she only saw him occasionally, she was more aware of the physical and mental changes in him. His illness now showed clearly on his face. Just a few months before, he could pass as a normal person until you tried to converse with him. But now his face had lost its expression and his eyes were often blank. It was obvious to anyone who saw him that something was seriously amiss.

He was vanishing. Bit by bit his personality was being rubbed away, leaving a shell that had once been her father. She had vague memories of being carried on his shoulders when she was young, of trips to the beach, of him laughing at something silly that she had done, but they were just fleeting images from the past. The man she had once called Daddy was no longer there. He had gradually slipped away and Lisa felt utterly helpless; she could do nothing to bring him back.

When she visited him, he no longer bothered to try writing things down. If he wanted to draw her attention to something, he just grabbed her arm and pointed. His hand, now very bony and thin, felt like a claw grasping tight, as if, by holding her arm, he was trying to keep hold of life itself. Lisa always looked where he was pointing, and tried very hard to understand what he was showing her.

If he pointed at the stove, she'd check to see if it had been left on, or if it was dirty, or if the gas was leaking. But maybe he was pointing at the stove because he wanted something to eat, or maybe he wasn't pointing at the stove at all, maybe he was pointing at the wall behind the stove, maybe the wallpaper was looking old and he was asking Lisa to decorate the kitchen. Simply pointing his finger could hold hundreds of meanings and Lisa's patience often ran out, so that she'd give up trying to discover which was the right one.

Sometimes, when she felt as if she was going to scream with frustration, she tried to walk away from him. But he never gave up. He'd shadow her around the house, standing close by until she had to come back to the spot he had been pointing at and try once more

to understand him. At times like this, she could feel
what was left of the man inside, feel him willing her
to try, because if she gave up, if she ignored what he
was pointing at, she'd be giving up on him.

Lisa couldn't begin to contemplate what he was like
at work. She didn't want to think about how hard it
was for him to keep going to the office every day and
work with the same people he'd worked with for years,
who'd known him before it all started, who had been
his friends and who now couldn't even look him in the
eye. The thought that he was aware of what he'd lost
was almost unbearable.

She knew he was aware, because in Tesco's one Saturday a man had come up to them and said cheerfully,
'Long time no see.' When Lisa's father looked at him
blankly, he added, 'Jim Peters — I was best man at your
wedding.'

'My dad can't talk any more. He's sick,' Lisa had
explained.

'I'm sorry to hear that,' Jim replied after a shocked
pause. He tried to smile and stayed a few moments to
exchange pleasantries, but his discomfort was clear.
Whether it came from pity or from the fear that
comes when you see someone your own age struck
down by something nasty, wasn't clear, but Jim had
been a lot less jaunty when he walked away than when
he approached them.

Her father had managed a slight smile to show either
that he was pleased to have bumped into Jim after so
many years, or that he had noticed Jim's reaction but
wasn't upset by it. Either way, Lisa had realised, he
was still very much aware of what went on around
him. The knowledge had haunted her ever since.

Living in Stratford, she'd been able to put her worries

about him to the back of her mind for much of the time. But now, as she lay there thinking about moving back to Baneham, they came back with renewed strength. What would happen when he couldn't look after himself any more? Who would take care of him? Lisa couldn't see herself as a full-time carer. She had compassion, but she didn't have the emotional strength, or the patience, to cope with such a huge task.

She knew she should talk things over with John before their father got really bad. They should work out a plan for the time when he was totally dependent on them. But John had detached himself from the situation by moving abroad. Dealing with sick relatives was not one of his lifestyle choices. Lisa wished she could detach herself too, but she found it impossible to switch off her feelings.

If she moved back to Baneham she would worry constantly. She seemed to be the only one willing or able to face up to the situation. Aunt Millie stayed with her father often, but she was ten years older than him and not in the best of health herself, as she often pointed out. Now that she had a taste of living with her baby brother, she'd told Lisa, she knew without a doubt that she wasn't strong enough to cope with staying with him all the time.

'He still insists on driving, you know,' she'd informed Lisa one Saturday afternoon.

'Well, he hasn't hit anything so he must be fine,' answered Lisa.

'Fine? He had his wipers on last time and it wasn't even raining.'

'It's a mistake anyone can make,' said Lisa, trying not to laugh.

'Some people put them on by mistake, but they don't

leave them on. The rubber was screeching back and forwards across the windscreen. Gave me a headache, it did.' Aunt Millie rubbed her temples at the memory.

'Well, you drive next time,' suggested Lisa.

'Me? Oh Lisa, dear, you know how I am with my nerves. I couldn't possibly.'

Aunt Millie is no Florence Nightingale, thought Lisa now, and the future flashed before her eyes: her father blind, deaf, paralysed and doubly incontinent, and herself the one who had to care for him. Lisa Soames, full-time carer. Life would pass her by as she, out of filial duty, spent her youth nursing her sick father. The vision frightened her. Would she be able to undertake such a role without being crushed by the strain of it all? She hoped the day would never come when she had to choose between caring for her father and caring for herself. She wasn't altogether sure which she would choose.

'That's my future,' said Lisa to herself, and at that moment she made a decision. Until the day came when her father really needed her, she wanted to live her life as enjoyably as she could.

She got up and went back to the kitchen.

When she'd sat down at the table and lit a cigarette she said, 'So tell me more about this flat, then.'

'I thought you weren't looking,' said Ron, pleased that she had calmed down.

'Well,' said Lisa, 'I've been at the bank six months, so I can get a mortgage subsidy now. What with all the overtime I'm doing, I could probably afford it.'

'It's not one of those luxury places.' Ron knew that Lisa was aiming for a Docklands flat. 'It's a conversion, above a shop. It's got a fitted kitchen and everything.'

*   *   *

'Everything' turned out to be a fresh coat of magnolia paint and four new lightbulbs, one in each room and another above the front door in the hall.

'It's very small,' said Lisa as they stood in the living-room. There would be just about enough room for a sofa and a small dining-table with two chairs.

'The ceilings are very high, though,' said Ron, looking up.

'Yes, they'd be perfect if I was a monkey and wanted to swing from the lampshades,' said Lisa sarcastically. She was disappointed, not just because the flat was small, but that this was all she could afford after six months of hard work in the City.

Ron tried to make the best of things. 'It's got lovely doors,' he said pointing to the glass-panelled door between the living-room and the bedroom. 'Makes it nice and light.'

'It also means that anyone coming in can see straight into the bedroom,' said Lisa.

'Not if you put a curtain up,' suggested Ron, 'although that would make it darker. But look at the fitted wardrobes,' he said going into the bedroom and opening the wardrobe doors. 'Look at the space in there.' He stepped inside and spread his arms out.

Lisa looked. It was a very large cupboard indeed, with shelves running down one side. 'It's nearly as big as the bedroom,' she admitted. 'It might actually be bigger,' she added ruefully.

'That's the spirit,' said Ron, relieved at her attitude. 'Let's take a look at the rest of it, shall we?'

'You make it seem like it's more than two steps away,' laughed Lisa.

She exaggerated slightly. It took four steps to get to the bathroom door from the bedroom. They looked

inside. There was no window, so they had to put the
light on.

'Where's the bath?' asked Lisa, she could only see a
shower, toilet and a sink.

'They didn't have room for one. Anyway, showers
are much more useful,' said Ron, pulling the curtain
back to expose the shower head.

'Especially if you happen to like showers,' agreed
Lisa, who liked a hot bath on a cold winter's night.
He's missed his calling, she thought, watching Ron test
the taps. He'd have made a fine estate agent.

The kitchen was what really brought her round.
It had been fitted out with new units, a stove, a
fridge-freezer and a washing-machine. Images of all the
meals she would be able to cook and eat with no one
to bother her were what clinched it. It wasn't a great
flat, and she hated the magnolia, but she imagined that
with a few coats of paint and the addition of curtains
and carpets, she could make it very cosy. It would only
take twenty minutes to get to work and there were lots
of shops nearby. She didn't think she'd find a more
convenient place, so she agreed to buy it.

Six weeks later, when she had moved in and was
sitting at her new dining-table eating a large plate of
spaghetti bolognese, she suddenly felt deeply lonely. She
didn't know what triggered it off. Maybe it was just
sitting there eating alone, or the fact that she had no one
to share her bottle of Chianti Classico with, or even that
she missed Mo's dog slobbering at her feet begging for
scraps. Maybe it was a combination of all these things.
Whatever it was, her mood plummeted and she found
herself thinking back to the not so distant past, to her
days at university when she lived with Ken.

She'd been so happy then that every bottle of cheap

wine they'd drunk tasted like champagne, and plain
lentil soup was eaten with relish because they were
eating it together. How different life is when you're
with someone you love, she thought sadly. At this
point she pulled herself together and poured another
glass of wine.

Memory plays tricks, she told herself sternly. It's easy
to only think of the good bits and conveniently forget the
pain. Ken, her first and only love. He certainly knew
how to stick the knife in and twist it, she remembered,
her melancholy growing stronger and stronger as the
wine in the bottle diminished, and she tried to put him
out of her mind. She knew that she wasn't the first
woman to be abandoned like that, but it didn't make
the humiliation any less.

They had met during Registration in their first year
at university. Ken was standing in a queue, and Lisa
asked him if it was the queue for the politics and
sociology course. He said yes, and Lisa took her place
behind him. He hadn't said anything else. He was into
Kafka in those days and saw unnecessary words as a
waste of his artistic potential. Lisa had considered him
either shy or rude.

That would have been that, as far as she was
concerned, but it seemed she was fated to have some
kind of relationship with him. They were placed in
the same tutorial group for political thinkers.

'Here's last year's exam paper,' said Professor Thomas,
handing it out to the eight students in his group.
'Take a look at the first question: "Is political thought
perennial?" For next week's tutorial, I want you to
prepare an answer to this question.'

Seven students nodded their head and noted the
question in their files. Lisa was still wondering what

'perennial' meant. If she couldn't even understand the words of the question, how was she going to cope with writing a paper to present to the group? The rest of the tutorial went over her head, because she had convinced herself that she wasn't clever enough to be at university and that very soon she would be sent home.

'How about a coffee?' Ken asked her as they left the room. Because of his artistic endeavours, he hadn't spoken to anyone for three days and now, pining to give his jaw some exercise, he picked her to talk to as she was the only familiar face in the room.

Coffee went well. They talked about where they had come from and what A levels they had studied, and Lisa even relaxed enough to ask what 'perennial' meant.

A few days later when she saw him sitting alone in the refectory, she felt no hesitation in joining him. 'Have you done the tutorial yet?' she asked.

Ken got out his file and handed her four sheets of paper: 'Before considering whether the history of political thought is perennial, one must first consider what is meant . . .'

Lisa was impressed. 'Where did you get this information?' she asked.

'I read the introductions of the core text books and then thought things through,' answered Ken smugly.

Lisa quickly finished her coffee, charged over to the library and got out all the textbooks on the reading-list. It wasn't until she'd read the introduction of the last book on the list that she understood what Ken had done. The fourth paragraph of the first page said, 'Before we can consider whether the history of political thought is perennial . . .'

When Ken arrived for the tutorial, Lisa was already standing outside Professor Thomas's office door. 'I know

what you did,' she told Ken triumphantly. 'I read it
as well.'

'Move over, squirt,' said Ken. They struggled in the
doorway for a few seconds, but Ken won and got the
seat next to the professor's desk so that he could read
his paper first. It didn't matter. Professor Thomas didn't
notice that their papers were the same. He'd given up
listening to freshers years ago.

Lisa and Ken became good friends after that. Lisa
gradually realised that she wanted him to be her first
lover, but as he never showed any desire for her, she
didn't let him know her true feelings in case it spoilt
their friendship. At the end of the first year they were
still just good friends.

In the second year they rented rooms in the same
house and spent many evenings pondering the meaning
of life and listening to the Velvet Underground. It took
a few bottles of wine and a joint one wintry night
for them to break the ice. They'd run out of 50p
pieces for the meter, and when the electricity went
off they lit some candles and climbed into Ken's bed
for warmth. Before long they were fumbling around
under the covers.

'I never said I loved you,' said Ken when they
broke up some months later. He had slept with her,
he had made her feel that she was loved, but he had
never said the words themselves. That was how he
justified himself when he left her for a six-foot blond
hockey-player called Paul.

So instead of Ken and Lisa it was now Ken and Paul.
The first time she saw them together in the refectory,
it had hurt very much. After the pain had faded, she
was thankful that at least he hadn't deserted her for
another woman. If he had, she would have had to

blame her figure, her face or her height for failing
to please. As it was, he'd had been after something no
other woman could provide.

She felt the loss of his friendship very much. She'd
been able to talk to him about anything and he was
very good at comforting her when she was down.
She'd enjoyed the sex, too. That was hard to admit
afterwards, because she had to wrestle with the notion
that he probably hadn't enjoyed it. When she could
separate her memories of sex from the knowledge
that her only experience had been with a man strug-
gling with homosexual tendencies, she realised that she
missed it a lot.

Lisa finished her spaghetti, did the washing-up and
then settled down on the sofa with a magazine and a
glass of whisky. She was not going to think about Ken
any more. She had her own flat. She had a good job.
She was getting on with her life. She was not going to
spoil the evening by thinking about the past. However,
as she turned the pages of the magazine, one thought
kept popping into her head. Sex. *Sex*. *SEX!* She hadn't
had it for so long, and right now it was all she could
think about. If she had a man to pop between the sheets
of her new double bed, she'd be contented. Sex would
cheer her up. Sex would put a stop to her end-of-winter
sadness. Sex would make her feel perky again.

Unfortunately, her present situation was rather like
being on a desert island: she was surrounded by water
she couldn't drink. In her case, the water was men. She
worked with them all day in the City, but she never
found one that she wanted to strike up a relationship
with. There were plenty who offered her sexual relief,
but Lisa wasn't used to separating the idea of having sex
from that of having a loving relationship. The thought

made her laugh, because the only loving sexual relationship she'd had had been with a closet homosexual.

She explained her problem to Jackie the next day when they met for a drink after work. 'The trouble is that I've never been your one-night-stand kind of girl,' she said. 'I like to get to know someone first before I have sex with them.'

'Yes, well, we all start off like that, don't we?' Jackie could even remember a time when a man's hobbies had seemed relevant to her. 'But during a dry spell, the urge becomes hard to deny and you have to take what you can get.'

'Well, I don't know about doing it with just anyone,' said Lisa, cringing at the thought of having sex with some of the men in the bar. 'But if I don't have it soon, I'll go mad — or,' she added, thinking back to last night's desperate activities beneath the covers, 'blind.'

'That bad, is it, kid?' said Jackie sympathetically. 'Well, your fairy godmother is here to help you.' She waved her hand as if it held a magic wand. 'Hubble bubble boil and trouble.' (That didn't sound quite right but she knew Lisa got the drift.) 'Send me a broker on the double.' She cackled with laughter.

'No, thanks,' said Lisa, imagining what would be said on the direct lines the following day if she did sleep with one. 'I don't fancy the whole market knowing what I do in bed.'

'Don't be silly. You're a dealer at Haru Bank. He wouldn't want to upset you, in case you ever get a really good dealing job,' said Jackie, speaking from experience. 'If you need to have a fling, your best bet is with a broker. You could get one easily.'

'You make it sound like fishing,' laughed Lisa.

'Oh it is, my dear,' said Jackie seriously. 'It is.

All you have to do is cast out your nets and haul
them in.'

'Very subtle, I'm sure,' said Lisa drily.

Lisa didn't follow Jackie's advice right away. She
intended to hold out for sex in a proper relationship.
However, as time went on and there was no sign of
a decent single man coming along to sweep her off her
feet, the idea of casual sex became more attractive, and
she began to look around for a likely candidate.

Bob was out of the question. He had recently started
dating a woman who lived next door to him, and
had fallen madly in love. On Monday mornings he
spent ages telling Lisa all the details of his romantic
weekends in places like Venice and the Cotswolds. Lisa
couldn't understand how he could see the Cotswolds in
winter in the same romantic way as Venice. But he was
American, and he was probably getting so much sex
on his weekends away that even Birmingham would
seem romantic to him. Lisa didn't dwell on a missed
opportunity. She knew Bob had only seen her as a
quick poke on their one and only date. She was too
short for him to whisk off for romantic weekends.

Admitting that her friend had been right, she turned
to Jackie for help and, after putting their heads together,
they selected Chopper, the broker at the Christmas
party who'd escorted Lisa out of the restaurant. Lisa
had heard that he was living with someone, but Jackie
said it was a minor matter as he wasn't actually married
and he didn't have any children.

'If a woman can't keep her man faithful when they
are only living together, they'll break up soon anyway,'
she said reassuringly. 'In any case, you're not aiming to
steal him, you just want to borrow him for an evening.'

Lisa saw the sense in Jackie's words and agreed that Chopper was a good choice. On many a drunken occasion he had suggested that they get off together and, as he was young and not too physically repulsive, she was prepared to lower her standards just this once. That he was one of Stephanie's brokers made her hesitate. What if the queen found out about it? Chopper would lose his line and Lisa would be . . . She usually stopped at this point because she couldn't imagine how Stephanie could become any more unpleasant to work with than she already was. She could, though, imagine what Leo would do, and the idea of him finding out, via Stephanie, that Lisa had slept with Chopper was bad enough for her to put her plans on hold for a while.

Fortunately, Chopper was moved off fixed-date dollars and put on to short-dates. He was now one of Andy's brokers and, seeing no danger there, Lisa decided to make her move. They met after work in a champagne bar at her invitation, although Chopper, having a generous expense account, was the one who put his credit card behind the bar. After two bottles of champagne and a bowl of peanuts, Lisa was sufficiently confident to proposition him.

'What's all this about, then?' he asked suspiciously. She had never taken his advances seriously before. Why the sudden change?

'I've got my own flat,' answered Lisa. 'I thought it would be nice to christen it.'

Chopper swayed slightly. He'd been out late last night, had had a three-hour liquid lunch today, and was topping it all off with champagne . . . What he really wanted was an early night, but Lisa was offering herself to him and he was never one to refuse a ride.

They jumped into a taxi and Chopper put his arm

round her, hugging her to him. Feeling his body close
to hers for the first time made her start having doubts.
In the early-evening light, he was not handsome. He was
a bit overweight and had that I-slept-in-this-shirt-last-
night look. Being so close to his armpits was decidedly
unpleasant, and she wondered if she could get him to
take a shower before he laid a finger on her. Once
in the flat, her doubts steadily grew. Chopper, having
been out the night before and having spent lunchtime
and the evening drinking, had terribly bloodshot eyes.
She wondered if he would be capable of indulging in
some erotic foreplay, let alone of sustaining an erection
for more than a few minutes. She sat him on the sofa
and went to the fridge to get a bottle of wine, hoping
a few more drinks would kill off her doubts.

'Come and sit by me, darlin,' he slurred, when Lisa
came back. 'Tell your Uncle Chopper what you like.'
He leered at her, and Lisa fancied she could see saliva
dripping from his mouth. Oh what big teeth you've got,
she thought, and she hoped the wine would make him
seem a little more streamlined and a little less sweaty.

She sat down next to him and poured the wine. He
drained his glass in one gulp, and leant over to give her a
wet, sloppy kiss, putting his tongue deep into her mouth.
Unfortunately, as he leant over he released the loudest
rip-roaring fart Lisa had ever had the misfortune to
witness. The blast of smelly fumes killed any sexual
feelings she might have had left, and she pushed him
away. This man's willy was definitely not going to be
pumping in and out of her vagina.

'I'm sorry, I've changed my mind,' she said, standing
up. She hoped Chopper wasn't going to turn into one
of those violent psychopaths she read about in Ron's
News of the World. What would she do if he tried

to force her to have sex? He was drunk enough to be dangerous. She backed away from him, clutching the bottle of wine firmly.

'Don't worry about it. I can't get it up tonight, any-way,' said Chopper, smiling apologetically and looking more like a huggy bear than a wicked wolf. 'Drank too much. Sorry.'

Lisa felt quite sympathetic. He must feel so embar-rassed, she thought. 'That's OK,' she said sitting down again. 'Do you want another glass of wine before you go?'

'Yeah, don't mind if I do,' replied Chopper, holding out his glass. 'And Lisa, I've just got one thing to say.'

'What?' asked Lisa, carefully pouring the wine.

'Get your kit off,' he ordered.

Lisa felt a moment of panic and nearly dropped the bottle. Should she just bolt for the door? She imagined being brought down by a rugby tackle and then being pinned underneath his sweating, heaving hulk of a body.

'I thought you said you couldn't do it,' she replied, wondering whether she would be better off trying to bang on the window for help.

'I don't think I can,' admitted Chopper, 'but that needn't stop me giving you a little pleasure, need it?'

Despite her reservations, Lisa felt the strange stirring in the pit of her stomach that signalled that she was going to have a good time. She took Chopper to the bedroom, they undressed and lay down on the bed. To the accompaniment of loud slurping, Chopper sucked all the important bits of her body for what seemed like ages, but in reality was only about fifteen minutes. Lisa enjoyed it, although she could have done without the sound effects. She didn't reach an orgasm because every time she got to the edge the memory of his fart came back and killed it. After extensive sucking, Chopper said he ought to be getting home. When he'd left, she lay on her bed, still tingling from his touch, sipping a glass of wine.

Jackie got a full report the following day and couldn't believe Lisa had come off so well. 'You were lucky he didn't just bonk you senseless and bugger off,' she said.

'He wasn't capable of going all the way,' said Lisa, smiling at the memory of his darting tongue — *that* certainly hadn't been affected by the drink.

'Oh, I doubt that. They usually manage to get it up somehow, especially when you don't want them to. What did he say when you told him you'd changed your mind?'

'He was fine about it.'

'I don't believe your luck. That's two you've stopped in mid-flow and neither of them minded.' Jackie shook her head: Lisa certainly wasn't playing by the rules.

'Perhaps it's because I'm so sweet and vulnerable,' said Lisa, giving Jackie her little-girl-in-trouble look.

'Yeah, right,' said Jackie, wishing she could still look virginal.

Lisa expected the market to be full of her recent indiscretion, but nobody said a word. Jackie was right about her luck. Like Bob, Chopper kept quiet. Lisa was convinced that her honest nature had gained the sympathies of her would-have-been but failed conquerors. She didn't realise either that Bob was frightened she'd reveal that he'd backed off at the last minute, or that the memory of the previous evening's wind problem was enough to keep even the loudest-mouthed broker quiet for some time.

Lisa didn't want to risk her luck on another pig in a poke, so that weekend she went up to Tottenham Court Road and bought herself a large vibrator with two speeds and five detachable heads. She went into the bookshop near the sex shop and picked out Nancy Friday's *The Secret Garden* and Anaïs Nin's *Delta of Venus*. Then she took a taxi to Marks & Spencer at Marble Arch, where she stocked up on wine and food before heading back home on the Central Line as fast as the noisy old train would carry her.

She spent a pleasant evening stuffing food, gulping wine and filling her head with erotic fantasies. The vibrator was a bit of a disappointment. When she switched it on it was so loud that she feared the neighbours would come to find out who was sawing her up with a chainsaw. The detachable heads were rather too easy to detach and she avoided putting the loud, shuddering tool inside her in case she was forced to head for casualty at Whips Cross hospital with half a vibrator stuck up her vagina. The clitoral stimulator was good, though. The first time she used it she had it on full-speed and she reached orgasm in less than thirty seconds. The force was so strong that she let out a very loud yell as she climaxed. If she hadn't removed the vibrator when she did, the neighbours would have had to peel her off the ceiling. On half-speed, though, the sensation was just right and that night, for the first time in months, Lisa slept soundly and without being tormented by torrid dreams.

She felt good when she headed for work on Monday morning. She had slept and eaten well all weekend, and she hadn't had to put up with Mo and Ron's arguments. She'd made the right decision in buying her flat, she concluded, even if she was a bit lonely.

When Leo came in, he was feeling very sorry for himself. He'd had a row with the Sow at the weekend over his excessive drinking, and she'd told him she didn't want to see him any more unless he cleaned up his act. He didn't tell Lisa any of this, but she heard him complaining about the Sow — or rather the Silly Fat Cow, as he called her this morning — to Stephanie, who showed her usual contempt for her own sex by sympathising with Leo and advising him to find a worthier partner. One would have thought, from what she was saying, that the queen of the dealing-room desired an alliance with the king, but her body language conveyed a different message. As Leo leant forward to talk quietly about his personal life, Stephanie gradually leant away. When she couldn't move any further without falling off her chair, she put her hand over her mouth and nose. Leo's whisky breath was bad enough to ensure their alliance was never sealed.

Lisa was sorry Stephanie was so unfriendly towards her. She was dying to find out whether she was sexually fulfilled or whether she was in the same state as Lisa. Stephanie was ten years older and had been a dealer for five years; presumably, at her age, thirty-two, she had achieved a satisfactory lifestyle. It was a shame that she was too mean to take Lisa under her wing.

She needn't have wasted time wishing for Stephanie's guidance. The only difference in their lifestyles was that Stephanie's seniority in the market gave her more money to cushion the pain of loneliness. Like Lisa, she had spent the weekend indulging in solitary pleasures, and if there was one piece of advice she'd have been willing to give her, it would have been the make of her vibrator. Its detachable heads were secure and it didn't roar like Lisa's, it purred.

Chapter 14

After the Easter holiday, Lisa arrived at her desk and found out that she didn't sit there any more.

'You are corporate dealer now,' Aki-san told her, pointing to her new place at the empty row by the window on the other side of Leo's desk.

She felt quite sad at leaving Aki-san. He had been severe at times, but she had got used to working with him and had even developed a strange affection for his despotic tendencies. It had been fun watching his face turn all the colours of the rainbow when he flew into a rage. There was something poetic in his stilted English, and the simple phrases he used often entered her mind as she worked, reminding her of the penalties she'd face if she made a mistake. He was hard to please and always very demanding, but on the rare occasions when he had said, 'You did good,' or 'Very well done,' she felt as pleased as if he had given her £500 as well.

She wasn't sorry to be moving to a different section from Leo, though. Now that she was no longer his junior, he wouldn't be able to order her about or make her fetch his coffee. The drawback was that her new desk was closer than her old one to his, and there was no one sitting between them. When it came to insults, he'd probably be even more of a nuisance than before.

When Mr Kimura arrived, he took Lisa round the bank and introduced her to each of the managers as the new corporate dealer. He had sold the idea of a Corporate desk to his superiors by producing lots of reports and diagrams which nobody read but which they all signed once they saw other signatures collecting on the bottom. At the senior managers' meeting, where the decision was formally made, his choice of the first corporate dealer raised a few eyebrows, but he managed to convince the doubters that Lisa had a natural charm which was wasted on the quick buy-sell of dealing. He said that on the Scandinavian trip she had shown a flair for coping with customers face to face, and he thought this would be an asset to the desk. She was a little unconventional, he admitted, but the customers seemed to like it.

As Mr Kimura had staked his reputation on the success of the desk, no one wanted to believe he had chosen Lisa for any reasons except those he had given, so she duly found herself on the corporate desk. She had a greater workload and slightly more prestige, but not so much as a penny's increase in salary. Next to her sat a fresh plant from Tokyo called Mr Kubo, who, having previously been in the accounts department at head office, had virtually no experience of handling corporates and even less in a dealing-room environment. But he could write reports in Japanese and was therefore considered a suitable manager of the new Corporate desk.

While Mr Kubo got busy writing, Mr Kimura took over the real job of managing the desk, taking great pleasure in the daily strategy talks that he insisted on having with Lisa. He was sure that their long discussions, as well as all the corporate entertaining they would have to do together, would give him even more opportunity to show off his assets and that it wouldn't be long before she succumbed to his charms.

At first, Lisa was overwhelmed by her new responsibilities. Until now, the customers had spoken directly to the different dealers whenever they wanted to do business. This meant that, if they had two or three deals in different currencies or different financial instruments, they had been transferred around the dealing-room accordingly. Mr Kimura's idea was that, instead of the customer calls being handled by all the dealers, there should be one person acting as an intermediary. If the customers knew that every time they rang Haru Bank they would speak to the same person, a stronger relationship could be developed. Lisa, as the new corporate dealer, was to be that intermediary.

She had a lot to learn. As well as taking care of BAs, she was also going to have to learn about money-market and FX dealing. She wasn't expected to increase the customer base yet; she just had to get everyone used to dealing with her. From her new desk by the window, she could shout to any dealer in the room to ask for a quote. In theory, the dealers had to answer her as quickly as they could so that the customer would spend less time on the phone than before. In practice, the dealers were often away from their desks getting coffee, going to the toilet or sorting out a problem in the back office, so Lisa often had to put the customer on hold as she tried to find someone to give her a quote. If the dealers were at their desks, they often ignored her first shout, either because they were in the middle of a deal or because they wanted to aggravate her. The

latter was common, because there was much resentment
of the attention being paid to one of the newest additions
to the dealing-room.

So Lisa found that not only did she have trouble
getting the dealers to respond to her shouts, which
became more piercing as the day went on, but she also
had to cope with the customers who preferred to deal
with the dealers directly. They couldn't understand
why they suddenly had to speak to a young girl who
obviously didn't know what she was doing and who
made them wait twice as long as they had before.
When they voiced their frustration — and they did so
quite frequently — Lisa had to leave her desk and walk
over to the other dealers in order to drag a response out
of them.

The Japanese managers, seeing what was happening,
tried to help her. Mr Kimura had made it very clear
that the Corporate desk was his pet project and that
if it failed he would blame them. Thinking they were
aiding her, they told the dealers in their sections to give
priority to her requests for quotes, but that only created
more resentment and the dealers thought up more subtle
ways to hinder her.

Luckily, Lisa's time working with Aki-san and Leo
had taught her how to cope in unfriendly waters, so
she was able to get through each day without having
a nervous breakdown and little by little she began to
find her feet and get the dealers to work with her
instead of against her. Time and time again, though,
she inwardly cursed Mr Kimura for the extra hassle
he'd caused her.

The only thing that didn't change was Leo. He
couldn't order her about any more, but he could still
abuse her in his free moments, and this he continued

to do with relish. Lisa spent a lot of energy fighting back. She knew his weak points now, and she targeted them remorselessly. She made fun of his beer-belly and she teased him about the bald spot on the back of his head, which he was finding more and more difficult to hide. When she was in a really good mood, she made fun of his height. She was less than five feet but she didn't care. Leo, who at five foot seven was average among the Japanese, looked short and squat down the pub among the local dealers and brokers. Lisa had sensed early on that he minded this a lot, and that his obsession with her height merely reflected his dissatisfaction with his own.

Behind the swagger, Leo was a bundle of insecurity. He was afraid that if he left tomorrow he'd be missed hardly at all; he knew there were lots of people eager to take over his job. Late at night he was often tormented by a little voice telling him that very soon he'd be bald and burnt-out as well as fat.

As a dealer, he didn't actually make anything. After a day's work, he couldn't stand back and look at something he'd created; he could only count the figures on his dealing-sheet. If he made a big profit he felt unnaturally high, and he used champagne to maintain the mood and to help him forget that he easily lose just as much, if not more, the next day. The bank rewarded his efforts with a large salary and a fat bonus, but these in themselves were becoming a burden because he knew no other job would pay him so much for doing so little, and the thought that one day he might be forced to seek a real job and be paid an ordinary salary terrified him.

Leo tried to banish his fears by seeking pleasure. He often got drunk, fed his sweaty face in a posh restaurant and then threw money away playing blackjack in a casino until the early hours of the morning. He eventually reeled home, fell face down on his bed to sleep and then, a few hours later, was back at his desk ready to start all over again. His body was beginning to protest at this abuse, and soon he'd have to start going to a gym after work to do boring things with weights, hoping that he, too, would one day look good in Lycra shorts and a shiny vest. Not long after that he'd take up golf and at weekends join a few other brokers and dealers for a round or two at an exclusive country club. At first he'd believe that hitting small balls into little holes on a Sunday morning was a pleasant thing to do and be thankful that he could afford it. However, at about the thirteenth hole of his fiftieth round, if he were lucky, he might realise what he had become, and make plans to bail out, hopefully turning into a decent person in the process.

Unfortunately Leo was still at the heavy-drinking stage, and it would be a long time before he could be considered even quite nice. He'd have been content to spend the period before his metamorphosis tormenting Lisa if she hadn't taken matters into her own hands first.

She had been trying for two days to get hold of Mr Peterson, a customer whom Mr Aono had recently met in Switzerland and who had expressed a desire to place deposits with the bank on a short-term basis. Mr Kimura had told her to get in touch with Mr Peterson within the next few days. 'I expect you to take a deposit from him very soon,' he said. 'Don't let me down.'

With Mr Kimura's words hanging over her, she had phoned Switzerland immediately. Mr Peterson was out, so she left a message; he didn't ring back. This was repeated several times: Lisa phoned; Mr Peterson was away from his desk; she left a message; no response. Mr Kimura had already asked her three times what was happening.

She was beginning to feel like giving up, when she at last got Mr Peterson on the phone. The line was bad, though, so she had to ask him to repeat himself a few times. Just as Mr Peterson started to give her the details for his first deposit, Leo decided to have a bit of fun.

'Oh, Dwarfie,' he said, poking his face over the top of her desk.

Lisa put her finger to her lips to show him to be quiet.

'Silly tart trying to deal again,' he teased.

Annoyed at the distraction, Lisa waved him away. 'I'm sorry, could you repeat that, please?' she asked Mr Peterson. He did so. 'Eight million,' she echoed, 'two hundred and twenty-three thousand, six hundred and sixty-seven dollars—Oh, sorry, four hundred and sixty-seven dollars.'

'Fucking useless,' said Leo, and he started making faces at her just as Mr Peterson was giving her the numbers for the second deposit.

Lisa had had enough: she slapped him firmly on the face. He backed off, clutching his cheek, and sat down at his desk without a murmur. He was so shocked that he couldn't think of anything to say, and he didn't want to make a fuss because it would be humiliating to admit that such a small person had dared to hit him. He concentrated on his screens and hoped no one had seen.

Aki-san had noticed, though, and he smiled to himself to see that Lisa had finally begun to handle Leo, king of the dealing-room.

After that, things markedly improved between Lisa

and Leo. He still teased her, but with more of a twinkle
in his eye. He knew he'd gone too far by making fun of
her when she had a customer on the line and the way
she stopped him made him respect her. Not enough
to stop teasing her, but enough to make him a little
less vicious.

Lisa often wished she could knock some sense into Mr
Kubo as well because he was worse than useless when it
came to covering for her if she had to leave the desk. She
tried to be patient with him. He was still suffering from
culture shock and, as his wife and baby hadn't arrived
from Japan yet, he was desperately lonely as well, but
his poor English and inexperience in the dealing-room
made him such a liability that she found it very hard to
be kind. Every day, when she went to lunch, she knew
that she'd return to find a pile of half-completed deals
and Mr Kubo looking as if he didn't know whether to
cower under the desk in fear or weep in gratitude that
she had come back.

'What's this?' she asked him one day, holding up a
deal slip showing no details except the amount and the
interest rate.

'One-month dollar,' he said nervously. He knew she
was going to get annoyed with him over this one.

'Is it a deposit or a loan?' asked Lisa patiently.

He didn't understand. 'Eh?'

'Did you take money or lend it?' asked Lisa, speaking
very slowly and clearly.

'We take.' He sighed with relief. He was over the
first hurdle.

'Good,' said Lisa. She knew they still had a long
way to go. 'Now, who did you take it from?'

'Switzerland.' Mr Kubo was pleased with himself.
He was definitely getting better at this dealing business.

'Good. We now have the country,' said Lisa ultra-patiently. 'Zurich, Geneva or Lugano?'

He knew he'd forgotten something. 'Eh?' he said again, not realising that this was the response most likely to make her lose her temper.

'Which part of Switzerland?' said Lisa loudly.

Heads turned to watch the show.

'I not know,' confessed Mr Kubo, deeply embarrassed at being the centre of attention.

'Well, what was it? A bank or a company?' demanded Lisa.

'Eh?' He was beginning to feel sick. She looked so menacing — he wished he was back in Japan with his wife.

Lisa could feel her fingers twitching. She was sure she'd get all the details a lot quicker if she just beat him around the head. But she controlled herself and carried on intimidating him until she had squeezed out every last drop of information.

Once they had got through the difficult task of sorting out his deals, Mr Kubo was able to bury himself in writing reports to Tokyo and pretend to be too busy to get involved with such traumatic things as answering the phone.

Apart from when Mr Kimura took an interest in her job, and her cleavage, Lisa was effectively her own boss. Gone were the days of shining shoes and fetching coffee for Aki-san. Gone, too, was the horrible changing of the tapes. Much to Andy's dismay, the task had reverted to him. Lisa celebrated her new status by buying some light suits for the summer, making her executive wardrobe extensive enough for her to look like an international businesswoman at least three days a week. A few more colour-coordinated outfits and she could look the part every day, but her credit card couldn't stand any more strain and, more importantly, she didn't want to sell out completely.

To prove to herself that she hadn't really changed since becoming a dealer, she always made a point of dressing down two days a week. Mr Kimura found the all-in-black days the most exciting, because when Lisa had her trousers and lace-up shoes on, she tended to put her feet on the desk, which made her look very powerful. It also gave him a good view of her short but strong thighs and he longed for the night when they would be wrapped round his waist.

The results of six months of heavy drinking, combined with all the recent corporate entertaining she'd had to do, soon began to show on Lisa's backside and thighs. She ignored what was happening for a while but one day, when she was cleaning her teeth, she noticed that she had a double chin that was threatening to turn itself into a triple. It made her realise why Leo had started to call her 'the fat dwarf' instead of 'the fucking dwarf'. He hadn't toned down his language, he was simply stating a fact.

She rushed to her bedroom and in the full-length mirror, one of the first things she'd bought for her flat, looked critically at her naked body. It was beginning to bulge in unseemly places, and when she held up a hand mirror she was just about able to get a rear view of her buttocks. They were now so wide that she could only view them one at a time.

During her lunch hour, she headed for the fancy City gym that gave a discount to Haru Bank staff. Despite the discount, the enrolment fee was so high that Lisa reckoned the stress of signing the cheque must have burned up five hundred calories at least. She filled in

a fitness questionnaire and then went to join her first
aerobics class. The room where it was held had been
designed as a punishment for the bodily challenged and
a paradise for those blessed with long legs, small, pert
breasts and little peachy buttocks. Along three of the
walls there were floor-to-ceiling mirrors so that one
could see oneself at every angle, panting and groaning
along to the irritatingly energetic tones of the instructor.
The fourth wall was plain glass so that those people
with no life who spent thirty minutes running on a
treadmill, or fifteen minutes on an exercise bike in the
gym next to the aerobics room, had something to look
at and keep themselves amused.

The room gave Lisa nowhere to hide and she was
dismayed to see, when they were urged to run on the
spot, that she was one of the wobbliest in the class.
Besides that, the mirror she faced seemed to be one
of those trick mirrors that distort you into a squashed
turnip shape.

'Up two, three, four. Keep it moving,' sang the
instructor; he wore shiny blue bike shorts that empha-
sised his teeny-weeny testicles.

'Fuck two, three, four,' moaned Lisa under her
breath, as every joint in her body began to ache and
her smoke-abused lungs got their revenge by sending
sharp pains bouncing about her internal organs.

By the time they lay down to do their stomach
exercises, Lisa was ready to be carried off on a stretcher,
but Mr Mini-Balls, determined that the flabby shrimp
with the huge buttocks wasn't going to ruin the look
of his class, kept her conscious and mobile by energetic
bullying and eventually, when she went completely
limp, physically pushing and shoving her in the right
direction.

Class over. Covered in sweat, Lisa headed for the showers. The naked women prancing around in the changing-room should have warned her: the showers were like the large, square communal horrors you get at school. But in these ones women stared at each other even more than adolescent girls do. Lisa felt very popular in the shower, because she could see the women looking at her and saying to themselves, 'Well, at least she's fatter than I am.'

It was most interesting to see the different shapes in which women had styled their pubic hair, courtesy of Bic. Lisa hadn't known that pubic-hair styling was so popular. She was the only one with an untouched, natural bush. The rule seemed to be the thinner the woman, the narrower the crotch of her leotard, so most of them had allowed only the tiniest bit of pubic hair to remain, covering the clitoral area. As Lisa was the fattest in the shower, it seemed fitting that her pubic hair reached her hip bones.

Showered and dressed, Lisa headed back to the bank, stopping off at a health-food shop to buy carrot soup, wholemeal bread and some orange juice. She wasn't sure whether the soup would sustain her the whole afternoon, so she popped into a newsagent's and bought herself a Crunchie and a packet of crisps in case she got peckish at around four o'clock.

When she got back to the dealing-room, her boiled-lobster face convinced everyone that she had spent her lunchtime over-indulging in alcohol. Getting drunk at lunchtime in the line of duty for Haru Bank was acceptable, but selfishly getting drunk for one's own pleasure was now forbidden. Everyone waited expectantly for Mr Kimura to summon her to his desk, which he did after only fifteen minutes. It took Lisa half an hour to to convinced him that her colour was due to healthy exercise, not alcohol. As evidence, Lisa pulled her sweaty leotard from her bag to show him. He fingered it lovingly and would have liked to sniff the fragrance of the crotch area but, consciousness of his position re-awakening, he stopped himself just in time. He had to make do with imagining her odour as he brought himself off in the toilets later.

A month of going to the gym three nights and two lunchtimes a week began to have its effect. Lisa's appetite was now huge. To get through the week, she had to eat twice as much food as before. She didn't lose any weight, but her buttocks, although no smaller, no longer wobbled quite so much. To celebrate, she shaved off one centimetre of pubic hair from each side.

Chapter 15

After a few weeks at the gym, Lisa felt very fit. She no longer slouched into the dealing-room each morning, she bounded in. She had acquired the spring in her step of a trained athlete and although she didn't have the figure to match, she sometimes believed she was well on the road to acquiring it. Not that she wanted a great figure in order to get herself a man. Lisa wasn't one of those women who worry about whether their bodies are attractive to the opposite sex. She believed firmly that if a man was worth having he'd want her no matter what she looked like. She went to the gym to get fit and healthy, though if she developed small, pert breasts, a firm stomach and little peachy buttocks she wouldn't complain.

One fine sunny day, when she bounded into the dealing-room she noticed a young man sitting with Mr Kimura at his desk. He was sufficiently handsome to catch her interest and, as from her desk she couldn't see him well enough to take in all the details, she went to get a coffee so that she could take a closer look on her way out of the room.

She liked what she saw, and when she got back to

her desk she got straight on the line to Jackie.

'Morning, Lisa,' said Jackie. 'You're a bit early for the rates.'

'Rates? Who cares about rates? There's a new guy in the office,' said Lisa excitedly.

'Well, from the sound of you, he must be quite something. Is he married, single or divorced?'

'God, is that all you think about?'

'And you don't, I suppose,' said Jackie.

'Not at all. Well, not usually, but this guy is quite a dish.'

Jackie was intrigued. 'What's his name? I might know him.'

'I don't know yet. Ooops! He's heading this way.' Lisa put on her I'm-very-busy face and said loudly, 'Thanks for the rates, I'll get back to you.' She clicked out just as Mr Kimura and the new addition to the dealing-room reached her desk.

'Lisa, this is Simon Russell,' said Mr Kimura, pleased that she was hard at work already.

Lisa stood up to shake hands, giving Simon her friendliest of smiles. 'How do you do,' she said, and then inwardly shuddered. He had a handsome face, but his hand was so soft and cold that it felt like a dead fish. If he hadn't given her a sincere smile, she would have taken an instant dislike to him. As it was, she tried to pass off the weak handshake as reluctance to crush her delicate fingers. She didn't want to judge him on that alone, especially as he was so good-looking.

'Simon will be with you on the Corporate desk,' said Mr Kimura. 'He has been working at a German bank and he has corporate experience. With your dealing knowledge and his corporate knowledge, you should make a fine team.'

Lisa's delight in Simon's arrival was wiped out by an immediate burst of insecurity. Why hadn't she been told about him before? She was too disturbed to say anything, so she just nodded.

'You must teach Simon everything you know,' ordered Mr Kimura. 'I want him to start dealing as soon as possible.'

'Certainly, Mr Kimura,' answered Lisa. A five-minute lesson would be enough to teach him everything she knew. Maybe she should act like Leo and, rather than admit she didn't know much, pretend she didn't want to give anything away.

Mr Kimura set off with Simon to introduce him to the other dealers. As she watched him shaking hands with them, Lisa tried to work out her feelings towards him. He was handsome, but she didn't trust really good-looking people, especially ones who were put on her desk without warning. Also, he was very tall. This was another good reason to dislike him. Tall people always acted as if they were in charge, and if they didn't everybody treated them as if they were.

Lisa looked hard to see any other faults that Simon might have. He was slender enough to be put in the weedy category, with light-brown hair (mousy, she decided) that was freshly cut and brushed off his forehead. Lisa imagined he'd carefully blow-dried and gelled to make it look as if he'd just run his fingers quickly through it when he got up that morning. He had pale-blue eyes which made him look cold even though he was smiling. His smile was restrained, probably because he was nervous. Or maybe he felt that he wouldn't look very manly if he smiled widely; instead, he half-smiled, which made him look very sincere. He was well dressed in a light grey suit that was creased in all the right places, with a lemon shirt and a blue and grey striped tie. She couldn't see much to fault there, although it was all a little too perfect for her liking. She stood up to catch a glimpse of his shoes and was surprised to see slip-ons with tassels. She had expected Mr Sincerity to be wearing lace-up brogues. She didn't trust tassels.

She pressed Jackie's button. 'He's on my desk and his name is Simon Russell.'

'Never heard of him. Is he married?'

'I only just shook his hand, for God's sake.'

'Well, was he wearing a ring?' Jackie would have noticed that straight away.

'I don't know,' said Lisa. 'I'll get him to come out with us at lunchtime and you can find out for yourself.'

'Sounds good to me,' said Jackie, hoping for another conquest. 'I'll talk to you later. Bye.'

Lisa got back to work. She noticed that Mr Kubo had moved his stuff one desk along and that Simon would be sitting between them. That made her even more upset: it had been considered necessary to move the manager of the Corporate desk in order to make room for Simon, but it hadn't been considered necessary to tell her he was coming. She couldn't understand why Mr Kimura had spent time recruiting and interviewing people without saying anything to her about an addition to the team. Was it because she'd been doing badly?

Leo made an unwelcome visit to her desk. 'I hear they're getting rid of you already, Dwarfie.'

'Fuck off, Fatso,' she said. It was typical of Leo to put her fears into words.

'Ooooh, what's up? Can't face the idea of hunting for another job?' jeered Leo.

'Drop dead,' she answered, too unnerved to think of a really clever put-down.

He went off, laughing, and Lisa was left alone to worry about her future. What if everyone except her knew she was getting fired for incompetence? It would be so humiliating. She tried to push the negative thoughts out of her mind. It couldn't be true. Mr Kimura had said she and Simon would be a team. Why would he lie to her?

Bob's light was flashing so she picked up the phone. 'Hi, Bob,' she said, without enthusiasm.

'Well good morning, little lady.' He sounded as cheerful as ever. 'You don't sound so great. A late night, I suppose?'

'No, I'm fine.'

'She says, sounding very down—'

'What do you want, Bob?' interrupted Lisa, not in the mood for his light-hearted concern.

'Ouch,' said Bob. 'You are in a foul mood. I'm looking for six months. Have you any interest at forty-four?'

'I'll have to get back to you.'

'Hold on there,' said Bob. 'I don't like to hear my favourite dealer so down. Tell me what's up.'

'There's a new guy on the desk,' she explained, 'I came in this morning and found him here. Nobody told me he was coming.' She knew she shouldn't really be saying anything to Bob about it, but she couldn't help herself.

'Well, that's too bad. Is he going to be doing the same stuff as you?'

'Yes, we're going to be a team,' said Lisa, spitting out 'team'.

It sounded ominous to Bob. 'Well, don't tell him everything. Keep him guessing and you'll stay ahead.'

'I don't know very much myself. He'll soon know as much as I do. Anyway, he seems quite nice. I'm not that worried,' said Lisa, trying to sound confident.

'The nice ones are the most dangerous. Don't tell him too much, OK, sweetheart?'

Lisa was amazed at Bob's advice. If it had been her brother, the Prince of Paranoia, imparting the same advice, she wouldn't have been surprised, but Bob always seemed so casual and relaxed about everyone. Perhaps he, too, thought she was for the chop, and was warning her. Lisa's fears began to grow. By the time Simon came back she had built up such a dislike towards him that she could barely bring herself to look at him, let alone speak. As he sat down, she pretended to be really busy and kept her eyes firmly on her screens. Every time a customer called she made a great show of shouting loudly for quotes and then speaking quickly on the phone to make Simon think that she was under tremendous pressure. He was suitably impressed and she could feel him looking at her with admiration. He was trying to be cool and nonchalant about sitting at a dealer's desk for the first time, but Lisa saw him surreptitiously trying to find out if his chair swivelled all the way round and looking very happy when he found out that it did. He stared at all the buttons before him and she could tell that he was itching to touch some of them. He put on his screens and a sterling futures page came up. He sat back in his chair and looked at the screens intently, as if they were the pages he'd intended to put up in the first place. Occasionally he glanced across at Lisa, and she could tell he was fighting the urge to ask how to change the pages.

Lisa sniggered. What an idiot. Why didn't he just

ask her? Why did he have to try to pretend that he knew everything? How typical of men, she thought, conveniently forgetting how reluctant she'd been on her first day in the dealing-room to ask questions and thus reveal her ignorance. She made up her mind not to tell him anything unless he asked her. That would serve him right for . . . for what? He hadn't actually done anything to her except be there.

Lisa suddenly felt a little bit guilty. It wasn't Simon's fault that she hadn't been told about him. She was acting just like Leo and Aki-san had when she started. She remembered how inadequate they had made her feel by not volunteering any information unless she grovelled to them. She wouldn't have survived if it hadn't been for Andy's kindness. She was far more likely to get on well with Simon if she helped him out. They were supposed to be a team, after all. If she treated him nicely, surely she'd benefit from his gratitude in the end.

Simon was older than her — he looked about twenty-five — but she was the one with the experience and he'd be relying on her to train him. She decided that, unlike Leo, she would be a kind and fair teacher. By acting unselfish and mature, she'd be able to develop a good relationship with him and they would indeed make a fine team.

'Just ask if you want to know anything,' she said condescendingly.

Simon looked relieved and Lisa, to prove how helpful she was going to be, showed him how to change the pages on his screen. She then explained how to use the phones and he immediately began to dial an outside number.

'Just calling my wife to let her know my telephone number,' he explained.

Lisa pushed Jackie's button. 'Bad news, I'm afraid. He's out of the market,' she whispered. 'He's married.'

'Nobody is ever completely out, my dear,' said Jackie, speaking from experience.

'So we're still on for lunch, then?'

'Of course,' said Jackie. 'How about the tacos bar?'

'Fine,' said Lisa. 'See you there at eleven thirty. Bye.'

Lunch turned out to be short. As soon as she found out that Simon's wife, Hannah, was not only his childhood sweetheart but was also a nanny. and, according to Simon, 'a lovely woman', Jackie made her excuses and left. Lisa was left alone with Simon as he described, in excruciating detail, the history of his relationship with the lovely Hannah. On the way back to Haru's, she managed to change the subject and get him to talk about what he had done at the German bank. She was relieved when he said he had been an accounts clerk. He had no dealing experience and very little knowledge of corporates: she had no real reason to be worried about him.

Lisa told herself the same thing over and over again during the next few weeks, as Simon quickly settled into his new job. He had none of the problems she'd had trying to fit in. On the contrary, the other dealers warmed to him and when, during lulls in the market, he went over to their desks they happily explained to him the ins and outs of their various markets.

Lisa was slightly jealous of his popularity and the ease with which he acquired information that she'd had to fight tooth and nail for. She tried to control her feelings by thinking about how she had benefited since Simon's arrival. She now had someone to share the workload with. Someone who happened to be

friendly and polite. As he was married and eager to
get home after work, he didn't go out drinking with
the other dealers and so hadn't become tainted with the
laddishness that affected so many of them. He shunned
their crass comments in favour of a more sophisticated
style of humour. He even kept Leo at bay by distracting
him with questions about the futures market whenever
he came over to the desk to tease Lisa.

Work had definitely become much easier since Simon's
arrival. His popularity meant that the dealers were more
cooperative towards the Corporate desk as a whole, and
now that there were two corporate dealers Lisa had
someone to share the burden of Mr Kimura's daily
pep talks.

Simon was very good at handling Mr Kimura and
he was quite willing to take Lisa's place at the senior
manager's desk, although he didn't sit quite so close to
Mr Kimura. Sometimes they sat talking for more than
an hour, and Lisa got a little paranoid, but then Simon
would return and make a disparaging comment about
Mr Slimy Kimura and she would be thankful that it
had been him rather than her who had had to endure
such a long discussion.

She quite enjoyed her job now and she enjoyed
being part of a team. Simon could be very amusing.
One afternoon when the market was quiet, he came
back from the toilet and told Lisa that there was a
pornographic magazine in there.

'It was by the sinks when I went in the cubicle.
When I came out it was gone. Somebody's picked it up
and is at this very moment sitting in the other cubicle
with it. Watch and see who comes out.'

From her desk, Lisa could just about see who went
in and out of the men's toilet. Normally, she wouldn't

have been the slightest bit interested, but now she leant forward to get a good look. After a few minutes, Mr Kimura came out.

'Surprise, surprise!' said Lisa, and she enjoyed a good chuckle with Simon.

Seeing them laughing, Mr Kimura came over to the desk. 'I'm very happy to see my Corporate team enjoying themselves. How is business today?'

'Very slow, Kimura-san,' answered Simon seriously.

'Well, you should both get on the phone and look for business. Be aggressive,' responded Mr Kimura sternly. He put his hand in his pocket and pulled something out. 'Here, Lisa, a little treat for you.'

Holding her hand palm upward, he cupped his other hand over it and slid it off slowly, leaving behind a toffee wrapped in shiny paper. He might enjoy talking corporate strategy with Simon, but Lisa was still the subject of his fantasies.

'Work hard this afternoon, please,' he said and walked away.

Lisa and Simon managed to hold in their laughter until he was safely back at his desk.

'I must go and wash my hands,' said Lisa, throwing the toffee in the bin.

'I'll just get on and ring all those customers,' said Simon, putting on an earnest expression.

'Yeah, right.' Lisa laughed again. Simon was so funny.

When she came back, she expected to carry on laughing, but Simon had a list in front of him and he was talking seriously on the phone.

Lisa waited till he had finished, then asked, 'What are you doing?'

'Mr Kimura gave me a list of UK corporates. He

wants me to call them up and introduce myself,' Simon explained. 'He said he wants me to expand the corporate base.'

'Don't you mean "wants us"?' asked Lisa, concerned that she hadn't heard about the list.

'Well, these are UK customers. He said I was to do the UK and you will cover the rest of Europe,' said Simon. 'He thought it would be more efficient if we split things up,' he added seeing that Lisa didn't look very happy about the new plans.

'When was this decided?' she asked, trying to sound cool.

'He told me a few days ago. Didn't he say any thing to you?' Simon looked very surprised and almost apologetic.

'He probably said something,' lied Lisa, 'but I must have forgotten.'

Simon turned back to the phones and all afternoon Lisa heard him saying, 'Good afternoon. My name is Simon Russell. I am calling on behalf of Haru Bank . . .'

His telephone voice was monotonous and it droned on and on. Lisa imagined that the people on the other end were bored senseless before he had finished his first sentence. She would have sounded much more lively and interesting. She was pleased to get the rest of Europe for her customers, because it was much more fun dealing with foreign companies. She did feel rather put out that, once again, she hadn't been told anything, but perhaps that was just the Japanese way of doing things, or perhaps Mr Kimura thought he had told her. That was probably it. He was busy and probably just forgot. She shouldn't resent Simon. He had done her no harm at all. It really wasn't his fault.

'You can speak either to me or to my assistant, Lisa Soames,' she heard Simon saying on the phone.

His assistant? How dare he call her his assistant? When Simon came off the phone she was waiting for him.

'What do you think you're doing?' she said aggressively.

Simon was shocked at the sudden change in her. 'What do you mean?' he said, looking bewildered.

'Your assistant? Are you mad?'

'Oh that,' he said, with a smile. 'It's just for the customers. The UK corporates will have more respect for me if they think I am more senior than you, that's all.'

'You get respect by doing a good job,' answered Lisa angrily. 'I suppose you'd like me to tell all my customers that you're my assistant.'

'If you must,' said Simon, still smiling. 'I was only thinking about what's good for the desk.'

Bollocks! thought Lisa. She wanted to argue with him but he was so calm, so smooth, that he made her feel she was being childish. She would have to keep a watchful eye on him from now on. There was definitely something suspicious about her teammate. His sincerity and charm could merely be hiding a devious mind.

Over the next few days, Lisa and Simon divided up their work. Simon set about writing reports on the companies he had telephoned and he spent a lot of time talking to Mr Kimura about the progress he was making. He didn't seem to be actually raising the level of business, but the busy way in which he created lots of impressive-looking paperwork, and the confident way in which he spoke about his activities, satisfied those at the top that he was being very successful indeed.

Chapter 16

———— ➤ ◆ ————

As Lisa tried to cope with her growing resentment against Simon, at the end of May there came another change to the dealing-room. Three trainees from regional banks connected to Haru Bank in Japan settled themselves into the empty desks on her row.

With the newcomers on her left and Simon and Mr Kubo on her right, she felt boxed-in and under scrutiny. The Corporate team had had a whole row of desks to themselves and she had got used to the privacy and the space. Now she would no longer be able to stretch out and put her feet up, she wouldn't be able to read magazines without being noticed, and conversations with Jackie would have to be censored; or so she thought when she was introduced to Mr Ishikawa, Mr Biwaki and Mr Wada.

It didn't take long for Big Jock, Tom and Frank, as they soon came to be called, to let Lisa know that her life in the dealing-room didn't have to change at all, as far as they were concerned. They were three guys from unfashionable regions of Japan who, having studied at no-name universities, now worked for small, mediocre banks. They saw their once-in-a-lifetime opportunity to

spend three months in Europe as a chance to find out
what life could have been like if they had managed to
swot themselves into one of Japan's prestigious universities and get jobs in famous companies.

Mr Kimura called them 'trainees', but these men had
all worked in banking for at least ten years and they
weren't interested in learning anything more about the
financial world. They had been given a three-month
'holiday' and they intended to have as much fun as
they could. That they were expected to submit regular
reports to their superiors in Japan did not deter them at
all. On the plane from Narita airport, they had decided
that, as they worked for different banks, they would
take it in turns to write reports and then give copies
to the other two, leaving themselves with enough time
for serious enjoyment. So the three trainees, in their
holiday mood, settled into the London branch of Haru
Bank. They brought to the dealing-room a lot of fun
and laughter, both of which had been sorely lacking
since the start of Mr Kimura's reign.

Big Jock, who sat next to Lisa, was the shortest
and the loudest of the three. He was about forty,
with a receding hairline and a big, round, shiny face
that rarely looked serious. He laughed and giggled
throughout the day and his good humour made him
a very popular drinking-companion with both the local
and the Japanese staff. He had earned the nickname of
Jock because of his love of whisky. Lisa had assumed
that the 'Big' was a joke about the fact that he stood
only a few inches taller than she did, but Jock assured
her it was because he was well endowed.

'Local staff men see me in toilet,' he explained. 'They
very shocked. They now call me "Big Jock".'

'If you say so,' said Lisa, doubting very much if it

was true. As his ears, nose and fingers were quite small, she imagined his penis was as well.

Big Jock's English was on a par with Aki-san's, but unlike Aki-san he enjoyed talking English and at every opportunity he tried to engage Lisa in conversation.

'Me love London life,' he said, as they shared a Kit-Kat.

'Oh yes, and why's that?' asked Lisa, more out of politeness than real interest. She was bored by these conversations because she had to speak very slowly in simple sentences in order to be understood. Having worked in the City for more than six months, she had got used to the bish, bash, bosh of dealing-room conversations, in which everything was said at top speed and you rarely paused before giving a reply.

'My wife not here, my daughters not here and my mother not here. They all in Japan,' said Big Jock with a wide smile.

'How many daughters do you have?' asked Lisa.

'Three. Oldest is seven, middle daughter is four and baby just one,' he replied.

Lisa did some calculating. 'Three years between each pair?'

'Yes, my wife very good planner. We live with my mother in my father's house. He is dead five years before.'

Lisa restrained herself from making a cheap joke of his grammatical error. 'So it's you and five females now,' she said. 'Lucky old you.'

'No, no,' said Big Jock. 'It very terrible life. Mother and wife, they fight very much. My children, they always screaming. My wife say no more children, so no more sex. Very sad for me.' He put on a gloomy expression.

'Poor Jock. Why don't you use condoms?' asked Lisa in sympathy, although she imagined that avoiding pregnancy was not the only reason for Big Jock's wife refusing to have sex with him.

'Me too big. My wife say they break,' he said, clapping his hands to emphasise his problem with bursting condoms.

'Yeah, right,' said Lisa, and got back to her work.

Next to Big Jock sat Frank. Standing over six feet tall, he was viewed as a giant by the Japanese. Tom and Big Jock had started calling him 'Frank' after they heard him singing 'My Way'. None of the English staff had heard him sing yet and, despite assurances from Big Jock, Lisa doubted very much whether his version of 'My Way' sounded anything like the real thing. What fascinated her most about Frank was the amazing efforts that had been made to save his teeth. Instead of giving up in the face of such terrible decay, the dentist had added large silver bits to his teeth to compensate for the areas that must have either rotted or been drilled away. The thought of the time and pain that must have gone into creating such an unattractive effect made Lisa cringe whenever Frank opened his mouth to speak. A good set of false ones would look much better, she thought, but she suspected Frank was too vain to accept them, as he wasn't even forty yet. When he spoke, the silver in his mouth caught the light and flashed. If he threw back his head to laugh, Lisa caught a glimpse of the butchery that had taken place in the name of Japanese dentistry.

Frank was the most unconventional Japanese banker she had ever seen. He wore coloured shirts, loud ties and a bottle-green double-breasted suit. Among the single-breasted dark greys and navy blues of the other

Japanese staff, his suit was outrageous. Not only that, but he wore sunglasses to the office and his hair, instead of being dead straight with a knife-edged side parting, had a distinct wave to it that definitely wasn't natural. The sunglasses and the curly perm were two pleasures denied him in Japan because they were associated with gangsters. Due to his attire in the London branch, the Japanese staff suspected that he had powerful connections in the Yakuza, the Japanese mafia. That would explain how such an unconventional man could find so-called employment in a bank. Some thought it possible that he didn't really work for a bank: he might be a gangster who had blackmailed the head of the regional bank into letting him pose as an employee in order to get a free vacation in London. Consequently, although Frank was always polite and friendly to the other Japanese staff, they feared him and left him and the other trainees alone to enjoy themselves. If someone had had the courage to call his manager in Japan, they would have found out that on his native soil he always went to work in a single-breasted navy suit with a white shirt and that he had never permed his hair or wore sunglasses. He had changed his image on arrival in London, knowing this was probably the only chance in his conventional life that he would get to pretend to be something more than he really was.

The third trainee sat at the end of the row by the FX section. His real name was Tomu but the local dealers had shortened it to 'Tom' because they were too lazy to pronounce the extra syllable. Tom had just turned thirty-two, although with his spotty skin and innocent expression he looked about twenty-one. He had got married at the beginning of April to one of the office ladies from his branch, and he was the only one of the three not to have been thrilled at being posted to London. He was still full of the joys of being a newlywed and to be separated so soon in his married life was, to him, sheer cruelty. His wife was anxious to have a baby, so she was willing to have sex as much as possible.

Tom knew that once she got pregnant his sex life would change for ever. In Japan, sex is discouraged during the first three and last three months of pregnancy, and babies sleep with their parents until the age of five or six. So, even if Tom's wife felt like having sex once they had small children, they would only be able to do it very quietly. Tom had been warned by his older colleagues about how quickly the period of sex in unlimited quantities passes. He couldn't believe that the one time in his marriage — probably in his whole life — when he had the chance to have as much sex as he wanted, he should be sent to the other side of the world.

He spent at least an hour every day on the phone telling his young wife how much he missed her. He also hoped and prayed that she wouldn't greet him with the news of a positive test result. If it hadn't been for Jock and Frank, he would have spent his time in London moping, but in the company of two such boisterous and fun-loving companions, he couldn't be down-hearted for long.

The trainees were impressed with Lisa. The women they worked with in Japan always wore uniforms and make-up. They were very polite and would never think of putting their feet on the desk or shouting across the room, as Lisa often did. They certainly never had the chance to talk to important customers or deal with large amounts of money. The women in their banks carried out menial tasks like photocopying and making tea. Lisa was only twenty-two and yet she was left practically alone all day to deal in large sums with many customers. They enjoyed watching her work and Lisa, sensing their admiration, used to give them something to talk about.

'Bob, what's your six months? I've got fifty.'

'Hang on, I'll ask Chuck . . . We're at forty-six.'

'Forty-six? Why are you at forty-six? Everyone else is at forty-five.'

'Maybe Chuck don't like the market.'

'Well, I'd expect him to be at the same level as everyone else.'

'Hold on, I'll talk to him . . . He said he can do twenty at forty-five. How's that, babe?'

'That's no good, I've got fifty. Don't worry I'll go elsewhere.'

'No, wait . . . We can do the fifty.'

'Great, that's fifty at forty-five.'

Frank was puzzled. 'Why you no deal with the people who said forty-five first?'

'Because I like Bob and nobody else gave me that rate,' replied Lisa.

'Why you say everyone at forty-five?'

'I lied.'

'You very strong woman,' said Frank seriously.

'That's right,' said Lisa, 'and don't you forget it.' She leant across her desk to answer another call. Frank said something in Japanese to Big Jock and Tom and they roared with laughter.

'Having a party?' asked the customer.

'No,' said Lisa, frowning at the trainees to quieten them. 'It's just some schoolboys on a tour of the office.'

They waved at her and Big Jock threw a paper pellet. It bounced off her nose and this brought more laughter. Lisa hurriedly dealt with the customer before they got even worse.

'Do that again and I'll bop you one,' she told Big Jock when she'd clicked out of the line.

'Bop? What's this bop?' he asked innocently.

'Like this,' said Lisa, slapping him on the back of the head. 'Only harder.'

'*Itai!*' said Big Jock, rubbing his head. 'You should not hurt me today, Miss Lisa. It my birthday.'

'Your birthday?' said Lisa. 'You should have said.' She jumped to her feet. 'Hey everyone!' she shouted. 'It's Big Jock's birthday. He's buying at lunch.'

The dealers all clapped and Big Jock stood up, smiling, to take a bow. He soon stopped smiling when he realised what Lisa's announcement would do to his wallet. At Haru Bank, those celebrating a birthday usually bought drinks for their colleagues. With about thirty people in the dealing-room it could work out very expensive unless a friendly broker offered to put his credit card behind the bar.

'Happy birthday, Jock,' called Leo. 'Which pub are we going to?'

'You very strong woman,' said Big Jock, narrowing his eyes at Lisa.

She ignored him, 'How about going downstairs?' she shouted to Leo. 'The nearer it is, the more people will be able to be come.'

As there were no figures expected, Big Jock's birthday party was well attended. The dealers had called their brokers and asked them to come too, saving him the expense of buying everyone drinks. Once he saw how many credit cards there were behind the bar, Big Jock relaxed and began to enjoy himself. He was enjoying himself so much that he didn't see the tall policewoman when she entered the pub. He soon noticed her, though, when she twisted his arm up behind his back.

'I've had a report that a short, fat Japanese man known as "Big Jock" fondled a woman's breasts as she came out of the toilets,' she said so loudly that everyone could hear.

'No, sir, please,' begged Big Jock, his birthday mood completely gone.

'Call me "officer",' she said menacingly.

'Please, officer, not me,' cried Big Jock.

'I'll have to punish you. Bend over!'

Jock obediently bent down and touched his toes. He howled as he received six swift, painful slaps on the backside. When he stood up again he was shocked to see the officer taking off her jacket and skirt to reveal a voluptuous body encased in black leather underwear. At this point, he suspected that something wasn't quite right, and he looked towards Tom and Frank for help, but they were too busy gazing at the policewoman's enormous wobbly breasts. He was on his own when dealing with this gigantic, terrifying native.

The policewoman took off Big Jock's jacket and tie, slowly unbuttoned his shirt and gave him lingering kisses from his forehead to his navel. He thought he would die of fright or shame, he wasn't sure which. He overcame his fear when she begun to tug at his belt. Determined that his important bits weren't going to be revealed to the laughing people all round him, he pushed her hands away and tried to make a quick exit. He was shoved back by the wall of spectators and made to kneel on the ground while the stripper danced round him. When she wiggled her backside in his face, he began to get the joke and by the time his nose was pressed firmly between her breasts he was smiling.

In the dealing-room later that afternoon, the party atmosphere continued. Mr Kimura was at a meeting and, as most of the dealers were too drunk to do much work, they leant back in their chairs laughing and joking. Lisa, who had organised the whip-round for the strip-a-gram, was very popular. It amazed her how much she had changed since leaving university. If someone had told her that, less than a year after graduating, not only would she arrange for a stripper to come to a lunchtime party but she would think the act highly amusing, she would have bet them a hundred pounds that they were wrong. The women's group that she had joined at the freshers' bazaar would have expected her at least to stage a protest outside the pub with placards demanding that the poor, exploited stripper be rescued from her life of sexual slavery.

Lisa couldn't have imagined rescuing the stripper from anything: she was one of the strongest women she'd seen in her life and seemed to have more power in her work than Lisa had in hers.

The trainees admired Lisa even more when they found out she was behind the lunchtime entertainment.

'Thank you for birthday present,' said Big Jock.

'Everybody paid, I just made the call.'

'I liked her breasts very much. My wife have no breasts. I like big, soft breasts.'

'I'm sure you do.'

'You let me touch your breasts?'

'In your dreams, you dirty old man,' said Lisa, bopping him for the second time that day.

Simon intervened before Big Jock could retaliate. 'Lisa, Mr Kimura asked us to call round the customers

this afternoon to give them market reports.' He thought
the trainees were making the Corporate desk look
ridiculous and that Lisa had done much less work
since their arrival.

Lisa was annoyed. 'When I need you to tell me how
to do my job, I'll ask you.'

'You're not doing your job,' said Simon coldly. 'You're
just acting like a child.'

Lisa felt like swearing at him, but she controlled
herself because she didn't want to fight in front of the
trainees. Instead, she lowered her voice and said calmly,
'The market is dead. No one is dealing. I only call up
my customers when I have something to say to them.'

'That's your trouble – you're too lazy.'

'Lazy? Me?' Lisa's calm went up in smoke. 'Bollocks!
I just don't believe in boring the customers to death like
you do. Why should I waste their time when I have
nothing to tell them?'

'You should use this time to get to know them
better. Just because Mr Kimura's not here, it doesn't
mean he won't know what you've been doing.' Triumph-
phant at having the last word, Simon reached out to
answer a call, leaving Lisa steaming as she pondered
his words.

The threat was there all right. If she didn't behave,
he'd tell on her. She wondered what else he'd been
saying to Mr Kimura during their long talks. All at
once she wished she was back with Leo and Aki-san.
Leo was a rude, arrogant bully and Aki-san ran a petty
dictatorship, but at least they were only horrible to her
face. She couldn't imagine either of them sneaking up
to Mr Kimura to tell on her.

'Miss Lisa,' whispered Big Jock. 'I sorry to get you
in trouble with boss.'

'He's not my fucking boss,' she replied, stomping off to get a coffee.

Despite being sworn at, Big Jock wanted to make it up to Lisa for getting her into trouble, so he asked her if she would go out with him, Frank and Tom that night to continue celebrating his birthday. Lisa rang Jackie and asked her along too.

They met Jackie in a wine bar after work and she presented Big Jock with a bottle of champagne. She then sat very close to Frank and tried to interest him in her charms. Frank wasn't much impressed with Jackie: she was too skinny for his taste. He could get plenty of skinny women in Japan. He was looking for someone a little rounder. Someone like Lisa. He had high hopes for a fling with her. Until now, she hadn't shown any interest in him, but he was confident that, once she had heard him sing some romantic Japanese songs at the snack bar they were going on to, she'd look at him differently.

'Why didn't you tell me before?' asked Jackie, when she and Lisa went to the toilets.

'What?' said Lisa.

'That Frank was such a dish.'

'A dish? Him?'

'He's got a great body and his voice is so sexy. You've been trying to keep him for yourself, haven't you?'

'You must be mad. Jaws would be more attractive than him. Imagine kissing all that metal.' Lisa shuddered at the thought of it.

'You wouldn't notice if you shut your eyes.'

'I bet that's what you say about all the guys you get off with.'

'Cheeky! Now don't forget, pout your lips more. It'll make men crazy for you.'

Jackie went out, and Lisa, who was brushing her hair, practised a few pouts.

In the taxi to the snack bar, Tom and Big Jock sat on the pull-down seats trying not to fall off every time the cab turned a corner. Lisa and Jackie sat on the back seat, with Frank in the middle. He was very busy. On his left side he was trying to move his thigh away from Jackie's as she attempted to turn him on by rubbing her leg against his, and on his right he was trying to awaken Lisa's desire by pressing his thigh against hers. He failed on both counts. Jackie just moved closer and Lisa scratched her leg and carried on talking, showing no sign at all that she realised what he was trying to do.

They could hear the terrible singing before they even got inside the snack bar. Japanese *enca*, to the untrained ear, sounds like a man howling in agony after catching his penis in the fly of his trousers. Once inside the bar, the trainees switched to talking Japanese and they seemed to grow a few inches in height and width. They were on their home ground now and it was their turn to take charge.

There were too many of them to be seated at the bar, so they were led to comfortable sofas near a giant karaoke screen. Frank ordered a bottle of whisky and some Japanese snacks. The latter arrived very quickly and they were in assorted shades of green and brown. Lisa tried one that looked — and tasted, as she found out after one bite — like very strong rubber. She pulled a face and Frank offered her a tissue so that she could spit it out.

'Why don't you try some *tako*? It very tasty,' he said, offering her a dish.

'It's octopus,' warned Jackie.

'Ha! Thought you'd got me there, didn't you?' said Lisa.

Frank hadn't the faintest idea what she meant. He would have asked her to explain but Jock had stood up to sing and it was polite to listen to the first line at least. He had chosen 'Subaru', a famous Japanese pop song. As Jock sang, Frank whispered a translation into Lisa's ear.

She began to feel a tingling in the pit of her stomach. It wasn't Jock's voice that moved her, although he did sing quite well and it wasn't painful to the ears when he reached the high notes. No, it was Frank softly whispering the words in English that caused the strange sensations down below. Jackie was right. He had a lovely deep voice and as Lisa felt his warm breath against her earlobe, she felt faint stirrings of desire. Frank moved closer and laid his arm along the back of the sofa so that it was resting lightly against her shoulders. The strong smell of aftershave momentarily put her off, but when she got used to it she found the closeness of Frank's body to her own rather pleasant, and she made no attempt to create a greater space between them.

Frank, seeing no signs of being physically or verbally repelled, found his confidence growing. Here he was, sitting very close to her, with his arm on her shoulders, whispering in her ear. She was melting already and he hadn't even sung yet. He sipped his whisky and plotted his next move.

Chapter 17

Frank wanted to get it just right. Lisa had to be impressed from the first song or else he might destroy the progress that he'd already made. Should he sing in Japanese or English first? He flicked through the songbook, looking for something with exactly the right tone, and selected a simple Japanese love song and his two favourite English songs, 'Love Me Tender' and 'My Way'. He wrote down the numbers, handed the piece of paper to a hostess and awaited his moment.

When his number came up, the hostess handed him a microphone and he stood up. When the music began, he started to sway his hips gently and, looking down at Lisa, lifted the mike and sang. She didn't have to understand the words to know what the song was about, because the pictures on the screen behind him made that very clear, and the way Frank stared at her left her in no doubt as to whom he was singing to.

He sang in a wonderful deep, rich voice that made her tingle from the top of her head right down to her toes. She told herself it was merely sexual frustration: her body must be so desperate that it was responding to any male attention, regardless of how desirable that man was.

Lisa sipped her whisky and looked up at him. In the dim light he didn't look too bad. He'd taken his jacket off and, apart from a slight paunch, his body was rather sexy, with wide shoulders and strong-looking thighs. He danced well, too. After another sip, he looked even better. When he held out his hand to invite her to dance through the last verse of the song, she found herself standing up, putting her arms round him, and slowly moving in time to the music.

'You're well in there,' whispered Jackie, when they sat down after the song.

'It was only a dance,' said Lisa. She was uncomfortable with what was happening to her, she certainly wasn't going to tell anyone else how she felt.

'Go for it,' said Jackie, not fooled at all.

Frank persuaded Lisa and Jackie to sing next. He soon regretted it: they stood up and screeched 'Like a Virgin'. Women should have soft, dainty voices he told himself looking at them in disbelief. They should not sound like a pig having its throat cut. One of the first things he would do with Lisa, he resolved, once the physical stuff was out of the way, would be to teach her to sing.

'Love Me Tender' was next. Frank had practised this song many times in Japan. The pronunciation was a little tricky. Too many Ls for his Japanese tongue, but after years of singing it, he was confident that he sounded like a native English-speaker.

To Lisa, the first line sounded like 'Rub me tender, rub me true,' but she was still stirred by Frank's rendition. When she closed her eyes, and forgot about the 'rub's, she could imagine that it was Elvis singing those lines to her with pure love in his heart. When she opened them, Frank was standing before her, staring at her, offering himself. Would he be worth the fuss it would cause at Haru Bank if she went with him? No, he couldn't possibly be, she told herself. She went to the ladies to splash cold water on her face and hopefully get rid of the temptation to do something really stupid.

It was getting late. The bar was full of drunken Japanese businessmen and a few English dealers who were murdering 'I Left my Heart in San Francisco'. Frank's last song finally came up on the screen and he stood up. He had danced with her. He had put his arm round her. He had stared deeply in her eyes. She hadn't shown any signs of resistance. He knew that, after this song, she'd be his for the taking.

As he heard the opening bars of 'My Way', he took a deep breath and began to sing, confident that this, his favourite song, would gain him the prize. The raw sexuality of Elvis gave way to the smooth maturity of Sinatra as Frank put all his efforts into winning Lisa over.

To Lisa, his voice felt like warm honey seeping down to the pit of her stomach. Why was this happening to her? To think that just a short time ago she had scorned any suggestion of a fling with this man, and now all she wanted to do was take him home and find out if he was as good at sex as he was at singing. It must be the drink, she told herself. Dealers usually found that the heavy drinking got to them in the end. She should stop before she did something that she would really regret. Lisa wrestled with herself as Frank sang, but the more he sang the more her resolve weakened, and when he reached the last line of the song she was ready and waiting.

Fortunately for her and unfortunately for Frank, the

cool night air that hit them when they stood outside
waiting for a taxi sobered her up. She looked down and
saw that her hand was in his. Did he think she'd take
him home with her? Had she said she'd spend the night
with him?

As soon as she saw an empty taxi come round the
corner, Lisa took her hand away and flagged it down.
She grabbed Jackie and pushed her inside. They had
slammed the door and driven away before Frank had
a chance to say anything. Lisa looked out of the back
window and waved. He was standing there with his
mouth open, looking very forlorn.

'Well, you certainly changed your mind fast,' said
Jackie, amazed at Lisa's sudden burst of sanity. 'One
minute you were on his arm with your tongue hanging
out, the next you practically pushed him in the gutter.'
Lisa made no reply, so she carried on. 'You shouldn't let
them think you're interested when you aren't. One day
someone'll get nasty.'

'I don't know if I was interested or not,' said Lisa,
who felt a bit guilty about what she'd done. 'It was all
happening so fast.'

'You've lost your chance now, anyway,' said Jackie
unsympathetically.

Lisa wasn't looking forward to seeing Frank tomorrow. She was ashamed of being tempted by him. She
hoped she wasn't becoming like Jackie, who found
anything with a penis and testicles attractive.

The trainees hadn't arrived when she got in the next
morning. She went off to get a coffee and when she came
back they were sitting at their desks with the previous
night's heavy drinking stamped all over their faces. Jock
was supporting his head with his hands, Frank was
leaning back in his chair pressing a wet handkerchief

to his forehead and Tom was face down on the desk with his eyes shut. Every few seconds, one of them emitted a groan.

Lisa said, 'Good morning,' and sat down. Underneath her newspaper she found a little box. It was beautifully wrapped and tied with a dainty pink bow. She looked at Frank and caught his eye. He smiled, indicating that she should open it. She didn't want to unwrap it in the dealing-room, so she slipped the box into her pocket and headed for the toilets.

Safely in a cubicle, she unwrapped the box and opened it. Inside there was a purple silk pouch embroidered with Japanese writing in orange thread. There was some white, silky string attached to the pouch so that it could be hung up. She didn't know what it was, but she appreciated the thought behind it and she was glad Frank wasn't angry with her.

He was waiting for her in the corridor when she came out.

'Thanks for the present,' she said, glad she could thank him privately. 'What is it?'

'It called an *omamori*. My mother gave it me when I left Japan. I give it you now,' said Frank softly. The sound of his voice brought back what she'd felt when she heard him sing, and it was all she could do to stop herself kissing him.

'You don't have to do that,' she said, stepping away from him. Much as she might want to, she wasn't going to kiss him in such a dangerous place.

'Yes, I want you have it,' insisted Frank. 'It give you luck. My mother got it at temple in Japan. You keep it with you and you lucky. Inside there is message written by priest.'

Lisa was touched to think he had passed on a present

from his mother — after she'd been so mean to him, too. It made her feel guilty for thinking that only large quantities of alcohol could make a Japanese man attractive in her eyes. Frank's gift showed he was clearly a gentleman, who respected her very much. He couldn't just be after sex, she thought. She found herself looking at and listening to him all day, and the more she did the more attractive he became.

Frank was relieved that he had listened to Big Jock's advice and given her the *omamori* rather than the box of chocolates he'd have chosen himself. He decided to wait for a couple of days before asking her out again. If they went out on Friday night, they wouldn't have to worry about getting up for work the next day. It was only three days away, and the waiting would make the conquest all the more sweeter. He smiled when he thought of Lisa's soft, naked body in bed beside him.

Lisa found it hard to concentrate on her work with Frank sitting nearby. Luckily, the market was quiet and many of the dealers were filling in the time by doing crosswords, phoning friends and arranging long lunches with their brokers. She wanted to laze around too, but Simon was working hard, or at least looked as if he was, and he told Lisa that she should be doing the same.

She wondered why he was so busy. His volume of deals was lower than hers, and yet he always acted as if he was doing twice as much work. In truth, he wasn't much of a dealer. Four years in the Accounts Department had placed him permanently in the report-and-procrastinate brigade, and his mind wasn't quick or sharp enough to cope with the cut-and-thrust of dealing. However, he was always very well turned out, his work was nicely presented and his desk was incredibly tidy. He was also good at creating the impression of useful activity by writing reports and arranging neat piles of statistical information on his desk. He would engage his customers in conversations by asking them what they thought of the market and then agree with them in such a way as to suggest that, by meticulous research, he had reached the same conclusion himself. He was excellent at sounding as if he knew what he was talking about, even though he had even less idea about the market than Lisa. If you didn't watch him too closely, and most people in the dealing-room had no cause to do so, he seemed the perfect example of an up and coming corporate dealer.

Lisa was not. She often came to work looking scruffy, her desk was so full of paperwork that she had to put her feet on it to stop everything falling off, and she didn't believe in pretending to be a financial expert. If she didn't know which way the market was going to go, she admitted as much to her customers and joked about it. Her customers, used to the unpredictability of the market and to corporate dealers whose confident forecasts were often wrong, admired her honesty and enjoyed her jokes.

Simon, who had in his mind an image, painted by Mr Kimura, of the ace corporate dealers who worked for Citibank, disapproved of her irreverent style when talking to the giants of the corporate world. His aim was to create something serious and competitive, and Lisa threatened to spoil it for him. He told her she ought to tidy her desk, he looked disapproving when she chatted to Jackie on the phone, and he suggested that she treat her customers with more respect.

'You should never say, "I don't know" to a customer. You should always let them think you have some idea of what is happening,' he said.

'Who died and made you God?' she retorted, fed up with his holier-than-thou attitude.

'Mr Kimura said we must build up good relationships and you don't seem to be trying.'

'You're unbelievable,' said Lisa, getting up to go to lunch. 'I'm going out with Jackie and,' she added, to underline the point that he wasn't her boss, 'I'm going to be late.'

'Oh, sign this before you go,' he said casually, handing her a report attached to a heavy clipboard.

Lisa turned to the back page as she usually did so that she could add her name to the many signatures at the bottom. Reports often came round from the other departments that met or conducted business with big companies. She didn't bother to read them because they were so dull, but something in Simon's casualness made her suspicious. Why was he so calm and smiling when she had just told him she was going out for a long lunch?

She looked at the first page and read the title. It said 'Monthly Report of the Corporate Desk'. It was the first she'd heard of such a report. She looked at it more carefully. It was about twenty pages long and there were sections devoted to BAs and to her European customers. The English was far too good for it to have been written by Mr Kubo.

'What's this?' she asked.

'It's just a little report. Mr Kimura asked me to do it,' said Simon, flashing her one of his sincere smiles.

'Why didn't you tell me about it?'

'I've just given it to you now,' said Simon defensively.

'But it's already been round the fucking bank,' said Lisa, her raised voice attracting several stares.

Just then a call came through, and Simon was able to escape by turning round to answer it. Suppressing the urge to force clipboard and report into his smug little

mouth, Lisa went off to meet Jackie for lunch. She'd
sort him out, she vowed, when she got back.

'What's the fuss about?' asked Jackie when Lisa told
her about the report. 'Mr Kimura probably knows you
don't like paperwork, so he asked Simon to do it.'

Lisa wasn't convinced. 'But why did Simon keep it
a secret?'

'He probably knew that you wouldn't be interested
that's all. Don't worry about him. He's a nice guy,
and he'll probably make a great manager,' Jackie said
with a smile.

'He's never going to be my fucking manager,' replied
Lisa angrily. 'What's he been saying to you?'

'Get a grip, Lisa. I was only joking. Forget about it.
Let's talk about Frank instead. Has he said anything
else today?'

'No, just the usual chatting.'

'Maybe he's waiting for you to make the next move,'
suggested Jackie.

'He'll have a long wait. I don't like asking men out.'

Heading back to the bank after a long but sober lunch,
Lisa wished she could spend the afternoon flirting with
Frank, subtly conveying that she was prepared to go out
with him. It would be a lot more fun than sorting Simon
out, but if she let him get away with this report
business, she'd regret it later.

Simon concentrated on his screens when Lisa sat down
beside him. He was eating sandwiches which he'd asked
one of the back-office school-leavers to get for him. He
didn't want to go out himself because he wanted to make
the point that while Lisa was off enjoying herself, he
was working as hard as ever. He was wasting his
efforts today, because nearly everyone was out for a
long lunch. Even Mr Kimura had come to realise the

value of business relationships formed in the restaurants and bars of the Square Mile, and on a quiet day when no figure was expected he was often out himself for a few hours.

Lisa ignored Simon and waited for Mr Kimura to appear. When he did, just before two o'clock, he looked slightly flushed and he strayed a little to one side as he headed for his desk, but he looked sober enough to talk to, so she stood up ready for action and went over to his desk.

'Can I speak to you?' she asked, smiling sweetly.

Mr Kimura looked up in surprise. 'Certainly,' he said, pulling his spare chair closer and patting it. 'Please sit down.'

'No, not here,' she said. 'I want to go into one of the meeting-rooms.'

Mr Kimura's face turned lobster red and he pulled at his collar to give himself more room to breathe. This was it! She was finally coming round to the idea of a relationship with him. It was typical of women to become interested once all hope seemed lost, he thought, smoothing his hair with his clammy hands and standing up to lead the way out of the room. He would have liked to have gone behind her to watch the gentle sway of her hips as she walked, but that would not be dignified. He was the senior manager, so he had to go first.

Lisa had the satisfaction of seeing Simon peering over the top of the desk at them. She gave him a little wave and he pretended not to notice.

In the meeting-room Mr Kimura was a little disappointed that Lisa chose to sit in an armchair rather than next to him on the sofa.

'I'm not very happy, Mr Kimura,' she said. 'I am having a few problems.'

'What's wrong?' he asked, his mood deflated. This was not what he had expected.

Lisa wasted no time trying to be subtle. 'Simon told me you asked him to write a report about the whole desk.'

Mr Kimura chose his words carefully. 'Yes, I asked him to make sure a monthly report was sent around the bank.'

'Did you ask him to do it without telling me, or were we supposed to do the report together?' asked Lisa.

Mr Kimura frowned. He was the senior manager and yet Lisa, no doubt aware of her sexual allure, was questioning him as if he was the junior. Why couldn't these local girls be more like the Japanese ones at home?

His mind filled with rosy pictures of his days at head office surrounded by delicate women in uniform who made his tea and wouldn't dream of talking to him the way Lisa was doing now. But then he remembered the fracas in the lift, and he realised that women all over the world were probably the same. They got poor men like him under a sexual spell and then dominated them mercilessly. Domination. Lisa would be so good at dominating him between the sheets. Why was she only interested in talking to him about work? Mr Kimura was caught for a moment in a fantasy in which Lisa had tied him up with leather thongs and was beating him with a bamboo cane. It was heaven.

'Mr Kimura?'

Lisa's voice brought him back to earth, and he remembered what they were discussing. He wanted to be angry with her, but she looked so fetching today and she had such a great cleavage. If only she'd allow him to touch it. He flexed his fingers and just managed to stop himself from reaching out.

'Lisa,' he said, 'I want to expand the desk. I want a whole row of corporate dealers. I can only get more dealers if the desk is successful, and Simon is doing his job very well at the moment.'

'So you asked him to write a report without telling me, is that it?' demanded Lisa, who was not going to let him lead her off the subject.

'I asked him to write a report on his customers. I assumed you wrote the part on yours,' snapped Mr Kimura. Better to lie than to upset her even more, he thought. After all, it was his word against Simon's.

'I see,' said Lisa. 'So will you tell him not to write one again without consulting me?'

'I will talk to him,' said Mr Kimura.

She wasn't satisfied. All they ever seemed to do was talk — that was one of the problems. But she could hardly demand that they stopped talking to each other.

Mr Kimura saw that she was unhappy. 'I need you to work together as a team. Simon is doing his job very well at the moment,' he said again.

'He is not doing better than me,' said Lisa defensively.

'He doesn't spend time playing around,' retorted Mr Kimura. 'He is using every moment to increase the customer base. You must work harder to do the same.'

Lisa felt defeated. Simon had got the upper hand and she was going to have to work very hard to even things out. She sat back in her chair and wished that she hadn't bothered to say anything about the report.

'Now, go back to the dealing-room and do your best,' said Mr Kimura, relieved to have regained control of the situation. Much as he liked Lisa, he couldn't put her before the success of the desk, because he had staked his reputation on it.

She didn't go back straight away. The meeting had

left her feeling very insecure. What if Simon got promoted and was put in charge? It would be so humiliating. She went for a caffeine fix to give her the strength to go back and sit beside him.

Frank and Leo were in the coffee room, and she tried to smile at them.

'Ooops, here's the dwarf waddling in,' said Leo with a loud chuckle.

'Nice to see you too, fat boy,' snapped Lisa and Leo, after picking up his coffee and muttering a quick, 'Fuck off,' left the room.

'Why he call you "dwarf"?' asked Frank. He knew that a dwarf was one of those little men in *Snow White*, and he couldn't see any resemblance between them and Lisa.

'He thinks it's funny that I'm short.'

'But he short too,' said Frank in amazement. 'He very rude man. In Japan you not so short.'

'Really? Maybe I should move there,' said Lisa.

Frank smiled down at her. 'If you came to Japan, I could show you all the beautiful places.'

'That would be nice,' said Lisa, brightening a little.

'Really?' asked Frank. 'You like to go out with me, then?'

'Yes,' said Lisa. She thought of Jackie's advice. 'How about tonight? I need cheering up.'

'I'm sorry, but tonight I am busy.'

How embarrassing, she thought. She'd obviously misunderstood him. 'Never mind,' she said. 'I'm tired, anyway.'

'Are you busy Friday?' asked Frank. 'How about I show you some good Japanese food?'

'Only if I can eat some as well,' laughed Lisa, relieved that he'd saved her dignity.

Frank looked puzzled.

'Don't worry, it was just a joke,' she explained. 'Can we keep this a secret? I don't want everyone teasing me.'

'Of course,' he said. 'Just you and I will know that we go out.'

A loud chorus of *Alleluias* sounded in Lisa's head followed by cannon-blasts and fireworks exploding into the air. The Japanese equivalent went off in Frank's and they both walked back to the dealing-room smiling broadly.

Simon, on seeing her face, was a little worried. What had happened with Mr Kimura? She ignored him and, as soon as he was busy with a customer, told Jackie about her date. Frank, noting that Lisa was busy on the phone, gave Tom and Big Jock the thumbs up.

On Friday morning, Lisa took extra care when getting ready. She wanted to look good but she didn't want everyone in the dealing-room to suspect she had a hot date. She settled for a navy suit and an emerald-green short-sleeved silk blouse. Underneath, she wore matching dusty-pink undies — lacy bra, suspender belt and French knickers — which she had bought on the way home the night before, with navy-blue stockings. Feeling a little trussed up by the unfamiliar suspender belt, she set off for work. By the time she arrived, the stockings were down by her knees and the suspender belt felt so tight that she was sure it was cutting off a vital part of her blood supply. She went into the toilets and took off the belt and stockings. She'd put them on later, when she didn't have to sit down so much.

The trainees were out visiting the Futures Exchange

with Aki-san that morning, so Lisa was able to concentrate on her work and show Mr Kimura that she too could look keen and busy. When they came back after lunch, a figure had come out and Lisa was rushing around so much that she had no time to take much notice of Frank. At five o'clock, she was still trying to get through her work, so Frank said he would wait for her down the pub. Lisa finished an hour later, put on her stockings and suspenders and went down to meet him. As it was Friday night, the pub was packed out with Haru Bank staff. Lisa found Frank standing with Stephanie, who was holding court among some of her brokers. Simon was there too, which was unusual on a Friday – he usually rushed off to start his weekend with Hannah.

'Where's Jock and Tom?' she asked Frank, hoping he wouldn't mention their date in front of everyone.

'They go see *Les Misérables*. I see it twice already. It very sad. Make me cry.' He winked, to show he understood the need for discretion.

'We're going up Thank God it's Friday soon,' broke in Stephanie. 'Why don't you come with us, Frank?'

'I very tired tonight. I go back for early night,' lied Frank nervously. He didn't like saying no to Queen Stephanie.

'You'll be all right once you've got a few drinks inside you,' said Stephanie, her smile making his knees tremble with fear. 'It's Saturday tomorrow you can sleep late.'

Trapped, Frank looked at Lisa for help.

She stepped in to rescue him. 'Can't you see the poor guy's tired? Leave him alone.'

Stephanie shrugged and turned back to her brokers, who were busy trying to show how entertaining they thought she was. Lisa was glad that she didn't deal through brokers. It would be too much to have a group of men at her beck and call, all pretending to adore her, when all they really wanted was to make sure she dealt with them more than anyone else.

She wanted to leave the pub. The longer they stayed, the greater the chance that Frank might be persuaded to forget about their date. She tugged at his sleeve and he leant down.

'You leave first and I'll follow in a few minutes,' she whispered.

'Yes, I get taxi,' said Frank, relieved that they'd soon be on their way. He finished his drink, gave a loud stage-managed yawn and announced he was leaving.

Lisa followed him out a few minutes later and found him waiting for her in a taxi. She got in and Frank put his arm round her and kissed her on the cheek. The taxi headed for the West End and Lisa relaxed back into the seat. She had a feeling it was going to be a really good night.

Perched on a high stool in a Japanese restaurant thirty minutes later, she wasn't sure whether the evening was going to be a good as she'd hoped. In front of them there was a large hotplate, and behind it a Japanese chef was making high drama out of chopping and cooking an assortment of meat and vegetables. It wasn't the most romantic of places to sit. The heat from the hotplates made their faces red and shiny.

As she got hotter and hotter Lisa felt the bare tops of her thighs becoming sweaty, and the places where lace met flesh began to itch terribly. The chef cooked so much food that soon her stomach swelled and the tight suspender belt began to cut into her waist. They were using chopsticks and drinking hot sake. The more she drank the worse she handled the sticks, and every few

minutes she dropped either a chopstick or some food.
She had a large greasy stain on her left breast where
she'd dropped a piece of steak and the floor was littered
with chopsticks. At first, she had got off her stool each
time to pick up a dropped stick, but the stool was very
high for her and when she got off and back on again, she
felt her stockings fall down a little further and her skirt
ride up a little higher. To keep her dignity, she decided
it was better to leave the mess on the floor.

The seating might be uncomfortable, but Lisa wasn't
disappointed with Frank. He talked just enough to be
interesting and was quite happy to answer her questions
about his life in Japan. She warmed to him even more
when she found out that he, too, had family problems.

'My life very hard. My wife left. I no see my son for
two years,' he told her.

'So you're divorced?' said Lisa.

'No,' admitted Frank.

'You're still married?' Lisa didn't like the sound of
this.

'No, my wife, she left me,' said Frank quickly.

'But you aren't divorced?'

'Not yet.'

Oh great, thought Lisa. He's married. Not only was
she embarking on an affair with someone from the
bank, someone Japanese, but he was married with a
child. Typical of her luck! Then good sense told her
that he had been separated for two years and his wife
had left him, so he was as good as single.

She'd always thought women who went with married men were foolish. What hope could they ever
have of happiness, when their relationship developed
under the shadow of deceit? Relationships were difficult
enough without trying to have one with a man who you

already knew could cheat and lie. She was thankful
Frank was separated.

'Why did your wife leave?' she asked, anxious to find
out who was at fault.

'She play too much *pachinko* and spend all our
money,' he explained sadly.

'*Pachinko*?'

'Yes, it game you play with little silver balls. You can
win lot of money.'

Lisa's sake-stoked imagination ran riot. Little silver
balls? She'd get him to draw a diagram later. 'But your
wife didn't?'

'No, she always drunk so can't hold the handle very
well. Then she take my son and go off with the boss of
the *pachinko* parlour. He very rich man. He Korean.'
Frank spat on the floor in disgust.

Lisa put aside the many questions rolling round her
head, and concentrated on comforting him. The poor
man had been abused by a terrible woman who wouldn't
let him see his son. It was very sad and Lisa's heart went
out to him. That such a kind and gentle soul should be
so badly treated was a crime.

Sake can make the simplest story into the biggest
tragedy. Aided by Japanese rice wine, Frank left the
restaurant with Lisa's heart firmly in his pocket.

Chapter 18

———— ————

'You want we go snack bar or we go somewhere else?' asked Frank as he looked out for a taxi.

Lisa's heart was where Frank wanted it to be, but her body was rebelling against their romantic restaurant experience. Her stomach felt full enough to burst through her navel, and the sake had made her so dizzy that she feared one puff of wind would topple her over. To add to her discomfort, her thighs were in itch-induced trauma and she felt as if she was being cut in half by her suspender belt. All she wanted to do was rush home, rip off her clothes and go to sleep.

'I'm very tired,' she said. 'I don't think I can go on any more.'

Frank couldn't understand what had gone wrong. He was sure he'd won her over with the story of his life, and yet in the time it took to finish their meal, pay the bill and leave the restaurant, she had tired of him. 'What's matter?' he asked. 'You no like me?'

Lisa squeezed his hand. 'Of course I like you,' she said. 'It's just that I've eaten and drunk so much that I feel tired' – *and slightly sick*, she could have added. 'Let's just call it a night and go out another time, OK?'

But Frank had geared himself up for sex and he was determined not to let her get away a second time. 'Come to hotel with me,' he pleaded. 'You lie down and you feel good soon. I got a nice room.' He bent and kissed her.

Jackie was right: when Lisa closed her eyes she didn't notice that he had a mouth full of metal. As she concentrated on his mouth, his tongue and his right hand, which was caressing her left breast, she saw the sense in his words and the thought of going home alone seemed ridiculous.

Feeling her response to his touch, Frank was confident enough to stop the kissing and the caressing so he could find a taxi before she changed her mind again. Luckily, one soon came, and he practically threw her inside.

'The Savoy Hotel, please,' he told the driver. Then he put his arm around Lisa and tried to kiss her again.

She pushed him off. 'The Savoy? I didn't think Haru Bank was generous enough to put you up there.'

'No, not Haru Bank,' said Frank proudly. 'I book room for tonight myself.'

'Oh, really.' Lisa was more than a little put out by his assumption that she'd sleep with him on their first date. 'How did you know I'd spend the night with you?'

The look on her face warned Frank to choose his words carefully. 'I didn't. But I just hope very much that you do. I get lovely room just in case.'

If Frank had lived in England, Lisa would have given him a harder time. But as he was only in London for a short period, she let him wriggle out of trouble quite easily. After all, she told herself, she'd intended to sleep with him tonight, and she could hardly blame him for reading what must have clearly shown on her face all week.

When they arrived at the Savoy and Frank checked in, Lisa stood behind him, hoping that she wasn't being mistaken for a callgirl. She felt naughty but quite safe, because it was most unlikely they'd been seen by anyone who knew them.

Behind her, Leo arrived with his ex-girlfriend. He was treating her to a romantic evening in the hope that she'd take him back again. He was surprised to see Lisa and Frank, but he didn't call out to them in case Lisa told his ex-girlfriend that he called her 'the Sow' when she wasn't around. Leo kept his head down and walked past quickly, and to his relief they didn't notice him.

Lisa and Frank were shown to their room by a porter. Frank immediately went to check out the bathroom. Hoping that he'd come back soon and give him a tip, the porter explained to Lisa how to use the television and showed her where to hang the clothes she'd have had if she'd had any luggage. They heard Frank turning on the bathtaps, so the porter explained how to draw the curtains and how to operate the light switches. When he had finished and was looking round for something else to do, Frank emerged from the bathroom.

'Can I get you anything, sir?' asked the porter, hoping Frank would hurry up and tip him.

'A bucket of ice, please,' said Frank. In Japan, tipping is almost unheard of, so he didn't know what the porter was waiting for.

'Certainly, sir. I'll have it sent up.'

The porter looked at Frank. Frank looked back. Lisa wanted to whisper about the tip but she didn't know how much they should give, so she said nothing. After a minute, the porter gave up and left.

Frank took off his jacket and tie and put them over the back of a chair. He checked his hair in the dressing-table mirror, ran his fingers through the side bits, adjusted his fringe and then turned to Lisa, who, her indigestion having subsided, was sitting on the edge of the king-size bed waiting to be seized in a passionate embrace.

'Come and look at bathroom,' he said. Not quite what she had expected, but she got up and followed him. The bathroom was big. As well as the toilet, bidet and sink, there was a huge bath with a shower head as big as a dinner plate.

'This very nice bath. Like Japanese bath. We bath together, OK,' he said excitedly.

'OK,' agreed Lisa. She didn't like the implication that she needed a bath before sex, but she had never shared a bath with a man before, at least not one like this, which looked big and deep enough to swim in.

She followed Frank back into the bedroom, removed her earrings and put them on the dressing-table then turned to watch as Frank took off his shoes, socks, trousers and shirt. To her disappointment, he was wearing a white vest and large boxer shorts. She was used to seeing the outline of vests under the shirts of the Japanese men at work, but she had hoped that Frank, with his perm and his unconventional clothes, would be bare-chested under his shirt. The vest, tucked into the huge boxer shorts, made his legs, which were slightly bowed, look very short. Not a good start, but she hadn't seen him naked yet.

Frank sat down on a chair and drew Lisa towards him. Humming 'Love Me Tender' softly, he started to unbutton her blouse. The last few nights, Lisa had often imagined being slowly undressed by him, and with the help of her little electric friend she had managed to work herself into the most satisfying erotic frenzies.

But now that it was actually happening, she wasn't aflame with desire. Frank undressed her so briskly that he might have been a mother undressing a child at bathtime. Never mind, she thought. When he got to her underwear, he'd be so overcome with passion that he'd throw her on the bed and do it there and then. The thought was exciting, even though it meant she'd be trapped in the killer suspender belt for a bit longer. But pain was tied to pleasure, and she'd probably have the most satisfying orgasms during the ordeal.

It didn't happen. Frank barely glanced at the lacy ensemble. He took off Lisa's bra and then, looking as if he was choosing a ripe melon, felt the weight of each breast in his hands, giving her nipples a gentle squeeze between thumb and forefinger. He quickly removed her French knickers and then paused to stare at the suspender belt and stockings. Not to appreciate them, but to work out how to remove them. One stocking was down by Lisa's knee. There was a patch of red on each thigh where she had been scratching, and when he located the hook of the suspender belt and undid it, there was a red line round her waist and a lacy imprint across her stomach.

'This what English girls wear all day?' asked Frank disbelievingly, holding up the the suspender belt, stockings still attached.

'Sometimes,' said Lisa feeling foolish. 'It's supposed to be sexy.'

'Really?'

'Don't they have them in Japan?'

'Not normal women.' He stopped to take a look at Lisa's body. 'I like naked best,' he said, running his hands down her back and feeling how firm her buttocks were.

He was about to stand up and take off his underwear when someone knocked at the door.

'It's the ice,' said Frank.

Lisa got under the bedclothes and he went to open the door. After placing the ice-bucket by the bed, Frank took off his underwear and led Lisa by the hand to the bathroom. She lifted her leg to climb into the bath but Frank pulled her back.

'No. I wash you,' he said. 'We don't get soap in the bath, so I wash you first.'

Lisa had heard about this Japanese custom, but she didn't think the Savoy would be very pleased if he splashed water all over the place. He squatted down by the bath with his legs wide open; an ugly position, but it gave Lisa a good view of his vitals as they hung down. Black testicles were not what she had expected. She had imagined them to be smooth and practically hairless like the rest of his body, but they were very dark and hairy, the skin looking as tough and wrinkled as an elephant's behind. His penis looked quite normal, though. No strange colour tones there, and the length was about average. She couldn't be sure until she got a chance to take a closer look and do the inch test with the top joint of her thumb, but from where she stood she could see it wasn't that small, which was a relief.

Frank wetted a hand towel, applied lots of soap and briskly scrubbed her from head to toe. His touch was firm but not painful, and it left her body tingling. If she had been washed by a fat attendant in a Turkish bath, she would have been more than satisfied.

Frank rinsed her off. 'Now get in the bath,' he ordered, holding her arm so that she could keep her balance.

'Shall I wash you first?' offered Lisa. She would

have been quite happy to wash him, concentrating on his dangly bits.

'No,' said Frank. 'I want to see you stretched out and relaxed.'

Amused that he wanted her to be passive, she put her foot in the water.

'*Aaaaagh!*' she screeched, taking it out again. 'Bloody hell, it's *boiling*! Didn't you put any cold water in?'

'Have patience,' said Frank, smiling. 'Your body will soon get used to it.'

Lisa wasn't sure about this but she thought that for his sake she'd give it a try. It was very painful getting in and stretching out. Her whole body went bright red and her nipples felt as though they were on fire — she was sure she was being boiled alive.

'Am I done yet?' she asked.

'Have patience,' said Frank, rinsing himself off. 'Soon you will feel very good.'

He was right. As she lay neck-deep in the water, she felt the stinging gradually subside and she began to relax. Frank finished washing and climbed into the bath. It was so big that they were both able to stretch out. He had very supple toes and he used them to stroke Lisa's erogenous areas. She'd never been touched up by a big toe before and she was amazed at how stimulating it was. She hoped his fingers were as effective as his toes.

Lobster-red and tingling all over, they got out of the bath. Frank dried Lisa with a towel and dressed her in a bathrobe. She wanted to pee, so she gently pushed him out of the room and locked the door. Respecting Frank's need for cleanliness, and wanting to find out if it was true about the pleasure of sitting on one, Lisa opted for the bidet rather than toilet paper. She went over and turned it on. The pleasure was intense, and she sat there for a few minutes laughing with delight until Frank knocked on the door and asked her what was going on.

When she opened the door, he picked her up, laid her on the bed and began to suck her toes, gradually working his way up her body – annoyingly, bypassing the bits her bathrobe covered – until he was kissing her on the mouth.

'I give you massage,' he said, and he removed the robe.

Lisa groaned in frustration. If he didn't start some serious foreplay in the next fifteen minutes, she was going home. It was all very nice so far, but it wasn't satisfying and she couldn't take the suspense much longer.

She lay face down on the bed while Frank, using a combination of pressing and rubbing, gave her the most delicious sensations all up and down her body. She wasn't too enamoured when he started to press and pummel her scalp, but the neck and shoulder massage that followed made up for the headache. Her back dealt with, he turned her over and began to work his way slowly over her front. She closed her eyes and allowed herself to relax completely under his touch. She was building up into the most delicious state of desire when she suddenly felt something very cold being rubbed against her nipples.

She screamed and sat up. 'What are you doing?'

'Ice. I saw man doing this in movie,' said Frank. 'It very sexy, no?'

'It's bloody cold,' said Lisa, taking the ice from him and throwing it on the floor. 'How long are you going to torture me?' she demanded.

Frank looked deeply disappointed. 'You no like it so far?'

'No,' said Lisa. 'Well, not the ice, anyway.'

'Not even this?' asked Frank. He took another cube from the bucket and slowly circled her belly-button with it.

Lisa pushed his hand away. 'I especially hate that. Now put down the ice and let's get on with it.' Passivity was all very well, but if it meant getting frostbite she wasn't going to play any more. She grabbed Frank by the penis and showed him what fun an assertive woman can be.

A few hours later, Lisa looked at the sleeping man beside her. She couldn't decide which bit of his sexual repertoire had pleased her the most and she couldn't think of anything he'd done, once they got down to it, that had disappointed her. She'd had a variety of orgasms. She'd been shown some very interesting new sexual positions, and right now she wanted to learn some more.

Frank, exhausted by the extra effort he had put in to satisfy his first ever foreign woman, was snoring gently in a deep sleep. Lisa reached over and started to rub his penis. It soon woke up, but Frank slept on. She shook him, but he still didn't stir. The remaining ice did the trick. Frank was woken by one piece in his ear, another under his armpit and a third between his buttocks. He made a great fuss, claiming that Lisa would make him catch cold.

'I thought it was a Japanese custom,' she said innocently.

'The film was American,' snapped Frank. He got up to find a towel.

'Oh,' replied Lisa, trying not to laugh.

Frank went and had a hot shower. When he came
back he was in a better mood and quite willing to play
a bit longer. By 3 a.m., however, he was wondering
exactly what kind of woman he had chosen. Was she
never going to go to sleep? He had cramp in his tongue
from licking so much, his penis felt blistered and he
was sure he was developing repetitive strain injury in
his right wrist. Lisa on the other hand, was in heaven.
If she could make this night last for ever, she would be
content for eternity.

When she heard Frank snoring between her legs, she
realised that she would have to be a little more realistic.
She removed her vulva from the vicinity of his mouth,
turned over and forced herself to sleep.

He was still out for the count when Lisa woke up
in the morning. She decided to let him sleep on —
they had the whole weekend ahead of them, after
all. She ordered breakfast, and by the time it arrived
Frank was beginning to stir. The night's activity had
given them both enormous appetites, and they gorged
happily on a spread which would easily have satisfied
a family of four.

'What shall we do today?' asked Lisa, when they
had finished breakfast and were leaning back on their
pillows feeling bloated.

'I go see Cambridge with Tom and Jock,' lied Frank.

Lisa was downcast. He couldn't have enjoyed himself
as much as she'd thought if he didn't want to spend any
more time with her.

'But I come back,' said Frank quickly, seeing her
disappointment. 'I come to you tonight.' He hoped his
body wouldn't let him down.

'OK,' said Lisa, smiling, 'I'll be waiting for you.'

She glowed all the way home on the train. So much

sex in one night and more to come. She didn't care that Frank was at least fifteen years older than she was, that — on paper, at least — he was still married, or that he wasn't in England for long. All she cared about was the immediate future and the fun they were going to have together. Her insane happiness cushioned her from the reality of the situation, and she sat on the train with an idiotic grin on her face, going over every tiny detail of their night at the Savoy.

Chapter 19

——— ◄———

Lisa spent Saturday having a good rest to prepare herself for another passion session.

Frank arrived at about eight thirty in the evening. He was clutching a guitar and wearing the same expression of fear that he had worn all the way from Bank station. As he'd travelled across London and entered the East End for the first time, he'd grown more and more agitated at the thought of someone pulling out a knife, robbing him of his valuables and leaving him to bleed to death in an alley. He was a big man, but at the slightest hint of danger he was apt to crumple into a ball and weep. When he got to Leyton station and left the relative safety of the train, he asked himself whether Lisa was worth all this danger. The route from the station to her flat was one of the most frightening of his life and he was profoundly relieved when he at last arrived alive and unhurt at her door.

'How you live in such a place?' he asked, as he went inside.

'What's wrong with it?' Lisa was insulted. Her flat might be on the small side, but it was freshly painted and looked clean and tidy.

'So many dangerous people,' he explained.

Lisa laughed at his expression. 'It's not so bad, I've never had any trouble. You just have to be careful at night and have strong locks.' She pointed to the chain, Chubb lock, two bolts on her flat door and Frank was comforted.

It didn't take long to show him the kitchen, living-room, bedroom and toilet with fitted shower unit but he was impressed. It would take years to afford a similar-sized flat in Tokyo and he wondered aloud how much she was earning. Lisa ignored the question, preferring to let him think she was rich.

To change the subject, she said, 'You've brought your guitar, I see.'

'Yes, I play for you tonight.'

'How lovely,' she said, but she thought, how corny. Would she have to sit there and gaze at him with a sickly smile while he strummed away? And how long did he intend to play for?

Luckily, Frank was hungry so he delayed his perform-ance while Lisa popped out to get a takeaway from the Chinese restaurant a few doors along. When she came back, Frank opened a bottle of wine and they sat down to eat.

'How was Cambridge?' asked Lisa.

'I no go. You made me very tired. I sleep very much.' He smiled apologetically. 'I think you are too young for me. I old man.'

'We should go to bed early tonight then,' suggested Lisa with a smile.

'You want me dead?' asked Frank. Oh well, he thought, if he had to die, at least it was a nice way to go.

Lisa laughed and he pulled her nose affectionately.

She felt relaxed with him. They had only been together one night, and yet they had already got past the stage of needing to fill every second with conversation and were quite comfortable with long pauses. That the pauses were due to Frank's difficulty with the language didn't occur to Lisa. She had never tried to converse in another language except when she went to France as a schoolgirl – and even then most people could speak a little English – so she didn't realise what a struggle it was for Frank. He could usually understand what she said, but when it was his turn to speak he couldn't find the words that would both express what he meant and also make him sound like an educated man in his late thirties. He often thought of something he wanted to tell her, but gave up before he'd started because he couldn't remember the correct form of a verb.

Food consumed, they retired to the sofa. Frank perched on the edge, picked up his guitar and sang some romantic Japanese songs. Lisa sat with a glass of wine in her hand, gazing at him with a silly grin on her face, quite forgetting that earlier in the evening she had winced at the thought of such a scene and also the strange things that wine and song had done to her emotions at the karaoke bar. And so Lisa, who'd have laughed if she'd seen an expression like hers on another woman's face, happily floated into a world of love, romance and passion as Frank strummed softly away on his guitar, secure in the knowledge that at this moment, in Lisa's eyes, he was the most wonderful man in the world.

The sex was good, too. Once they had washed each other in the shower, they were ready for action, and now that they were familiar with each other's likes and dislikes, they were both able to perform

with confidence. In her own home, Lisa was more
comfortable and shrieked and moaned in pleasure whenever Frank touched her sensitive areas in exactly the
right way.

After a few hours of this, the neighbours started
banging on the wall. Lisa was eager to let them know
that she didn't go to bed alone every night so she made
even more noise. Frank was mortified, and tried to
quieten her down by placing his hand gently across
her mouth. The pain when she sank her teeth into his
thumb convinced him immediately that it was better to
put up with the noise and the embarrassment than to
risk losing a chunk of important flesh. So Lisa shouted
and moaned and Frank got used to it.

They spent all that night and most of the next day
in bed. Frank wanted to stay on Sunday night with
Lisa, but he had aggravated an old knee injury and his
lower back was killing him so, he kissed her sadly and
went back to his hotel to recover his strength.

On Monday morning, Lisa floated into the dealing-
room on a cloud of fulfilled lust. She didn't notice Leo
and Stephanie deep in conversation. They noticed her,
though, and as she walked across the room, Stephanie
stood up, pointed at her and shouted, 'What were
you doing checking into the Savoy with Frank on
Friday night?'

'You can't wriggle out of this one, Dwarfie,' added
Leo. 'I was there too.'

All heads turned.

Laughing outside, but dying inside, Lisa sat down
at her desk and concentrated on turning her burning
face back to its usual colour. The room was buzzing
in delight at such a scandal. All around her, Lisa
saw people looking and laughing. She wished Frank

would hurry up and get to work. With his support it wouldn't seem half so bad. The news quickly spread around the bank and the market, as the dealers relayed the information to the brokers and the back-office staff. Within fifteen minutes, anyone in the City who knew Lisa also knew that she had slept with one of the Japanese trainees.

The words 'dog', 'tart', 'whore', 'slapper' and 'slut' came up frequently. Although Lisa had got used to being referred to by these terms, as any woman dealer must if she is to remain in the market, it was harder to hear them now because people believed the words to be true. Her reputation, whatever that was supposed to be, was now damaged. Frank, by comparison, was treated like a conquering hero when he arrived at work with Big Jock and Tom.

Contrary to Lisa's expectations, he did not go straight up to her and show everyone that he was proud of what had happened at the weekend. He merely said, 'Good morning,' to both her and Simon, took off his jacket and settled down at his desk to read a Japanese newspaper. Lisa, aware that everyone in the room was looking to see how Frank behaved towards her, despised him at that moment. He was man enough to put on his own condom, she thought, but not man enough to support her in public. She gritted her teeth and choked down the urge to scream at him.

'Lisa.' Simon's voice broke into her thoughts. 'Bob's just given me the rates. He wants to know why you haven't picked up his line yet.'

Lisa hadn't expected sympathy from Simon and he didn't surprise her by showing any. He pursed his lips in disapproval, and went back to his work. It wasn't his style to join in the kind of teasing that followed

Stephanie's exposure of the affair, but his coldness towards Lisa made it very clear that he wasn't on her side. She guessed that, being devoted to his wife, he was disgusted at her for succumbing to lust and temptation. Of course, she thought angrily, it's easy for someone in a long-term, steady relationship to condemn the unattached for their 'immoral' behaviour.

She couldn't believe her affair with Frank had been found out so soon. It was plain bad luck that Leo had seen them. It wasn't surprising that he'd told Stephanie. But that she should stand up and screech about the affair in such a way was unforgivable. Lisa could have understood if it had been Leo who had done the shouting. He was a man and he had never hidden his contempt for her. But Stephanie was the only other woman dealer. Did she feel so threatened by Lisa that she took pleasure in hurting and embarrassing her? Stephanie herself must secretly have slept with someone in the market at some time. Didn't she have any belief in female solidarity?

These thoughts allowed Lisa to blame Stephanie for her misery. She was determined not to let Leo and Stephanie know they'd scored a victory over her, and she certainly wasn't going to let Frank think she was bothered by his coolness. She was made of better stuff than that, she told herself, blinking away a rush of tears. She picked up her telephone and got on with her work.

The Japanese staff had mixed reactions to the affair. Some managers, like Mr Sumida on FX, were thrilled. Now that he knew she was available to Japanese men, he decided to pay special attention to her. Frank would be gone soon and she'd be searching for another lover. Maybe he'd be the next lucky one. By the look of Frank, and from reports in the toilets by Tom and Big Jock, Lisa was certainly worth the wait.

Mr Kimura, on the other hand, was very upset. They had shared three whole days together in Scandinavia and she hadn't even given him a glimpse of her under- wear, let alone allow him to get inside it. And yet here was Frank, who worked for a mediocre bank at home, who had managed to have her with almost no effort at all. Mr Kimura couldn't understand it. Was it Frank's height? Or was it his singing? Perhaps if Mr Kimura had sung to her too, she might have been more accommodating. His 'Tie a Yellow Ribbon round the Old Oak Tree' had always impressed his wife, so maybe he should have sung it to Lisa.

He cursed himself for neglecting her recently. If he hadn't been so obsessed with his dream of building a Corporate team, she might have succumbed to his charms and he'd be the one sitting here looking like a cat that had overdosed on fresh whipped cream. Frank, despite making every effort to look as if nothing had happened, had about him the air of a man who'd been to heaven and back several times over the weekend.

On the Futures desk, Aki-san was furious with Mr Kubo for being such a weak manager. He was sure Lisa wouldn't have dared act like that when she'd been under his command. He looked across at Mr Kubo and sneered when he saw that, as usual, he had his head down and was writing reports. He probably hasn't even heard about the affair yet, thought Aki-san.

The clock played tricks with Lisa that morning. Whenever she glanced at it, she could have sworn that the hands were moving backwards. She was desperate for lunchtime to come so that she could escape from the room and fortify herself with some alcohol. Without

it, she doubted she would get through the afternoon.
Frank's behaviour was bitterly disappointing. He'd
avoided her eye all morning, and he made no attempt
to follow her when she went to get a coffee. They'd
been so close at the weekend, and they sat so close
to each other in the dealing-room, but they might as
well have been sitting on opposite sides of an ocean.
The public knowledge of their affair sat between them
like a huge barrier preventing them from drawing any
comfort from each other's presence.

Lunch with Jackie brought little relief. Jackie was
only interested in hearing the details of Frank's sexual
technique. If she'd realised how hurt Lisa was, she'd
have been more sensitive, but she had slept around for
so long now that she'd forgotten what it feels like to
lose your reputation in the market.

'So when are you seeing him again?' asked Jackie.

'I don't know. He won't even look at me.'

Jackie was surprised that Lisa looked so unhappy.
'He was that good, was he?'

'Yes, he was.'

'Oh really? Tell me more,' said Jackie, leaning forward across the table.

Lisa didn't want to give Jackie a light-hearted
rundown of what had happened. Her feelings for Frank
had started as just sexual attraction, but some time over
the weekend, probably when he played his guitar to
her in her flat, Lisa had felt the potential for much
more. And now it had all been turned into something
seedy, and Frank was treating her as if he didn't even
know her first name. It was too much to take.

'Jackie,' she said, 'I'm sorry, but I can't talk about
it now.'

Jackie was concerned, 'I didn't know you felt so—'

Lisa raised her hand. 'Don't. It's not your fault. Let's just call it a day, shall we?'

On her way back to Haru's, she bumped into Andy.

'Well, you certainly know how to create a storm,' he said. When Lisa didn't reply, he went on, 'I can't believe you were so unlucky. Imagine Leo of all people seeing you there.'

'I know. I can't bear to think about it,' said Lisa sadly.

'How's Frank taking it?'

'Like a man. A typical fucking man.'

'Poor guy, he's probably so embarrassed.'

'Well, what about me? Do I look like I'm having a great time?' Lisa didn't need to be told how bad Frank was feeling: he couldn't feel any worse than she did.

'Point taken.' Andy realised he'd only upset her more. 'How about a drink after work?' he suggested. 'It'll make you feel better.'

They went into the bank and got into the lift. As the doors began to close, they heard someone shout, 'Wait!'

Andy opened the doors, and Aki-san got in.

'Thank you,' he said to Andy. Then, to Lisa, 'I hope you are working hard. You are not here to play games.'

Simple words, but they were loaded with meaning and Lisa, bright red, held her breath and concentrated fiercely on the numbers over the doors. Right now, crawling up the stairs would have been preferable, even if she'd had to go up to the twenty-fifth floor and not just the sixth. Anything would have been better than standing with Aki-san in the lift. His disapproval was so strong that the air was heavy with it and the lift, usually so quick, seemed to slow down to give her a few extra seconds of agonised embarrassment. When they got to the sixth floor, Aki-san got out and walked quickly to the dealing-room.

'Are you sure you can get through the afternoon without taking a swing at someone?' asked Andy as they walked along the corridor.

'I think so,' said Lisa, managing a weak smile. 'The trouble is that there are so many people to chose from.'

'Well, you just behave yourself and we'll have a nice drink later,' said Andy kindly, giving her shoulder a squeeze.

It was easy for him to be kind and sympathetic to Lisa, he thought guiltily. As long as people focused on her as a source of amusement, they wouldn't bother about him. For two years he'd managed to work in the City and keep his little secret. In any other workplace, what he did wouldn't raise a single eyebrow, especially in this day and age. But he wasn't in any other workplace, he was a dealer, and the other players in the market were ruthless to anyone who slipped off the path of what they considered normal, acceptable behaviour. As long as he worked at Haru Bank, it was vital that no one knew about his life outside the City. He cringed when he thought what the reaction would be if it became known at work what he did three nights a week and all day Saturday. He didn't think he would be able to bear the insults so well as Lisa.

It would have been sensible for Lisa to have gone straight home after work to avoid the inevitable teasing in the pub. But she preferred to hear what was being said about her, hoping that if she faced everyone now they would soon tire of the affair and leave her alone.

So that evening she gritted her teeth and headed down the pub with Andy.

Laughing and joking with Andy's brokers was quite easy once she was on her third vodka and tonic. It wasn't so easy to keep up the smiles when Frank, Big Jock and Tom came in and went and joined Simon, Stephanie and her brokers.

'Judas,' said Lisa to herself, but she wasn't sure who had betrayed her the most; Frank, her demon lover? Simon her teammate (what was he doing down the pub on a Monday night, anyway)? Or Stephanie, the traitor to her own sex?

Just then, Frank smiled at something Stephanie said. There was no doubt about it: he was the one who'd really put the boot in. Lisa turned away and tried to look as if she was having a good time, but every so often she heard laughter and she imagined that they were all standing there saying bad things about her. By the time she was on her fourth vodka and tonic, she was about ready to burst.

'Calm down, Lisa,' said Andy, noticing that she looked on the verge of an explosion. 'You don't want to do something you might regret later. Just play it cool.'

'I don't know how to any more,' said Lisa. 'I just want to see him suffer. The swine! He even looks like he's enjoying himself.'

'He looks embarrassed to me,' said Andy, sorry for Frank in spite of his behaviour towards Lisa. 'I don't understand why he came down here. Maybe he just wants to be near you.'

'I don't think that's likely, do you?' answered Lisa. 'Look at him – he's even laughing now.'

She was right. He was laughing. Stephanie had said

something amusing and, although Frank hadn't understood the joke, he politely managed a slight chuckle
that would have gone unnoticed by anyone except a
recently abandoned lover who was watching his every
move. Then Frank made a classic mistake: he let Lisa
know he was aware of her scrutiny by catching her eye
and giving her a little wave.

'Bastard!' said Lisa. She picked up her drink and
went purposefully towards him.

'Lisa, don't!' cried Andy.

Too late. She flung the contents of her glass in
Frank's face. Then, without a word, she put the glass
down, grabbed her bag and stalked out of the pub.

Frank stood there, speechless, with vodka dripping
off his face and everyone laughing. The day in the
office had been humiliating, but this was far worse.
He looked at Big Jock and Tom for help, but they were
laughing too.

It was Andy who stepped in. 'I'd go after her, if I
were you,' he advised. 'She's very upset. You ought to
make sure she's all right.'

'Yes, I will,' said Frank, who thought a quick
exit was the best idea. He wiped his face with a
handkerchief and, with the laughter ringing in his
ears, left the pub.

He found Lisa looking very sorry for herself on a seat
on the Central Line platform at Bank station. He sat
down beside her and waited for her to start talking.

'I was hoping you'd drowned,' she said, sniggering
at the memory of his startled face.

'No, I still here,' said Frank. 'But you make me
very wet.'

'Good. You deserved it,' said Lisa, her anger ris-
ing again.

Frank was shocked and upset at her tone. 'I don't understand.'

'Do you think I would sleep with just anyone, is that it?' snapped Lisa, infuriated by his mock innocence.

Frank looked at her and she looked back at him, waiting for him to redeem himself. She thought he must understand, even without her spelling it out, how cruel he had been to her all day. Frank, however, being Japanese and having a totally different way of looking at things, couldn't understand what she was making a fuss about. He had spent the whole day avoiding her so as not to cause them both further embarrassment and now, instead of being grateful and thanking him for his conduct, she was actually angry.

'What I do?' he asked, his eyes wide with astonishment.

'You bastard! Are you sick or stupid?' Lisa's face, all screwed up with rage, was not a pretty sight.

'You no want me to come with you tonight?'

'No, I bloody don't,' she said. But she was lying. In spite of everthing, she still wanted him to stay the night at her place.

'I sorry. I think you like me.'

Frank looked so sad that Lisa softened. 'You know I do,' she said quietly. 'But you made me look like a fool today.'

'Forgive me,' he said, bowing his head. 'I thought it was for the best not to talk to you. I make a mistake. I'm very sorry.'

Lisa's anger turned to tears, and by the time the train came she was weeping. Frank had to suffer even more humiliation as she sobbed loudly on his shoulder all the way to Leyton.

Inside the flat, Lisa opened a bottle of wine. 'Now,

Frank,' she said as she poured, 'I've just got one thing to say.'

She sounded so calm and and sane that Frank could hardly believe this was the woman who had wept on his shoulder all the way home.

'Yes?' he asked cautiously.

'If you want to carry on with this, you have to stop avoiding me at work. We're both single, so why should we be ashamed of what happened?' she said.

Frank could think of many reasons why he should be ashamed, but he thought it better to keep quiet. He hadn't the strength to cope with an argument. He just nodded.

Lisa took that as a yes and went into the kitchen to find some food. She wasn't totally happy with the way things had turned out. He'd let her down when she needed his support, and that worried her. Was his behaviour today due to his culture or was he just a weak man? He'd lost some of the magic that he'd acquired over the weekend. But not enough to snuff out her feelings for him. She was looking forward to having sex again, once she'd had something to eat.

Chapter 20

Call it love, call it the result of plenty of sex, call it misguided . . . whatever it was, it changed Lisa. Her life before Frank had felt like a long, hard trudge through sticky mud with several large wooden crosses hanging around her neck. Now she felt like a ballerina pirouetting across the stage. She was triumphant at work with Frank sitting beside her, expecting that soon everyone would stop their malicious gossip and teasing now they knew the affair hadn't been just a quick fling. She glowed with happiness as she sat at her desk dealing with her customers.

Frank's feelings were more complicated. Half of him was thrilled to be having an affair with a young Englishwoman. Whenever he looked at Lisa, he couldn't believe she had chosen to sleep with him. However, he wished they'd been able to keep it secret. He wasn't too concerned about what the local staff were thinking, because he wouldn't be in London long enough for their opinion to matter but his Japanese colleagues made him uncomfortable. They didn't blame him for having an affair — after all, how many of them would have acted differently? — but they blamed him for not

being more discreet. Having such a public relationship
with one of the local staff did not meet with their
approval.

He also worried about what would happen when he
had to leave London. How would he separate himself
from her if she developed a strong attachment to him?
His life in Japan would not be able to accommodate her.
The sensible thing would have been to stop seeing her
as soon as the affair became public knowledge, but Lisa
was fresh and young and it was years since he had met
with such sexual enthusiasm. Wouldn't it be wrong to
deny himself this experience? He'd be forty soon. This
was probably his last chance to have such uninhibited
sex with a young, relatively firm body before middle age
set in. And those breasts: where in Japan would he ever
be able to find such breasts?

Lisa had no idea what Frank was going through.
She felt so at ease with herself, and so right sitting
beside him, that she wanted to believe very much that
what had started off as a bit of fun, was turning into
something much more serious.

Work became more pleasant now that Frank was
by her side. Leo no longer came over to tease her,
Mr Kimura kept his distance, and Simon stopped being
so interested in how she acted towards her customers,
preferring to put his head down and concentrate on
his own work. He was as conscientious as ever, but
he had given up trying to get Lisa to work in the
same way as he did. He realised she found it impossible to think seriously about making money when
the man she had been having sex with the night
before was sitting right beside her, and he wasn't
going to waste his energy trying to get her to work
harder.

The person whose behaviour changed towards Lisa the most was Stephanie. When Lisa went over to give her a deal slip one day, Stephanie said, 'I see you've worked out your little problems with Frank.'

'Yes,' said Lisa. 'Although no thanks to you.' She was still angry about the way Stephanie had broadcast news of the affair to the whole dealing-room.

'Point taken,' said Stephanie. 'I was out of order. I didn't think about what I was doing.'

Lisa had never thought she'd see the day when Queen Stephanie apologised for something. It was a huge comedown, and Lisa found it surprisingly easy to forgive her.

'Well, I suppose it sounded funny when Leo told you,' she said.

'Yes, it did,' said Stephanie, relieved that Lisa was taking it so well. 'How about I make it up to you? I'm having a big night out with my brokers on Wednesday. Why don't you and Frank come along?'

'Yes, I think we will,' said Lisa, happy to accept the olive branch.

'Guess what?' she said to Frank when she got back to her desk. 'Stephanie's invited us out tomorrow night.'

Before Frank could answer, Simon butted in. 'She's not asked you as well?'

'Oooh, hark at big ears! Don't tell me Hannah's letting you off your lead again?' said Lisa, laughing. The invitation had lost some of its appeal now that she knew Simon was going, but she didn't want him to know that.

'She's in Barbados for a few weeks,' said Simon frostily. 'She's there with her boss's family to take care of the children.'

'All right for some, isn't it?' said Lisa. 'I suppose you're taking the chance to play the field while she's away.'

'Don't be ridiculous,' snapped Simon.

On Thursday morning, despite being seriously hungover, Lisa didn't regret having accepted Stephanie's invitation. The queen had been very friendly, and her brokers had only teased her and Frank for the first hour or so. Simon, so cold at work, warmed up a lot and became much friendlier after a few drinks, and Lisa had quite enjoyed his company. It had been a good night, but now they were all paying for it.

As she sat sipping her coffee and eating a chocolate croissant Frank had treated her to, Mr Kubo came over.

'Why you no send New York a telex about the six-month deal you did on Monday?' he demanded.

'Because I didn't do any six months, that's why,' Lisa answered, mildly irritated that he assumed the fault was hers.

'I look in the BA file last night and there was this deal.' He showed Lisa a deal for $25 million, done with a Spanish bank over the Reuters. 'Maine Weavers went to collect the paper and it hadn't been issued. It was a very big problem. Mr Kimura is very angry.'

'Hold on,' said Lisa. She turned to Simon. 'Did you do this on Monday?'

Simon glanced at the file and then looked straight ahead as if he was slowly cranking the memory-wheel back three days. 'No, it wasn't me,' he answered eventually. 'Is there a problem?'

'Yes, New York weren't told about it and they didn't make the issue in time,' said Lisa.

'Mr Kimura is very angry,' said Mr Kubo again. He had been shouted at by Mr Kimura for twenty minutes the night before and he wanted to shout at Lisa now, but he was a little scared of her, especially with Frank sitting there.

'Rather you than me,' said Simon.

'Thanks for the sympathy,' said Lisa. She turned back to Mr Kubo. 'I'll have to check what happened. I'll get back to you when I've found out the details.'

Mr Kubo would have liked to remind her that, as he was the manager, he was the one who should decide when things would be discussed, but she had already turned away from him and the moment was lost.

Lisa looked at the deal slip. The BA had been issued to Jackie's security house so she went into her line.

'Morning,' said Jackie. 'I hear there was a bit of trouble yesterday in New York. What's been going on?'

'It seems like I did a deal, covered it with you and then forgot to tell your New York about it. I must be losing it, I can't even remember doing the deal in the first place.'

'That's because you didn't,' said Jackie.

'What?' Lisa felt a surge of relief.

'No, I did it with Simon.'

'Are you sure?' asked Lisa, who couldn't believe her luck.

'Yes, positive.'

Lisa clicked out of the line and turned to Simon, who was looking intently at his screens. 'Jackie said you did this deal,' she said accusingly.

'What deal?' asked Simon, keeping his cool.

'The six months that was done on Monday.'

'I thought you said Tuesday,' he replied.

'How many drinks did you have last night?' asked Lisa, so relieved to be in the clear that she was happy to tease him.

'I can't remember. I can't even remember getting home.'

'I'm not surprised, the way you knocked back those cocktails.' She looked at him more closely. 'Didn't you wear that shirt yesterday?'

Simon looked down and saw how creased it was. 'Oh God,' he said, burying his head in his hands. 'I feel like death.'

'You'll feel worse when Mr Kimura gets in,' said Lisa. Then she remembered what Simon had said to her earlier. 'I'm glad it's you and not me,' she added smiling.

'Thanks,' said Simon.

Lisa took great pleasure in telling Mr Kubo it was Simon who had been responsible for the deal. She then sat back to wait for Mr Kimura's arrival. Simon was always so smug about his work that she reckoned he deserved a little hassle now and again. She was therefore very surprised when it was her and not Simon who was called over to Mr Kimura's desk an hour later.

'Sit down, Lisa,' said Mr Kimura grimly. He waited for her to take a seat before continuing. 'There was a very big problem in New York yesterday.'

'I know, Mr Kubo has already told me,' answered Lisa.

Determined to go over every last detail with her, whether or not she already knew it, Mr Kimura carried on. 'Maine Weaver went to collect some BAs and New York knew nothing about them. Mr Kubo looked in your file and you dealt on Monday twenty-five million dollars in the six months. You forgot to tell New York—'

'I didn't do it,' broke in Lisa. 'Simon did the deal and then forgot to tell me about it.' She knew she sounded like a schoolgirl, but it was not her mistake and Mr Kimura should know that.

He didn't care who had done the deal. 'You are the BA dealer. It is your job to make sure that New York is told about all the deals. Did you ask Simon before you left on Monday if he had done any BAs?'

'No,' said Lisa, 'but he should have told me.'

'It is your responsibility to find out,' said Mr Kimura.

Lisa could see the conversation turning into a panto-mime if she persisted; the words 'Oh no, it isn't' sprang to mind and she imagined Mr Kimura in drag as the Widow Twanky, shouting, 'Oh yes, it is,' back at her. She smiled at the image.

Mr Kimura lowered his voice and spoke with icy calm. 'I know that you have problems that are making you behave very strangely. You are not concentrating on your work. From today, you must get Simon to check all your deals, then we won't have any mistakes.' The injustice wiped the smile off Lisa's face. She wanted to protest, but his expression told her that it would not be wise to say any more.

Dismissed, she headed to the coffee machine. She couldn't believe Simon had come out so well. What a snake, she thought. He had wriggled his way out of this one. 'Bastard, bastard, bastard,' she said aloud, thumping the buttons.

'Now, now, Lisa, don't take it out on a harmless machine,' said Andy, coming up behind her.

'I suppose you were listening again,' she said, spilling some coffee on the floor as she took the cup out of the machine.

'One of the perks of sitting by the boss's desk,'

laughed Andy. 'You don't do yourself any favours, do you? You should have just said sorry.'

'I didn't do anything wrong,' said Lisa, 'And I'm certainly not going to apologise for someone else's mistake.'

Andy wondered if he had ever been so naive about work. 'That attitude will get you nowhere,' he said firmly. 'The BAs are yours, so anything that goes wrong is your fault. That's the way the Japanese look at it. Mr Kubo got a bollocking just for being your boss.'

Lisa didn't care about Mr Kubo. All she could think of was that how Simon had come off better than she had. 'Typical,' she said. 'Simon causes the problem, and everyone else suffers. I'm beginning to hate him.'

'He's not a bad chap. He's just conscientious,' said Andy.

'And I'm not, I suppose?'

'Well, to be tactful,' said Andy, without having any intention of being so, 'they don't think you can be doing your job properly while you're sitting next to Frank.'

'I didn't even make the Mistake,' said Lisa bitterly, it having acquired a capital letter in her mind.

'You should have checked with Simon before you went home,' said Andy, and Lisa walked off in a huff.

'I still don't think it's my fault,' she said to Frank that night. 'He should have told me he'd done the deal. I always tell him when I deal with his customers.'

They were in her kitchen and she was chopping onions for bolognese sauce. Frank, who wasn't sure if the tears running down her face were caused by the onions or by her frustrations at work, was trying yet again to make her understand why she'd got into trouble.

'Lisa,' he said gently, 'I try one more time then I finish. I don't want to talk about Simon any more.'

'That's fine by me. I'm sick of him, anyway,' said Lisa.

'You are the BA dealer,' said Frank. 'If there is a problem, it is your fault.'

'Not if I wasn't the one who did the deal,' said Lisa, chopping the onions with unnecessary force.

'Why can't you see?' said Frank. 'Mr Kimura was told off by general manager, and then Mr Kimura told off Mr Kubo. Don't you see why you were told off too?'

'When is Simon supposed to get told off?' asked Lisa.

'Why are you thinking of him? It is not important what he does. It is what you do.' Frank was losing patience.

'So Simon can mess up my work and I have to take the blame for it. Is that what you mean?' demanded Lisa, waving the knife as she spoke.

'If you worked properly, there would be no problem. You always playing, you very lazy. Simon work very hard,' shouted Frank, edging towards the door — it might act as a shield if she threw the knife at him.

'If I haven't been working well, it's because of you.'

'So it now my fault!' cried Frank. 'Why you not take responsibility?'

'Oh shut up,' said Lisa. 'I'm sick of talking about work.' She turned back to her cooking and didn't say another word until the food was on the table. As they sat down, she said, 'I suppose you intend staying here tonight then.'

'Yes, of course,' said Frank.

'Are you sure you wouldn't rather be with Simon?'

'Does he have nice breasts?' asked Frank, and they both laughed.

She found it impossible to be angry with Frank for long. It took only one little joke or a note of a song and she found her anger melting away. It was disappointing that he didn't take her side against Simon, but everyone else had been fooled by the snake and it was hard to blame Frank for being taken in too. She was not the sort of woman who needs her man to fight her battles for her, and was quite prepared to cope at work without Frank's help.

Chapter 21

———— ◆————

Six weeks after Lisa and Frank had started their relationship, she saw her father waiting in the lobby as they were leaving work one night. She felt a moment of fear as he approached, because there must be something seriously wrong if he wasn't rushing to catch the 5.15 from Fenchurch Street as he always did.

'What's up, Dad?' she asked.

He held out a letter. Lisa took it and began to read. It was from the personnel office in his bank and said that, following the recommendations of the bank's doctor, the date of his retirement had been set for 31 August.

'Early retirement? I didn't know about this,' said Lisa, giving the letter back to him. As soon as she'd spoken, she realised how stupid she was being. How could she have known? She'd been so preoccupied with Frank that she hadn't been to see her father for over a month. He couldn't talk on the phone and he couldn't write to her, so he had no way of telling her any news. She felt guilty at how easily she had managed to put him out of her mind recently.

Lisa looked at her father closely, trying to see signs of how he felt. Was he relieved that he'd no longer have to go through the trauma of work every day, or was he upset that his disease had progressed so far that he wasn't seen as fit even to do simple checking? Did he want sympathy or encouragement? His face gave no clues.

She decided to be positive. 'God, Dad, you're so lucky! You don't have to work any more and you're not even fifty-five yet.' It sounded false even as she said it, and she wished she'd said something else.

Her father tried to smile — or she hoped he did. She badly wanted to believe he was happy with early retirement. Surely it would be good for him not to have to work any more, she told herself. His life would be much easier.

His life. What kind of life did he have? He lived alone, he was gradually losing himself, and now he wouldn't even have to leave the house to go to work. After he retired, the only company he'd have would be herself and Aunt Millie.

Lisa promised herself that, when Frank went back to Japan, she would start taking better care of her father, even if it did mean eventually moving in with him. But she at once realised it was an empty promise, because if things carried on with Frank the way they were going, she could see herself going to Japan to be with him. She was just going to ask her father if he wanted to go for a drink, when he pointed to his watch. It was ten past five. If he ran, he might just make the 5.15 train.

As he sprinted away, Frank turned to Lisa. 'Why he no talk?'

'He's got something wrong with him,' she said. She knew her answer wouldn't satisfy Frank, but she didn't want to go into the details. She was angry with herself for being so selfish. If she'd been a decent person, she

thought, she'd never have let her father go home alone.
She should have insisted on going with him, even if it
meant sprinting all the way to the station. She despised
herself for preferring to be with Frank than going to
Baneham to comfort her father.

'I need a drink,' she said, and she led Frank downstairs to the pub.

'Tell me more about your father,' said Frank, when
they'd sat down with their drinks. 'You not talk very
much about him.' In fact, beyond explaining that her
parents were divorced, she'd said virtually nothing
about them. It hadn't occurred to him to ask before,
but now that he had seen her father he was curious.

'What is this?' snapped Lisa. '*Twenty Questions*?'

'I just like to know about you, that is all,' he
said gently.

Lisa calmed down. It was guilt, not Frank's questions,
that was making her irritable. He had every right to
know about her family, she thought, especially as one
day they might be his family too. 'Why don't we go
and see my father at the weekend?' she suggested. 'You
can find out about him for yourself.'

'No,' answered Frank.

'There's no need to say it like that.' said Lisa,
offended that he disliked her father after only seeing
him once.

'No,' said Frank, 'I mean, I can't go. I'm going
to Europe branches with Tom and Jock. We go to
France, Spain, Switzerland, Italy and Germany,' he
said counting them off on his fingers. 'We go on Friday
for two weeks.'

'Two weeks?' said Lisa, dismayed. 'Why didn't you
tell me before? I can't believe you'd just go like this,
without telling me.'

'I no want to upset you.'

'Upset me? How can I not be upset? You've only got three weeks till you go back to Japan. If I'd known, I'd have taken some holiday so I could come with you,' she said, wondering if it might still be possible.

'You can't do that,' said Frank. 'What would every-one say?'

'I don't care what everyone says,' said Lisa; but she knew he was right. Besides, she didn't trust Simon enough to leave him alone on the desk for two weeks. She'd just have to bear the separation as best she could.

Frank's absence that weekend allowed Lisa to play the dutiful daughter and visit her father. He couldn't tell her how he felt about his impending retirement, but he spent the weekend in the usual way, so she concluded that he wasn't particularly upset and might even be looking forward to a life of leisure. She hoped he'd spend his days pottering about happily in the garden, or perhaps take up a hobby like fishing or golf. She had an image of him in a comfy sweater and jeans, sitting in a rocking-chair in the shade of a big tree, smoking a pipe and looking at ease with the world. The fact that he'd never fished or played golf in his life, and would certainly never smoke, didn't cross her mind. She wanted to believe that he was going to have a happy retirement, so she did.

Freeing herself from worry about her father, meant that she was able to concentrate on her own life without feeling guilty. On the train on Monday morning, she thought about Frank and his trip. Why had he left it till the day before his departure to tell her he was going? Was this the Japanese way of breaking bad news? Or was it that he wanted to make sure there was no chance

of her joining him? Would he have acted like that if
he felt as strongly about her as she did about him?
She wouldn't find out the answers until he got back.
In the meantime, she would have a good indication of
his feelings for her by the number of times he phoned.
He'd rung her at work on Friday afternoon when he
arrived in Italy, but as she'd stayed at her father's for
the weekend, and had forgotten to give him the number,
she hadn't heard from him since then.

When she was really truthful with herself, she
admitted there were some things about Frank that
troubled her. Why had he never taken her back to his
hotel? He'd told her it was a really cheap hotel and he
only had a single bed, but was that the real reason? The
other thing she found suspicious was that he hardly ever
spoke about his life in Japan. She knew nothing about
his home, his work or the town where he lived. He
talked of general things like food or the weather, but
when it came to personal details his English suddenly
got very bad or he changed the subject. Lisa had thought
their relationship had become quite strong during their
six weeks together, but now she wondered whether
they knew each other at all. Their time together had
been mostly taken up with sex. Was that all Frank
wanted from her? If so, would their relationship end
as soon as he went back to Japan?

Lisa could have occupied herself all morning with
her doubts, but Simon soon obliged her to concentrate
on her job instead. He had a customer coming for an
in-house lunch so, between lengthy consultations with
Mr Kimura and Mr Yoshida, he fussed around, finding
glossy Haru Bank brochures and making sure the gift
pens were wrapped in blue Haru Bank gift paper with
a silver ribbon. That was normal, and didn't bother

her. What did bother her, although she tried hard not
to let it show, was a small box of new business cards
for Simon which a messenger delivered to the desk.
Simon was busy gathering market tips from each of
the dealers, so that he could pass them off as his own
to the customers, so Lisa had to sign for the delivery.

She knew at once that she was in trouble. On the
cards was written in shiny black ink:

Simon Russell
Assistant Manager
Corporate Dealing Section
Haru Bank

At that moment, Simon came back, saw the cards on
his desk and started to put some of them into his wallet.
'Thank God for that,' he said. 'I thought they weren't
going to come in time.'

'I see you're now an assistant manager,' said Lisa,
trying not to choke on her words. 'When did that
happen?'

'Oh, that,' he said dismissively. 'Mr Kimura just
thought it was a good idea to put it on the cards so
that the customer would think I had a higher status.'

'I'd better get mine changed, then,' said Lisa, relieved.

Simon didn't think that was a good idea. 'You'd
better use up the ones you've already got first. You
know how they are about waste. In any case,' he
added, 'I don't know if Mr Kimura wants everyone
to be assistant managers.'

'Fine,' said Lisa, as if she really didn't care either
way. She didn't trust herself to say anything else because
she knew she'd only sound bitter or jealous.

She listened to him as he read out the *FT*'s market

forecast to a customer. He'd given up writing his own, because they were always wrong, and now usually read straight off the Reuters or from the *FT*, pretending it was his own market view. Lisa had laughed about it at first, but today, watching him sitting there so confident in his deception, she felt very uneasy.

The more she thought about him, the more she became convinced he was up to no good. When she arrived in the mornings he was always sitting at his desk, and he'd begun finding excuses to stay later than her in the evenings. She hadn't taken much notice before, because she'd been only too happy to leave early with Frank, but now she realised he must have been staying late to show Mr Kimura how hard he was working. He'd also started trying to answer the Corporate desk's phones before she did and then, instead of passing the call straight over if the customer was one of hers, doing the deals himself. If she'd thought, as everyone else did, that he was a nice guy, she'd have taken it that he was trying to be helpful. But now she realised he was being underhand.

She thought back to the Mistake. At the time, she'd been angry about getting into trouble over an error made by him, but it had never occurred to her that his failure to tell her might have been deliberate. After all, how could he have known that the Mistake would be blamed on her, not him? She supposed he might have a better understanding how the Japanese look at things. Or maybe it was just that he had been in banking longer. Was it a feature of the Japanese or was it a tradition in banking that meant people got blamed for someone else's mistakes?

She knew the Corporate desk needed a proper man-ager, but she'd thought Simon was too young and too

inexperienced to be given the job. Mr Kubo held the
title, but he knew nothing about corporate dealing
and spent the day writing reports. In cases where
the Japanese manager was simply a plant from Tokyo,
there was usually a local staff member with the title of
assistant manager, and this was the person who really
controlled the section.

Until now, the real manager of the Corporate desk
had been Mr Kimura; he had directed everything from
his desk on the other side of the room. Did he intend to
promote Simon? If not, maybe Simon was out to convince
Mr Kimura that he should. It was the type of thing
that tall people did – they always felt entitled to be
the leader. Well, she wasn't going to accept it. Lisa
decided to start a guerrilla-warfare campaign designed
to throw Simon off the fast track to the top. She began
by playing 'Let's see who can be first in, last out'.

She usually arrived at work just before seven o'clock
but, as Simon always seemed to get there before her, she
decided to arrive at 6.30. The look on his face when he
came in and saw her already at her desk was worth
the loss of twenty minutes' sleep. The next day, she
beat him again. On the third day, when she expected
Simon would get in really early to make sure he was
first, she didn't arrive until just before seven. Thinking
that her two early days were a fluke, Simon relaxed
again and on the fourth day he arrived at 6.50. When
he saw her sitting at her desk, he was in a bad mood
until lunchtime.

Lisa had fun in the evenings too. Simon had given up
leaving at five o'clock weeks ago and, no matter how
late she stayed, he always made an excuse to stay later.
She suspected that this was another ploy to make it look
as if he was working much harder than she was. To test

her theory, one evening she pretended to leave, waited in the toilets for five minutes, and then went back into the dealing-room. Simon had put his jacket on and was just switching off his screens. When he saw her, he turned to his customer files, pulled one out and then sat at his desk pretending to read.

'I forgot to finish that report for Mr Kimura,' said Lisa, getting out some papers from her drawer.

'I'm just researching a customer I plan to call tomorrow,' said Simon. 'I like it when the room is quiet. I can think better.'

'Me too,' said Lisa.

They sat side by side, concentrating on what was on their desks, each determined not be the first to leave. Lisa knew it was petty, but she had nothing better to do while Frank was away. She was lonely without him, and her campaign against Simon gave her something else to think about. It was healthier than hitting the bottle.

By 6.30 all the other local dealers, except Stephanie, had gone. The Japanese managers were still there. They always stayed late, because it wasn't polite for them to leave before Mr Kimura, and he never left before 7.30 to show that he was working hard, even if he wasn't.

Simon was beginning to look agitated. Lisa noticed him looking across at Stephanie, who was getting ready to leave. Just before she walked out of the door, she turned around and mouthed something to him. He nodded in reply and turned back to his report.

'What did Stephanie say?' asked Lisa.

'What?' Simon looked furtive for a second, then controlled himself and gave her one of his sincere smiles. 'I'm having a quick drink with her and some of her brokers tonight.'

'What, again?' said Lisa. 'You've been going out a lot lately.'

'Not really. I just get on with that crowd, that's all.'

'I see.' It sounded suspicious to Lisa, and she was determined to find out what was going on. 'I'll come too,' she said. 'I could do with a drink.'

He went pale. 'I don't think I'll go now,' he said, looking at his watch. 'It's getting late.'

But Lisa wasn't going to let him off that easily. 'Stephanie will never give us a quote again if you let her down,' she insisted. 'You know what she's like.' She stood up to go and Simon put away his report.

When they left the building Simon didn't head for the dealers' usual pub, but started walking towards London Bridge. He strode along fast and Lisa had almost to run to keep up.

'What's up with Stephanie?' she asked. 'It's not like her to walk this far. She usually gets her brokers trotting over to meet her.'

'I suppose she wanted a change of scene,' said Simon, looking slightly uncomfortable.

They came to a little pub tucked away off King William Street. Simon led the way down to the basement, where they found Stephanie on her own.

'God, Stephanie, you are losing it! Where are all your fans?' joked Lisa.

'They had to work late,' said Stephanie evenly.

Lisa was astonished. It was unheard-of for Stephanie's brokers to keep her waiting — if they did she usually refused to deal with them for a few days. Lisa was about to make another joke, but she caught a silent exchange between Simon and Stephanie and knew she'd stumbled onto something. Simon and Stephanie: who would have

guessed? And how long had it been going on? Lisa
remembered that Simon had been with Stephanie in
the pub the evening after the queen had broadcast the
Lisa-and-Frank news. The hypocrites! They'd been at
it all the time.

The 'quick drink' turned out to be very quick indeed,
because Simon and Stephanie drained their glasses before
Lisa could even finish chewing her cherry. They waited
for her to finish and then they all left together. Lisa
followed close behind and saw them into a taxi which
they said they were sharing to London Bridge Station; in
fact, Lisa knew, Simon always went home via Liverpool
Street. She decided that next day she'd stand up and yell
across the dealing-room, 'What were you two doing in
a taxi together?'

In the event, though, she didn't. She was too superior
to play that game, she told herself, and in any case there
was nothing wrong with sharing a cab. It would be
more fun to keep quiet and watch them trying to keep
the affair under wraps.

Simon had been convinced Lisa had guessed about
him and Stephanie, but that morning, as she showed
no signs — nudges, winks or crass comments — that she
had, he decided his secret was safe: she was so wrapped
up in Frank that she hadn't noticed anything. He spent
much of the morning enjoying his lucky escape.

Lisa wasted no time telling Jackie the details at
lunchtime. 'You were right when you said no one is
ever out of the market,' she added.

'The rotten swine!' exclaimed Jackie. 'And to think
that I walked away from him.'

'I still can't believe it,' said Lisa, shaking her head.
'I thought he and the lovely Hannah were as strong as
you can get.'

'Apparently not. What a creep!'

'It makes you lose your faith in men, doesn't it?'

'Not at all. Give up on men and you're really in trouble,' said Jackie firmly.

Lisa was surprised; she'd never imagined that Jackie was a starry-eyed romantic. 'I thought you gave up on them a long time ago,' she said.

'No, not really. I suppose I'm just like any other woman. In the back of my mind there's always the hope that out there somewhere is somebody perfect just waiting for me,' answered Jackie dreamily.

'Oh yes, I know that hope. It goes alongside winning the lottery or becoming a film star,' said Lisa.

Back at her desk that afternoon, Lisa thought over the conversation. Much as she had laughed about men, she knew she wasn't indifferent to them, and deep down she hoped that Frank was right for her, although since he'd been away she'd started to have a few more doubts. He hadn't rung her as often as she thought he should have — well, actually he'd only rung once — but she'd had a postcard signed 'Love, Frank', so she knew he was thinking about her. She just didn't know whether he was missing her as much as she was missing him. She comforted herself with the thought that he'd be back next week, and then she'd find out how he really felt. Who knows, she might even end up as his wife. She laughed at the possibility of that ever happening.

To take her mind off these doubts, and now that she was sure about Simon's true nature, she stepped up her campaign against him. She had great fun hiding his *FT* so that he couldn't give market forecasts, cutting his customers off whenever she passed a call over to him, and hiding the chocolate he brought in for his mid-morning snack. He would narrow his eyes and look at her for a few seconds, trying to decide whether she was upsetting him on purpose or whether she was just naturally careless and irritating.

To Lisa's annoyance, her tactics only made a slight dent in his image. He still managed to impress the senior managers, and this was brought home when Lisa told Mr Kimura she was planning to take two Swedish customers out for drinks. They were flying in that evening from Stockholm and they had asked her to meet them. Normally, a Japanese manager would have accompanied her, but this time Mr Kimura said that Simon should go with her and later that day, as if to show who he thought was the real host for the evening, he gave Simon the expenses application form to fill out.

To prevent people being extravagant when entertaining on expenses, Haru Bank had a policy whereby a request had to be made in advance to the general manager for a sum of money; on the request form the staff had to estimate how much they would need. The day after the event, they had to produce their receipts, and then, providing they'd spent no more than they had applied for, the bank reimbursed the money.

Simon started to fill out the form. 'What time are the customers coming?' he asked Lisa in a managerial kind of voice.

She had to swallow hard to prevent herself from spitting at him. 'They're checking in at the Hilton at eight.'

'Are they expecting us to take them to dinner?'

'No,' lied Lisa. 'They said they'd be eating on the plane and would just like one or two drinks. They want an early night because they have a busy day tomorrow.'

'Two of us and two of them, two drinks each . . . I'd say fifty pounds will be plenty,' said Simon, writing in the amount on the form.

'Fifty'll be more than enough,' Lisa assured him, trying not to laugh. He's so arrogant, she thought. Let's see how arrogant he is tomorrow morning.

Having been an accounts clerk at his old bank, Simon hadn't done much corporate entertaining, nor had he been on any foreign business trips. So he had no idea that when people say, 'Let's have a couple of drinks,' what they really mean is *Let's go out, get very drunk and spend lots of your company's money*; to him, 'a couple of drinks' meant a couple of drinks. Lisa was happy to let him go on thinking that way for the time being.

Simon and Lisa arrived at the Hilton at 7.45 and decided to have a drink each before the customers arrived. Lisa ordered a vodka and tonic and Simon went for a whisky and soda. The colour left his face when he saw the prices. At this rate, they'd only be able to afford one round when the customers came. But he was determined not to let Lisa see he was worried: he couldn't stand the thought of her triumphant little smile if he admitted that he hadn't applied for enough money.

'Is there a pub near here?' he asked casually. 'The atmosphere would be much better' − meaning *much cheaper*.

'I don't know this area at all,' said Lisa. 'Anyway, it's raining now. I don't fancy walking about, do you?' She feigned an innocent expression and Simon reluctantly agreed that they should stay where they were. Noting that tension had made him tight-lipped, Lisa smiled to herself. She was going to enjoy this evening a lot.

By 8.30 Lisa had finished her drink and chewed her ice cubes and was now sucking her slice of lemon. Simon looked as if he'd been sucking one for quite some time. He knew he should offer Lisa another drink, but if he did he'd have used up most of his expense allowance, and the Swedes hadn't even arrived yet.

Lisa lifted her glass and tilted her head back, and Simon watched as the last drop of liquid rolled slowly down into her mouth.

'Very nice,' she said, plonking her glass down on the table and looking pointedly towards the bar.

'Do you want another?' asked Simon through gritted teeth.

'Yes, why not?' said Lisa gaily. 'The bank's paying, after all. We might as well enjoy ourselves.'

Simon ordered another vodka and tonic, but decided not to have another whisky just yet. If he waited, the rest of the ice cubes in his glass would have melted and it would look as if he hadn't finished his first.

'Drink it slowly,' he said to Lisa when her vodka came. 'You don't want to be drunk when they arrive.'

At 8.45 the two Swedes at last arrived. They apologised for being late, and expained that their plane had been delayed. Introductions were made and, as they were all young, they were soon on first-name terms. Ingrid and Peter were very friendly. That this was due to the free in-flight champagne was obvious to Lisa, who delightedly noted their flushed cheeks and wide grins.

'Would you like a drink?' asked Simon, taking the lead.

'How about some champagne?' added Lisa, grinning wickedly when she saw Simon frown at her.

'That would be great,' said Peter.

By the end of the second bottle of champagne, Simon's frown had turned into a scowl.

Lisa decided to turn up the pressure. 'Shall we get something to eat?' she asked.

Ingrid and Peter said yes, and Simon, making a big effort to smile sincerely, asked Lisa, 'Where do you suggest?'

She could see the 'I'm going to throttle you, you little midget' glare in his eyes, but she didn't care. If he thought he was going to walk all over her at work, he deserved to suffer.

'I don't know this area very well,' she answered as innocently as she could. 'Why don't we go to Covent Garden? There are some good places there. Or perhaps we should eat here?' she said, looking towards Peter and Ingrid for their approval.

'I hear there is a very fine restaurant on the roof,' said Peter.

'Yes, the Rooftop,' said Lisa. 'That will do nicely.'

Simon gasped. He'd have to take out a mortgage to cover the cost of dinner for four.

Lisa led the way to the lift and Simon brought up the rear. His gloomy countenance was ignored, because Lisa was loud enough and jolly enough to push him firmly into the background and the two Swedes had enough alcohol in them to blind them to the feelings of others.

'Shall we have a drink first?' asked Lisa, when they'd been shown to their table.

'They don't want to drink, they want to eat,' muttered Simon.

She ignored him. 'How about some wine? Or maybe another bottle of champagne?' Peter and Ingrid nodded. 'Champagne it is, then,' said Lisa, smiling even though

Simon had taken the desperate measure of pinching her thigh under the table.

As Simon was using his credit card, albeit very reluctantly, he got to choose the champagne. 'I'm not drinking any more, so that leaves three of you. I'll order a half-bottle,' he said.

'He loves his little joke,' said Lisa. 'We want a *big* bottle, Simon.'

Everyone laughed except Simon, who was busy hunting for the cheapest one. They turned to their menus. Being the guests, Peter and Ingrid looked to Simon for some guidance.

'We don't need a starter, because it's late,' he said firmly.

'I want one,' said Lisa. She wondered how long it would be before he started crying. He was a bit pale, but not so much that the customers would notice under the dim lights.

'OK, we'll have a starter,' said Simon tensely.

Peter, Ingrid and Lisa chose with regard to taste rather than price and Simon, trying to cut corners, chose soup. Lisa thought the main courses looked very inviting but, as Simon was now applying fierce pressure to the toes of her left foot with the heel of his shoe, she agreed to share one with him. Poor Hannah, she thought. He probably ties her to the bed and whips her if she doesn't put the toothpaste lid on properly. Lisa wasn't downhearted, though. They'd already finished the champage (their third bottle altogether) and more was on its way.

She was so hungry that she finished her starter in a couple of bites. When the main course came and Lisa saw how little of it there was, although it was very nicely arranged, she couldn't stop laughing. How would

they divide up the cob of baby sweetcorn? She stabbed
at it with her fork and Simon made a rush for the two
mangetout. He only got one because Lisa speared the
other with her knife. Conversation was halted as they
tussled over the breast of chicken that was hiding under
a sprig of parsley — at least, Lisa thought it was parsley,
but she couldn't be sure because Simon shoved it in his
mouth so fast that all she saw was a flash of green.

'Well, I'm having a sweet,' she declared, looking at
the trolley, and moving her feet under her chair.

'No,' said Simon. 'It's very late, and Peter and Ingrid
must be tired.'

'Not really,' said Peter. 'I would love something
sweet.'

Lisa called the waiter and the sweet trolley was
brought over. As Lisa, Ingrid and Peter chose freely,
Simon's face began to crumple. The bank was bound to
refuse to pay for all this. What would Hannah say?

'Are you all right, Simon?' asked Ingrid. 'You look
quite ill.'

'I think I'm coming down with something,' said
Simon, feeling his forehead to see if he had a tem-
perature, although he knew that it was the thought
of the bill that was making him sweat.

'He used to be in accounts,' said Lisa. 'He can't
handle the pace yet.' She patted him on the back
condescendingly. 'After the coffee and brandy, we'll
call it a night.'

When the bill came, Simon whimpered. He handed
over his card and prayed that there was enough left
on his limit. He waited nervously for it to come
back and felt half relieved and half anguished when
it did.

Peter and Ingrid got out of the lift at their floor. As

the doors closed behind them, Simon sank to his knees
and put his head in his hands.

'That bad, is it?' asked Lisa.

'The bank won't pay for it. What shall I do?' he
moaned.

'Just explain what happened and maybe they'll give
you half the money,' said Lisa. She despised him. Didn't
he know that dealers were supposed to act rich, even if
they weren't?

'They'll never let me take anyone out again,' said
Simon, more to himself than to Lisa. 'They'll insist on
a Japanese manager coming as well.'

Lisa offered some words of fake comfort. 'Simon,
you're just a junior member of staff. They don't expect
much of you anyway.'

Simon groaned. The words 'junior member of staff'
stabbed him like a knife. He'd assured Hannah that
he'd be assistant manager by Christmas, and now this
little setback might cost him his promotion. He walked
away sadly and Lisa, proud of her evening's work, took
a taxi all the way to the chip shop near her flat.

The next morning, Simon, for want of a better
alternative, went to Mr Kubo for help. He showed
him the request form and the place where he had
written £50 and then presented him with the receipts
that showed the actual cost of the evening. When he
understood what he was seeing, Mr Kubo laughed
loudly, and three of the Japanese managers came up
to the desk to look and laugh too. Simon smiled with
relief. Being made to look ridiculous wasn't exactly
comforting, but at least no one was angry.

'Simon, amount not important, ' said Mr Kubo. 'This
happen to junior staff many times. You must ask Mr
Kimura to sign a new form for you.'

'Yes, Mr Kubo,' said Simon, relieved that he would
get his money back but upset to be reminded again that
he was a mere junior.

Lisa smiled to show that she was pleased he wasn't
out of pocket. Inside, though, she was angry that he
had slithered his way out of trouble again. Still, he'd
had one night of worry and he'd been made to look
very stupid, so her efforts hadn't been wasted.

Simon wasn't sure whether Lisa had landed him a
large bill on purpose. Maybe she'd just been playing
the good host or had been too drunk to realise what
she was doing. He slid a sideways look at her. She
was leaning back in her chair, her feet resting on an
open drawer, and was chatting away to Jackie. Her
desk was a mess as usual and she'd made no attempt
to study the market. Simon shook his head. She was
a nice enough girl, but she needed a firm hand. When
he became assistant manager of the desk he'd soon show
her how to behave. Until then he was happy to let her
neglect her work, because it would make Mr Kimura
more determined to have some one responsible in charge
of the desk.

He, Simon, could only benefit if Lisa was seen to
be doing her work badly. He decided to do his best
to make sure that she was. She was so caught up in
her own world that she'd never notice if he set her up.
She hadn't guessed about him and Stephanie, even when
the evidence was right in front of her nose. It would be
easy to make her look bad.

Two happy dealers sat at the Corporate desk that
morning. Simon imagined his new plan would win him
his promotion quickly, Lisa was in good spirits because
not only had she managed to humiliate her loathsome
colleague, but also Frank would be back soon. The

contented pair sat looking at their screens, so lost in pleasurable thought that they didn't notice they had a call on one of their outside lines.

Mr Kubo noticed it, though. 'Simon,' he said, relieved to see that both local dealers were free to answer the call, and that therefore he himself needn't, 'line two.'

Simon went into the line, and while he was dealing with that customer Lisa answered another call on line one.

'Corporates,' she said in her I'm-so-busy-I-can-only-say-one-word voice.

'Hello, Lisa. Is Simon there?'

Lisa recognised 'the lovely Hannah's' voice straight away. 'Yes,' she said, 'but he's on the other line at the moment. How's it going?'

'Well, if I wasn't throwing up every five minutes, I'd say not bad. Can't complain, though, only another six months to go.'

'It must be hard working at the same time,' responded Lisa, as if she'd heard already from Simon that Hannah was pregnant. He must be keeping quiet about it so that Stephanie wouldn't find out.

'Yes, especially looking after young children. I can't wait for my maternity leave,' laughed Hannah.

'He's free now,' said Lisa, who suddenly felt sick herself. 'Take care of yourself. Bye.' Poor lovely Hannah, she thought. So happy to be pregnant, and all the time her husband was cheating on her. She wasn't sure what to think about Stephanie. Lisa knew what it was like to be lonely, so she supposed Stephanie couldn't help herself, although that was no excuse. As for Simon, did he feel any guilt at all? She hated him at that moment. There he sat, pretending to be so nice and sincere, when all the time he was a liar and a cheat.

Her little campaign seemed pathetic now. How could she match such a man? He was so smooth, so good at lying, she'd never be able to beat him. She'd been merely an irritation, a fly buzzing round his ears. If she didn't do something soon, she'd be squashed flat.

Chapter 22

Lisa didn't dwell long on Simon's moral deficiencies. She knew he had to be watched carefully, but once Frank came back they'd have only one more week before he returned to Japan and she didn't want to waste precious time on workplace disputes. When it came to choosing between her man and her work, Lisa made the same choice as many intelligent, well-educated young women. You can work any time, she told herself, but who knows how long a relationship will last? She tried not to be too optimistic about Frank; however, she'd had plenty of time during their two-week separation to fantasise about the future. Late at night, when she tried to fill the emptiness of her double bed with a couple of pillows, she even let herself hope that Frank would solve the Simon situation by asking her to go and live with him in Japan.

On the day of Frank's return, when she knew he was already on the plane to Heathrow, she decided that after work she'd go to his hotel in Paddington and surprise him. She didn't know the address, but she had the number, so she rang up and asked for directions. At five o'clock, she raced over to the hotel and, after checking whether Frank was back, phoned up to his room from the lobby.

'Hello. Wada speaking.' The familiar sound of his voice made her smile.

'Hi! It's me!' she said excitedly. 'Welcome back.'

'Hello, me,' laughed Frank. 'It is very nice of you to call. You have missed me very much, I think.'

'Oh yes, I have,' said Lisa still smiling. She knew his English wasn't good enough for him to know that what he'd just said made their relationship sound very one-sided. 'I can't wait to see you.'

'I just get back,' said Frank. 'But I can come later. I be in Leyton about eight thirty.'

Lisa enjoyed teasing him. 'I can't wait that long,' she said. 'I need to see you now.'

He was flattered. 'I take a taxi and get there a little earlier,' he promised.

'No,' said Lisa. 'I can't wait any more. I'm coming up now.'

'What?' asked Frank.

'I'm in the lobby,' laughed Lisa. 'I thought I'd surprise you.'

'I very surprised.' Frank sounded more shocked than anything else. 'Wait there. I just had bath. I put clothes on and come downstairs. Don't come up. I come down to you very soon.' He hung up, cutting the line and Lisa's excitement in one go.

It wasn't supposed to be like this, she thought heading for the lift. He was hiding something and she wasn't going to give him time to get rid of the evidence. When the lift stopped at Frank's floor, she half expected to see three callgirls in fake furs and leather bikinis waiting to go down. It had to be something kinky and sexual, she told herself, trying not to panic as she rushed

up the empty corridor. I hope it's not another man, she
prayed, banging on the door. She couldn't take it if
Frank turned out to be another Ken.

'Open the door!' she shouted, banging louder when
Frank failed to appear. 'It's me!' she added needlessly.
'Let me in!'

She heard the key turn, and when the door opened
Frank stood before her in his shirt and boxer shorts.

'I not ready yet,' he said making no sign that he
wanted her to come in. 'I come down very soon.'

There was no hug, no kiss and no smile of welcome.

'You're hiding something,' said Lisa. She pushed past
him into the room, headed for the wardrobe and flung
the doors open. There wasn't a naked woman sheltering
inside. There wasn't even a naked man. All she could
see were clothes on hangers and some bags of duty-free
goods on the floor.

She turned and looked at Frank. He looked back
impassively. 'The bathroom,' she said, and went to
look. It was empty. Lisa was struck by its elegance
and how nicely decorated Frank's room was with —
surprise, surprise — a double bed. 'You said it was a
cheap, horrible hotel and that you only had a single
bed,' she said accusingly. She still had the feeling he
was hiding something.

'No guests allowed,' explained Frank, colouring
slightly. He sat on the bed to put his trousers on.
As she watched him, Lisa noticed that the door of
the bedside cabinet was slightly open and a card had
slipped out. She went over and knelt down to pick it
up but Frank, seeing her move, quickly reached forward
to close the door. Suspecting she was on to something,
Lisa twisted his ear to move him out of the way. He
automatically raised his hands to protect himself and

Lisa was able to get the cabinet door wide open and
see what was inside.

There were photographs, some loose and some in
frames, three or four birthday cards and some pictures,
obviously drawn by a child. She didn't get a chance to
examine everything carefully, because Frank began to
cry and she got up to find out what was wrong.

If she had known that in Japan crying expresses
a range of emotions, from sadness at a loss for the
volleyball team of one's old school to happiness at
winning fourth prize in a golf tournament, and that
genuinely awful events, like death and natural disasters,
are usually met stoically and with dry eyes, she would
have stayed by the cabinet. But she didn't know, so she
sat down by Frank and gently rubbed his ear.

'Does it hurt that much?' she said, afraid she'd done
some real damage.

'Yes,' sobbed Frank. 'But it not make me cry. I'm
sorry. I hurt you very much.'

'What's wrong?' asked Lisa. He wasn't making any
sense, but she feared he was going to tell her something
terrible. If it's AIDS, I'll kill the bastard, she thought,
trying to remember if any of the condoms they'd used
had burst . . .

'It my birthday tomorrow.'

'I know,' said Lisa. Not only did she know but she'd
bought him some presents and was planning to cook him
a special dinner.

'Tonight, when I get back,' he continued, pausing
to blow his nose on a tissue, 'I get cards from Japan.
Cards, photographs and drawings.' He pointed to the
bedside cabinet and the things that had spilt out. He
picked up one of the drawings. 'Look at this,' he said,
and was overcome by fresh sobbing.

'How nice,' said Lisa, glancing at it. From the lines and the choice of colours, she could tell it was the work of a very young child. It was cute, but she was too concerned about the implications of Frank's grief to take much notice of its artistic potential.

'I not think I get anything because soon I be in Japan. It very expensive to send things,' said Frank between gut-wrenching sobs.

'Yes, yes. How nice for you. Now get to the point,' said Lisa impatiently. She felt like crying herself.

'My wife, she send me the things,' said Frank, and he took a deep breath in anticipation of an explosion.

'Did she know you were here, then?' said Lisa, still in the dark.

'Of course.'

Lisa looked at Frank and he looked back at her for a few seconds, then put his face in his hands and carried on sobbing. She thought back to the sad story he'd told her about his wife. Two years, he'd said. The drunken, gambling-addicted slut had left him two years ago for the Korean owner of a *pachinko* parlour. Now she was sending him things on his birthday. 'Does she want you back?' she asked.

'She never left me,' sobbed Frank. 'I make story. I love my wife. I no want leave me.'

'You lied to me?' Lisa was beginning to understand.

'Yes. I no have son. I have two daughters.' He showed her one of the photos. 'Look at their lovely faces.'

'Fuck the photos!' said Lisa angrily. 'Your wife never left you?'

'Yes,' said Frank quietly.

At a moment like this you can make certain choices. You can, with dignity, stand up and leave. You can sit

and cry. Or you can do something very nasty by way
of revenge.

Lisa chose the first option. 'Frank,' she said, getting
to her feet, 'give me one last kiss and I'll get out of
your life.'

Relieved that she'd taken things so well, he stood up
too, and opened his arms to give her a final embrace.
'*Aaaaaaaaaaaaaagh!*'

She'd meant to choose the first option but the third
one came more naturally. Kneeing Frank in the groin
and watching him fall to the floor in agony was far
more satisfying than simply keeping her dignity.

'Take that back to your wife, you bastard!' she said,
and she slammed out of the room.

Frank lay there, groaning and temporarily paralysed.
Why had he told her the truth? he asked himself. He
should have told her the things were from his sister.
If he hadn't panicked, she'd have believed him and he
wouldn't be in agony now. She must really like him
to have reacted like that. He was in pain both from
the assault on his testicles and from the loss of such
a passionate young woman. One more week, that was
all they had left, and he'd gone and ruined it.

Lisa stormed out of the hotel and hailed a taxi.
'Leyton, please,' she told the driver.

'What, in this traffic?' he said. 'You'd be better off
going on the tube.'

'Are you refusing to take me?' Lisa asked.

'No, love.' The driver saw her eyes fill with tears
and he decided that if she thought she could afford it
he'd take her. 'Cheer up! It can't be that bad,' he said
as the tears started to fall.

He had a most entertaining journey, because he heard
the whole story as they inched their way eastwards.

When Lisa came to the bit about how she had kneed Frank, he winced. 'You women certainly know how to do a man in, don't you?' he said, squirming in his seat.

'He deserved it,' replied Lisa bitterly.

'Well, he deserved something all right,' agreed the driver, though not necessarily, he thought, what Lisa had given him. 'How old did you say he was again?'

'Thirty-seven,' said Lisa, 'or at least he will be tomorrow.'

'The dirty sod,' said the driver, thinking that Frank was a lucky man to have dazzled a young girl, and he wasn't even rich. 'Well, you're well rid of him now. You just make sure you get a better one next time.'

The taxi pulled up outside her flat and she got out to pay the fare.

'Are you going to be all right?' asked the driver.

'Yes, I'll be fine,' said Lisa, and she gave him a large tip.

The phone was ringing when she opened the door. She guessed it was Frank, so she ignored it and went into the kitchen to pour herself a large whisky. After a while it stopped. Five minutes later it started up again and she decided to answer it.

'Hello,' she said as casually as she could.

'Lisa?' said Frank, glad she'd got home safely. 'You were so upset when you left, I was worried about you. I am sorry to hurt you.'

Lisa hesitated. She was still angry with him, but the concern in his voice softened her a little. 'I'm fine,' she said eventually.

'I think we should talk more,' he said. 'I want you to understand everything.'

'What is there to understand? You're married and

that's that,' replied Lisa. It was over; she just had to
get used to it.

'But I want to see you,' said Frank. 'I don't want
things to end like this. We can still have a good time.
Can you forgive me?'

'It's a bit soon to be asking that, isn't it?' snapped
Lisa. 'You've just told me that everything you said on
our first date about your family was a lie, and now you
want me to forgive you, just like that. What do you
think I am?'

'I just want to see you again,' pleaded Frank. 'You
so good to me. You come to give me a lovely surprise
and I spoil it all. I am so sorry. I want to make you
happy again.'

'And how do you think you're going to manage that?'
said Lisa sourly. 'You love your wife and don't want to
leave her and you're going to make me happy as well.
Dream on, Frank! It doesn't work like that.'

'We have one more week,' he persisted. 'I can give
you a very good time and then when we say goodbye
we have happy memories of each other. If we finish
like this we have nothing but pain.'

Lisa didn't know what to say. It was easy finishing
with Frank in her head, but now that he had said sorry
and wanted her back, albeit for just one week, she was
ashamed to admit she was tempted to accept.

'I'm too tired for this now, Frank,' she said, hoping
that she would have the strength to do the right thing
if she gave herself more time. 'I'll have to think
it over.'

'I understand,' said Frank disappointedly. 'If you
want to talk to me, I be here.'

That night was torture for Lisa. She rapidly drained
the whisky bottle, raging all the while against herself

and the world for her bad luck. She couldn't believe she'd been stupid enough to fall for a man like him. The thought that everyone except her probably knew he had a wife and two daughters in Japan was too humiliating. And now, to make things even worse, he'd said that he needed her for that last week and, instead of telling him where to put his happy memories, she'd told him she would think about it.

A week of pleasure he had offered her. Was his ego so large that he thought he could wipe out the pain of his lies with a week of pleasure? Lisa thought of their nights together. Could seven nights of sex with a middle-aged, married Japanese man who sang like Elvis possibly make up for the hurt she felt now?

The answer came loud and clear: yes. At this point she realised that she was a very sad case. She thought about her short but disastrous relationship history. She thought of Ken and how he'd deceived her. 'Bastard,' she said cursing his memory. Then she thought of Frank. Frank, who was married with two daughters. Frank, who had sung to her and made love Japanese-style. Frank, who was a lying, cheating swine. Just like Ken. 'Bastards!'

At four in the morning she was woken by the urge to drink a bucket of water. She staggered to the kitchen, got a bottle of mineral water from the fridge and then headed to her bedroom. Having quenched her thirst, she was able to think more clearly, and she came to a decision.

Frank was fun to be with. She'd enjoyed their affair very much. She'd even thought she loved him, although now she wasn't sure about that. Everyone at work already knew about their relationship, so all the damage had been done. Why should they stop now just because she knew he was married, not separated as he had told her? It seemed silly to deny herself pleasure for the sake of mere pride. Frank was right. They should spend their last week having fun, and when he left she'd put her life straight. The truth was that she couldn't face going back to her lonely life quite so soon. Having a man had been a refreshing change, and she wasn't yet ready to renew the batteries of her vibrator. Her pride could be shelved for a week, she told herself firmly. Besides, work would be unbearable if he was there and not with her any longer — everyone would wonder what had happened and maybe they would guess he was married, if they didn't already know, and that would be even more humiliating. Lisa was sure the local staff didn't know about his wife, because if they did they would have teased her about it by now.

Lisa thought about Stephanie and could understand why she was having an affair with Simon. There are times when you just can't help yourself. Lisa knew she should turn her back on Frank, but she didn't feel able to. She'd been angry with him at first and had wanted never to see him again. But now, sitting alone in her flat, all she wanted was to feel his arms round her.

On the way to Frank's hotel a few hours later, Lisa rationalised her behaviour. It all seemed very simple to her. Forget what had happened and carry on having fun. What was wrong with that? What harm would it do to stay with him for one more week? Six weeks of orgasms had distorted Lisa's sense of reality, and by the time she reached Frank's room she had convinced herself that she was doing the right thing.

He was waiting for her. 'I hope all night you come, so I sit up all night,' he said, opening his arms to give her a hug.

Lisa pushed him away. 'Not so fast. You haven't apologised properly.' She didn't really need to hear Frank say 'Sorry' again, but she thought that, for the sake of her dignity, he ought to suffer for a little longer.

'I understand,' he said. 'Let's kneel down and I give you proper Japanese apology.'

'OK,' said Lisa, slightly amused, and she knelt. 'I hope this isn't one of your sex games?'

'No, I very serious.' said Frank, his face twisting in pain as he knelt opposite her.

'Does it hurt?' asked Lisa, glad that it did.

'Yes, you hurt me very much,' said Frank, 'but I think they still working.'

'Well, that's nice to hear,' said Lisa. There wasn't much point in being with him if he couldn't perform, even if he was good with his hands. 'Happy birthday, by the way.'

'Thank you,' said Frank. 'Now I start.' He leant forward and put his hands on the floor in front of him, then bowed down until his forehead touched the floor. 'Please forgive me,' he said, his voice muffled. 'I tell you lies and I hurt you very much. Please forgive me.'

Lisa liked seeing Frank on his knees before her. It made her feel powerful, and she was able to convince herself that she hadn't lost any dignity at all by coming back to meet him.

'Very nicely done,' she said, ruffling his hair. 'You can get up now.'

Frank sighed with relief. 'Thank you very much,' he said getting up. 'Now you get in bed and I cook breakfast.'

Lisa took off her shoes and got into bed. Frank poured boiling water onto two cups of instant noodles.

They weren't her first choice for breakfast in bed on a Saturday morning, but she saw how tenderly he stirred them and how much care he took when placing the little polystyrene cups on the bedside cabinet, and she felt affection flood through her. She still adored Frank, even if he was a lying, cheating swine.

Frank almost snuffed out Lisa's candle of affection when he started eating. He slurped up nearly half the noodles in one go, without stopping for breath, and the noise was tremendous. That Mo should stick with Ron, despite his revolting table manners, wasn't so hard to understand now – after all, Lisa was doing much the same thing. When the last noodle had disappeared into his mouth, he lifted the pot to his lips and loudly drank the remainder of the soup. Thank God that's over, she thought, smiling at him.

He, not knowing how close he had come to putting her off, reached out and gently stroked her cheek. 'I sorry I lie to you. It all my fault.'

'Yes, I know. Don't do it again,' said Lisa sternly, although she didn't feel stern, she felt relaxed and comfortable being with him again.

'You no hurt me any more?' asked Frank, his testicles twingeing at the memory of last night's assault.

'I don't know. It depends on how you behave, doesn't it?'

'From now, I will be very good,' he promised.

'So will I then,' she said, crossing her fingers.

They made love, very careful and gently so that Frank's pain was minimised.

As they lay dozing in each other's arms afterwards, they were woken by a knock at the door. It was Big Jock and Tom. Frank hadn't told Lisa, but he'd spent the previous night drinking whisky with them and

pouring out his woes. They were here to see if he had
recovered, and couldn't understand what Lisa was doing
in his bed. Well, they could see what she had been
doing, but according to Frank she'd viciously assaulted
him the night before and now here she was in his
bed, naked.

Frank shuffled them outside the door while Lisa
put on some clothes. When she was decent they came
back in.

'Good morning, Lisa. Are you OK?' asked Big Jock.

'Yes, I'm fine. And you?'

She smiled at them and they backed away. How
could she be smiling after what had happened? Was
she mad? They could see that Frank was still limping
slightly. She was definitely a dangerous woman. Had
she smiled like this just before her knee hit his groin?

'We just here to see if Frank want come to Kew Gar-
dens. We go now. Goodbye,' said Jock, and they fled.

'What's wrong with them?' Lisa asked.

'They think you hurt them too because they no tell
you I married.'

'Maybe I will later.'

Frank looked so startled that she laughed. To show
that he understood her English joke, he laughed too,
but he didn't find it funny. He couldn't understand
how she could laugh about an act that had caused
him such pain. Then a terrible thought struck him.
She'd come back to him and she was being very
loving, but she hadn't actually said she'd forgiven
him. She was smiling now, but she might be acting
out some terrible plan to take revenge on him. She
was a powerful woman with strong emotions; had
she really accepted the present situation? He hoped
she had, but he couldn't be sure. He decided that

he'd treat her very, very carefully over the next seven
days.

They went back to Lisa's flat, where she gave Frank
a very happy birthday. He got a double cassette of *The
World's Greatest Love Songs* and two pairs of high-cut
briefs from Marks & Sparks. She'd bought him a new
watch as well, but now that he was only a short-term
lover she decided he wasn't worth the expense. She'd
try to get her money back on Monday.

Frank spent the evening wiggling his hips in his new
briefs and miming to the songs on the tape, while Lisa
prepared a romantic dinner for two. The meal was a
great success. She'd bought a selection of Indian food
from M&S and pretended to Frank that it was all her
own cooking. He said it was the best food that he'd
tasted since he'd been in England and that he was very
happy she'd accepted his apology.

He went back to his hotel on Sunday morning, saying
he was worn out from his trip. Lisa was sorry to see
him go. While she was with him, she could convince
herself she was doing the sensible thing, but once she
was alone again she was plagued by guilt, anger, sorrow
and any other negative emotion that felt like making an
appearance. She doubted whether she'd be able to cope
with the week at work. Not only did she have Simon
to think about, but she'd also have to try to keep calm
about Frank.

As it turned out, the trainees weren't in the dealing-
room. During their last week, they had to spend a day
in each of the other departments to get to know more
about the London branch. Mr Kimura had anticipated
a rough time on the Corporate desk, and he wanted to
remove Frank from the danger zone.

The first indication Lisa had that things were going

to be a lot tougher than she thought was on Tuesday morning when Simon was called over to Mr Kimura's desk and told that Mr Aono was planning a visit to a major car manufacturer in Turin in a few weeks' time. Mr Aono had suggested that one of the corporate dealers go out there next week to have a preliminary meeting, and Mr Kimura had chosen Simon.

'If you do well,' he said, 'it will be very good for your future here.'

Simon took this to mean that he'd be promoted if the trip was a success, and couldn't hide his triumph when he asked Lisa for the car manufacturer's file.

'It's where it always is,' she replied. 'Why do you need it? Did they call when I was off the desk?' She'd never managed to deal with them and she hated to think that Simon had succeeded where she had failed.

'No,' he said. 'I'm visiting Turin next week, so I need to read the file.'

'But they're non-UK. Why are you going?' demanded Lisa.

'I don't know,' he said, shrugging.

Lisa badly wanted advice on how to handle the situation. She thought about asking Frank, but he hadn't been very supportive so far and she didn't want to argue with him again. Mr Kubo would take half the day to understand that there was a business trip and the rest of the day to understand that Simon was going instead of her. She looked around the dealing-room. Andy had been very helpful when she was new, but he liked Simon. Leo would just laugh at her. Perhaps if she told Stephanie about Hannah, she might be on Lisa's side? But then again, she might already know and just think that Lisa was being a bitch.

Her eyes settled on Aki-san. He'd hardly spoken to

her since she left the Futures desk, but she knew he
hated Mr Kimura. Maybe he hated Simon as well? Even
if he didn't, he would at least tell her his honest opinion.
When he went out to get a coffee, she followed him.

'Can I speak to you?' she asked.

'Yes, but quickly. I very busy today.'

'Well, I need some help.'

Aki-san looked at her coldly. Her affair with Frank
had disappointed him. 'You should speak to Mr Kubo.
He is your manager now.'

'I know, but I don't think he can help.' Lisa tried
not to sound too pathetic. Aki-san trod on the face of
weakness, but if she stood firm he might bend a little.

Aki-san gave a grim little smile. It was true: Mr Kubo
could barely help himself, let alone look after Lisa. He
should never have been made her manager. 'Is this
about work?' he asked, suddenly hit by the thought
that Frank might have made her pregnant.

'Yes,' said Lisa.

'That's good,' said Aki-san, meaning it was good she
wasn't pregnant, but not that she had trouble at work.
When he saw her puzzled look, he wanted to explain
what he meant, but he didn't know where to start in
English so he just said, 'Lunchtime, we go for a pizza
and we talk, OK.'

'Thanks, Aki-san,' said Lisa with relief.

Sitting opposite him, with a large hot-and-spicy
between them and half a pint of lager each, Lisa
was reminded of the first occasion when she'd had
her throat scorched by chilli peppers. He had been very
tough with her then. Maybe it wasn't such a good idea
to confide in him now.

'What is your problem Lisa?' asked Aki-san.

There was no turning back, she realised nervously.

'Simon is going to Italy next week on a business trip.'

'Why is that a problem?'

'It's my customer. I should go,' answered Lisa.

'You had trip last year,' replied Aki-san. He already knew about Turin, which had been discussed at the managers' meeting. Simon had been seen as the best choice because he would soon be in charge of the desk and he needed some experience of foreign business trips.

'That's beside the point,' said Lisa. 'I deal with non-UK customers, so I should be the one to go.'

Aki-san took a bite of his pizza and chewed as he slowly digested what she'd said.

'You both Haru Bank dealers,' he said eventually. 'It not important who go.'

His words were a blow, but Lisa refused to give up yet. 'So why did Mr Kimura divide up the desk?' she asked. 'Why did he say that I should deal with non-UK and Simon should deal with UK customers?' She was getting cross with herself for asking Aki-san for help. She should have known he wouldn't support her.

Aki-san took another bite of pizza. He had been at the London branch for three years but, try as he might, he could not get used to the attitude of the local staff. In Japan, it had taken him five years to be posted to head office and another three years before he was dealing. Yet, here was Lisa, younger than he'd been when he started at the bank, who had in less than one year, started dealing, gone on a foreign business trip and got a good job on the Corporate desk. Didn't she realise that the women graduates at head office had no chance of getting a job like hers? She was very lucky to have got this far so quickly. Why couldn't she be content? Or at least why couldn't she behave herself?

'You forget everything I teach you,' he said, cursing his poor English. There was so much he wanted to say to her but couldn't.

'You didn't actually *teach* me anything,' answered Lisa before she could stop herself.

'I teach you to think for yourself. I teach you to work hard and no make mistakes,' replied Aki-san icily despite the hot chillis he'd been eating. 'But you forget everything. You disappoint me.'

Lisa bent her head. Aki-san despised her and he wasn't going to help at all. She had never actively sought his good opinion, but now she knew she didn't have it she realised how much she valued it. Perhaps the Mistake really had been her fault. Perhaps Simon wasn't really bad. Perhaps she was just paranoid.

Aki-san realised he had been a little too severe. He liked Lisa. She had been amusing to work with and he wanted to see her do well. 'You must accept things,' he said gently. 'Simon is older than you. He is married. He is very careful with his work and so he is the best choice to be assistant manager.'

'What?' said Lisa, looking up sharply. 'Assistant manager?'

Aki-san cursed himself again. His flow of English had seemed too good to be true. Now he had said too much. 'Simon will be assistant manager soon. You must accept this.'

'No way!' said Lisa shaking her head.

'This is Kimura-san's choice. Simon not real manager,' he said, in an effort to soften the blow, 'only a title.'

'If it's only a title, why can't I have it too?'

She was impossible, thought Aki-san, and he said sternly, 'You must behave and work hard.'

Lisa knew it was time to grovel. 'Aki-san,' she said meekly, 'I know I've let you down recently, but I will try very hard to be better. Can't you ask Mr Kimura to give me a chance to show I can do my job well?' She didn't really care about doing her job well, she only wanted to prevent Simon from being her superior, but she couldn't admit that to Aki-san.

Aki-san looked at her consideringly. Lisa tried not to crumple under his gaze and put all her efforts into looking like someone he could depend on. It worked. 'I help you this time,' he said at last. 'I talk to Kubo-san and we will see Kimura-san together. You must promise to make no mistakes, OK.'

'I promise,' said Lisa, beaming at him, and to show she meant it she took a large bite of hot-and-spicy.

It was worth the pain. The following day Mr Kimura called Lisa over to his desk. 'The managers and I think that you should go to Turin. You have experience of foreign business trips and so you are the best person to go.' He didn't add that if the trip was a disaster it would show everyone he was doing the right thing by promoting Simon.

'Thank you, Mr Kimura,' murmured Lisa. Up yours, Simon, she said to herself, and she got up to return to her desk.

'Just one thing, Lisa,' said Mr Kimura, indicating that she should sit down again. He leant over and lowered his voice. 'If you don't do well, I will be very unhappy with you.'

Lisa understood his threat completely. 'I won't let you down,' she said, hoping she could keep her word.

Mr Kimura watched as she walked back to her desk.

How he loved the sway of her hips. How he wanted
to plant soft kisses on the back of her neck. If she'd
been an office lady at the head office, he might just
have tried.

Simon was quick to go to Mr Kimura's desk when he
heard about the change of plans. He couldn't understand
how Lisa had managed to pull this one off.

'The desk cannot be left without our best dealer,'
explained Mr Kimura, and Simon, although disappointed at missing out on Turin, was flattered that
he was seen as indispensable.

Aki-san had known that the way to get Lisa on
the trip was to say that Simon couldn't be spared.
He realised she wouldn't be pleased if she knew how
he'd persuaded Mr Kimura, but that couldn't be helped.
She'd got what she wanted, and it didn't matter how
he had achieved it. All she had to do now was to prove
that she was just as capable as Simon when dealing with
important customers. As she would be saying goodbye to
Frank this weekend, Aki-san didn't hold out much hope
for the success of her trip, and he didn't look forward
to being in the same room as Mr Kimura if she did mess
things up.

Chapter 23

———— ————

Two days before their departure, the trainees were given a riotous farewell party down the pub under the bank. Three strip-a-grams were hired and each one, aware of the competition, became more outrageous than the last. Frank had to use his teeth to remove a banana from the fur panties of a jungle woman, Tom got a traffic warden who took his trousers down and spanked his bare buttocks, and Big Jock, who had the misfortune to be last, was stripped naked by an enormously fat lady wearing only a string bikini and six-inch stilettos.

Now that they had more experience of the English sense of humour, the trainees could see the funny side of being sexually humiliated in public, although Big Jock wasn't too happy about his wares being exposed to everyone in the pub. Drunk as he was, he didn't fail to notice that people now wiggled their little fingers at him and called him 'Wee Jock'. Tom, despite having a sore backside, had found the experience strangely thrilling and he looked forward to introducing this form of sexual stimulation to his wife in Japan. Frank was just thankful that he had managed to remain fully clothed.

The party moved on to a spare-rib restaurant in the West End, where everyone sat with plastic bibs and greasy fingers, chomping their way through piles of ribs and having drinking-contests with exotic-sounding cocktails. They got louder and louder until eventually they were asked to leave. A few people were still willing and able to go on, so they decided to go to a casino on Park Lane. Frank was eager to go along, but Lisa pulled him back. She had laughed and had fun with everyone throughout the evening. Now it was time he paid her some attention.

In the taxi on the way to Leyton, they didn't talk very much. Frank was so drunk that he had forgotten how to move his lips and Lisa, aided by alcohol, was feeling all dramatic and tearful. She didn't trust herself to talk, in case she started begging him not to leave.

Once inside the flat, Frank collapsed into a heap and Lisa spent their precious time together trying to get him undressed and into the bed. He was too heavy for her to move, so she left him on the floor with his trousers round his ankles.

The next morning, when the alarm went off, Frank woke up feeling as though he had been run over by a herd of elephants. 'What time is it?' he said feebly, trying to sit up.

'Six o'clock,' said Lisa loudly. She'd drunk plenty of water before going to bed, so she only had a mild headache.

The room was spinning, so Frank lay down again. 'My head,' he moaned, clutching his forehead.

Lisa stood over him. 'You shouldn't have drunk so much,' she said unsympathetically. As she looked down at him, she thought what an inviting target he was for a good swift kick. Unfortunately, she was barefoot and she didn't want to risk injuring her toes, so she just trod on his chest as she stepped over him.

Frank moaned again. 'Why you hurt me? I have pain in my head, I no want it on my body.'

'Look at the state of you,' said Lisa in disgust. 'Our last day and you're like this. Typical.' She went into the bathroom and slammed the door.

When she came back into the bedroom to get dressed, Frank had shed his trousers and managed to haul himself into bed. To increase his suffering, she went to the window and wrenched the curtains open. As the bright sunlight poured into the room, Frank sank under the covers and begged for mercy so pathetically that she took pity on him and made him some black coffee and a slice of dry toast.

'Ring me when you get back to your hotel,' she called out as she left for work.

Frank didn't have to go in, because it was his last day in London. He was going to go back to the hotel to pack, and would meet Lisa in the evening at Covent Garden. He hadn't told her, but he had arranged a very romantic evening. They'd start off at a cocktail bar, then go to the restaurant he had taken her to on their first date. Their last date would end perfectly, with a night at the Savoy.

Apart from his hangover, he was in good spirits. Only one more day till he went back to his family in Japan. Before that happy time, he had Lisa to take care of. Their affair was coming to an end and, although he was sorry to be saying goodbye to her, he was relieved it was almost over. Being an adulterer was too much of a strain. He shuddered when he thought how difficult things would have been if the affair had taken place in his home town, where his wife and his girlfriend might well have run into each other.

He could understand why some of his friends had lovers, though, because despite the risks there was something very satisfying about being desired by a young, attractive woman. Lisa had made him feel alive again and he felt he owed it to her to make up for the hurt she'd feel when he left. If he made sure that their last evening together was perfect, she'd have good memories of him, he thought, smiling as he remembered all their wonderful times in bed. When she was alone at night, she'd be comforted by those memories.

His only worry was that she might be so upset at his leaving that she'd cause a scene. He pushed firmly from his mind nightmare images of Lisa hanging on to the taxi door as he left for the airport, or, even worse, following him to Heathrow and wailing loudly as he went through the departure gates. Everything will be fine, he told himself firmly, trying to shut out his nagging doubts.

Lisa had intended to take the day off and luxuriate in the melancholy caused by Frank's decision to abandon her and return to his wife and children, but the Turin trip meant that she couldn't. Instead of spending the day hanging on Frank's arm, making his sleeve damp with her tears, she had to trek into the City, to her desk at Haru Bank, where she was so busy that apart from a brief wallow at lunchtime she had almost no chance to think about Frank.

'You will fly to Milan on Tuesday evening,' said Mr Kimura, during the first of a series of preparatory meetings. 'You will stay the night in a hotel and on Wednesday morning Mr Takahashi from the Milan office will collect you and you will go to Turin with him. You will fly back to England on Wednesday afternoon and come to work on Thursday.'

Where you will be exterminated, said Lisa to herself, thinking of what would happen if she cocked everything up. All the same, she was looking forward to going to Italy, and a few days' sightseeing might help her get over Frank. 'It seems a shame to go for only one day,' she said. 'If I book some holiday, can I stay until Sunday?'

'This is not a pleasure trip, it is work, and you must come back to report on the meeting,' said Mr Kimura, shocked that she should even consider enjoying herself.

'I could do that by fax.'

'You must come back on Wednesday. Our insurance doesn't cover you if you stay any longer,' explained Mr Kimura, frowning. 'I can send someone else if you aren't serious about the trip.'

'No, that's all right,' said Lisa hastily. 'I'll come straight back.'

'Now, you must study the market carefully so that you can give sensible predictions. You must also learn about the history of Haru Bank and the recent developments in the Japanese economy.'

'Yes, Mr Kimura,' said Lisa. She tried to sound as if she meant it, but she'd already decided to leave the Japanese economy and the history of Haru Bank to Mr Takahashi.

'You must also arrange a meeting with Mr Yoshida, who will tell you exactly what is expected from you. Do you have any questions?' asked Mr Kimura, expecting her to have a list of questions already drawn up.

'Yes,' said Lisa.

He smiled. She had obviously learnt a thing or two from the Scandinavian trip, he thought proudly.

'When I get to Milan on Tuesday evening,' continued Lisa, 'will the bank pay for my evening meal?' She was looking forward to a night out on the bank's money.

'Certainly not,' snapped Mr Kimura. 'You will eat on the plane.'

'I see,' said Lisa. Tuesday night looked like being an early one.

Mr Kimura was beginning to wish that he hadn't listened to Aki-san and Mr Kubo. 'Now, go back to your desk and start your preparations,' he said wearily.

Lisa didn't get much opportunity to follow any of Mr Kimura's orders. There was a figure out that afternoon, and she was too busy to do anything except answer the phones and deal, all the time keeping an eye on the clock to make sure she finished by five; she had no intention of staying late on Frank's last day. What with market forces and the allure of her soon-to-be ex-lover, all her good intentions about getting ready for the trip came to nothing, but she wasn't too concerned because she still had Monday and Tuesday.

Over cocktails, in a jungle-themed bar in Covent Garden, Frank told Lisa of his plans for the evening and rather than being thrilled, as he'd expected, she was horrified. The memory of their first night together was very special. They'd had some good times, but nothing had compared with that night. To return to the same places, knowing he was leaving the next day, would be unbearable.

'I don't want to go,' she said firmly.

'I already checked in and moved my things there. Please come,' pleaded Frank.

'No, I couldn't bear it,' said Lisa, and her eyes filled with tears.

He leant forward and stroked her face. 'I know you upset, but I give you a wonderful last night. You be very happy after.' *And I won't have wasted my money*, he said to himself. 'It not the same room,' he added, as if that made all the difference.

'You make it sound so simple.'

'It is,' said Frank, sensing that she could be persuaded to change her mind. 'Think of the lovely big bath, the warm, soft double bed — and,' he added with a chuckle, 'the lovely bidet. I think you enjoy that very much.'

Lisa smiled at the memory. 'Keep going,' she said.

'I can give you lovely massage and then we can make love all night with no worries about your neighbours. After, we lie in bed and drink champagne. Then maybe we can have another bath. Sounds good, doesn't it?'

'I suppose it does, when you put it like that,' said Lisa. 'All right, you win. But you have to promise one thing.'

'What's that?'

'No more buckets of ice,' said Lisa. They laughed and Frank, relieved that the plans had not been altered, bought two more strawberry margueritas.

Later, as they sat in the restaurant, Lisa found it as hot and uncomfortable as before, but this time, having slept with Frank so often, she'd chosen her underwear with regard to comfort rather than sex appeal so she wasn't bothered by itchy thighs or a too-tight suspender belt. She'd also eaten enough Japanese food to have become a dab hand with the chopsticks, and she picked up the assorted bits of meat and vegetables with confidence. Tonight, their last night, there'd be no greasy stains on her bosom and no mess on the floor.

She thought back to the first time she had sat there with Frank surrounded by fallen chopsticks and dropped pieces of food. He'd told her about his wife running off with the *pachinko*-parlour owner and she, believing his every word, had felt sorry for him. His vulnerability was one of the things that had attracted her to him. Lisa looked at him. He'd recovered from his hangover and he'd taken the trouble to look his best for her. She remembered how she'd felt about him when she first knew him, how all she'd noticed were his flashing teeth, his curly perm and his bad taste in suits. It was amazing how a few romantic songs had transformed him into someone desirable. She wondered if she'd have felt anything for him if she hadn't heard him sing. Probably not, she said to herself, seeing, as only a 22-year-old can, the lines round his eyes and the grey hair at his temples.

'What are you thinking?' asked Frank, noticing her scrutiny.

'I was just thinking about your voice,' answered Lisa. 'I was wondering whether we'd have got together if I hadn't heard you sing.'

'Of course,' he said confidently. 'I have many good things about me, as you have found out. You would have liked me even if I hadn't sung. Or if not you, someone else,' he added with a smile.

'What did you say?' asked Lisa.

'Just a little joke,' said Frank hastily. 'I would not play with just any woman.'

He lifted Lisa's hand and made to kiss it but she snatched it back. His little joke had hit a sore spot, and she guessed there was some truth behind what he said. He'd probably made up his mind to have an affair with someone before he'd even got off the aeroplane.

If she hadn't gone out with him he would indeed have tried to find someone else.

She suddenly felt very foolish. Here she was planning to spend a night with Frank, when she knew that tomorrow he would leave her and go back to his wife. Had she no pride at all? If she had, she'd have finished with him the week before, when she found out he was married. It wasn't too late to save her dignity: she didn't have to stay with him.

'This is a mistake,' she said. 'I ought to go.' She stood up to leave.

'No!' Frank was horrified. He grabbed her wrist to stop her walking away. 'Please, Lisa,' he begged. 'Just a stupid joke. I no mean anything. Of course you are special. You and I, we have had too much to drink and it makes us say foolish things. Please don't go.'

Lisa was slightly mollified, but not enough to sit down again.

Seeing her hesitate, Frank thought he was close to appeasing her. He took a deep breath and softly began to hum 'Love Me Tender'.

Lisa knew that she should clonk him on the nose for presuming she could be so easily persuaded, but there was something about his voice that moved her. Instead of wanting to leave, she now wanted to sink into his arms and be held. It couldn't hurt her pride that much to have one more night of fun with him.

'Oh what the hell,' she said. 'Let's just go for it.'

Frank had thought Lisa demanding on their first night, but on their last night, she was not just demanding, she was awe-inspiring. As they indulged in furious foreplay and lusty love-making Frank feared for the cartilage in his knees, the muscles in his back and his heart, which beat a louder and louder accompaniment

to Lisa's unrestrained moans and shrieks of pleasure.
'Let me live long enough to see Japan, once more,' he
prayed silently. But he didn't really want it to end.
This night marked the start of his path to old age
and retirement. He'd soon be forty. Never again in
his life would he experience such agonising pleasure.
He looked at Lisa and loved her − really loved her −
for the first time. He loved the way she moved around
without embarrassment. He loved her for giving herself
to him again, and he loved her for being so young and
so fresh.

Lisa didn't know if it was love that she felt, and
anyway she had no time to think about it. She was
too busy milking the pleasure from Frank, too busy
bouncing off the walls. Boing! There goes an orgasm.
Boing! and another, boing! and another. On and on until
she passed out from sheer enjoyment.

The next morning, Lisa was the first to wake up.
She looked at Frank sleeping beside her, and felt deeply
sad that this was the last time they'd share a bed.
She made herself get up and moved around quietly,
putting her clothes on and picking her things up,
being careful not to wake Frank. She thought of
his wife in Japan, who'd be cleaning the house in
preparation for his arrival. She imagined the excited
faces of his daughters as they opened the presents he
had bought for them, and she started to cry. She cried
because she had to say goodbye to him and she didn't
want to. She wanted him to chose her instead of his
wife and his children. But he hadn't, and now he was
leaving.

In the bathroom, she looked in the mirror and
forced herself to stop crying. 'Pull yourself together,'
she ordered her reflection. 'He's a thirty-seven-year-old

married banker with two kids. You don't want to spend your life with him, do you?'

Dressed and ready to go, she looked once more at Frank. She didn't want him to wake. If he did, she'd find it even harder to let him go. It was better this way. She sat down at the desk and began to write.

Dear Frank,
I'm sorry to leave without saying goodbye.
Please forgive me.
        Love
Lisa

She read the letter through, then crumpled it up. Why should she apologise? He was the one who was leaving her. She took a fresh piece of paper and tried again.

Dear Frank
I hope you'll rub me tender again some time.
Have a nice trip.
        Love
Lisa

That was more like it. She put the note on the pillow and quietly left the room.

Frank woke up ten minutes after she'd gone. He saw the note, read it and wept.

Lisa's message might have been light-hearted and flippant but her real feelings were very different. She spent a dreary weekend mourning the loss of what seemed like the great love of her life. As she drowned Frank's memory in alcohol, she became more and more pessimistic about the future. She wondered how many

failed relationships it would take for her to end up
like Jackie, who never sought emotional involvement
with the bodies she went to bed with — for her, men
were for sex and nothing much else. Since the average
male's sexual technique is no more than a quick rub
on the clit, a squeeze of the nipples and then three
minutes' thrusting in the vagina, Lisa found the prospect
depressing.

On Monday morning she phoned the office and said
she was sick.

Jackie heard the news and rang her at home. 'Are
you all right?' she asked.

'No. I feel awful,' replied Lisa in her best hoarse
whisper. 'It came on all of a sudden.'

Jackie laughed. 'All of a sudden, my eye. You're not
sick at all.'

'Yes, I am,' said Lisa. 'I'm sick of men, I'm sick of
work and I'm sick of my life.'

'Oh dear.' Jackie was more amused than sympathetic.
'You *have* got it bad. I suppose you've been making
yourself feel worse by hitting the gin as well.'

'Whisky, actually,' said Lisa.

'Well, you'd better stop. You're going to Italy tomorrow. You're supposed to be impressing the bosses.'

'Don't remind me,' groaned Lisa. 'They'll walk all
over me.'

'Nonsense,' said Jackie briskly. 'Just pull yourself
together. There's plenty more fish in the sea. Don't mess
everything up just because he's gone back to his wife.'

'All right, all right, I get the message,' said Lisa. 'I'll
be in to work tomorrow.'

'Wearing lipstick,' said Jackie.

'Yes, wearing lipstick,' laughed Lisa, 'and I'll even
shave my legs.'

'That's the spirit.' Jackie was pleased to hear her bouncing back. 'Speak to you tomorrow. Goodbye.'

Lisa was as good as her word. She took extra care with her appearance, because she wanted to show that it wasn't only Simon who could put on a fine outer show. Mr Kimura was pleased to see that she was taking his words seriously although, in reality, he would prefer her to mess things up so that she would be forced to accept Simon's promotion without complaint.

She was briefed in the morning by Mr Yoshida about what she should and should not say at the meeting. Lisa wasn't worried about this aspect of the trip. In Scandinavia she'd learnt how to talk a lot without saying anything at all, and thought she'd got quite good at it. What did worry her were the gifts. Mr Yoshida gave her a selection to put in her briefcase.

'Only give the pens to the right kind of people,' he said. 'If they aren't the right kind, just give them a scarf or tie, depending on their sex.' He had been very good at English grammar at school, so he could speak in long sentences, confident that his verbs, nouns and prepositions were where they should be.

'The right kind of people?' asked Lisa.

'Yes. We don't want to waste money by giving them to the wrong kind of people,' he said. 'Those people should just be given the scarves or ties.'

'I'm sorry,' said Lisa, 'but could you tell me who are the right kind of people?'

'The senior ones,' said Mr Yoshida, frowning a little. She seemed too inexperienced to be allowed to go on a business trip alone. 'Look at their business cards and then give them their gift accordingly,' he explained, wishing she would stop wasting his time.

Lisa knew it wasn't that easy, because it wasn't

always clear from the titles on the cards exactly who was the senior manager and who was a junior, especially if they came from different departments, but something in Mr Yoshida's expression told her it wouldn't be advisable to pursue the issue.

She thought she'd better change the subject. 'What time should I take the taxi to Heathrow?'

Mr Yoshida gave a grim laugh. 'Taxi? It take too long in the daytime. You must not waste Haru Bank's money. I always travel by the underground, and so should you. What time is your flight?'

'Seven o'clock,' said Lisa.

'If you leave at four thirty you will have plenty of time,' he said.

'What about when I get to Milan? How do I find the hotel?' asked Lisa.

'You take a taxi,' replied Mr Yoshida. 'In a foreign country, the bank's policy is different. You must take a taxi because it is the safest way for you to get to your hotel. If you don't take a taxi and something happens that is bad, you will be in very big trouble.'

'I see,' said Lisa. How fond managers were of the term 'very big trouble', she thought ruefully. She hoped she wouldn't do anything on the trip that would mean finding out what they did to young bank workers who crossed the line between plain old 'trouble' and that which was 'very big'.

'Well,' said Mr Yoshida, 'that is all. You can go now.'

'Thank you very much,' said Lisa sarcastically and, gathering up the assorted gifts, she went back to the dealing-room.

The BA market was busy that day, as the rates were very attractive against ordinary interest rates.

By three o'clock she was worried that she wouldn't be able to get all the paperwork done in time to leave at 4.30. She thought about asking Simon for help, but he hadn't forgiven her for talking her way onto the trip and was being uncooperative in his own subtle way, so she decided to put her head down and work flat out. At four o'clock, when she still had a lot of paperwork to finish, she got a phone call from reception.

'Lisa, there are two men from EPS Belgium here to see you for your meeting.'

'Are you sure they want to see me?' asked Lisa

'Yes,' said the receptionist stiffly. 'That's why I'm calling you.'

'Hold on.' Lisa looked at Simon. 'EPS Belgium are downstairs. Do you know anything about it?'

'Oh yes, I forgot to tell you,' said Simon, slapping himself on the side of the head. 'They rang on Friday and said they wanted to meet you today. So I booked them in for four o'clock.'

'Well, that was clever,' said Lisa. 'I haven't got time to see them now. You'll have to go.'

'It's your territory, Lisa. I don't want to get into trouble,' replied Simon with a smile, and he got up to get a coffee.

Lisa swore at his back and looked around for Mr Kubo. His seat was empty and she couldn't see him in the room. How dare he leave the desk? she thought angrily. There was nothing else for it, she would have to go herself. 'I'll be right down,' she told the receptionist and, swearing under her breath, she shot off downstairs.

Lisa had a good telephone relationship with EPS, so she thought it better to come clean and say there'd been a mix-up and she could only talk for about fifteen minutes.

It made Haru Bank look very bad, but she didn't know what else to do. Fortunately, the customers had come just as a goodwill gesture, not because they had anything major to discuss. They thought Lisa was cutting things at bit fine leaving at 4.30. They thought she should have left at four.

'This is a Japanese Bank, and we like to do everything at a trot,' explained Lisa, and with that the customers said goodbye and were off. Back in the dealing-room, Lisa rushed through her paperwork. By the time she'd finished, it was five o'clock. She still hadn't telexed New York about the BA deals she'd done. Simon hadn't come back to the desk – she suspected he was avoiding her to make things difficult – and Mr Kubo wasn't there either. If she stayed any longer, she might miss her plane, so she scribbled on a Post-it, 'Please send BA telex to New York. The deals are in the file on my desk,' and left the note on Mr Kubo's desk. Then she ran for the lift.

Chapter 24

The tube journey to Heathrow took much longer than Lisa had expected. She kept looking at her watch, and willed the driver to cut out all the intervening stops so that she could catch her plane. It didn't happen of course and so she reverted to prayer. Please let me get there in time, she begged silently, each time the train stopped at yet another station.

She got to Heathrow at 6.20, leaving her only forty minutes to check in and go to the boarding-gate. She felt a fleeting panic when she looked around and couldn't see the right check-in counter, but she soon located it and there were only three people ahead of her. Three people who took a very long time: it was 6.40 when she handed her ticket over.

'I'm afraid there's no time for you to check in here,' she was told. 'You'll have to run to the boarding-gate.'

Lisa had mistaken the time. The flight was leaving at 6.50, not seven o'clock: she only had ten minutes to get to the gate. Ten minutes is not a long time when you are handicapped by short legs, a pair of court shoes, a heavy briefcase and a well-stuffed overnight bag. After banging into at least five people who were selfishly standing still on the moving walkways, she decided to stop apologising and save her breath for running. If she missed the plane, she'd probably find herself sharing chocolate digestives with the other failures in the back-office graveyard. That image was scary enough to give her the extra speed she needed: she reached the boarding-gate just as they were about to close the doors.

Sitting panting heavily on the plane, she hoped that this energetic start to the trip wasn't an ominous indicator of things to come. Fortunately, dinner was good and she struck up a conversation with the Italian businesswoman sitting beside her that lasted until they landed in Milan. By the time she set foot on Italian soil, she was faintly optimistic.

She got a taxi to the hotel and cheered up even more. She had expected that someone of her rank, travelling alone, would be booked into a cheap *pensione*, but the bank had chosen a top-class hotel. She checked in and went up to her room. Her mood took a dip when she opened the door. With its dim lights, modern decor and huge double bed, it was the perfect room for lovers . . . Lisa suddenly felt very much alone.

In search of company, she went downstairs to the hotel bar. She perched on a high stool and poked at the ice cubes in her drink. She hoped someone would come and talk to her but, as the only other people in the bar were a middle-aged couple talking quietly in German, that was unlikely. After twenty minutes, she was bored of staring at her reflection in the mirror behind the bar so, feeling flat and lonely, she finished her drink and went up to her room to bed.

The phone by the bed rang quite a few times before Lisa registered that the strange buzzing was indeed a telephone. She fumbled for the receiver in the dark. 'Hello,' she answered sleepily.

'Lisa, this is Kimura speaking.' He sounded tired and angry.

Lisa came instantly awake. She sat up, switched the light on and, aware that she was naked, pulled the covers up to her chin.

'It's very late,' she said, looking at the digital clock on the bedside cabinet: it said ten past one. 'Is anything wrong?'

'We have a big problem,' he said sternly. 'You didn't send the BA telex.'

'I know, I didn't have time,' she said, relieved that it wasn't anything serious.

'Mr Kubo said you left before talking to him.'

'He wasn't at his desk, so I left him a note asking him to send the telex,' explained Lisa.

'Mr Kubo didn't say anything about a note.' said Mr Kimura. 'New York rang us this evening asking for the BA deals. Simon had gone home. I had to go to a reception with the general manager, so now I have come back to look.'

'The deals are all in the file on my desk,' said Lisa wearily. She should have known better than to leave things to Mr Kubo. She should have asked Aki-san.

'I can't see it,' said Mr Kimura.

'Try the drawers,' suggested Lisa.

There was silence, while Mr Kimura tried all Lisa's drawers and then Simon's.

'I can't see it,' he said at last. 'What colour is it?'

'It's green and it says "BA File" on the spine.' Lisa was getting worried.

'No, I cannot find it. You should have told Mr Kubo where you were going to leave it.'

'I told him in the note,' insisted Lisa. She realised she had left herself wide open to one of Simon's schemes — oh God, she should have been more careful. 'Look, Mr Kimura, I left that file right on my desk and I stuck a message on Mr Kubo's desk. If they aren't there now, it isn't my fault and there's nothing I can do from here.'

'The New York office is waiting for my call,' said Mr Kimura.

'The deals don't come into effect until Thursday. If you find the file tomorrow they'll still have time to issue the paper,' said Lisa tiredly. She was due to meet the bank's Milan rep at 7.30 in the morning, and at this rate she'd get no sleep at all.

Mr Kimura realised she was right. 'This is a big inconvenience for everyone,' he said. 'But you can do nothing now. Go to sleep and have a good meeting tomorrow.'

'Thank you, Mr Kimura. Good night.' Yes, thank you for calling me in the middle of the night, thought Lisa as she hung up. She drifted off to sleep.

It seemed only ten minutes later that she was woken by her early-morning alarm call. The bright, sunny weather and the sounds of the city outside should have lifted her spirits, but Mr Kimura's call and the prospect of the meeting ahead put paid to that. For a moment she planned to leave it all behind and run away, but then she thought of her mortgage and how, if she abandoned it, she would probably never be able to borrow money again.

She was becoming a true banker: the health of her finances was taking precedence over her spiritual well-being and she wasn't even twenty-five yet. She felt very old and sorry for herself. When she put on her make-up, she half expected to see wrinkles and grey hairs peering back at her.

After breakfast, she checked out and found two men, an Italian and a Japanese, from the Milan office waiting for her in the lobby. They introduced themselves as Paolo and Mr Fuji, and led her outside to a chauffeur-driven Mercedes. Mr Fuji got into the front, and Paolo sat next to Lisa on the back seat.

'What happened to Mr Takahashi?' asked Lisa. 'I was told that I would be going with him.'

'He very sick today. I come instead,' answered Paolo. 'I am head of administration.'

Lisa didn't like the sound of that. 'Do you know anything about dealing?' she asked.

'No. I do maintenance,' he said.

'How about you, Mr Fuji?'

He turned round and smiled at her. 'No English,' he said. 'Sorry.'

'Well, I can't speak Japanese or Italian, so can you interpret for us, Paolo?' asked Lisa.

'Sure, but don't worry,' said Paolo, smiling at her. 'Mr Fuji just here to see Turin. He not know any dealing.' Seeing the look of horror on her face, he didn't add that Mr Fuji couldn't speak much Italian either.

Help! thought Lisa. Stop the car right now and let me out. She'd expected Mr Takahashi to lead the meeting and had thought she'd be able to get away with saying very little. Instead, she was going to have to take control. Immediately, all the knowledge she'd gained during the last year at Haru Bank flew out of the window. A screech of *I know nothing, I know nothing* went round and round in her head until she thought she was going to be sick. She couldn't go through with this.

She was a useless failure. Perhaps it would be easier just to accept Simon as her manager.

Just when all seemed to be lost, she started to hear another voice in her head. It began very quietly, gradually getting louder and louder. *I teach you to think*, it said over and over again, and Lisa pictured Aki-san with a huge slice of hot-and-spicy pizza in his hand. Aki-san, who had got her on this trip. What would he say if she failed? 'You disappoint me,' she said quietly to herself.

'Sorry?' asked Paolo.

'Oh nothing,' she said, quickly pulling herself together. 'Have we got time to stop for a coffee before the meeting? We should talk about what we're going to say.'

'Sure, I know just the place,' answered Paolo and he leant forward to give the driver directions.

Lisa forced herself to think positively. She was going to take charge today and show everyone exactly what she was made of. In the coffee shop, she told Paolo and Mr Fuji what she wanted to achieve and explained as clearly as possible, given their lack of knowledge, the kind of business she was aiming to set up.

She needn't have bothered. Paolo took one look at Mr Calabrese, the customer's finance manager, and gave a cry of pleasure. Mr Calabrese looked blank for a moment and then, smiling widely, embraced Paolo, and there was a flood of excited Italian.

'This,' said Paolo in English after a few minutes, 'is a very old friend of mine. We lived in the same block of apartments when we were boys. I haven't seen him for over twenty years.'

'How lovely,' said Lisa smiling with relief. She'd thought maybe hugs, kisses and excited chatter were the usual way of doing business in Italy, and had prepared herself for similar treatment. But this news was even better than a warm embrace. She could relax now; everything would be fine.

The meeting turned into an hour-long chat as Paolo and Signor Calabrese – or Alfredo, as he said Lisa should call him – reminisced about things they used to do and people they both knew. Lisa and Mr Fuji simply sat there and smiled. Not one word was said about business, but afterwards, when they'd had a good, lengthy lunch at a restaurant and downed a few bottles of wine, Alfredo, who had received all Lisa's pens, promised to phone her when she got back to London.

She felt very confident arriving at work on Thursday. The meeting had gone well, and she was sure that all would be forgiven once she did her first deal with Alfredo.

Simon was at his desk, eating a bacon sandwich for breakfast. When he saw her, his face became very grim.

'Morning,' said Lisa cheerfully. 'Who burst your balloon?'

Simon put down his sandwich to give her his full attention. 'Do you know what trouble you caused us? We ran all over the bank looking for your file.'

'Did you find it?' asked Lisa, avoiding his gaze concentrating hard on removing the lid from her polystyrene coffee cup.

'Yes, but not until late in the afternoon,' he replied. 'The New York office were furious.'

'They'll still be able to issue the notes on time,' said Lisa.

'That's not the point,' said Simon pompously. 'Everyone is very annoyed with you.'

'Oh well, it's not the first time and it won't be the

last, I expect.' She wasn't worried. The issue would be made in time, and once Mr Kimura knew how successful the Turin trip had been he'd forget about everything else. 'Where did you find the file, anyway?'

Simon looked steadily at her. 'It was in that meeting-room that you went in on Tuesday afternoon. You must have taken it with you when you went to meet EPS.'

'Yeah, right,' said Lisa sarcastically. They stared at each other. Simon looked away first. What a bastard, thought Lisa. He really had tried to drop her in it. She couldn't wait to see his face when he saw how pleased with her Mr Kimura would be over the Turin trip.

As soon as Mr Kimura arrived, he summoned Lisa to his desk.

'Good morning,' she said smiling at him. 'You'll be happy to hear that it went very well yesterday.' Even as she spoke she was horribly aware of how sycophantic she sounded. I'll be bringing him shiny apples next, she thought and for the second time in three days she was conscious of how much the City was changing her for the worse.

Mr Kimura wasn't softened by her good news. 'It is no use being successful on a business trip if it means causing everyone else trouble while you are away,' he told her sternly. 'Your carelessness caused much trouble.'

Lisa's mood took a dive. 'I wasn't careless,' she said calmly. 'I left a note for Mr Kubo and the file was on my desk.'

That was about the worst thing she could have said.

'It was not on your desk,' shouted Mr Kimura. 'We look a very long time for it and it was a very long way from your desk.' He paused, realising how badly his anger was affecting his English. 'You caused a lot of trouble and inconvenience. You must apologise to the New York branch.' He slapped the table for emphasis. 'Then to me,' and he slapped the desk again, 'and to Simon and Mr Kubo.' He finished with two loud, finger-throbbing slaps, making his temper even worse.

If it hadn't been for the injustice of it all, Lisa would have been amused by his display, but instead she was annoyed that he'd vented his anger so publicly. She'd expected applause and compliments after her triumph in Turin, and it was unfair to be told off after all the effort she'd put into making her trip a success. 'I don't see why I should apologise, when I did nothing wrong,' she said stubbornly.

Mr Kimura was furious now. 'You didn't do your job properly,' he said very quietly, fighting to control himself. 'You must apologise or there will be very big trouble! Now go and think about what I have said.'

Lisa walked back to her desk, aware that everyone was watching her. As she passed Aki-san, she caught his eye. She wished she hadn't. His cold stare left her in no doubt that he, too, would demand an apology. She felt sick at heart. Simon would be made assistant manager now, and she'd be just his side-kick. It was humiliating to have been beaten so easily. She'd given him a perfect opportunity for one of his dirty tricks, and he'd grabbed it. Mr Kimura hadn't even asked her how the trip had gone.

She sat down at her desk and, ignoring the Serpent, who made no attempt to hide his glee, tried to get on with her work. She managed to look as if she was concentrating, but all the time she dealt, her head was full of rebellious thoughts. She'd already made up her mind that she wouldn't apologise, no matter what the

consequences. It was bad enough that Simon would be in
charge, without having to humiliate herself with false
apologies.

By eleven o'clock, as she hadn't approached him, Mr
Kimura decided to go over to her desk and insist that
she follow his orders. Lisa saw him coming and shot
off to the coffee room.

She found Aki-san and Andy there.

'How was Italy?' asked Andy, giving her a friendly
smile. He sat close enough to Mr Kimura's desk to have
heard every word of the conversation that morning,
and he wondered how Lisa had the nerve to deny
everything. She obviously hadn't learnt that with the
Japanese it was better to admit everything and say sorry;
then it would all blow over quickly. He couldn't say
anything while Aki-san was there, but he made up his
mind to talk to Lisa later.

'You're the first person who's asked,' replied Lisa.
'It went very well, actually.'

'I'm glad to hear it,' said Andy. 'Well, better get on,'
and he went out.

Lisa stared intently at the paper cup that was slowly
filling with coffee, willing it to go faster. She didn't
dare look at Aki-san, but she could feel his eyes on
her as he stirred his coffee. At last, the cup was full
and she quickly took it out of the machine. She gave
Aki-san a quick nod and turned to go.

'Lisa.'

Never had her own name sounded so ominous. She
turned round and forced herself to look Aki-san in the
eye. 'Yes?' she said nervously.

'We go to meeting-room and talk,' said Aki-san. Lisa
followed him out of the room feeling as if she was being
led to the gallows.

In the meeting-room, they sat down opposite each other and Lisa waited for Aki-san to start. She knew that what he had to say would probably upset her, but she didn't think it could make her feel worse than his silence did.

'Lisa,' he said eventually, 'why you no apologise?'

'Because I didn't do anything wrong,' she answered. She'd hoped he'd ask for her version of the story, but his question made it clear that he'd already judged her and found her guilty.

'How can you say you did nothing wrong?' he asked in amazement. 'You left the dealing-room without finishing your work.'

'I left a note for Mr Kubo,' insisted Lisa.

'That is not the point. It is your job to do the BAs. You must make sure that everything is done before you leave.' Aki-san was getting angry now. She had forgotten everything he had taught her.

'If I had, I'd have missed the plane.'

'That your fault,' said Aki-san. 'You bad at planning.'

'No, I'm not,' insisted Lisa. 'It wasn't my fault! Simon scheduled a meeting without telling me, and I didn't have time to finish everything because—'

'You bad at planning,' interrupted Aki-san coldly. 'You must apologise for the trouble you have caused.'

'No,' said Lisa folding her arms.

'You are a very stubborn girl. If you were my daughter I would hit you,' said Aki-san.

'I'd hit you back,' replied Lisa.

Aki-san smiled grimly, it was hard not to find her amusing. Nevertheless, she had to do the right thing. 'You must apologise. Everyone is waiting,' he said firmly, getting up to go. He though it best to leave Lisa alone with her thoughts.

Once left, she put her head in her hands and cried tears of anger and frustration. She knew she'd lost. Everyone had made up their minds that she was at fault. It was so humiliating and there was worse to come. Not only would she have to say sorry to Simon, knowing he had set her up, but she'd also have to accept him as her boss. If she couldn't, she'd have to leave the bank.

That thought sobered her. She stopped crying and went to the ladies to splash some cold water on her face. The sound of vomiting came from one of the cubicles. So as not to be seen, Lisa dived into the other cubicle and locked the door.

'Oh God, I'm dying. Help me,' a voice groaned.

'Stephanie?' said Lisa in astonishment. 'Are you all right?' Forgetting her own troubles, she left the cubicle and waited for Stephanie to emerge. When she did, she looked awful: her eyes were streaming and her mascara had run down her face. There was vomit in her hair and her skin had turned pale green.

'Did you have a late one last night, then?' asked Lisa, relieved that even the queen of the dealing room let her crown slip sometimes.

'Never again, never again,' moaned Stephanie, clutching her head as if she had a major hangover.

Lisa smiled and verbalised a wicked thought. 'Hannah told me that she's been throwing up a lot too,' she said before she could stop herself, 'but that's because she's three months pregnant.' She couldn't believe it when she'd said it. But it was too late to take it back now. She watched in horror as Stephanie's complexion turned vivid purple.

Stephanie stared at Lisa and Lisa stared back fearfully, trying her best to look innocent.

Stephanie fought hard to regain her self-control. 'I shall have to go and congratulate him,' she said menacingly.

Lisa followed as Stephanie went stomp, stomp, stomp through the bank towards the dealing-room. The sight of the queen in such a rage sent shivers of fear down the spines of all who looked upon her, but she didn't notice. Stephanie was a very angry woman. So angry that she was blind to everyone except Simon.

When she entered the dealing-room she headed for the Corporate desk. Seeing Simon on the phone, she reached over his desk and with one hand cut off the call while with the other she grabbed him by the hair and yanked him forward until his face was unpleasantly close to hers. Simon, caught completely off guard, could do nothing but whimper.

'You said you hadn't had sex with her for six months,' shouted Stephanie, underlining each word by banging his head against his computer. 'You said you'd leave her by Christmas.' She pulled his hair even harder — 'Ouch!' he squealed — and yelled, 'You said you'd give my baby your name, you bastard! Well, let me tell you now, I don't fucking want it!' With that, she released him, snatched up her things and stormed out of the room.

Simon was left crimson-faced and with a big tuft of hair sticking up from the top of his head. At first all he felt was physical pain, but slowly it dawned on him what had really happened. Ever anxious to look the professional, he tried frantically to think of a way of diminishing the damage to his reputation. Ignoring the open-mouthed amazement all around him, he picked up the phone and dialled his customer's number.

'Hello, it's Simon Russell,' he said shakily. 'Sorry about that — we got cut off.'

At the sound of his voice, the dealing-room was jolted back to reality and gradually everyone went back to their work.

Lisa quietly sat down at her desk, not looking at Simon. She was well aware that she'd scored a mammoth victory but she didn't feel good about it. She despised herself for the dirty trick she'd played.

At lunchtime, badly in need of a drink, she met Jackie and told her what had happened.

'Did Stephanie come back?' asked Jackie, who'd thoroughly enjoyed the story.

'No,' said Lisa, wondering if they'd ever see Stephanie again. 'She must have gone home. I feel so sorry for her. Imagine having his baby when he's still married and his wife is pregnant. What a bastard!'

'Well, I doubt if he did it on purpose,' said Jackie, laughing at her outrage — it wasn't so long since Lisa had been playing around herself. 'I feel quite sorry for the guy.'

To their surprise, Leo interrupted them. 'Can I buy you slappers a drink, then?' he said brightly.

'Hello, Leo,' said Lisa unenthusiastically. He was the last thing she needed today. 'I thought for a minute it was Prince Charming,'

'And so I am, dear girl. Fancy a bottle of champers?' he replied, laughing, and without waiting for an answer he went up to the bar.

'What's come over him?' asked Jackie.

'You tell me,' said Lisa. 'It's too early for him to be drunk. Perhaps he's on drugs.'

'Or he's bumped his head.'

'Maybe it's both. High and brain-damaged — that

must be it,' said Lisa. They laughed loudly and Leo, coming back, joined in.

'I must say, Dwarfie, that was a nice one you pulled this morning,' he said.

'What, with Stephanie?' she asked. She was surprised that people already knew that she was the one who'd revealed Simon's little secret.

'No, with Kimura. They're bound to fire you now. I bought this to celebrate.'

'You bastard!' said Jackie laughing.

'No, not really,' said Leo smiling at her. 'I'm just happy.'

'And what have you got to be so happy about?' asked Jackie.

'Why wouldn't I be happy working for Haru Bank. It is such an interesting place, don't you think?' He put his arm round Lisa and gave her a squeeze. 'First we get Dwarfie and Mr Kimura having a barny, then Stephanie tries to kill Simon. Who needs a telly when you can get entertainment like that in one day?' He smiled at Jackie and she gave him one of her meaningful stares.

Lisa had had enough. Not only had she coped with all the events of the morning, but now she was sitting with a super-friendly Leo who seemed to be trying to charm Jackie at the same time. It was all too much. She suddenly felt very tired and slightly sick.

'I'm not feeling so good,' she said, pushing Leo away. 'I have to go home.'

'Don't be silly.' He poured her some more champagne. 'Drink this. It'll make you feel better.'

'No,' said Lisa, shaking her head. 'I have to go.' And she got up and left before Leo or Jackie could say anything more.

Lisa took to her bed that afternoon. She was physically and mentally exhausted. Knowing she had nothing to fear from Simon was no comfort, because she hated what she'd done to beat him. She'd never have done anything like that before coming to work in the City, with its weird code of what was right and what was wrong. If she wanted to be herself again — and she wasn't sure if she knew what that meant any more — she'd have to start thinking seriously about getting out, because she didn't like what she'd become.

No one in the dealing-room commented on her absence that afternoon. Simon was too busy keeping his head down, and Mr Kimura was still in shock. He had sat at his desk all through lunchtime and thought about what he should do. In a hurried consultation with Mr Aono and the other senior Japanese managers after lunch, Mr Kimura found that, even though everyone expressed disgust at Simon's behaviour, nobody knew what to do for the best. If Simon was fired, shouldn't Stephanie be fired as well? If they both were fired, would it create bad feeling between the local staff and the Japanese staff? England seemed to be a very immoral country, so maybe this kind of behaviour was normal? The managers had all nodded solemnly at this. England was a terrible place. So much sex and scandal in such a small country. Each of them, while condemning the locals' immoral behaviour, easily forgot his own tumbles from the straight and narrow path of good clean living over the years.

Unable to reach a unanimous decision on suitable punishments, they had decided that this latest example of lewd behaviour by the local staff should be ignored for the time being. As long as Simon and Stephanie's work didn't deteriorate, nothing more would be said about the matter. It went without saying, though, that promotion for Simon at this time, or indeed at any other time, was out of the question.

Mr Kimura felt some relief that he hadn't promoted him earlier. The humiliation of having two of his staff involved in such a scandal would have been far greater if Simon had been an assistant manager.

His relief was short-lived. Mr Aono made it quite clear that he blamed poor leadership for the troubles on the Corporate desk. First Lisa and now Simon . . . There would have to be big changes, to ensure there were no more sordid scandals. From now on, Mr Aono said, he would be keeping a close eye on Mr Kimura's department and if any more problems arose he would arrange to have Mr Kimura sent to the office in Colombia — a posting which required the issue of a specially made Haru Bank bulletproof vest in small, medium or large.

With Mr Aono's warning fresh in his mind, Mr Kimura acted fast: as soon as he got back to the dealing-room, he called an emergency managers' meeting.

All the trouble on the Corporate desk was Mr Kubo's fault, he told the meeting. If Mr Kubo had taken proper control of the desk, Simon and Lisa would have behaved properly. What was needed on the desk was a more forceful personality. Someone who would be a real manager. Someone who wasn't afraid to take charge.

The next morning, when Lisa and Simon arrived at work, they found a new manager awaiting them. He had moved Simon's things to Mr Kubo's old place and had settled himself at the middle desk so that he could sit between his two morally defective juniors and make sure they caused no more trouble. Mr Kubo had been moved to a new manager's post in the back-office graveyard.

Before they started work, Simon and Lisa were given a pep talk by their new commander.

'Today you work hard, you make lots of deals and you no make mistakes,' he said sternly.

'Yes, Aki-san,' they chorused meekly.

Chapter 25

——— ———

While Aki-san was laying down the law to the Corporate dealers, Stephanie arrived. She was pale, and the smell of bacon and egg sandwiches that hit her as she walked past the FX desk nearly made her throw up in Mr Sumida's wastepaper bin, but her head was held high and she looked as fierce as ever.

'Morning, Steph,' said Leo with a welcoming grin, as she took her seat. 'You're looking very lovely this morning.'

'I always look lovely,' she said coldly, picking up the phone and going into one of her brokers' lines to show Leo that he might have time to stand around chatting but she certainly hadn't.

'Good morning, David,' she said into the phone. 'Can I have the rates, please?'

Everyone in the dealing-room had looked up when she came in, but as soon as they realised that she was not going to do anything dramatic, they began to relax and get on with their work. The only two who couldn't relax were Simon and Lisa. Not only did they have Aki-san breathing down their necks, but they were worried about what Stephanie would do when they had to ask her for a quote.

Luckily for Lisa, the first customer to ask for a six-month deposit rate was one of Simon's.

'Stephanie, what's your six months?' he called, his voice cracking a little under the strain of trying to sound as if today was a pefectly normal day and Stephanie hadn't banged his head against his computer yesterday. Silence gradually fell as everyone waited to see how his pregnant ex-mistress would react.

Just as usual, the queen went straight into the brokers' lines to check the rate. After three calls, she put down her phone, picked up her pencil and slowly wrote 'FUCK YOU' in huge letters on her dealing-sheet. All eyes focused on Simon, to see his reaction to the delay.

'Stephanie, six months, please,' he said, cringing at the thought of another scene.

She turned to face him, glared for a few seconds and then asked very slowly, 'I'm sorry. What did you say?'

Simon's face burnt bright red. 'What's your rate for twenty million in six months?' he asked again, saying each word very carefully.

Stephanie continued to glare at him. Everyone's eyes were now on her. What would she do next? She turned back to her dealing-sheet, read what she had written on it and then with a grim smile said quietly, 'Nine and a half.'

There was a collective letting-out of breath, and gradually the noise in the dealing-room rose to its normal level.

Lisa was amused that Simon had been humiliated again, but she worried about how Stephanie was going to treat her when she had to ask for a rate. She soon found out. Her next call was from a customer looking for a one-year dollar deposit. She didn't want to shout across to Stephanie and suffer the same embarrassment as Simon. There would be far less chance of that if she went over to Stephanie's desk, although the risk of physical assault would be much increased. Lisa reckoned the risk was worth it . . .

Stephanie was inputting some deals into her computer.

'Can you give me your one-year?' asked Lisa quietly. 'The customer has fifty to place.'

'Hold on.' Stephanie clicked into the brokers' lines to check the rate. 'Nine and a half,' she said eventually.

'Same as the six months?' Lisa suspected a trap.

'That's right,' said Stephanie, looking her straight in the eye.

'OK, nine and a half it is then,' said Lisa. 'Thanks.'

'No,' said Stephanie. 'Thank you,' and she smiled.

Lisa had an idea. 'Do you fancy coming to lunch with me?' she asked. 'I'm going for a drink with Jackie from Maine Weavers.'

Stephanie thought for a moment. 'Well, I'll be on orange juice, but I'd like to come along.' She smiled again and Lisa, pleasantly surprised, smiled back.

In fact, Stephanie was genuinely grateful that Lisa had let her know the truth about Simon before she lost all her self-respect. She realised Lisa'd had ulterior motives when she told her about Hannah, but Stephanie had exposed Lisa's affair with Frank, so she could hardly blame Lisa for not caring about her feelings. In Lisa's situation she'd probably have done exactly the same thing.

Stephanie knew that her dislike of Lisa when she first came into the dealing-room had been because until then she'd been the only woman in the room and had felt special. When Lisa started working on the Futures desk, she'd felt threatened and, yes, she had to admit it, a bit jealous. Lisa was so young, so fresh, so ignorant about life in the markets, that it made her feel old and jaded, and she was reminded of how she had been, all those years ago, before dealing had worked its way into her system. Now, however, pregnant and constantly at the mercy of her hormones, Stephanie was grateful that there was another woman in such a chauvinistic environment.

Not only that but, as Lisa had also had an affair with a married man, she understood exactly what Stephanie was going through. Stephanie was sorry she'd always been so cold to Lisa. Maybe if they had supported each other, or rather if *she* had supported Lisa when she was new in the dealing-room, they wouldn't have both made such a mess of their personal lives. Instead of being the subject of gossip and ridicule, as she was now painfully aware they'd become, they could have been a strong, united team terrifying all the other dealers. Well, it was too late for that now, she thought, but it wasn't too late for them to be friends.

'Well, this is nice,' said Jackie, filling Lisa's wine glass. 'Here I am with the two most scandalous women in the market. I only hope it doesn't give me a bad name.'

Lisa and Stephanie laughed.

'You're one to talk,' said Lisa. 'You've been with half the men in this bar.'

'Cheeky,' said Jackie. Then, lowering her voice, 'Now that I'm in a steady relationship with a *single* man, that kind of comment is not allowed.'

'Since when?' asked Lisa in surprise. As far as she

knew, Jackie's love life was as sad as her own. 'It's the first I've heard of it,' she said to Stephanie.

'Since yesterday,' Jackie said. 'We went out last night and, although it's early days yet, I think we've clicked. I'm seeing him again tonight.'

'Sex with the same man two nights running. It must be love!' said Lisa.

'Or lust,' suggested Stephanie.

'Actually,' said Jackie, 'I didn't sleep with him. We just went to dinner, and we chatted for hours. They even had to ask us to leave the restaurant because we were the only two customers left and they wanted to go home.'

'My God!' said Lisa in mock horror. 'This sounds serious. Do we know him?'

'Yes, but not as well as you think,' said Jackie. She paused for effect, then said, 'It's Leo.'

'Leo!' shrieked Stephanie and Lisa.

'You mean, our Leo? Horrible, rude, slobby Leo? Leo who goes out with . . .' Lisa turned to Stephanie. 'What's her name? I only know her as the Sow.'

'Jane,' said Stephanie. 'It finished weeks ago. Where have you been, Lisa?'

'Yes, that's the one,' said Jackie. 'But he's not as bad as you think. Once he's out of the City he's another man altogether. He's a real softie at heart.'

'He'd have to be,' said Lisa, and Stephanie nodded in agreement.

'If that's how you both feel, I'm not saying another word,' said Jackie haughtily.

'I'm sorry,' said Lisa, afraid she'd gone too far. 'If you say he's nice, we'll take your word for it. I just can't picture him at a romantic dinner for two, that's all — not without spilling something down his shirt, anyway.'

'Nor did I until we met him at lunchtime yesterday,' admitted Jackie.

'Oh yes, that's right,' said Lisa, remembering. She laughed. 'It's all your fault, Stephanie. I was telling Jackie about what happened with Simon, and Leo came over to talk about it.'

'That's right, blame me,' said Stephanie. 'I suppose if they get married that'll be my fault too.'

'Not much chance of that,' said Jackie.

Lisa thoroughly enjoyed that lunch. The three of them talked and laughed about the men in their lives or, in Stephanie's and Lisa's case, the men who had been in their lives and she was relieved to have two older women friends who made the same mistakes as she did.

But as she sat at her desk that afternoon, an unpleasant thought struck her. If Jackie and Stephanie were still making those mistakes after more than ten years in the City, what hope was there for her? She didn't want to be like them. It wasn't that she didn't admire them for having survived in the markets for so long, it was just that she didn't want to end up with a personal life which seemed terribly amusing after a few glasses of wine, because she knew that, once the wine wore off, what had been funny would look pathetically sad.

Lisa didn't know what she wanted out of life, but she knew that what she had now would never satisfy her. She had to think of something else to do, she had to act before she got so used to the City and the money that she couldn't imagine doing anything else. But what could she do? Her spirits sank as she considered the careers open to her and, one by one, rejected them all.

She wasn't the only Corporate dealer whose mind wasn't on work. Simon had stayed at his desk all through lunchtime. After being humiliated by Stephanie for the second day running, and then seeing Stephanie and Lisa go to lunch together, he was deeply anxious. Would they tell Hannah? He could just see them plotting how best to ruin him. Not satisfied with wrecking his chances of promotion, they'd probably destroy his home life as well. He couldn't bear the thought of Hannah divorcing him. He saw himself as a victim; his fate was in the hands of three women, one he loved and two he feared.

Simon twisted and turned on the line he had hooked himself upon. He'd wanted a little excitement before settling down to fatherhood. He'd risked everything just to relieve his boredom. What had he been thinking of? He wondered whether he should confess the affair to Hannah before she found out from someone else. If she really loved him, she'd forgive him and they could put it all behind them. He shook his head. That was too risky. What if she left him? He couldn't bear the thought of life without her. No, she mustn't know about the affair. Whichever way he turned he saw himself in trouble, so there wasn't much he could do except hope. Hope that Stephanie had calmed down enough not to seek further revenge, and hope that he'd get through this crisis with the lovely Hannah still by his side.

Life in the dealing-room calmed down after a few days. When everyone realised that Stephanie was going to ignore Simon and that there wouldn't be any more drama, their affair stopped being the main topic of conversation at the coffee machine.

Lisa found that she couldn't cheer herself up, though. Things had improved a lot at work. She no longer feared being set up by Simon, and whereas in the past Andy had been the only friendly person in the dealing-room, now Stephanie and Leo were warm to her as well. Leo in particular, now that he was deeply in love with Jackie, had become friendly, and not only to Lisa. He was pleasant to his brokers, even when he was losing money. He no longer stood up shouting and snarling after a figure. Instead, he sat at his desk and said calmly, 'Buy, please,' or 'Sell, please.' It transformed the atmosphere of the dealing-room.

Before he met Jackie, his main after-work activities had been drinking, eating takeaway curries and sleeping in his suit. Now, the two of them went to the theatre, the cinema or to cosy restaurants where they could talk about their future together.

That Jackie had found her Prince Charming should have given Lisa hope that she too might live happily ever after, but she had doubts about that. For one thing, Leo's transformation probably wouldn't last for ever: she expected the warty toad to re-emerge any day now. Besides, living happily ever after would take more than merely finding a man to settle down with. She felt so wrong sitting at her desk each day that she couldn't imagine ever being really happy unless she escaped from the City.

Since Frank had left, she'd been so lost and lonely that she'd felt compelled to visit her father more often. Contrary to her expectations, the change in his routine after he retired hadn't caused a complete mental breakdown. At first, the novelty of not having to work seemed to agree with him. It probably helped that his retirement coincided with some fine weather: he sat in his garden relaxing and getting brown, putting behind him the struggle of communicating with the outside world. Lisa thought he'd even improved a little. He gained some weight, his face filled out and with his suntan he looked as he did in photos taken ten years ago.

Unfortunately, once the weather cooled, he began to fade again. His work routine was replaced by another, equally rigid, routine, encompassing everything from brushing his teeth to buttering a slice of bread, and he got very distressed if it was broken. If interrupted, he kept on trying, oblivious of anything else, until he had completed his task in the set way. After dinner, he got up to do the washing-up as soon as he had finished chewing his last mouthful. He filled the bowl three-quarters full with hot water, added a little cold and then one tiny squirt of washing-up liquid. Cups had to be washed first and then placed upside-down on the draining-board. Plates came next and they were leant against the cups. After that knives, then forks, then spoons and last of all saucepans. If Lisa was still eating when he started the washing-up, he'd take her cup away at the cup-washing stage, then come back for her plate at the plates stage and so on until she'd given him everything. It was fine if she was eating a sandwich, which she could hold in her hand, but if it was fish fingers and baked beans and she didn't eat quickly enough, he simply took her plate away and scraped the uneaten food into the bin. At times like this, when his habits seemed designed to annoy her, her patience was sorely tried and it took every last ounce of self-control not to lose her temper. But she reckoned it was worth the effort, because as long as he filled his day with petty, routine tasks, he would be too busy to sit and think about his life.

She tried to do the same herself, keeping busy at work in the daytime and then getting drunk in the evenings so that she could blot out the calls for change that dominated her thoughts. She'd probably have carried on like this until her liver gave out, if it hadn't been for Andy.

The news took a few days to get around the market. It would have gone around faster if Andy had told one of the local staff, but when he handed in his notice the only person he told about his plans was Mr Kimura.

After recovering from the shock of finding out that quiet, steady Andy Rolfe was really Adrian Starre, champion ballroom dancer, and that he intended to set up his own dancing-school in Croydon, Mr Kimura held discussions with the Japanese managers about possible replacements for the short-date dollar position. Then he called Stephanie, his senior dollar dealer, to his desk to hear her opinion. It was after that meeting, when Stephanie loudly told Lisa by the coffee machine about Andy's resignation, that the news began to spread quickly.

If Lisa had thought she had suffered after everyone found out about her and Frank, it was nothing compared to the jokes and insults heaped on Andy. Every time he got up from his desk there were whistles, catcalls and comments about the way his hips moved. When he asked his brokers for quotes, they often called back down the boxes with fruity voices and made queer jokes. Leo, the master of abuse, reverted to his old self in the dealing-room to make sure that Andy's last month at work would be truly unforgettable.

Andy took the abuse very well. He merely smiled when Leo jeered at him, and he never retaliated. Leo got bored taunting someone who didn't react, and the abuse soon faded away. Lisa fervently wished she'd been able to act like Andy when Leo teased her.

'It's a shame you had to resign before you could come out,' said Lisa when she went to lunch with Andy one day.

'God, Lisa! You'd better get out of this place before you become like all the rest of them,' said Andy seriously. 'I never said I was gay. I'm just going to open a dancing-school.'

'Well, why haven't you told everyone that?' demanded Lisa. 'Why do you let them think you're gay when you're not?'

'I'm a ballroom dancer,' said Andy. 'The meatheads in the market couldn't imagine that I could be anything else but gay.'

'No, I suppose not,' she agreed. 'But you can't blame them. It's not like you've ever been out with anyone or anything.'

'How would you know?' asked Andy. 'Just because I don't tell the whole world what I'm doing doesn't mean I don't go out with women.'

'I wouldn't like you any less if you didn't,' said Lisa.

'You're not listening to what I'm saying, are you?' said Andy irritably. 'I've been going out with someone for two years now. Her name's Fiona and I am setting up the school with her.'

Lisa wasn't sure she believed him. 'Why didn't you tell me about her before?'

'Because I like to keep my private life separate from work. I'd have thought you, of all people, would understand the importance of that,' said Andy pointedly.

Abashed, Lisa lowered her eyes and concentrated hard on her lunch.

Chapter 26

——— ◄———

'Dad's dead.'

Lisa had wanted to break the news gently to John, but when she heard his voice on the other end of the line, those were the only two words that came out.

'What?' said John.

'Dad's dead,' she said again. 'He fell under a train at Baneham Station.'

'Fell under a train?' John could hardly take in what she was telling him. 'When?'

'This morning,' said Lisa. 'You know what he's like, always standing with his feet close to the edge. Well, he stood too close this time and that was it.' She felt as though it was someone else saying the words. She was still too shocked to believe what had happened. She knew her father was dead but she couldn't feel anything yet.

'What was he doing at the station? I thought he was retired,' said John.

'He is.' She couldn't yet speak of her father in the past tense. 'But he had a suit on, apparently. Maybe he just forgot he doesn't work any more.'

Did he jump or did he fall? The question hovered unsaid between them. After so many years of leaning back slightly when the train came in, could he have got muddled up and leant forward instead? Had he woken up and forgotten that he had retired? Or did he wake up and decide that he'd simply had enough?'

'What about the body?' John's voice broke the silence.

Lisa saw images of shattered, bloodied limbs, and shuddered. 'I'm trying not to think about it,' she admitted. 'When can you come home? There's so much to do. I can't cope on my own.'

'I'll be back as soon as I can,' said John. 'I'll ring you when I know what flight I'll be on.'

During the next few weeks, Lisa's dreams were dominated by macabre images of her father. She never saw him intact: part of him was always missing. Over the years, he had gradually become detached from himself. His illness had taken the man from the body. Now, because of the way he'd died, his body became detached as well: scattered bits reattached themselves in all the wrong places, and he started searching for the fragments of his personality that had been lost as his illness progressed.

She thought these dreams were a warning of what might happen to her if she didn't take control of her life. She had to change it but she didn't know what she wanted to do and, in any case, her father's death haunted her so much that she couldn't think clearly about her own future.

Did he jump or did he fall? Lisa asked herself the question over and over again. Other people never asked her. Suicide implies that those left behind aren't worth the struggle to keep alive, and it is cruel to suggest to grieving relatives that the dead person didn't love them enough to do them the favour of staying alive. 'A tragic accident' was what everyone called it. A gust of wind must have pushed him forward just as the train came in. Perhaps they were right. Certainly the Essex winds are notorious for propelling people to untimely deaths.

It couldn't have been suicide. He wasn't the type.

Lisa wanted to believe that he had jumped. That he'd got up that morning, followed his normal work routine right up to the moment when he aligned his feet with the edge of the platform, and then, as the train came in, shouted, 'Fuck it!' and leapt forward. In her mind, he always spoke the words loudly and clearly. She wanted to believe that the rage caused by his illness had given him back his voice in the final moments of his life. Refusing to fade away until there was nothing left, he'd taken control and ended it himself. She didn't want to believe that he had just gone along with what was happening without making any kind of protest. She refused to accept that he had fallen silently in front of the train.

Lisa didn't allow herself to grieve very much. By believing that he had made the choice to die, she was able to convince herself that his death was a good thing. He hadn't let himself simply be pulled along the path that fate had laid down for him. He had made the final choice.

She couldn't say this to anyone. The people who spoke to her about her father didn't want to hear about the details of his death or how she really felt. Death as a topic of conversation is full of pitfalls. She knew that when people offered condolences they were terrified in case she broke down and cried. When they asked how

she was getting on, they didn't want a full explanation
of her emotional state; they expected a dignified reply
like 'Thanks for asking. I'm bearing up very well.' They
liked to be thanked for their sensitivity but they'd have
felt thoroughly uncomfortable if she'd given them an
honest answer. It was as if they were relying on her
not to embarrass them, not to demand more from them
than they could give.

Within a month people had almost forgotten about
her father's death, and they stopped asking Lisa how
things were. She did her job, she looked the same and
she didn't seem to be undergoing an emotional crisis, so
people treated her as they normally would have. But
she'd changed. She was no longer prepared to put up
with what was happening to her. Her father's death
had stopped the rot, and made her determined to take
responsibility for moulding her own future. She would
shape her life into what she wanted it to be. She began
to feel stronger and more cheerful, and even started to
laugh again.

Jackie, sensing that it was now safe to meet her,
asked her out for a drink one lunchtime. Not having
suffered the death of a parent, she'd had no idea
how to cope with her friend's bereavement. When
Lisa came back to work after the funeral, Jackie
had offered condolences like everyone else, but then
she had backed off.

'You seemed depressed before, so I didn't want to say
too much,' she explained, pouring the last of the wine
into Lisa's glass.

'Depressed?' Lisa was affronted. Jackie made it sound
as if it was her fault that she'd been unhappy.

'Yes. I was worried, but I didn't want to upset
you.'

'Upset me?' Lisa knew she sounded like a parrot, but she thought Jackie could have tried a bit harder.

'By saying too much.' This meeting was much harder than Jackie had expected. Lisa obviously hadn't recovered, even after all this time.

'By saying too much?' Lisa looked at Jackie as if she was absolutely crazy.

Jackie looked away. 'Do you want another drink?' she said, and fled to the bar.

If it had been a 'nice' death, like a heart attack or a stroke, Jackie would probably have been a better friend to Lisa. But her father's death had a question mark over it, and Jackie was too frightened of saying the wrong thing to say anything much at all. Besides, she didn't know what kind of support to offer because Lisa had always kept her feelings about her family to herself. When they had talked about her father before his death, Lisa had acted as if she didn't care about him. Jackie loved her own father very much, and didn't mind telling everyone she did. She didn't understand that Lisa had always coped by locking her feelings about her family firmly inside herself and pretending that what was hidden didn't exist.

When Jackie came back from the bar, she decided for Lisa's sake to be upbeat and change the subject.

'Leo wants to move in with me,' she said.

'The question is, do you want to live with him?' asked Lisa. She knew what her own answer would have been.

'The way things are,' said Jackie seriously, 'I can't imagine being with anyone else. He's everything I've ever wanted in a man.'

'Well, then, I suppose you'd better go for it,' said Lisa. She wished she could be happy for Jackie, but she wasn't: she was sad. Up to now Jackie had slept around indiscriminately. Lisa had hoped she would be more discerning when choosing the man she wanted to spend her life with.

'How about you? Have you got your eye on anyone?'

'I'm not even thinking about it,' said Lisa. 'I've got too many other things to consider.'

'Like what?'

'I'm leaving.'

'Leaving?' Now it was Jackie's turn to be the echo. Had what she'd said earlier offended Lisa so much that she was going to walk out? 'Don't go,' she said hastily. 'I've just bought a drink. I'm sorry, I'm not very good with deaths.'

Lisa laughed at her friend's horrified expression. 'No, not now, not here. I mean I'm leaving the City.'

Jackie calmed down. 'When?' she asked.

'When I've sold my flat.'

'And then what are you going to do?'

'I haven't decided. I've got to sell my flat first, then I'm going to leave Haru's. Maybe I'll go abroad.'

Jackie smiled. Dealers were always threatening to leave, but they never did. The money was too good. They always had some excuse for staying. Lisa had her flat – that was a good excuse. She wouldn't be able to sell it and she'd spend the next few years grumbling to Jackie, 'If I could only sell my flat . . .'

But Lisa was serious. 'I'm going to sell my flat, leave my job and start again.'

And she did.

Epilogue

———— ◆ ————

Lisa looked in the mirror. Her hair was having a
good day, although she could have done without
the flowers stuck onto the headband, which was digging
into the skin behind her ears. She didn't mind the
neckline of her dress, which did justice to her cleavage
without being so low that she daren't bend over in case
something fell out. But the big puff sleeves were too
much. As for the full skirt with its lace petticoats, the
bride certainly had some explaining to do.

'Did you have to have hoops?' she asked.

Jackie, who was sitting on her bed, was too busy
opening a bottle of champagne to answer.

'Hoops and puff sleeves are not for short people,' Lisa
complained.

The cork popped, and Jackie took a long swig
from the bottle. 'Don't be silly,' she said. 'You look
adorable.' A drop of champagne ran down her chin
and she wiped it away with the back of her hand.
'It really suits you,' she added not very convincingly.
'Everyone will love it.'

'Everyone will laugh, you mean,' answered Lisa.
'Well, at least you'll look good.' She looked over at

the silk wedding-dress hanging on the front of the wardrobe. 'Although should you be wearing white with your track record?'

'They didn't have them in red, and ivory made me look yellow,' said Jackie, reaching for her lacy stay-ups.

'I can't believe you're going through with it,' said Lisa. 'I mean, you and Leo. I don't think I've ever got over the shock.'

'He's a reformed man,' said Jackie, pulling up a stocking. 'He hardly drinks now, and he's started playing golf so he's lost weight. More importantly,' she added, smiling, 'he's a real tiger in bed.'

'I don't want to think about it,' shuddered Lisa. 'Have another drink. A few more swigs and you'll be able to plead drunkenness when you file for a divorce.'

'Will you stop it,' laughed Jackie.

Since Lisa had left the City the two friends had seen hardly anything of each other, so Jackie was especially glad Lisa had agreed to be her bridesmaid. 'How's work? Have you done any enemas yet?' she asked.

'It's not all poop and bed baths you know,' replied Lisa haughtily. 'Nursing is a highly skilled occupation – even if we don't get paid much.'

Nurse Lisa Soames. It didn't sound as good now as it had when she'd started her training. The truth was that Lisa disliked nursing even more than she disliked dealing. She hated the smells, the doctors were arrogant, and being in a hospital all day depressed her; she just didn't bond well with sick people. No, nursing was definitely not for her. Very soon she'd be on the move again. She refused to admit this to Jackie, though, because she wanted everyone from the City to think she was deliriously happy with her new life, at least until her plans to visit John in Singapore and then travel around Asia had been settled.

'Let me know when you get fed up with it,' said Jackie, who wasn't fooled at all. 'I'll get you a job at our place.'

'No thanks,' said Lisa firmly. 'I've already made that mistake once.'

Jackie didn't believe her. She was certain that having less money, and therefore less success, must be making her short friend regret her foolish decision to walk away from Haru Bank.

'I bet you miss it really, and—Oh God! I've got to go again.' She dashed out to the toilet, leaving Lisa to chew over her words.

'I don't miss it at all,' she told her reflection in the mirror. She did sometimes worry about money, and occasionally she remembered the excitement of a big figure, but she had no desire at all to be back at the Corporate desk.

The only person to voice strong opposition to her resignation had been Aki-san. 'You will be very sorry after you leave,' he said.

Mr Kimura, who still hadn't got over the shock of Andy turning out to be a ballroom dancer, put up hardly any resistance at all. 'We will be sorry to see you go,' he had said, 'but you have made up your mind so I wish you good luck.' He did regret missing the chance to fondle her naked body, but regret was soon overtaken by anticipation of the enjoyment he would have looking for her replacement. He set his heart on a blonde with large breasts and rounded hips who also happened to be qualified to work alongside Simon and Aki-san.

While Mr Kimura was daydreaming about Marilyn

Monroe lookalikes, Aki-san did his best to persuade
Lisa to change her mind. One lunchtime, over a large
pepperoni pizza — chosen to reflect his conciliatory tone
— he tried in vain to make her understand what a big
mistake she was making.

'You waste everything,' he told her. 'You waste
your money, your experience and you waste the time
of everyone who trained you.'

Lisa laughed ruefully. 'No one trained me,' she said.
She was pleased that Aki-san cared enough about her
to try to get her to stay, but she wasn't going to let him
get away with comments like that. 'You and Leo made
things very difficult for me,' she said, but she smiled
to show she'd forgiven him.

'That was your training,' he snapped. 'It made you
strong. It teach you not to make mistakes. It make you
a very good dealer.'

Lisa was moved. She knew how difficult it was for
him to pay compliments. 'I didn't know you thought
I was good,' she said. 'It's nice to know that, but it
doesn't make any difference. I'm still going.'

Aki-san gave up. 'You a very foolish young woman.
You will be very sorry after,' he said angrily, and that
was the last he said about her decision to leave.

But he was wrong. Lisa hadn't yet found a solution
to her life but she wasn't sorry to have left the
City. She was much happier away from the world
of moving currencies, fluctuating interest rates and men
who thought breaking wind was an acceptable way to
punctuate a conversation. She knew she'd been right
to give up her job at Haru Bank. She just wondered
how long it would take her to reap the rewards of
that sensible decision.

'I hope they've got some toilets in the church,' said

Jackie coming back into the room. 'You won't believe how many times I've been this morning.' She took her wedding-dress off its hanger. 'Help me on with this, will you?' She stepped into it and Lisa zipped it up.

'I have a confession to make,' said Jackie, watching Lisa closely in the mirror. 'I noticed you didn't have a date for the wedding, so I fixed you up with someone.'

'Yeah, right,' said Lisa, who knew Jackie's sense of humour. 'Don't tell me. It's the best man and he's the spitting image of Leo.'

Jackie laughed. 'I think I can safely say that he's nothing like Leo and you'll be very surprised when you see him.'

'You're being serious, aren't you?' said Lisa. She wasn't pleased at being landed with a blind date, especially one picked by Jackie.

'I ran into him a couple of weeks ago in the City. His bank has opened a new branch here and he was delighted when I told him I knew where you were,' said Jackie gaily. 'Now don't ask any more questions. I want it to be a surprise.'

Before Lisa could beat the information out of her, there was a knock at the door.

'Are you ready, love?' called Jackie's father. 'We really should be setting off now.'

'Well, this is it,' said Jackie. 'You'd better go. You're supposed to be in the first car.'

'Good luck,' said Lisa, and in a rare moment of sentiment she gave Jackie a big hug and a kiss on the cheek. 'You make a beautiful bride.'

'Get out before I'm sick,' said Jackie.

Lisa went to the church in a white limousine with Jackie's mother, who was wearing a very large hat which she'd regret buying once she saw the wedding photos, and a floral two-piece which would ensure she stood out as the mother of the bride, if nothing else. She was very emotional to see her only child finally married at thirty-six.

'Such a lovely boy,' she told Lisa. 'I believe you worked with him.'

'Yes, I did,' said Lisa, not willing to shatter the poor woman's illusions. 'A lovely boy, indeed. He has a real way with words.' She remembered the first time she'd seen Leo. There he'd stood, the king of the dealing-room, bacon sandwich in one hand and phone in the other, wearing a stained candy-striped shirt and loud braces, and with his beer-belly hanging over his trousers. 'Oh my God!' he'd shouted. 'They've employed a dwarf!' Lisa could still feel the embarrassment of that moment and she wondered if today she would see the man that Jackie claimed he'd become or whether, apart from the grey morning-suit and top hat, he would essentially be the same as ever.

Jackie's mother broke into her thoughts. 'I bet there'll be a lot of those Japanese at the church,' she said. 'Leo insisted on inviting them. It didn't please my Uncle Thomas. He was in one of their camps in the war and so he's refused to come. I tried to get him to change his mind. "It's in the past. You've got to move on," I said. "Look at us, we got bombed out by the Germans three times and yet we talk to them when we go to Majorca." But he wouldn't budge. Very stubborn he is. We all are on my mother's side.' Her ramblings made Lisa long for the silence of her father. Even Mo's short, sharp acidic comments were preferable. She was relieved to see the church coming into view.

'Well, here we are,' said Jackie's mother. 'Look,

there's one of those Japanese chaps over there.' She pointed to the steps of the church and Lisa looked out of the window hoping that it wasn't Aki-san waiting to ask her how she was getting on.

He was standing at the foot of the steps, a little apart from the other guests. Permed hair, sunglasses, loud shirt and a new suit with a matching waistcoat. Lisa gasped. How could Jackie do this to her? Frank looked absolutely wonderful and she was about to emerge from the car in a peach dress with puff sleeves and hoops.

She was dismayed at how upset she was. It was more than a year since he'd left and she'd convinced herself she'd got over him. But now, seeing him standing there, she had to admit that she still cared about him. So much that she was determined not to let him see her get out of the car in her bridesmaid's dress.

She held her bouquet in front of her face and edged her way along the seat. If she could just get up the steps and into the church, she thought, she'd be fine. The shock of seeing him again hadn't robbed her of her wits. She knew she couldn't avoid him for the whole wedding, especially as he was almost certainly her surprise date, but she hoped that if she had a little time to compose herself she'd be able to keep her dignity when she first spoke to him. She certainly wasn't going to cry, 'Oh Frank!' and fall into his arms as she imagined everyone expected her to. He'd abandoned her and gone back to his family, and if he wanted her to be nice to him he'd have to do a little bit more than get all dressed up and turn up unexpectedly at a wedding.

She got out of the car and, still hiding her face and keeping her back firmly to Frank, made her way crablike up the steps of the church. She hoped the wind wouldn't blow her skirt up high and make her look even more ridiculous than she did already. She imagined that he must have seen her and expected him to call her name, but he didn't. Half of her wanted him to shout something, the other half wanted him to make it easy for her by staying silent.

He did neither. Very quietly, his voice quivering with nerves and embarrassment, he began to sing.

She kept on up the steps. 'It'll take more than a few bars to make me turn round,' she told herself, determined to be strong.

She was nearly at the top. Frank sang more loudly, drawing the attention of the other guests. As his confidence grew, he threw himself into his performance, standing arms outstretched towards Lisa as if pleading with her to acknowledge him.

The rubs finally got to her. Lisa had forgotten how his deep, rich voice invaded her body, making her feel warm and tingly all over. It was impossible to keep walking away. She turned and looked down at him.

She thought back to the first time she had slept with him at the Savoy, to the snack bar on Jock's birthday, to the fun they'd had together. Then she remembered that it had all been based on a lie. Did she still feel the same way towards him? She'd thought she'd lost him for good, and yet here he was serenading her on the steps of the church in front of Leo and all the wedding-guests.

'Sing to me again after the wedding and I'll let you know,' she called down, and with her head held high she walked to the church door.

Just before she went inside, she turned and looked at him again. Frank stood on the steps looking up at her, flushed and smiling. Lisa wondered if, this time, she was being extremely wise or very foolish.